Also by Albert Shansky

Extinction of Illusion

Shinran and Eshinni

An American's Journey into Buddhism

Two Trips in Search of the Buddha

A Trio of Zen Buddhist Stories

The Roshi, The Japanese Castaway,
Escape from Exile Island

Albert Shansky

iUniverse, Inc.
Bloomington

A Trio of Zen Buddhist Stories
The Roshi, The Japanese Castaway, Escape from Exile Island

iUniverse books may be ordered through booksellers or by contacting:

iUniverse
1663 Liberty Drive
Bloomington, IN 47403
www.iuniverse.com
1-800-Authors (1-800-288-4677)

ISBN: 978-1-4620-0647-2 (pbk)
ISBN: 978-1-4620-0648-9 (ebk)

Printed in the United States of America

iUniverse rev. date: 3/23/2011

Introduction

Zen Buddhist stories are usually thought of as mythological tales such as those found in the book of Jataka Tales. They are often thought of as metaphors for abnormal behavior or perhaps a short fictitious narrative from which a moral or spiritual truth may be drawn. In that sense these three stories, The Roshi, The Japanese Castaway, and Escape from Exile Island fulfill that description. The mores in these stories are in conflict with the Buddhist Dharma which teaches that sexual misbehavior, covetousness, stealing and killing are against the tenets of Zen Buddhism. Nevertheless, they are neither metaphors nor parables. They are depictions of the deviousness of society and the outcome of the predicaments that demand solutions. These three stories are a view of the human lot and the dynamics of coping with it. Despite the pragmatic mode in being concerned with problem solving in these stories an unknown and unforeseen factor always creeps in to upset some of the best laid plans. The protagonists in these stories are then forced to confront their individual situations and predicaments.

The story, The Roshi, reveals that no matter which way one turns the ultimate end is usually the same. The story answers the question, "What if?" that despite the turn of events in one's life the end is always the same.

In The Japanese Castaway one finds a unique reliance on faith. After suffering excruciating physical harm and pain the protagonist keeps his salvic faith until rescue is achieved.

Escape from Exile Island is the most severe revelation of aberrant behavior of an individual deviating from truth and rectitude including murder, theft and deception where, in the end, evil is requited with truth through the death of the protagonist.

I recognize it might be erroneous to call these stories Zen Buddhist stories since they are not connected to each other and therefore can stand alone as novella. But they do bring to the fore and show the necessity of calmness, habitual sobriety, and freedom from agitation in one's life – all teachings of the Buddha.

Albert Shansky,
Norwalk, CT – January 15, 2011

Dedication

This book is dedicated to my wife Pearl Brody Shansky with love and gratitude.

She has tolerated my obsession with my work with general good humor and has helped provide the warm environment, in which I have been able to write this book,

Acknowledgements

This story is a work of fiction. The characters, names, incidents, dialogue, and the plots are entirely the products of my imagination. Any resemblance to actual persons, companies, temples, or events are purely coincidental. Some names of actual places have been changed or used fictitiously to protect the innocent. It was not intended to besmirch or ridicule anyone.

My close friend, Dr. Maurice Siegel, helped me plan the format and made many worthwhile suggestions. For this he has my thanks and unwavering gratitude.

THE ROSHI

**The Adventures of a Wayward
Zen Buddhist Priest**

In two parts

Albert Shansky

PART 1
I

What have I done? Why are they so angry with me? It seemed to me she was willing. Yea, she was very willing. She came on to me; didn't she? I asked her to be certain. Nothing could dissuade her. She wanted me. So what did I do so wrong? She started the whole affair. Yet, I am blamed. Is it because more is expected of me? I am so confused with these priggish rules in America. In Japan this would never have happened. It certainly would never have come to this. Sexual activity is not sinful in Japan. Prostitution and homosexuality has been tolerated ever since the Tokugawa Period in the seventeenth century.

Oh my, it's so cold sitting in this zendo (Zen practice place) I should have worn a shawl over my robes before I sat in zazen (seated meditation). Did I break my ordination vows? The first precept says – do no harm. Who did I harm? No one was harmed; unless it was her husband, Mr. Kangetsu. He was just cuckolded. The poor man; may he rest in peace? But it wasn't me. It was she. She harmed him. The real tragedy is the effect on Myoko and Serena as a result of my actions. The fourth precept says – do not engage in sexual misconduct. Well, having sex with a willing partner certainly is not sexual misconduct. It isn't as if I attacked Serena or abused her. It was a simple matter of my satisfying her lust. As for Myoko, I am in love with her. Yes, I am still in love with her and sex was a natural outcome of my passion for her.

Now, all has been revealed. It seems so cruel to be exposed by some nosy body; for what purpose? It seems the intention was to injure me. More so, it was to injure Serena. Does she have such enemies? It is hard to believe that a gossip's tattle could cause so much damage and injury. It could only be done by a very callous person. But, I should have thought about the consequences before getting involved. Yet, I have wronged two women with my behavior. How can I deserve any benevolence? Now, I am interlocked in a stupid conflict. What am I to do? Will this scandal ever subside? Yes, my arrangement with Mr. Chigesu to return to Japan is the best way out. I am really grateful to him for arranging transport for me on a freighter for tomorrow. Perhaps I can start over when I am back in Japan? Yes, that is the only way open to me. How did it all begin? Let me think. Let me think......

1

II

I was standing on the Yokohama dock waiting to board the Umi Maru for Honolulu, Hawaii. It was a day of great excitement. I had been ordained as a Buddhist priest just the month before and decided to try and locate a congregation in America. I was very committed to starting an ecclesiastical unit even though I knew it was attended with risk and peril. Some friends and family came to see me off with good wishes for a happy journey. Everyone was gleeful, cheerful, and engaged in merriment, "Have a good trip, Jiun," they shouted with backslaps and bows. I was given presents which was added to my luggage. Then suddenly it was 'all aboard' and I walked up the gangplank with a wave of my hand leaving my friends and family behind.

I made my way to my to my stateroom which was one of only three guest cabins. This ship was a cargo steamer which took on limited passengers. The trip would take about twelve days to Honolulu. The accommodations were less than luxurious and the meals were simple fare. For this reason it was the least expensive way to travel.

I unloaded some of my bags and began to partake of a *bento* (box lunch) which I acquired on shore. After lunch, I made my way to the deck and at the railing began to follow the rippling water. Looking at the endless water I found myself getting bored and the trip has just begun. I am glad I brought along some books. It was obvious that reading would become my main occupation. I returned to my cabin which contained a bed, a table and a chair in a ten feet square room. There was a clothes closet in one corner and a separate small bathroom with a sink, a toilet commode and a shower stall all crammed together. The cabin was made somewhat hospitable by a small porthole which let in light and air. Meals were to be taken three times a day with the crew in the galley below deck. I am used to these hardships having spent six years in a monastery in Japan.

I removed my Buddhist robe and put it away for special occasions in the future. I donned my *samu-e* (Buddhist everyday/work clothes) and immediately felt that I was a different person.

There was a knock on the door which I opened to find a man standing wearing a seaman's uniform. He touched his cap visor with his right hand and said, "May I be of help to you Nakahara-san (Rev. Nakahara)?" [My name is Nakahara Jiun (last name first)] He was a man of about 5'6" tall with a tawny complexion and a flowing black mustache. His eyes were mere slits which seemed to form a perpetual smile.

"No thank you," I said. "I am just getting settled.'

"Well, I came to give you the meal schedule. We dine tonight in the galley at 6:00 pm. A bell will alert you."

"Thank you." I replied. "I hope to meet the other guests and the crew at that time."

He was silent for a moment then slowly answered, "The crews eat at a separate table. The guests have their own table."

"That will be fine," I retorted realizing I made a slight faux pas.

After a long silence he hastily added, "We've never had a priest on board before."

"Well I am sure there is nothing to concern anyone. I am only a passenger."

"In that case I will leave you and look forward to seeing you this evening at dinner," He said as he stepped backward with a bow out of the doorway. I suddenly felt very much alone. In order to keep busy I began to open the gifts given to me by my friends and family on shore. There was a pair of house slippers, a box of candles and incense, a string of *Ojusu* (Mala beads), a black wool sweater, and a copy of the *Shobogenzo* (a type of Zen Bible). All these things were practical gifts and would come in handy in the future. I then began to distribute the contents of my luggage throughout the closet. Having completed this task, I sat at the desk and began to read one of my books. After a while, there was a feeling of ennui which came over me. I could not concentrate on my reading. I just hung my head to try and overcome the feeling of weariness which beset me.

I then grabbed the Mala beads and began to recite the 108 evil passions to which humans are subject. Moving the beads between my thumb and forefinger gave me a sense of fruition. I slowly began to shake off the tedium after what seemed like a long time of manipulating the beads. After completion I sat back and stared fixedly at the ceiling as through wonder.

Then, I heard a bell ringing outside and someone shouting, "Dinner, Dinner." I realized I had been sitting at my desk for hours. I shook my head to clear my thoughts, went to the sink to wash my face. I donned my *hippari* (small coat) and made my way to the galley.

The galley was a small room containing two tables. As I entered, I noticed all the people at the two tables rise and bow in obeisance. I returned the bow with a *gassho* (palms together) saying, "Please it is not necessary to accord me such special respect. I am a passenger just as you are."

The naval officer who came to my cabin approached me as I began sitting. "Nakahara-san, may I introduce your fellow passengers?" He said with a slight bow. I was half erect then settled back. "Of course, that would be welcome."

3

He began in a matter-of-fact manner. "Next to you are Mr. and Mrs. Kangetsu of cabin 2 and across from them are father and son Chigesu of cabin1."

"Thank you," I exclaimed to the naval officer. I then turned to the table, "I am glad to meet all of you. I wish you all a pleasant voyage."

Food was brought to our table by a man who carried bowls of cooked rice and steamed vegetables. He was a short man with a rotund stature and small limbs. He had a round face with severely slanted eyes which seemed closed. His face was puffy, his neck thick and pink, and his chin was doubled. He was as bald as a knee with a head that looked like a peanut. He had a slightly pocked-marked skin on his cheeks and neck. As best I could tell his age was probably in the late fifties.

The large bowls contained large wooden flat spoons for dispensing the vegetables into our plates and the rice into small individual bowls. After much courtesy was exhibited people began to eat with *hashi* (chopsticks) in a slow deliberate manner. Then in a few minutes the cook brought an iron tea pot which he set on the middle of the table. Tea was dispensed into our handle less cups by the passengers to their neighbors; each proffered some to the other.

Mr. Chigesu was making a sucking noise by slurping his tea, shortly followed by Mr. Kangetsu. I had all I could do to contain myself from laughing at this synchronous display. After all were sated, a conversation began by my asking Mr. and Mrs. Kangetsu, "Are you going to Hawaii on vacation or business?"

"Oh no, we live in Honolulu. We just returned from visiting my mother in Chichibu," replied Mrs. Kangetsu.

"Chichibu, where is that?"

"It's a short train ride north of Tokyo," she continued, "She is very old and we wanted to see her before she died."

"I see. What about you, Mr. Chigesu?" turning my head as I spoke.

"We are only stopping for a short time in Honolulu and then we are going on to San Francisco. We have business there."

"I hope to go to San Francisco after a short stay in the Emerald Sangha in Honolulu." I continued, "Forgive me for asking but what kind of business do you have?'

"My son and I are in the import/export business. We arrange for the shipment of various kinds of goods from Japan to America."

"Thank you. I was just curious. When will you go to San Francisco?"

We will arrange for transportation, probably by boat, as soon as we land. It may take a day or two to get a proper berth on a boat."

"I see. I shall be staying with fellow monks at the Emerald Sangha in

Honolulu but only for a short while until I can arrange with the captain of this ship for my final destination in San Francisco."

Suddenly there was a lacuna in our conversation when the cook arrived to announce, "All must leave now so I may clean up. Sorry. Sorry."

We left the galley and appeared on deck where we continued our conversation at rail side. There were some deck chairs provided for our use and comfort. Mr. Kangetsu lit up a cigarette and began to smoke while he talked, "Hawaii is a most beautiful island. We have a small house on a hillock outside of Honolulu surrounded by bougainvillea. In every place throughout the year there are changes in the weather called seasons: winter, spring, summer, and fall. In Hawaii we only have two: the dry, sunny season and the wet, rainy season. When we arrive it will be the rainy season. In Hawaii and elsewhere in the tropics, the change in seasons often goes unnoticed but we know the subtle details in the world around us – plants, animals, and weather patterns. There is a large Japanese community where we live. We have a statue of *Jizo* in front of our house. *Jizo*, one of the most beloved Buddhist deities in Japan is known primarily as the guardian of children and travelers. But we look to him for protection. If you are able please come and visit us." With that he handed me an address card using both hands and a bow in a very formal manner.

"Thank you," I said as I reached for the card.

Since our start the weather has been delightful and the sea was very calm. I found myself getting very tired so I bade my compatriots good night and returned to my cabin. I decided to sit *zazen* (seated meditation) for an hour before retiring. I removed my *samu-e* (work clothes) and put on my *kesa* (meditation robe) and sat on one of the cushion/pillows with a straight back in rigid condition. I placed my right foot on my left thigh and thence my left foot on my right thigh and thus was sitting in full lotus position. I placed my hands on top of each other in my lap with thumbs touching as if carrying an egg and began a rhythmical breathing with my eyes half open. Thoughts kept racing in my head but after a few minutes I felt very calm and little by little whatever thoughts would enter would quickly disappear.

Halfway through my zazen a great lurch of the boat threw me off my cushion. I sat up startled as I heard thunder and saw lightning through the porthole. I got up to close the porthole to prevent the rain from coming in but was thrown back by the jerking and tossing of the ship. Obviously, we were in the middle of a squall. I grabbed the desk which was apparently fastened to the floor to steady myself but the ship was continuously tossed from side to side with great thuds by the storm. This rocking motion continued for what seemed like an unusually long time. Then it stopped as quickly as it started and the ship seemed to sail smoothly once again.

I found myself breathing a sigh of relief. Could this incident at sea have been my demise? No, No I thought. Buddha has greater plans for me. The cabin was in severe disarray as I looked about. Everything was tossed about in disorder. I picked up the cushion and sat once again to continue my *zazen*. As I sat I could hear the rhythmic thumping of the engine. All seemed to be well again, but I was distinctly apprehensive. After completing *zazen*, I straightened up the room and prepared for bed. That night I dreamed sweet dreams of my future.

The next day, after a breakfast of *congee* (rice porridge) and pickled vegetables followed by *ryokucha* (green tea), I went out to the deck for a stroll. To my surprise I found Mr. Kangetsu leaning over the railing retching repeatedly. Meantime his wife was patting his back.

"Are you unwell?" I enquired as I approached him cautiously.

Holding a large handkerchief at his mouth he straightened up and looked at me with a weary look in his eyes. "I think I'll return to my cabin and lie down, "he said with downcast eyes as he strolled off holding his wife's hand.

III

I was sitting at my desk reading the *Shobogenzo* (Buddhist Bible-like book) when I heard a faint knock on the door. I arose from my concentrated state and went to the door. On opening it I noticed Mrs. Kangetsu standing at the threshold. She immediately bowed her head as she spoke, "Sumimasen Nakahara-san." (Excuse me Reverend Nakahara). My husband is sleeping and I became very bored. May I keep company with you?"

I was stymied for the moment still having the words of the Shobogenzo in my mind. But I stepped back with a flourish to allow her entry. "Of course, come in. Have a seat." I blubbered with some awkward hesitancy.

"I thought we might just talk, but if you are busy I shall leave." She started to remove her coat off one shoulder.

I hurried over to her, "No, No, please come in. May I help you?" I reached from behind to remove her coat. I noticed she was wearing a red silk dress cut in close conformity to the lines of her body. She turned immediately and faced me as she raised her hand to clasp my face on each cheek. Her hands felt warm and smooth. With that she pulled my face close to hers and planted a kiss on my lips. I was confused and startled, but responded by grabbing her waist and returned the kiss with a force of passion. I felt a surge in my loins and held her close to me. She dropped her hands and placed her arms about my back and pushed her breasts into my lower chest. We stood in this hugging position for a few minutes in total silence. I began to feel my member stiffening so I grabbed her rump and lifted her while walking to the bed. Having placed her on the bed I asked in a whisper, "Do you want to undress?"

"Yes, I do not want to ruin my dress." She raised herself off the bed as she spoke and began to disrobe. I noticed her underclothes were also made of silk. She removed these as well leaving her standing totally naked. Her skin was creamy white like porcelain and her floss was black and curly. I felt somewhat embarrassed observing her nudity. I removed my *samu-e* (everyday clothes) and my underclothes and immediately took her in my arms. I could feel the pulsation of her body as my member pressed against her thighs. I was in a state of extreme passion. With one hand she stroked my member as we slowly, very gently fell onto the bed. She continued to stroke my member as I moved between her legs with my body. It was then she inserted my member into her moist vagina. The gyrations and movements were smooth and slippery. I reached coitus almost simultaneously with her at which point I pressed my lips against her mouth and inserted my tongue into her wet buccal opening. We were both spent but held each other for a few moments.

We unscrambled and disengaged rapidly in order for her to proceed to the bathroom in haste. I dressed again and waited for her to come out. Some time elapsed as she lingered in the bathroom while I heard the water running. I could only imagine what she was doing. The bathroom door opened slowly and she methodically grabbed her underclothes and the red dress and was quickly attired in a presentable fashion. Nothing was said in all this time. Now, she looked at me with eyes that radiated like pools of fire. "Did you like that?" she said in a low sibilant rustling sound.

Half-chokingly I uttered, "It was wonderful."

She came up to me and with one hand stroked my shaven head and then touched my cheek. Touch is the sense most treasured by lovers.

"I hope you don't hold me in contempt," she said.

"What are you saying," I exclaimed. "We had a sympathetic understanding. We both wanted it whatever our individual reasons. Having ardent affection for each other is a natural feeling. We both took delight in such mutual pleasure." I stopped talking when I saw tears glitter in her eyes. I took her into my arms to console her as she heaved with each breath. "There, there, why are you crying?" I soothed her with a repeated thump of my hand on her back.

"I feel so ashamed but I could not control myself. I am lonely. My husband is impotent and does not crave sex. I, on the other hand, enjoy sex. But most importantly I had a deep, abiding affection for you since we first met. I hope these words do not offend you; after all you are a priest."

"No, I am really very flattered." I said with faint conviction.

"I must go now to see if my husband has awakened from his troubled sleep. He may need my help," she explained in an unconvincing voice as she bowed and let herself out.

Left alone I returned to my desk and spied the open book – Shobogenzo – at the page *shoakumakusa* (refrain from evil). I began reading: Ancient Buddha said, "Refrain from all evil, practice all that is good, purify your mind: This is the teaching of the Buddhas." A shudder ran through my body, "what have I done?" I rested my head on my arm on my desk.

IV

I did not go to dinner. Instead I sat zazen for one hour and then went to bed. In the morning I went out on deck to breathe the invigorating sea air. I did not go to breakfast using this as a sort of penance. I watched the wake of water flowing against the side of the ship. The Pacific Ocean seemed calm and quiet and it put me in a reverie-like mood that tended to release me from reality. I thought about Mrs. Kangetsu and the incident of last night. Would she approach me again? What would I do? The thought of it became a nettlesome problem.

I was unaware that Mr. and Mrs. Kangetsu were approaching me from the rear until I heard her voice. "*Ohayo, Nakahara-san* (Good morning, Reverend Nakahara), "we missed you at breakfast."

I turned around to find Mrs. Kangetsu strolling arm in arm with her husband towards me. He still looked unwell with a pale complexion and rheumy eyes. He shuffled along using his wife's arm for support. I suddenly felt sorry for this man whom I cuckolded. He reached me with extended arm and attempted to speak with a toothless maw, "I am happy to see you, Nakahara-san. I had a terrible time yesterday but I am much better now."

"I am glad *Kangetsu-kun* (Mr. Kangetsu) maybe the sea air will help you." In the meantime I noticed there was no unusual sign of recognition from Mrs. Kangetsu. She simply gave a fawning smile as she trudged along holding her husband as if nothing was unusual or different. I felt smothered by the helplessness raging inside me. In a way, however, I was content with this attitude knowing I shall make payment through penance.

"Please sit down, husband, on this chair," she said as she maneuvered him to the seat.

I approached to help but only moved in an obsequious way.

She looked up and suddenly pointed to the distant horizon, "Look, look, there is a whale!"

I turned in time to see the fluke of the whale beating the surface of the water with a gigantic splash; then in a few minutes it rose to the surface with a fountain of water expressed through its blow hole.

Mrs. Kangetsu clapped her hands and squealed with gleeful joy. For a moment I felt a gnawing erotic desire at her pleasurable emotion. I quickly put these thoughts aside and joined the people in empty conversation. This went on for a few hours until she asked in a spirited tone, "Will you be joining us for dinner this evening, Nakahara-san?"

Nothing was said while I mulled over the question. I looked at her pleading eyes as I said, "Yes, I believe I shall."

With that she attempted to help raise her sickly husband out of the chair, "Well then, we shall meet at dinner." She said as they shuffled once again to their cabin.

I remained on deck until the last wink of the fading sun before it disappeared beneath the horizon. I wondered what will come next as I entered my cabin and prepared for dinner,

At dinner we all expressed the customary gentility. I looked at Mrs. Kangetsu with a questioning frown on my brow.

"My husband has remained in the cabin. I am afraid he is still too weak to join us," she hastily stated apologetically.

"I am sorry to hear that, Mrs. Kangetsu is there anything I can do?" I offered.

"Thank you, no, Nakahara-san. I am sure a good night's sleep will help him," she replied.

"Well if you need help please be sure to call on me," I tendered once again.

"Thank you, I shall," she demurred.

After dinner we all parted the galley heading for our individual abodes.

Within the hour I heard a soft knock on the door. I rose from my chair and opened the door to discover Mrs. Kangetsu looking resplendent in her red silk dress. "Come in, come in," I whispered anxiously while looking outside in both directions. Satisfied that no one was about I ushered her into my cabin.

"What about your husband?" I asked with a fearful look on my face.

"He is sleeping. I couldn't stand the heavy breathing and snoring. He vomited his dinner again. I am really concerned. Do you have any suggestions for me?" she stated in a forthright manner.

"Maybe, he shouldn't eat for a while. Food obviously doesn't agree with him. Just give him hot tea for a while until he improves," I proposed tentatively.

She looked at me with her intense gazing eyes, "Do you think so?"

"Yes, it would be better," I assured her.

"Thank you. May I stay here for a while?" she requested politely.

"Yes, indeed," I said hurriedly while offering her the chair.

She sat down while smoothing the silk of her dress and said, "I am always afraid of creasing my dress."

"If it bothers you why not take it off," I suggested in an innocent voice.

"Would that be alright? I mean would you mind?" she asked coyly.

With shrinking modesty I answered, "I not only would not mind but would enjoy it."

After a bit of silence, she rose and began removing her dress.

"May I help you?" I asked gallantly.

"No, I can manage," she quickly responded.

After removing her dress she stood wearing only her silk panties and a brassiere which supported her rather small breasts.

I gazed at her with amatory admiration and astonishment at my immediate sexual arousal. I could feel my member becoming hard and swollen. I went over to her and exposed my member to show her the state of my erection. She giggled like a young child as she touched it, "Let's get into bed," I pulled off her brassiere and began to knead her breasts with my hands.

"Please stop; let's get into bed," she spoke as she went to the bed. I removed her panties and my hand opened her legs. I began having her with thrusts that were somewhat violent. On completion I rolled off her body with a low groan. I found my body shaking and sweating. I rested on my back looking upwards before speaking, "I am sorry if I was rough."

"She immediately responded, "Oh, not at all. I really enjoyed it." We lay side by side looking in each others eyes. Nothing was said for a long while until she fidgeted in a restless movement onto her side. "I must go. My husband may need me," she spoke as she raised herself to a leaning position on her elbow. I watched her sleek body in motion as she went to the bathroom to perform her ablutions. Meanwhile, I dressed and waited for her to come out. She eventually dressed and parted with a kiss full on my mouth. "May I come tomorrow?" she asked with a beseeching look in her eyes. Then I knew she would fulfill my sexual desire and become my paramour.

And so it went for the remainder of the trip. Mrs. Kangetsu visited me every night. Mr. Kangetsu never left his cabin. Mrs. Kangetsu brought him food and tea daily.

Apparently he was seriously ill. When the ship docked in Honolulu harbor he was taken off on a stretcher by a waiting ambulance crew.

V

I went by taxi to the Emerald Sangha where I was greeted by the head monk, Koichi Kagaguchi, "Welcome, Nakahara-san. I am delighted to see you. I rejoice that your ship has brought you to us safely. Did you have a good trip?" he sputtered hastily as he bowed deeply with a gassho.

I acknowledged his softness of manners and returned the courtesy with a deep bow and gassho. "The voyage was both uneventful and enjoyable, Koichi-san, but I am now most happy to be here," I feigned with dissembled reasoning. We walked off together while a young novice carried my luggage. Koichi, the head monk showed me to my room. The guest room was small with the *tokonoma* (alcove for a hanging scroll) facing the inner room. It was a room of the plainest description; it was severe in its simplicity. The *chigai-dana* (shelves for articles) was next to the veranda. The recesses were quite deep – the *chiga-dana* having a single broad shelf. A little bamboo flower-holder was hanging on the post. The floor of the room was permanently covered with *tatami* mats made of straw. I could see that this was a 'six mat room' or about nine feet by twelve feet. The mats are laid side by side; two mats in one way and the third mat crosswise at the end. This is repeated in an opposite direction with the three remaining mats. A futon is rolled up in a small closet under the shelf of the *chigai-dana*.

I thanked the novice who placed my luggage on the floor as he parted with a bow and gassho. Koichi Kagaguchi, the head monk, addressed me with an angelic look on his cherubic face, "I hope you will be comfortable here, Nakahara-san. Please rest the remainder of the day. A bell will summon you for dinner,"

"Thank you, this will be fine." I declared as I looked about me and surveyed my surroundings. Koichi Kagaguchi left with a shuffle of his bare feet. He retrieved his house slippers on the outside of the *shoji* (sliding paper door) and swaggered off with his head held high and his hands held on top of each other against his chest.

I began to remove clothes and items from my luggage to stow away on the *chigai-dana*. Suddenly I heard a muted voice on the outside of the *shoji*, "Sumimasen, (excuse me) Nakahara-san, I have brought you a thermos of hot water and some tea."

I went to the door and slid open the *shoji* door to find the novice waiting with a tray in hand. He stepped over the threshold and entered with a bow; shuffling with bare feet to the only piece of furniture in the room. He set the tray down on the small, low table and turned towards me to gassho. I returned the gassho and said, "Thank you very much. What is your name, please?"

"My name is Watanabe, Junjiro."

"Your accent sounds strange."

"I am Nisei. I was born in Hawaii."

"Then you are American?"

"Yes, I am training here in the Emerald Sangha."

"Very good, I thank you once again."

He then turned and left after closing the *shoji*, leaving me to prepare the tea. I sat cross-legged before the small table and placed a teaspoon of the green tea shreds into the earthenware mug, added hot water from the thermos and allowed it to steep and settle for a few minutes until the essence extracted from the soaking tea leaves was evident. In raising the mug to my lips I was able to sip the hot brew with contentment. I closed my eyes as the warm liquid coursed through my body offering full gratification. Images of past events began to pass through my mind. Among the jumble of mind-pictures, I had a view of Tomoko Kangetsu. Will I ever meet her again? She is what is known as *genki no obasan* (healthy old lady). I laughed inwardly in merriment. What am I thinking? Maybe I am too harsh. I think she is a sprightly and fit woman in her fifties; a *musume* (young girl). I shook my head back and forth to quash her appearance. I wanted to suppress thoughts of her. I had more important things to think about. Now that I am in this monastery I shall do my priestly duties. Tomorrow I shall help with morning services.

After a while the dinner bell sounded and I proceeded to the dining room. The head monk, Koichi Kagaguchi, seated me next to him at the head table. All the others were at a table arranged perpendicular to the head table. The tables were low to the ground and we sat with folded legs in half-lotus posture. I was introduced as a visiting priest from Japan. Koichi spoke in Japanese and English since many of the members were English speaking Americans. A meal *gatha* (prayer) was chanted before eating.

The dinner was eaten deftly in *oryoki* bowls (nested concentric bowls) and consisted of boiled rice, boiled vegetables and fish. There was complete silence during dinner except for the occasional clang of utensils.

At the conclusion of dinner I joined the others in clean-up; after which I went into the *zendo* (meditation hall) to sit zazen for forty minutes. After zazen I went to the bath house to bathe and soak away all my cares and concerns. That night I retired early being tired from the day's travel and the shift of milieu. I slept fitfully having dreams of strange and weird circumstances of Tomoko Kangetsu and even Mr. Chigesu, the other passenger, traveling with his son, on board the Umi Maru.

The wake up bell sounded at 4:00 am. I put on my robes and returned to the *zendo* for zazen. On completion, I went to the *hatto* (services hall) for morning service. I contributed to the service by taking the lead position. This was an honor usually bestowed on visiting priests. Having completed the services, I joined in the routine clean-up, and then returned to my room. I removed my robes and replaced them with a samu-e. While I was rolling up my futon I heard a soft knock on my door followed by a voice which said, "Excuse me, Nakahara-san. You have a visitor in the anteroom."

"A visitor, did you say a visitor?" I queried as I slid open the *shoji* door. There stood the novice, Watanabe. "Yes, he replied. She is waiting in the anteroom. May I lead you there?"

"Thank you, I shall follow you immediately," I hastily replied. On arrival at the anteroom I saw a woman dressed completely in black sitting in a chair. At first I did not recognize her but as she arose I saw that it was Tomoko Kangetsu.

She spoke very softly with a tear in her voice, "Forgive me for disturbing you, Nakahara-san but I have just become the victim of very sad news."

"What is it?"

"Mr. Kangetsu died."

"Died?"

"Yes!"

"When?"

"Last night."

I stopped questioning since I noticed she was beginning to sob. I inquired in a sympathetic voice, "I am sorry." Then I hesitated but, continued, "What did he die of?"

She looked at me with her wet eyes as she spoke, "He had a large tumor in his stomach which the surgeons tried to remove, but the surgery was unsuccessful and so he died." There was silence for a while. I noticed she was daubing her eyes and cheeks with a small handkerchief. "I am sorry for your bereavement. Is there any way I can help?" I asked.

"Yes, you can," she quickly replied. "Would you perform a death service at his cremation?" She looked at me with tearful eyes as she said this.

"I would be honored to perform such a service," I spoke with genuine sympathy. "When is it to be?" I asked.

She spoke quickly with a note of anxiety in her voice, "This afternoon. I have a taxi waiting outside. Would you join me now?"

For the moment I was taken aback but recovered quickly,"Of course, but first let me get some things and I will meet you outside." I had to redress into my robes and pick up my *Shobogenzo* and my mala beads. The taxi drove us for about a half hour to a large building in what appeared to be an industrial neighborhood. We entered the building and were led to a waiting room where a small group of people congregated. I surmised they were friends. A man wearing a black, three-piece, pencil-stripped business suit with a white carnation in his lapel took Mrs. Kangetsu's hand and spoke to her with a lowered head in an inaudible whisper. Then he came over to me and bowed with his chin against his chest, "Welcome, honorable priest. May I take you to the crematory?"

I nodded and accompanied him and Mrs. Kangetsu into another room some distance down the hallway. "We shall start the cremation now," he said as he pointed to a doorway of the furnace. A sudden roar indicated that the fire was starting up. I immediately held my hands in gassho as I repeated the ancient prayer, the Heart Sutra, known to all Buddhists, from memory. I spoke in a low, steady voice, "This is the Prajnaparamita Hrydaya Sutra." I stopped for a moment and turned to look at Mrs. Kangetsu. Her head was low and she did not meet my gaze. I turned back and continued in a low steady voice, "When the Bodhisattva Avalokitesvara was coursing in the deep Prajna Paramita he perceived that all five skandas are empty. Thus he overcame all his suffering."

I turned to look at her again. "Oh Sariputra, form does not differ from the void, and the void does not differ from form. Form is void and void is form. The same is true for feelings, perceptions, volitions and consciousness."

I stopped to clear the frog in my throat, "Oh Sariputra, the characteristics of the voidness of all dharmas are non-arising, non-ceasing, non-defiled, non-pure, non-increasing, non-decreasing."

I continued, "Therefore, in the void there are no forms, no feelings, perceptions, volitions, or consciousness, no eye, ear, nose, tongue, body or mind: no form, sound, smell, taste, touch or mind object; no realm of the eye, until we come to no realm of consciousness."

I could hear a loud sobbing to my right where Mrs. Kangetsu was standing.

"No ignorance and also no ending of ignorance, until we come to no old age and death and no ending of old age and death."

The sobbing was getting louder, "Also there is no truth of suffering, of the cause of suffering, of the cessation of suffering, nor of the path. There is no wisdom and there is no attainment whatsoever."

I became convinced that the loud sobbing was being put on, "Because there is nothing to be attained, the Bodhisattva relying on Prajna Paramita has no obstruction in his mind. The Buddhas of the past, present, and future, by relying on Prajna Paramita have attained supreme enlightenment."

I hesitated but continued," Therefore, the Prajna Paramita is the great magic spell, the spell of illumination, the supreme spell which can truly protect one from all suffering without fail."

I next spoke in a loud voice, "Therefore he uttered the spell of Prajnaparamita, saying: gate, gate, paragate, parasamgate, bodhi, svaha."

I turned to Mrs. Kangetsu, "The above mantra said in Sanskrit is now said in English (Japanese): Gone, gone, gone beyond, gone utterly beyond, perfect wisdom, so may it be.

At the conclusion of the service, we were led back to the waiting room. I began to thumb my mala beads one at a time while reciting the 108 evil passions in a low whisper. I was in an oneiric state of repose sitting in full lotus posture on the floor. Mrs. Kangetsu, sitting next to me on a chair, was quietly sobbing as if it was natural accompaniment to my recitation. Then after a rather long while the same man, with the three piece suit, arrived carrying an urn which he placed in the open hands of Mrs. Kangetsu saying, "May your husband's soul reach the Western Paradise."

This produced a torrent of tears from Mrs. Kangetsu as she accepted the urn. It piqued my immediate attention at this unusual and unworthy remark. But I said nothing.

Mrs. Kangetsu introduced me to various people attending the service. Some people were munching the provided rice cookies and partaking of the refreshments. I found myself bowing and gasshoeing to everyone as they left with sympathetic gestures and statements to Mrs. Kangetsu. I stood back as they all finally parted.

"Would you like to come to my home?" she said with a pleading tone in her voice.

I looked directly at her before remarking, "I am sorry I must return to the Emerald Sangha to continue my priestly duties."

She hesitated before continuing, "Well then can I expect you one evening? I would like to see you again."

I breathed deeply with great courage, "No, that is all over. I shall only be in Hawaii a short while until I travel on to San Francisco."

We rode back to the monastery and I began saying farewell to her when she suddenly and without warning reached across the seat and grabbed my head while planting a long steady kiss on my lips. "Too bad, we could have had a very beautiful life together," she demurred.

"Goodbye and may great fortune be with you," I said as I alighted from the taxicab and headed into the monastery.

VI

Now that I no longer had a paramour to distract me I focused on the duties of a visiting priest at the Emerald Sangha, so called because of its surrounding verdure, I knew that if I took up with Mrs. Kangetsu again I may have been completely diverted by her widowhood and I would possibly forget about my calling. This is known as *shitsuren* or a broken affair. I was sad at this loss of love so I threw myself into my work for the remainder of the week until I would leave for San Francisco on the Umi Maru. When we landed in Honolulu the captain had told me it would take about a week to unload the cargo, clean the ship, and take on new cargo.

I spent my time during the layover helping with morning services and preparing *teisho* (sermons) to be given after the morning service. One day I gave a sermon on the individual self. It reminded me of the traditional Vedanta story so I used it in my sermon.

"Ten men on a journey came to a river. They swam across, and once on the further bank they counted to ensure that all had survived. Each time they counted the answer was nine. When they concluded that one had drowned, they wept at the loss of one of their number. A wise man happened to meet them, and enquired why they were lamenting. They said that one of their friends had drowned. He told them to stand in a line. Then he counted them, tapping each on the shoulder in turn with his stick. Finally he tapped the last man and pronounced them to be ten in number. Happy that none were lost, they thanked him and went on their way."

The point of the story is that each man had forgotten to count himself. The wise man reminded each one of his own self. What the wise man revealed was that we ignore the self that we really are – the true self. So who or what is the true self? The self is spirit. The self is transcendent. The self is universal. The self is space. Like space the self is one. The universal self is like space. It has no limits. After all, if the self is contained in the body, then a surgeon could easily find it. Perhaps he cannot do so because it is invisible; but then if it is imperceptible to all five senses, why should we expect to find it within a perceptible thing like a human body? That is why in Buddhism we say there is no self (*anatman*), one of the three marks of human existence, which also includes *dukkha* (suffering) and *anicca* (impermanence). It is a fundamental perception in Buddhism that since there is no subsistent reality to be found in or underlying appearances, there cannot be a subsistent self or soul in the human appearance.

One day a messenger came from the captain of the Umi Maru, "The captain said we will be outfitted by the ship's chandler and ready to leave at 4:30 am. The ship will not wait for you so please be on board." I thanked him and assured him I would be on board. I next went to the head monk to thank him for his courtesies with a promise to write him after I became settled. "I shall be leaving very early in the morning, before zazen and I wanted to thank you for your kindness to me."

He bowed with a gassho, "Go in peace, my friend. May your trip be pleasant and safe? May your life be fruitful and rewarding?" I returned a very low bow and gassho and went to my room to pack my things. At about 3:00 am I taxied to the dock and boarded the ship. I went to the wheelhouse and found the captain at the binnacle. "Good morning, Captain," I shouted, "I'm aboard." He turned with a scowl which quickly became a smile, "Good morning, honorable priest. Welcome aboard. You may have the same stateroom you used previously, we have no other passengers." He turned back to his work in haste and so I prepared to leave him." Thank you," I said. I left him with a bow and a gassho and returned to my old stateroom.

Since the trip will only take a little more than two days, I didn't bother unpacking. I then began to sit zazen for one hour. In a while I felt a lurch and could hear the engines revving as the ship began to move. We were on our way. The motion of the ship caused me to nod off and I fell asleep on the floor where I sat. After about an hour I arose, removed my clothes and got into bed. I had a fitful sleep dreaming of weird things and strange people. At about eight o'clock there was a knock on my door, which jolted me upright. On opening the door I saw the young messenger carrying a tray of food and tea. He exclaimed, "The captain's compliments. He did not want to disturb your sleep with a morning call to breakfast. I was astonished at this kindly gesture but took the tray from his hands with a recital of gratitude, "Thank you very much and, please, thank the captain."

After finishing breakfast, I dressed and made my way to the deck where I was immediately reminded of Mrs. Tomoko Kangetsu. I shook my head to disperse these old images and began to notice and appreciate the merging of the blue sea with the blue sky at the distant horizon. The ship was sailing along at a smooth steady pace and I enjoyed the cool air flowing against my face. I left the railing and sat down on one of the deck chairs. Soon I dozed off. Thoughts of the future entered my mind. *How will I obtain a position of head priest for a Zen temple? How does one start a Zendo?* These and other questions began to smite me. Since I was advised by the head monk of the Emerald Sangha to visit the Zen temple in Japantown, I felt his kindly manner assured me of my future. Suddenly a chill ran through my body so I decided to return to my cabin. I became depressed at being alone causing me to reach for the Shobogenzo to be in Dogen's company. I knew I could have a friendly intercourse with Dogen, as I read I could hear the creaking of the vessel as it swayed from side to side. It seemed to be speaking to me. More than once I looked up from the book to see the swinging of the overhead lamp. The room seemed to be alive with mystical noises and obscure movements. *Who? What?* I was in an apparent state of alarm. The dread and disquiet of loneliness seemed to be overtaking me. I rushed to the bathroom to wet my face. *Ah, that's better.* I calmed down. Now I could read the Shobogenzo with ease. Then I heard an inner voice: *You are not alone. Dogen is sitting with you.* I have been having these daytime images very often recently. The nightmares were even more terrible. They were usually excoriating scenes with the failure of people to communicate with each other.

After two days at sea we finally docked in the San Francisco harbor. I made my way to the captain's bridge to say goodbye but he was very busy giving orders to his men. Everyone was scurrying about. I bowed to him with a gassho, "Goodbye Captain. I hope our paths will cross in the future." He turned around with a blank stare on his face, "Goodbye priest. I hope we meet again."

With that I left the ship and hailed a taxicab to take me to the Zen temple in Japantown.

VII

The temple which is known as *Kinoji* (neighborhood temple) is on the corner of Laguna and Post Streets in what is called Japantown. The structure was a typical American style building used for churches and the like. It had no particular architectural reference to Japan. After alighting from the taxicab I climbed the few steps up to the front door and rang the bell. In a short while an older lady came to the door, "May I help you?" she said with a quizzical expression on her face. I bowed with a gassho and slowly responded, "I am here to see Reverend Fukuzawa, Kanako. My name is Nakahara, Jiun." She was startled and immediately bowed. Holding the door open wider she admitted me with a flourish of her right hand. "Come in, come in, Reverend. I will tell Fukuzawa-san you are here. Please wait in the front room while I bring in your luggage."

After removing my shoes, I sat on a chair in the front waiting room and looked about me while musing at the wall hangings. I could hear the shuffle of feet and the murmuring of voices as the Reverend Fukuzawa arrived with a deep bow and gassho. "Welcome, Nakahara-san. You came sooner than I expected. But you are most welcome." He was a rather tall man, at least taller than the average Japanese, wearing black robes and a silver *rakusu* (a symbolic tattered robe of the Buddha). His head was completely shaven and he wore black framed, very thick eyeglasses. His face was smooth with jowls that shook like jelly and with thick lips which fluttered as he spoke. He could be described as rotund with a protruding belly.

I rose and returned the salutation, "I am most happy to be here. I extended my hand which contained a beautifully wrapped box, "I brought these dried fruits from Japan for you. It contains peaches, apricots, pears, kiwis, berries, and grapes grown in the sacred soil of Japan. I hope you will enjoy them." He accepted the gift with a quaver in his voice, "Thank you. I am most delighted. Please sit. I shall order tea. He turned to the entrance way and shouted, "Tea please." I heard a rustle and then feet scurrying off.

The same older woman returned with a tray containing the tea and several pieces of china. "Thank you, *jochu* (maid servant). Please put it on the table." While we sat and sipped our tea I began the conversation with an inquiry. "Do you have a room in the temple where I may sleep?" He stared at me with a puzzled look on his face, "I am afraid not. This building has an office, a kitchen and a very large *hatto* (services hall). There is no place to put a sleep room for you. When you contacted me I thought you had sleep accommodations. You must make some other accommodations."

"I see," I said pensively.

He continued, "Don't you know anyone in San Francisco who could put you up?"

"Well no." I thought. "But I have the business card of Mr. Chigesu who I met on the ship coming over." I extended my hand with the card to Fukuzawa-san.

"Would you like me to call him on the telephone?" he questioned while perusing the card. "If you don't mind that would be very kind of you," I said.

He reached for the telephone and began dialing. "Hello, hello, Mr. Chigesu? My name is Fukuzawa, Kanako. I am sitting here with Reverend Nakahara. He would like to speak with you." He handed me the telephone with a broad grin on his face. I immediately began speaking, "Hello Chigesu-kun (Mr. Chigesu). How are you? I have just arrived in San Francisco. I am now at the Kinoji Temple. Oh, you know it. Well it seems I have a bit of a problem. You see the temple has no place for me to sleep. What? What did you say? Are you sure? I don't want to inconvenience you. Yes, Yes. Alright, I'll meet you at 6:00 pm this evening for dinner. Thank you, thank you very much. Goodbye." I hung up the receiver with a grinning facial expression. "He said he can put me up. I am to meet him at his home this evening for dinner."

"I am happy for you Nakahara-san. "That is a good omen for your stay in San Francisco." He said with a broad smile.

VIII

I received directions from Fukuzawa-san and I began the bus trek to reach Mr. Chigesu's house at the appointed hour of 6:00 pm. When I approached the house I found it to be particularly unpretentious. Of course, the front had a variety of plantings and flowers such as azaleas, rhododendrons and hastas. It was a low level house with a separate garage connected by a breezeway, typical of California architecture. The whole property, of about two acres, was surrounded by a low stone fence. The surprise came on passing through the front entry. The inside of the house was decorated with the finest of Japanese furniture, most with inlay and marquetry. The walls carried many scrolls and paintings of ancient Japan. There was statuary and sculpture on pedestals. But the biggest surprise was the grounds surrounding the back of the house. Mr. Chigesu offered to show me around the various installations. As we toured the property he spoke with mild enthusiasm.

First, to the left, is the waterfall garden in which a tiny stream tumbles down a miniature mountain planted with mountain laurel and ferns into a streambed of mossy stone. Mr. Chigesu explained," Water is essential to the vibrancy of the garden. It echoes the flow of energy through all life and its source is mysterious." He continued, "The stream flows from east to west, following the sun to draw the purity of a new day into the garden."

Next, to the right, is a pair of ginkgo trees – male and female- presiding over an area of gravel, sand and stone. This is the Zen garden, or *karesan-sui*. It is an example of the style that developed around Buddhist monasteries during the 15th century as an aid to meditation. Mr. Chigesu explained once again, "This abstract, minimalist garden uses the most basic of elements to convey the essence of nature, much as Japanese *sumi-e* painters suggest a whole world with a few brushstrokes. The rocks are "planted" in allegorical reference to a Buddhist tale – in this case the upright stone represents heaven with man and earth to either side. The sand is gently raked into patterns to suggest water or clouds.

We continued walking as Mr. Chigesu spoke with great pride about the gardens and his love of nature. Following the path counter-clockwise around the pond he pointed to the Katsura trees to our right. Katsura trees are native to Japan but apparently grow well in California. I was told that as the leaves yellow and drop in autumn, they give forth a wonderfully sugary scent and reveal the intricate structure of the trees. A slight breeze stirred the bamboo grove just ahead, creating a sound like rushing water. Mr. Chigesu told me that because of its many virtues, bamboo lore reaches deep into Japanese culture. A proverb suggests that a man who has bamboo will want for nothing.

As we walked I could see the pond. Surrounded by yellow flag iris and strewn with water lilies, the pond teems with life: frogs, fish and turtles which add cheerful animation to the garden. Mr. Chigesu spoke with great enthusiasm," The design device known as "hide and reveal" keeps the pond from being seen in its entirety." In the middle of the pond, slightly eccentric is the island. The island is reached by crossing a low stone bridge. Islands are considered sacred in Japanese mythology and are offered to the spirits as a resting place on their journeys,

During the tour of the garden, Mr. Chigesu told me that he brought a Japanese landscape architect from Japan to plan and supervise the construction of the garden. He seemed very proud of his accomplishment as he said," I have a local gardener coming in once a week to keep the place clean and trimmed." As we walked together inspecting the garden I was amazed at all this opulence. Having traveled on a tramp steamer I would have assumed that Mr. Chigesu was less than affluent. We then returned to the house to sit down to dinner.

The table was set in Western style with linen napkins and silverware. Mr. Chigesu began talking enthusiastically as we sat down, "The basic principles of Japanese garden design are balance and harmony. To achieve balance, designers employ yin/yang to represent the complementary aspects of life; male and female, positive and negative.

"Is that so? I had no idea that garden design was so spiritual."

"Yes, indeed. Each object in the garden is placed not only to be looked at but to be looked beyond. Using the design device *shakkei*, the surrounding landscape is "borrowed" and framed by stones or the branches of trees."

I stared at him unquestioningly when suddenly his son came in with a broad smile on his face. He had straight black hair and dark eyes which were almond shaped. His face was flat and was completely hairless. He was rather tall and would probably be described as handsome by Western standards. Mr. Chigesu looked up and said in a loud voice, "Ah, Koichi, come in. Say hello to Nakahara-san."

Koichi came toward me with a low bow and gassho, "How are you Nakahara-san. I am sorry to be late but I had last minute duties in the office." He then sat down and removed the napkin to his lap. I followed suit then I perked up my head as I heard Mr. Chigesu ask, "Have you seen Mrs. Kangetsu since our landing in Honolulu? I saw her husband being removed by stretcher after we landed."

"It was a very sad circumstance. Her husband died of stomach cancer.

I officiated at his cremation and to the best of my knowledge she is now alone."

I could hear him sounding tsk, tsk as he heard me speak. He stared at me for a long time without saying anything, and then the maid came in with the plates of soup.

After we finished eating our dinner, curiosity forced me to ask Mr. Chigesu. "Forgive me for asking Chigesu-kun but you seem to be a man of means. Why did you travel on a tramp steamer?" He raised his voice and roared with laughter while he slapped the table with his right hand. "Not at all, not at all. It is a logical question and there is no shame in asking."

He then looked me straight in the eye and in a serious tone he explained, "I am on the Board of Directors of the Yamato Steamship Company, which owns the Umi Maru as well as other ships. My business, Chigesu and Son, Importers and Exporters, has a business contract, in perpetuity, with the Yamato Steamship Company. I often use their ships for my travel needs. I go to and from Japan quite often. I find the sea voyage leisurely, restful, and comforting. Of course some ships are nicer than the Umi Maru but I am not fussy."

I hung my head in a consciousness of guilt and said, "Thank you. I did not mean to be nosy."

"Very well, now let me have my son, Koichi, show you to your quarters. I have arranged for you to occupy the small apartment above the garage. It was formerly occupied by my chauffeur but he is not here now. He is in Japan and will not return until next month."

I was startled in hearing this kind offer and could do no more than bend my head in supplication. I muttered quietly, "Thank you, Chigesu-kun. I am most grateful."

"You will be able to take the bus to Japantown every morning and return to us every evening for dinner."

I was aghast at this generosity and could only manage to say, "Thank you."

With that we rose from the table and I bowed with a deep gassho and went along with Koichi to the garage. While walking to the garage I said to Koichi, "I left my luggage at the Temple."

"Do not worry, Nakahara-san, I shall send someone to retrieve it for you."

"You are most kind. I appreciate it very much."

Koichi led me up an outside stairway to the room on top of the garage. It was quite nice with one large bedroom and a small kitchen and bathroom. The floor was covered with a Persian rug and the windows were curtained. The kitchen had utensils and dishes and the bathroom was provided with towels. The bed was equipped with linens and blankets. I noticed the clothes closet had a number of suits and coats hanging as I opened the door. Koichi was quick to say, "Those items belong to the chauffeur. Please disregard them and push them aside so that you can hang your things."

"Yes, thank you."

Koichi became restless, "I will leave you now. The messenger should be here soon with your luggage. I hope you have a good night's sleep. I will see you tomorrow at dinner, Konbonwa (good night)." He bowed with a gassho and retreated from the room.

I sat on the edge of the bed pensively waiting for the arrival of my luggage. After a while there was a knock on the door. I got up and hurried to open the door to find, in full view, a young man carrying my luggage bag.

"Good evening, Nakahara-san I have your luggage," he said.

"Thank you very much. Would you like to come in?" I asked.

"Thank you. I do not wish to disturb you."

"Come in you are welcome."

The young man came across the threshold carrying my bag. He was tall, about twenty years old, of slight stature, with a full head of black hair and a somewhat cherubic face. I watched him curiously as he toted the bag and placed it on the floor near the bed.

"What is your name?" I asked.

"My name is Tak Yamamoto," he answered.

"Ah, are you Nisei?"

"Yes, my parents were born in Japan, but I was born in San Francisco. I work for Mr. Chigesu as a messenger."

"I see. Well, thank you for your help," I said with a deep gassho which he returned in a vacillating falter, after which he left the room. I then began to empty my bag by placing items in the drawers and closets. When I completed this task, I sat on the floor in a full lotus position while holding my mala beads to practice one hour of zazen. It was so quiet I could hear the rustle of leaves in the garden occasionally interspersed by the deep croak of a frog. When I finished zazen I decided to go to sleep considering I had to catch the first bus of the day in the morning at 5:00 am to take me to the temple in Japantown. It was a full day with much to think about. Things moved so fast, having just arrived from Hawaii and meeting Fukuzawa-san at Temple Kinoji then coming here to the home of Mr. Chigesu. I slumbered off and began to dream of Mrs. Kangetsu.

She stood before me in her red silk dress. I grabbed her and tore her dress off. She shrieked, "Why did you tear my dress?" I began to paw her clumsily, amorously, and rudely. She began to flail and grab me wildly. We finally embraced and my swollen member was inserted in her vagina. I ejaculated and awoke with a sudden and violent start. "What happened?" I said aloud as I wondered at the outcome of this world of illusion and fantasy. Then I drifted back to sleep and shortly awoke to the set hour of the alarm clock.

I showered and rinsed out my *zubon* (sleep trouser) and hung it up to dry. I made a cup of tea in the kitchenette and afterwards hurried to the bus stop. I made a mental note to buy some comestibles for my morning breakfasts.

It was still dark when I reached the bus stop. I was the only person waiting. The bus came along in a few minutes and I was aware that there were only a few people on the bus. "Good morning," I said to the driver as I boarded. He returned the greeting "Good morning, Reverend. Are you going to the temple in Japantown?"

"Yes, I am. How did you know?"

"I saw that you were wearing your Buddhist robes," he responded.

I sat down feeling very pleased with this recognition and courtesy. This is what would have happened in Japan and no fare would have been taken.

The bus stopped at the corner of Laguna and Post streets where the temple is located. I alighted and hurried into the zendo where I encountered Fukuzawa-san. We greeted each other with a gassho and a bow.

"Good morning, Nakahara-san. How is your accommodation at Mr.Chigesu's house? Are you comfortable there?" Fukuzawa said in friendly voice.

I told him of the good fortune in being provided with a place to stay for at least one month. He nodded his head in agreement and made a clucking sound with his mouth as he said, "What luck. This is a good omen. You will probably have many more favoring chances in your future."

And so life went on.

I officiated at services and helped with instructions for novices. Once -in-a-while I delivered a *teisho* (sermon). I enjoyed working in the temple and often mused of the day I would have my own temple. In the meantime, I enjoyed living at Mr. Chigesu's house. The only time I saw him was in the evening at dinner after which we would stroll through the garden and discuss various matters.

One day he said to me, "Nakahara-san I regret to inform you that my chauffeur will be returning from Japan next week. I know this will inconvenience you but I have a suggestion to make to you." When he said those words I was dumbstruck by the inevitability. "Please do not fear, I have an idea which you may consider," he said with the smile of a Cheshire cat. I raised my head to hear his proposal without muttering a word. He cleared his throat as he puffed his cigar. "I have a friend who lives on the East coast in a town called Fort Lee, New Jersey. I spoke with him recently and he agreed to put you up until you can locate a temple. I would buy your airplane ticket to make your transition to New Jersey easy. What do you think?"

I was startled out of my wits. I was unable to respond properly. "You are most kind Chigesu-kun. I am speechless. I only hope this is not too great a burden for you," I expressed this sentiment in a faltering way.

"Then if you agree, I shall confirm matters with Mr. Fujimori, Ichiko in Fort Lee."

I looked at the twinkle in his eyes. It was obvious to me that he was enjoying this gesture of generosity. I find it remarkable that even though I had a paltry relationship with him on board the ship Umi Maru he became a friend and sponsor for no other reason then pure kindness and graciousness. I could never hope to repay his generous disposition to be helpful to me.

IX

It was my first ride on an airplane. The airplane was crowded and I was seated between two very large men in a squeezed position with no ability to move. There were two small children in the seats in front of me who insisted on turning around to face me and make funny faces and do other silly disturbing things. The mother seemed oblivious to all this. The man on my left, in the window seat, was asleep with his right arm pushing my left shoulder. The man on my right, in the aisle seat, was staring at me constantly and tried to engage me in conversation.

"Are you Chinese?"

"No, I am Japanese."

"Why are you dressed like that?"

"These are my robes."

"What do you mean robes?"

"I am a Buddhist priest and I am wearing my Buddhist robes."

He stopped his inquiry for a minute but then continued, "Are you the same as a Catholic priest?"

"Not really but similar," I answered with hesitation.

He kept questioning me with the same curiosity and tolerance for most of the trip. When he was not questioning me he offered opinions and told small tales. I was attentive but dispassionate, concerned but cool. It just did not seem worth it.

When the plane landed in Newark International Airport, I debarked and hurried to the baggage lounge where I was to meet Fujimori, Ichiko. I retrieved my bag and looked about for a sign of recognition. Suddenly, I heard a plangent cry and saw a man in the distance waving his arms, "Nakahara-san, Nakahara-san, over here." I walked towards him and dropped my bag as we approached each other. We both began to bow very low; each of us bobbing up and down attempting to bow lower than the other.

"*Jocoso* (welcome), *Okeiri nasai* (welcome home), Nakahara-san," he said with the palms of his hands tightly together. I thanked him and as I looked up I noticed that he was a man of medium height with a thick head of black hair and a glistening, tawny skin. His eyes were mere slits and his face was completely hairless and smooth. He extended his hand in the Western manner which I grabbed with a warm feeling.

"I am happy to be here, Fujimori-kun," I said to which he responded, "I am happy to have you. Shall we go to my car?"

It was about a forty-five minute ride from Newark Airport to Fujimori's house in Fort Lee. He kept talking all the way to introduce me to my new surroundings. "This neighborhood is populated by very many Japanese people," he said. "Not only is it comfortable being amongst our own people but we also have a very large shopping area called Mitsuwa Marketplace in Edgewater, New Jersey which is close by. There you can get all sorts of foods that are Japanese as well as household items and gifts made in Japan."

Finally, we arrived at his house. It was a plain rather small cottage with a front garden containing perennial flowers and a small grass lawn. Inside the house was simple decor with Western furniture and an occasional Japanese scroll hanging on the wall. He introduced me to his wife who was a petite woman of middle age. I was startled to see that she was wearing a traditional kimono with an obi. It apparently was something she brought with her to the marriage to be worn on special occasions. She bowed low and hissed in a sibilant tone, *"Konnichiwa* (Good day) Nakahara-san." I returned the gesture but said nothing.

Fujimori showed me to my room which was in the finished basement. "Make yourself comfortable and rest for a while. We will go to dinner this evening to a restaurant called Matsu Sushi owned by a friend.

In the room I found a convertible couch which could be made into a bed at night. There was a closet, a night stand, and a small TV. After a while I was called by Fujimori to dinner at his friend's restaurant. "My wife will not accompany us tonight. She will prepare linens and towels for your comfort."

"Thank you for your help and generosity," I said.

On entering the restaurant, Fujimori was warmly greeted by the proprietor. He sat us at a very nice table and Fujimori ordered our dinner after introducing me.

"Let us start with noodle soup. Which do you prefer udon or soba?"

"Oh, soba, of course, I really enjoy soba noodles."

"Good. Would you prefer teriyaki, negimaki, or tempura?"

"Oh, I don't know."

"I have an idea. Why don't we order one shrimp tempura, one chicken teriyaki, and one beef negimaki? Then we can share all these dishes. It is an American custom to eat this way."

"Is it really?"

"Yes, they have assumed this custom from eating in Chinese restaurants. They always share their dishes."

We ate a very filling meal. The main dishes plus rice was more than we could finish. The proprietor gave Fujimori the surplus in a container together with two *Matsu* rolls containing tuna, salmon, yellowtail and scallions for his wife. He thanked the proprietor for the gift and wished him a good evening.

"Thank you for a wonderful dinner," I said as we ambled to the car. "I feel bad that I came without a gift for your wife. Could we stop at a *hanaya* (flower shop) to get a bouquet of flowers for your wife?"

"Oh, it is not necessary."

"Yes, please, I would like to do it."

"OK, I know a place."

In the flower shop I bought a bouquet of a dozen red roses. We then continued on our way to Fujimori's house. We were met at the door by Fujimori's wife, whose name was Michiko. I was surprised to see that she had changed into Western garb.

"Good evening, Fujimori-*okusan* (wife) I bought these flowers for you. I hope you enjoy them," I said as I handed the bunch to her. She seemed to be startled with wide eyes and a dropped jaw as she accepted the bouquet and began to smell them. She spoke in a very low voice, "*Domo arigato gozaimasu* (thank you very much). I hope you had a nice dinner. I prepared your room Nakahara-san. I hope you will be comfortable while you stay with us."

We then bowed to each other and I noticed in some ways Michiko was very pretty. She was rather small but for a Japanese woman this is not a defect. She had a round face with a small pug nose. Her lips were pink and cupid-shaped. Her eyes were almond shaped with black dots for irises like a Renoir portrait. Her skin was milk-white and very smooth. I began to feel an emotional link to her. It was amazing to me the difference in sexiness between traditional Japanese dress and conventional American dress. She was like a different person.

Suddenly I was brought out of my reverie by the voice of Fujimori. I looked at him and said in wonderment, "What did you say?"

"I said are you tired? Would you like to relax in your room?"

Did he notice my staring at his wife?

"Yes, yes, I am tired. Please excuse me." I bowed to both of them and I started to go down to my room to prepare for the evening when Fujimori began speaking,

"Tomorrow we shall review the best way to find you a position in a temple."

I stopped, turned around and said, "That would be wonderful." Then I continued to my room. Fujimori called after me, "Breakfast is at 8:00 am."

"Yes, yes, thank you."

That night I dreamed about Michiko Fujimori.

X

The next day at breakfast we spoke about my future and how to prepare for it. Fujimori suggested that we call on the local priest at his temple. I agreed that this was a good place to start. Fujimori called the local priest, Aoyama, Yuko and made an appointment. The local temple was in a house formerly occupied as a dwelling. It was severely renovated to appear like a Zen temple of Japan. It did not have any decorations. There was a wooden sign out front in Japanese characters which said, Zen Temple. The ground floor was gutted to reveal a large unobstructed room used as the *zendo* (prayer hall). The floor was highly polished and in the front was a table on which was a statue of the Buddha next to which was a pot for incense. Some were still smoldering and there was a pervasive sweet smell of the incense.

The kitchen was maintained as a place for refreshments. It was here that we sat with Aoyama-san at a large table on which was a pot of *ryokucha* (green tea). This was an unusual venue since one is usually entertained in the priest's study. I must admit I felt much more comfortable in the kitchen. We sipped and talked and Aoyama-san kept saying, "Ah, so" to every answer I gave. After much discussion he asked me," Would you be interested in leading a congregation of *gaijin* (foreigners)?"

At first I didn't understand his question.

"What do you mean?"

"Buddhism is becoming very popular in America. There are many Americans who are interested in learning Buddhist ways, in particular Zen."

"Is that so?"

"Yes, I know of one possibility. There is a very rich gentleman in Connecticut State who has contributed money to the Soto Zen cause. He has expressed a desire to establish a Buddhist temple in Connecticut State."

Do you mean he will build a temple and start a group?"

"Yes, something like that."

"I see."

He quickly interjected," I realize it is a challenge and there are many obvious cultural differences as well as some language obstacles, but I believe you have the ability to handle all of these problems."

I became very pensive and did not respond for a while. I just kept looking at the geometric design of the floor covering.

"I am not sure. May I have some time to think about this?"

"Of course, take your time. Let us get together next week."

Riding back in the car with Fujimori, I asked, "What should I do? I am not certain that I will be able to connect or fit in with *gaijin*. Since I came to America I have only associated with Japanese people. I don't even speak their language very well. I haven't had the opportunity to practice. I might embarrass someone if I say the wrong thing."

"Oh well, I don't think you should worry about that," he said in a low spirited and disheartened way.

"Well I am concerned about making a fool of myself," I quickly responded.

"Look, Nakahara-san, Buddhism came to America by Japanese priests who could not speak any more English than you. They formed some of the biggest temples and monasteries all over this country. Somehow they were sponsored by some of the richest people in the country. Now this is happening to you. Think of this offer as an opportunity."

"Is it really?"

"Yes, it is"

When we arrived at home, I decided to sit zazen and contemplate the problem much like trying to solve a koan. I noticed Michiko in the kitchen and walked in to speak with her about my dilemma. Ichiko Fujimori was putting the car away so I felt free to approach her.

"Good evening, Michiko."

"Good evening, Nakahara-san. Where is Ichiko?"

"He is putting the car away in the garage."

I noticed she was wearing a small apron about her waist which emphasized her hips and a form fitting sweater-blouse which stressed her bud-like breasts. I was so stunned by her personal charm and sex appeal that I could barely continue speaking.

"I was given a possible offer today which troubles me. Could I have your opinion?"

"Well, I am very busy making dinner just now. Could we possibly discuss this at the dinner table?"

"Oh, of course, I am sorry to disturb you. I can see you are busy."

I left with a bow and went down to my room. I removed my street clothes and put on a *kesa* (ceremonial robe) and prepared my cushion to sit zazen. I no sooner got myself into proper lotus position when I found my mind racing. I had to focus. *I had to focus.* After a while a mental picture of a new temple formed in my mind. *I shall call it Kinjoji* (neighborhood temple), I thought. *Oh, if I could only have a wife like Michiko Fujimori. I would be the happiest man alive. To have a new temple and a new wife would be beyond my wildest dreams. She is young and beautiful; the very thing I look for in a woman. Is this offer of a new temple the wisest step for me to take? But is there a real offer? I only know that Aoyama-san said that it is possible. Nothing concrete has been stated. I really know nothing of the place. Where is it? What is it? How do I know they want me? Is there really an offer? Who is making the offer? Certainly, Aoyama-san is not making the offer. He is just saying it is possible. Oh dear, I am putting the cart before the horse. I must get more information.*

Just then the incense stick sputtered out indicating that forty minutes had passed. I arose with a slight kink in my right hip. On standing and bowing the kink disappeared.

I think I better see this place and meet the sponsor before I make any decision.

Michiko called at the top of the stairs for dinner. I came up wearing my *kesa*. Ichiko greeted me with a broad smile on his face, "Come in Nakahara-san. Have some saki before dinner." We all sat down and Michiko filled our small porcelain cups with warm saki.

"Kampai," we all shouted as we raised our cups. Then Michiko served the broiled salmon and mustard greens into our plates, accompanied by individual bowls of *gohan* (cooked rice). Fujimori asked, "Have you thought about the offer?"

"Yes, I have. First there is no offer, only a possibility. I think I need to see the place and meet the sponsor before I can consider this possibility."

"Very wise," piped in Michiko to the astonishment of her husband. "Please Michiko; you do not know all the facts." Her face reddened giving a warm glow to her complexion. "I just mean that Nakahara-san should meet this sponsor before he makes any decision," she said. I quickly agreed with a face-saving comment, "Yes, Michiko, you are right. That is what I shall do. Thank you." Fujimori was taken aback, "I see; then I shall make arrangements with Aoyama-san for an appointment with the sponsor."

We continued eating silently until dinner was finished and the last cup of tea was consumed. I offered to help with the dishes but Michiko would have none of it. I went into the living room with Ichiko Fujimori where we each had a bottle of beer and enjoyed watching a baseball game on television.

Fujimori said, "I love baseball. Did you know the Japanese learned it from the Americans during the occupation? Now Japan has baseball leagues just like here in America."

"Is that so," I said in amazement. My eyelids became heavy and I felt myself dozing off. "I think I better go to sleep. I am feeling very tired," I said with a yawn.

"Yes, you look sleepy. I'll call Aoyama-san tomorrow morning to make an appointment with the sponsor."

"Thank you," I said with a mild torpor in my voice. "I'll see you tomorrow.

Thank you for your help today." I went into the kitchen to thank Michiko for the dinner. I found her at the sink washing pots. "Thank you, Michiko, for the wonderful dinner." She turned and looked at me with her dazzling eyes and said in a slightly sibilant voice, *do itashimashite* (you are welcome)."

I continued, "I am grateful for your advice tonight."

"Oh, it was nothing. I wish I could be of more help."

I watched her lips moving as she spoke and wondered what it would be like to kiss her smooth pink lips. A warmth of emotion began rising in me. I knew I should leave before my ardor became uncontrollable. I bowed again and turned to leave. She called after me, "I'll see you tomorrow at breakfast. I am making *congee* (rice porridge)."

I went down to my room carrying a deep feeling for Michiko. This was a real case of unrequited love. Yes, I began to believe that I was in love with Michiko. Oh, well I said, as I prepared for bed, "Tonight I shall dream of Michiko Fujimori."

I arose in the morning, took care of my toilet, sat zazen; read a little while then went upstairs for breakfast. Michiko, looking lovely as usual, was in the kitchen setting the table and spooning out the congee into bowls.

"Good morning Michiko, good morning Ichiko, "I said with exuberance in my voice. They both answered in like manner. I sprinkled some ground sesame seeds onto my congee. It gave the porridge a nutty flavor. The porridge was delectable and I could not resist a second helping. After breakfast Ichiko Fujimori called Aoyama-san to arrange a meeting with the sponsor. Having done this he dropped me at the Mitsuwa Marketplace and then went off to work after arranging to meet me at lunchtime. At the Marketplace I looked at all the vendor's stalls which contained items and articles from Japan. All the shoppers inside were Japanese and they all appeared to be young with children. There was a large supermarket which contained comestibles of Japanese origin. The vegetables were of the type used in Japan but I assumed they were grown here in America. I have been told that some Japanese families have farms like those in Japan where they grow vegetables and sell them at roadside stalls. At least that was the way on the West coast.

I made my way to a tea shop where I ordered a pot of green tea and sat at an unoccupied table to rest and sip. After a few minutes a young girl attempted to sit at my table. She bowed with a gassho and spoke to me in Japanese, "May I join you, Reverend?"

I rose and returned the bow saying, "Yes, indeed, please sit."

She placed her tea and a bun on the table and sat across from me. "I am sorry to intrude, Reverend, but the other tables were all taken."

"Please, my name is Nakahara, Jiun. I am a Zen Buddhist priest. I am just visiting this marketplace until my friend will pick me up," I said in a hurried manner.

She looked at me with an intense stare, "I see, Nakahara-san. Is this your first visit to the Mitsuwa Marketplace?"

"Yes, it is. As a matter of fact, it is my first visit to the East coast. I came from California a few days ago."

I looked at her with curious delight. She was no more than twenty-five years old with lovely black hair and a slightly tawny skin. Her eyes were exceptional in that they appeared to be brown pupils in a sea of milk. She sat with a straight back and suddenly extended her hand saying, "My name is Yamaguchi, Myoko. You may call me Myoko."

I took her hand in a Western handshake and felt the softness beneath my fingers. It stimulated my emotions. I began to stammer, "I am happy to meet you, Myoko. I notice you have an Osaka accent. Are you from Osaka?"

"No, I was born here. My parents were from Osaka. We only spoke Japanese in the house. My mother is very old. My father is dead now. He is buried in a cemetery in Connecticut."

"Did you say Connecticut?"

"Yes, I did. Why?"

"Well, it just so happens that I may head a temple in Connecticut."

"Really; that's a coincidence. I live in Fairfield, Connecticut. I just came here today to do some shopping. Where in Connecticut will your temple be located?"

In a slightly embarrassed way I responded, "I don't really know I will find out soon. I am to meet my sponsor soon,"

She looked at me with her bright eyes and said, I have been looking for a good temple for some time now. How do I find out where your temple will be located?"

"Well let me give you the telephone number of Mr. Ichiko Fujimori with whom I am staying." With that I took out a small pad and pencil which I kept in my inner pocket and wrote out Fujimori's telephone number. I gave the slip of paper to her. "He will know when and where this temple will take place."

"Thank you," she said as she took the paper and placed it carefully in her purse. She kept up a droning conversation which I barely heard. The murmuring sound of her voice did not register with me. My only interest was in looking at the beauty of her face and the movement of her full lips and pink tongue over her pearl-like teeth. It gave me an exciting sensuous and aesthetic pleasure. She was an exquisitely charming and elegant woman. I noticed she did not wear a marriage band on her finger. This gave me further encouragement.

We sat and talked for several hours. I was most grateful for this female company. Life for me has been a series of lonely isolations. I entered the monastery in Japan at eighteen and after six years was ordained a Buddhist priest in the Soto Zen tradition at the age of twenty-four. Now I am twenty-five and I hunger for female companionship having been without it for so many years. Myoko was very pleasant to be with despite her American ways. Her manners were uninhibited and she adopted a friendly mode when encountering various situations such as ordering more tea from the waitress or waving to people and children as they passed by. She was completely American and knew little of the social rules of conduct or the prevalent customs of Japanese women.

I did not realize it was so late until I spotted Ichiko Fujimori coming in to the tea shop. He bounded over to our table and stood before me with a wide grin on his face. "Hello, Ichiko. I am glad you came. Please allow me to introduce Yamaguchi, Myoko. We were having tea together."

I was very surprised to see Ichiko extend his hand in a Western handshake and say in English, "I am happy to meet you." She answered with a single unpropitious word, "Likewise."

Ichiko sat down and I explained that Myoko and I met and enjoyed tea together. I also told him she would call him when I got settled in Connecticut. He agreed to all of this by nodding his head and saying, "I see. I see." After which we all parted. I grabbed Myoko's hand and in a frail pleading voice said, "Please call Ichiko in about two weeks; I should be settled in Connecticut by then, Goodbye and thank you for a very pleasant day."

In response she squeezed my hand and replied with a smile, "Thank you and I shall be sure to call Ichiko in about two weeks. I wish you the best of luck."

Ichiko and I left in his car. When we arrived at his house his wife, Michiko, looking at both of us said, "There was a message from Aoyama-san, please return his call.

XI

Fujimori dialed the telephone to Aoyama-san and after the usual greetings handed the telephone to me, "Hello, Aoyama-san. How are you? Good! Yes, I am well, thank you. Oh, you received some information from the sponsor. What? His name is what? Oh, I see, Dr. Hugo Bremer. Where? Narack, Connecticut. What? Oh, I see, the Bremer Chemical Company. When? He would like a meeting next Tuesday at 10:00 o'clock in the morning. Yes, I think so. I will speak with Fujimori to see if he can drive me. Yes, yes it's very exciting. Thank you very much. I am most grateful to you. Yes, I will surely call you when I return from Narack, Connecticut.

I hung up the telephone and turned to look at Fujimori saying in an excited voice, "The sponsor's name is Dr. Bremer. He is the owner of the Bremer Chemical Company in Narack, Connecticut. He wants to meet me next Tuesday morning.

Fujimori clapped his hands and shouted, "Oh, how wonderful."

"Would you be able to drive me?"

"Of course, it's only about an hour away."

"Thank you. I am such a burden to you. I hope it all works out."

"Not at all and it will work out. You must have patience and resolve."

Next Tuesday, Fujimori and I left his house at 8:30 am heading up the Palisades Interstate Parkway across the Tappan Zee Bridge to Connecticut. We arrived in Narack in less than an hour and parked the car in the parking lot of the Bremer Chemical Company. It was a magnificent structure which had a beautifully decorated entrance and lobby with statuary and paintings throughout. Having given our names to the receptionist we were asked to wait, actually we were about thirty minutes too early. We sat on a couch and a young woman came over saying," May I get you anything, coffee or tea?" We both refused. She then turned and left. In a little while another young lady arrived and escorted us to Dr. Bremer's office. It was a large cavernous room with very large windows overlooking a formal garden. We walked up to the massive oak desk from which Dr. Bremer rose and offered an extended hand.

"Welcome to both of you."

I bowed and accepted his hand in mine saying, "Good morning, Dr. Bremer, my name is Nakahara, Jiun. I am happy to meet you."

"Yes, indeed, I am happy to meet you. You speak English very well."

"No, not at all but I try."

He pointed to the couch saying, "Please sit." Looking at Fujimori he extended his hand and said, "Welcome to you, sir. Please join us."

The two of us sat on the couch facing him sitting in an upholstered chair of Queen Anne vintage. He was a tall man of slim build. He wore a gray pencil-striped flannel suit with a pink button-down shirt and a red tie. His face was freshly shaven with a few wrinkles on his cheeks and crow's feet at the eye area. His hair was a mixture of gray and black strands maneuvered to cover a growing bald pate. He had a thick mustache which covered his lips. He had gray, bushy eyebrows. His eyes, with intense blue pupils, seemed to dance as he talked.

"Gentlemen, please relax. May I offer you some refreshment? Perhaps you would like a coffee or tea? No, really. OK then let's begin." Dr. Bremer straightened up in his chair, pulled his jacket closed and began speaking in his booming voice, "Let me start from the beginning." He cleared his throat with a loud *harrumph* and continued, "I am the CEO of the Bremer Chemical Company, which grosses about four hundred million dollars annually. We manufacture surfactants and emulsifiers in a plant in Wickham, Kentucky. This building is our corporate headquarters. Across the road we have a ten acre property on which is the Bremer Library which formerly housed my collection of First Edition science books and ancient manuscripts and treatises on science. I say formerly because I have now donated the entire collection to the Connecticut Institute of Technology where they reside amongst their holdings for use by scholars."

He looked at us and said, "Any questions so far." We both shook our heads negatively as we sat in wonderment. He continued, "The Bremer Library is now empty except as a venue for an occasional concert. My daughter and I became interested in Buddhism many years ago as a result of extensive travel through the Far East. It is our desire to bring Buddhism to America. What we intend doing is donating the ten acre site which has a parking lot, a three bedroom house and the Bremer Library on the property plus a three million dollar endowment to form the Buddhist temple. It is our feeling that the head priest would live rent free in the house and would supervise the renovation and eventual maintenance of the Bremer Library building into a Buddhist temple. He also would be granted a stipend for living expenses."

He stopped speaking abruptly and looked at us as if examining a specimen under a microscope. "Well what do you think?" I was non-plussed and silent for a while. I was grateful that Fujimori said nothing. It was up to me to comment. I looked at Dr. Bremer and began stammering, "It, it sounds, uh, very generous. I would like to see the place before commenting further.

He smiled and said," Of course, but first let me hear your credentials and what your focus would be."

I nodded and began speaking slowly, "Please excuse my bad English. I lived in the Shujoji Monastery for six years after high school and eventually was ordained as a Zen priest. I received the *inka-shomei* (seal of recognition) from my master and now I am authorized to train others. It is my desire to run a meditation hall for the public regardless of their birth religious persuasion. I also intend eventually training the interested members of the laity into lay ordination and thence into full Buddhist monk ordination. Most important I would make every effort to become recognized by the Sotoshu Shumucho Administrative Headquarters of Soto Zen in Tokyo and hopefully become an affiliate." I stopped speaking and the room turned eerily silent,

Finally, Dr. Bremer said, "Shall we go across the road and look at the property?"

Yes, indeed," I replied eagerly. We walked across the road and up a flagstone path to view a very beautiful building standing like a beacon on a grassy knoll. The architecture was magnificent. The edifice of concrete, steel, aluminum, glass, fiberglass, and oiled walnut is suspended from a quadripod frame that allows the full upper floor complete freedom from internal supports. A separate full area is directly below which could be used as an unrestricted zendo. The upper area has a suspended balcony walkway and mezzanine around the periphery from which one could enter into several separate rooms.

The entrance comprised a heavy-looking, sculptured oak door with side vertical window lights of leaded, beveled glass. This led into a foyer with small offices on each side. A pair of French doors containing windows of leaded glass with geometric designs allowed one to enter the large expanse which is to be used as the zendo. Another double French doorway led to a back terrace surrounded by a garden. The library had several side windows made of stained glass with arched tops. The structure contained a full basement which was presently used for storage but eventually could be finished and used as a combination social hall and lecture hall. On one side of the building was the large parking lot. On the other side was the three-bedroom ranch-style house.

I was dumbfounded and totally amazed at what I saw. I looked at Dr. Bremer and said, "It is very beautiful."

"You really like it, huh?"

"Yes, indeed, it is beyond my wildest expectations. It has so much potential."

"Good, let us return to my office then."

We walked back to Dr. Bremer's office chatting in small talk all the way. Dr. Bremer told me about his daughter Serena who had a great interest in Buddhism and would like to learn and practice and is looking forward to converting the library into a Buddhist temple. He excused her absence saying that she had to visit some friends but would meet me the next time I returned.

In his office we took the same seats as before. Dr. Bremer ordered tea and we relaxed as we continued our conversation. Once again, Dr. Bremer spoke in his booming voice, "May I assume that you are interested in the position of head priest?"

I looked at him in a serious, convincing way, "Yes, indeed, I am."

"Alright then tell me what's to be done in the conversion?"

"Well, first we must install a large Buddha in the zendo. We must also consider installing a Buddha Stupa at the side of the front entrance with an appropriate sign. The floor of the zendo must be scraped and polished to a high shine. After that no one will be allowed to enter with shoes on because the zendo will become hallowed ground. Therefore, one of the offices at the foyer must be outfitted with shelves for shoes. We need to buy zafus and zabutons for the practitioners. They must be black in color and filled with kapok. In the beginning we will need only thirty each. We will also need a dais in front of the Buddha for the leader to conduct services. In addition, we will need a bell, candle holders and incense censors."

"OK, you can work with my construction engineer and purchasing agent to help you. I shall alert them that you will contact them," he said in an authoritarian way.

"Thank you very much for all kindness," I said as we stood up to leave.

I then turned to Dr. Bremer and asked, "Would it be alright if I moved into the house in a few days to relieve my friend Ichiko Fujimori the burden of putting up with me, "I laughed as I turned and pointed to him.

"Of course, we will get it ready for you immediately and stock the refrigerator too. Your stipend will start immediately as well." Dr.Bremer walked us to the doorway to his office. We all shook hands and said goodbye. Dr. Bremer handed me a card saying, "The phone number on this card is the best way to reach me quickly if necessary.

"Thank you." With that the same young woman who brought us up to his office brought us back to the front entrance. "Goodbye!" she said. We left to retrieve the car and rode back to Fort Lee. Fujimori was very excited as we talked.

"It is a golden opportunity Nakahara-san. I know that you will be very happy in your new venture. Of course, Michiko and I will come to practice when the temple is completed and ready."

"I owe much to many people but I shall never forget your kindness and that of Mr. Chigesu. I could never have been given this opportunity without your help. Thank you, dear friend," I said with moist eyes.

When we arrived at Fujimori's house, Michiko was waiting for us. I noticed that she wore a new dress as she bowed to us. She looked lovely with her long black hair now placed in a bun at the nape of her neck. "Tell me all about it, "she exclaimed in an almost childish way. Ichiko began talking in an excited way covering all of the events of the day. Finally, she questioned in a disappointed tone, "You are moving there, when?"

"I looked into her disbelieving eyes and hesitantly said, "In two days." She appeared devastated by this remark, "Why so soon?" I could tell immediately from the remorseful tone of her voice that she was sad at this prospect. I, too, became a little distressful since my departure would mean I would not see her again for a long time. I quickly put this out of my mind by thinking of the new temple about to be. "Do not fret," I said, "We shall see each other from time to time." Even while saying this, I was aware that this infrequency was not what either of us wanted. I knew I would miss her delicate and exquisite beauty. But, I had no other choice. My life's work lay ahead of me.

I went downstairs to my room to gather together the few simple possessions I had. I am to leave for Narack the morning after tomorrow. The events of the day had caused a high energy level in me that I wanted to quash, so I prepared to sit zazen until these feelings were suppressed. After one hour I knew the high emotional state was quelled. I then came off my cushion and prostrated myself on the floor and repeated aloud the ancient asseveration of all Buddhists. It is a solemn promise of fidelity and constancy said in *Pali* (the everyday language of Sanskrit).

Buddham sarinam gatchami
Dhammam sarinam gatchami
Sangham sarinam gatchami
I take refuge in the Buddha
I take refuge in the teachings
I take refuge in the community of monks

Having expressed my vows I felt better and began to slowly rise with a gassho and a bow to an unseen Buddha. I now believed that my life was going to take a fortuitous turn.

Suddenly, I heard the sibilant voice of Michiko, "Dinner is ready." I shook my head in order to confront reality. I could see that Michiko made a special dinner with the unique dishes of Japan. Was this in celebration of my good fortune or was it a farewell dinner? In either case I was happy to enjoy this unusual dinner with my friends. The food was Japanese home cooking starting with Miso soup with Tofu and Wakame, followed by an appetizer called Takiawase (dried bean curd with shrimp balls). The main dish was Teppan-yaki (grilled meat and vegetables) together with Aomame Gohan (cooked rice with green peas). It was a meal fit for a king, *Oishi* (delicious). I haven't eaten a meal like this since I lived at home with my mother.

Before eating Ichiko Fujimori filled my small porcelain cup with sake. He also filled Michiko's cup and finally his own, "Let us salute Nakahara-san for his good fortune," he said as he raised his cup. All of us raised our cups and said, "*Kampai* (a toast to one's health)." I was really touched by this extraordinary kindness, after all they hardly know me and were only recently recommended by Mr. Chigesu. The next day, Ichiko dropped me and Michiko off at the Mitsuwa Marketplace. Michiko had to go food shopping and I offered to help her. This was a most valuable opportunity since I would be alone with her most of the day. Ichiko said he would pick us up midday after lunch. Now, I could have her all to myself even for a little while. I was in heaven.

"First, let us go to the food market. I need vegetables, a twenty five pound bag of rice, a bottle of soy sauce, a bottle of rice vinegar, and a bottle of canola oil. Is there anything in particular you need," she said as she looked at me anxiously. I shook my head from side to side. I was satisfied just to look at her as she reached for the vegetables and then spoke Japanese to the grocery clerk for the remainder of her order. I helped her bag her items at the check-out counter. She paid for everything with a credit card. Everything was placed in a rolling cart which I pushed over to the household department. She said that she needed candles and incense. While watching her discuss the various aromas of the incense sticks with the proprietor, I could not help noticing the back of her head, where the hair bun occupied a prominent spot. Her ears were small and back close to her head and I deliriously thought of biting them. Her back was straight as a board and her dress was so tightly form fitted that I could make out the image of the back strap of her brassiere. Her legs looked like the smooth, straight legs of American girls not the often seen bandy legs of Japanese women. A sudden frenzied excitement overcame me such that I had to excuse myself and walk out of the candle shop for a minute. She followed me, "Are you alright? Is something wrong?"

"No, no I just wanted to get some air."

"Good, I'll be finished in a minute, and then we can go for some tea."

A sudden thought flashed through my mind. *What if we bump into Myoko Yamaguchi?* What silliness. So what if we meet her. Anyway she lives in Fairfield, Connecticut and probably does not come here very often. I wonder if she will call Ichiko Fujimori in two weeks. I really liked her and would enjoy seeing her again.

When Michiko was finished we ambled over to the tea shop. We selected a table and ordered a pot of tea and two sweet buns. It was delightful to watch her chew the bun and sip her tea. I particularly enjoyed watching the movement of her mouth and the occasional wipe of her full lips by her pink tongue. I could barely eat I was so intent on watching her. We chatted in small talk which I honestly could not fathom.

"Are you happy to be going to Narack?"

"Yes."

"I shall miss you."

"I shall miss you, too."

Then she blurted out, "It seems so unfair that circumstances have thrown us together and we are only limited to our vision and thoughts of each other." I was stunned to hear this and could not respond. I was afraid to say something offensive or inappropriate so I said nothing. Apparently my silence stimulated her to quickly add, "*Sumimasen* (excuse me) I did not mean to offend you. You are a spiritual person and have a committed life."

I answered with great thought and deliberation, "I am not offended. I am human. Even spiritual people have needs. I admire you very much and perhaps in a different life we can overcome the boundaries of our restrictions." She seemed to accept this and did not respond. She held her head down as she sipped her tea from the cup which she held nervously with both hands. Then she raised her head and looked directly into my eyes uttering a very daunting remark, "I am pregnant." For a minute I was speechless but finally I gathered my courage and smiled while saying, "How wonderful. Now you will have a family. Congratulations. I am happy for you. Have you told Ichiko, yet?"

"Yes, I told him last night. Please keep it as a secret. Do not let Ichiko know that I told you."

I saw her blush slightly which brought a nice hue to her cheeks. "I will not, of course, I won't. It will be our secret. When are you due to give birth?"

"Not for a long time. The doctor said in about eight months."

"Well, let me know if I can be of any help."

"Thank you," she said in a quiet demurred way. We continued talking for about another hour after ordering a second pot of tea. I felt very comfortable sitting across from her listening to her speak with that characteristic sibilant tone of her voice. The mood of musing was broken by a loud exclamation by Ichiko who was walking towards us, "Nakahara-san, how are you?" My state of being lost in thought evaporated quickly at the sight of Ichiko. "Ichiko, aren't you early?" He laughed as he responded, "I was able to get away. Let's load the car and go home.

XII

I had made arrangements for Ichiko to drive me to Narack the nest morning. I called Dr. Bremer the night before to expect me. Dr. Bremer told me the caretaker, Tony, would meet me at the house and give me the keys to the house and the library building.

I turned to Michiko to say goodbye, "Thank you for all your kindness. Being here in your home was one of the significant moments of my life. I wish you all the happiness you desire." I bowed to her but she extended her hand instead. I grabbed it as she said with tears in her eyes, "Good luck, Nakahara-san. I hope our paths will cross sometime in the future. I left and got into the car with my bag.

When we arrived at Narack, Ichiko deposited me at the house. He extended his hand and wished me luck. I spoke of my gratitude to him. Then he moved closer and whispered, "I would like you to know that Michiko is pregnant. I would like very much to name the child, Jiun, which is a neutral name fit for a man or woman. I looked at his smiling face and said, "Thank you. It is a great honor." He then left and I went to the house and met Tony, the caretaker. He gave me the keys and told me that the maintenance crew will care for the house and library, including a groundskeeper for the plantings and a maid will clean the house once-a-week.

I told Tony that the library shelves had to be removed and shelves for shoes had to be installed in the left side room of the foyer. I wanted the wooden floor in the main room of the library scraped and finished with a high shine. I also wanted a sign painter to make and install a sign for the front with incised, gilded letters stating, NARACK ZEN CENTER.

In the house I decided to use one bedroom for myself which will eventually contain only a futon and a tea table. The second bedroom will be used as a library/sitting room/office. The third bedroom will be a spare bedroom for possible guests. The dining room is to be converted into a conference room. All eating will be done in the kitchen. I prepared a list of items for the purchasing agent of the Bremer Chemical Company to order from Japan:

A six foot Buddha made of bronze to sit on a four foot lotus pedestal.

A three foot stone Buddha to be put inside a Stupa made of sandstone blocks.

I need an additional pair of winter and summer priest's robes.

I also need three pairs of samu-e garments and two pairs of house slippers.

A bell, candlestick and censor with a table are needed for services inside the zendo.

We need thirty zafu cushions and thirty zabuton mats for practitioners made with kapok.

At the conclusion of my visit with the purchasing agent, he told me that Dr. Bremer wanted to speak with me. I was led to his office and was received with a warm greeting and handshake.

"I just wanted to tell you a few things. First, I have arranged for a personal stipend of $25,000 per year for you. Also, you will live rent free in the house on the property. I have established a checking account in your name with our corporate bank. Here is the passbook. A monthly check will be deposited in your account based on your annual stipend. Second, our attorney copyrighted the names Kinjoji and Narack Zen Center. They are now the property of the Narack Zen Center which also has been incorporated. Third, we have established a three million dollar endowment to be administered by a committee of three people headed by me. Fourth, we shall give you a work contract establishing you as the head and leader of the religious segment of the temple. I shall be the administrative head of the business end of the temple. You take care of their souls; I'll take care of their bodies. We have already applied for tax free status with the proper municipalities. I have arranged for a driver and automobile to be available to you should you need one. As soon as the changes and modifications of the library into a Buddhist temple are completed, I would like to have a meeting with you and my daughter to discuss plans for a "grand opening" with the local media. We will devise some publicity regarding a dedication ceremony by some well-known Buddhist celebrity – perhaps the Dalai Lama, Ha! Ha! OK any questions?"

I could not contain myself. *$25,000 a year is a very large sum of money of which I have no need. I am a simple monk who has learned to do without worldly possessions. All of my formative years in the monastery we monks were self-sufficient, even growing our own food.* I could not understand his generosity. *Well, as they say in Daoism, go along with the flow.*

"No, I have no questions. But I am sure they will come up in the future."

"Well, when they do use the phone number I gave you. Do not hesitate to contact me. This venture is personally very important to me."

For the next few days found me working with the maintenance crew in both the temple and the house. The main room in the temple was being worked on by carpenters, painters, and floor mechanics. Computers and business equipment including desks and chairs were ordered for the reception office in the foyer, and one of the offices in the upper gallery of the temple, and for the office/library/sitting room in the house. By the end of the week the sign for the front was ready and installed on the left side of the entrance path near the roadside. It was beautifully completed in excised, gilded letters on a green verdure background, saying NARACK ZEN CENTER. I had the purchasing agent order twenty *Shobogenzos* (the words of the Zen Patriarch, Dogen) in English from Japan for use in special classes much like bible study. Also, I ordered several Buddhist books in Japanese and English plus the complete set of the *Pali Canon* (the orthodox canon of Buddhism) for my library in the house.

Everyone was busy getting things ready for the opening day. Sometimes curiosity seekers came by to inquire about the activity. The sign in particular attracted many young people. I spoke to them and after taking their names and addresses promised to send them an invitation when the temple officially opens.

I had two different meetings with Dr. Bremer during this activity to review the requirements for the opening. He told me with great bravado that he intended to invite Mayor Richard Fokachi as a speaker, "Never fear, His Honor will accept. It is a photo opportunity and a chance to get his name in the paper. Now, who can we get to bless the temple?"

"I was thinking of asking Reverend Yoshio Fujioka, the Administrative Head of the North American Soto Zen Headquarters in San Francisco to preside as the principal speaker," I said timidly.

"That's wonderful. I am thinking we should have three speakers, The Reverend, the Mayor, and if I am lucky I will try and persuade Senator William Boggs. I'll leave it up to you to get the Reverend." I agreed and so he asked me to prepare my list of guests for the meeting to come with his daughter, Serena.

One day while resting in my room in the house, a workman came to see me. He said with tremulous motion, "There is a young lady to see you at the front door."

"Did you say a young lady?" I asked quizzically.

"Yes, she says she knows you."

"OK, I'll go see."

As I headed for the front door I could not help a feeling of forbearance. There she was. I recognized her immediately as I approached her even though I had only seen her for a little while previously. It was none other than Myoko Yamaguchi. "Welcome, it is good to see you. Come in, please. To what do I owe this pleasure," I said trying to make a fine showing.

"Hi, Jiun, I called Ichiko and he told me where you were hiding. Are you glad to see me?" With a dauntless display, I said, "Of course, I am glad to see you. I've thought about you since we met in Fort Lee at Mitsuwa Marketplace. Aren't you working?"

"No today is my day off."

I found myself thinking in Japanese despite speaking with her in English which she seems to prefer. "Come in we'll have tea and talk some more." I led her to the kitchen and put up the pot to boil the water.

"Are you hungry? I have a refrigerator full of food."

"No thanks, I had lunch. But tea will be fine."

While pouring the boiling water into the earthenware mugs which contained the tea leaves, I told her of some of the events that happened to me. I allowed the tea to macerate a moment before serving the mugs then I sat down next to her to continue our chat. I looked at her intently and saw her long black hair flowing about her face and down to her shoulders enclosing her face like a frame. She noticed me staring at her so she began to laugh. "Ha! Ha! What are you staring at?"

"You are so lovely. I am so glad you came. I really like you very much, "I said with a certain naiveté.

"Yes, I like you too. I am so glad things are working out for you. I brought you a gift. It is by the door, "Oh, you shouldn't have," I called after her as she ran to retrieve it. She came back carrying a big box. "What is it?" I asked.

"It's a rice cooker."

"Did you say a rice cooker?"

"Yes every Japanese household has a rice cooker. I'll show you how to use it and stay for dinner. Is that alright?"

"Yes it's more than alright. Can you stay the whole night?" I said with some apprehension. She turned to look at me and then slowly moved towards me and put her arms around my neck and kissed me full on the lips as she said, "I wondered which one of us would ask first." I moved my arms around her back and drew her towards me tightly. Our embrace seemed to last a long time. I was deliriously happy. I never knew a feeling like this. I returned the kiss and felt her tongue darting in and out of my mouth. *Oh, bliss I think I love this girl.* We kept this embrace for a long time. Suddenly, she reached down and began rubbing the protrusion of my swollen member and laughingly said, "Later, after dinner."

I laughed in unison with her as I released her saying, "After dinner then." Myoko put the water and the rice in the cooker which was on the stove. She then got out a package of frozen peas from the freezer and placed them in a pan and put them on the stove to cook. In a few minutes both the rice and the peas were ready and so she mixed them together in a bowel and spooned in a heaping tablespoon of hoisin sauce. "This is called Gohan Aomame," she said. Meanwhile, in the same pan formerly used for the peas she boiled two hard-boiled eggs. We then sat down to eat our meager meal. Looking at each other as we ate we smiled and munched knowing what would take place after

47

dinner. "This meal is very tasty," I said. She looked at me very thoughtfully and commented, "It isn't much but at least it's vegetarian."

"Are you vegetarian?" I inquired.

"I am a sometime vegetarian. I do not eat meat but I do eat fish and chicken. I am not a vegan who does not eat meat, fish or chicken and, indeed, does not eat products of animals such as eggs, cheese, and milk."

"I believe Jains are vegans," I added.

"Is that so?"

"Yes, they, of all religions, respect all animals' life including insects and mice."

"What about Buddhists?"

"Buddhists have a prohibition against killing animals but will eat animals that someone else kills. They are not necessarily vegetarians, but some of them are."

After dinner I suggested to Myoko that she put her car in the garage of the house saying, "It will look very suspicious if it is seen outside overnight. I will go down and open the garage door for you.

"OK" she said and left to get her car. I met her in the garage and after it was safely put away we returned to the kitchen to wash the dishes and have our tea. While sipping our tea I began our conversation, "Tell me, darling, where do you work?"

"I work for the Fairfield Flag, a local newspaper. I do reporting, copy writing, and editing. I am a sort of all around journalist. I earned an AA degree in journalism from Narack Community College. It is my hope to transfer my credits to a four year college some day. In the meantime I am gaining valuable experience in the workings of a newspaper.

"That sounds wonderful. Do you live at home?"

"Yes, but I do not have to account for my time. I come and go as I please. My mother is an aged Japanese person who has no clue as to the American way."

"I see. So no one will worry if you stay overnight."

"No."

We kept up this banter for a little while until I said," I usually bathe before bed. Would you like to join me?" She laughed and clapped her hands, "What fun. That would be a great idea. Let's go." So we went into the guest bedroom and disrobed. I was immediately struck by her lithesome body. It was smooth and supple. Her breasts were like little hills with deeply magenta-colored teats. Just below her abdomen was the slight molding mound of her belly which was a curved protuberance begging for a kiss. Her thighs were smooth, sleek, and round and between each captured her floss made of black, soft, downy silk. I was fascinated by the sight of her. She approached me with short steps, holding out her arms and muffled something like 'I love you' in a dull sound as she embraced me. I held her tightly as I planted a wet kiss on her full lips and then moved my lips over her face and to her throat. I repeated, "I love you." We then went into the bathroom and ran the tepid water into the tub while giggling and tittering with short convulsive breaths. I entered the tub first and found there was hardly any room for her. Despite the limited room she got in and placed herself in sitting position on my lap. We then began to soap up. I ran my soapy hands over her body feeling her soft, silky skin. I explored all parts of her body with my fingers discovering unknown openings and bulges. My member swelled to unbelievable proportions. She held it and began moving the skin back and forth across the stem. I felt my brain exploding with uncontrollable emotion. She kept up this movement while occasionally sucking on my nipples. It was too late to stop. With an upward thrust of my back I released semen in short bursts while my whole body felt the exciting convulsive tremor of coitus. She laughed and kissed me as I began to relax while my member receded.

She said in an excited way," Let's shower and then get into bed." I agreed and released the tub water after we stood up. I opened the shower valve and hugged her as the cool water flowed over our naked bodies. We kissed and moved our hands over each others bodies. Being highly pleased, she almost made an oblation, "It will be my turn in bed." We towel dried and got between the sheets of the bedding to hold each other with giggles and kisses.

After quieting down I held her head against my chest and said in a muffled voice, "I truly love you. I have never felt this way about any other woman." She smiled and snuggled against my chest as she reached for my member which began rising from its slumber. "I feel so uninhibited with you. There is no obstacle, no hindrance to my love for you. I love you totally and with all my heart," she exclaimed. I lifted her head and kissed her lips. While doing this my member swelled in her hand. She moved on top of me and inserted my member into her moist, warm vagina and began a back and forth motion and gyration while I placed my mouth over her left breast and sucked on the teat. I felt her body stiffen and she let out a little cry, "Oh, oh, oh." Then her thighs tightened on my member in a squeeze-like vice which made me ejaculate with spurts of semen. I had reached the point of issue and fell back on my pillow.

I was breathing hard and uttered in a voiceless whisper, "I love you." She responded by breathing gently on my mouth and licking my lips, "You are my one and only love." She then released me and arose to walk into the bathroom to wash. Afterwards she returned to bed and we fell asleep in each other's arms.

In the early hours of the next morning after washing she began dressing.

I then got out of bed and had my turn at washing in the bathroom. I then started dressing when I heard her in the kitchen preparing breakfast. "Good morning," I said to her as I grabbed her around the waist and planted a kiss on her neck. She turned around and kissed me fully on the lips. "I made toast and found a jar of marmalade for breakfast. Is that alright? In the future I will make a real Japanese breakfast," she explained. I responded by saying simply, "That's fine."

After eating she arose to announce, "I must be off to work. Shall I come back this evening?" I hesitated before answering but held her hands and slowly said, "Much as I would love it, I think we should be very careful and wait a few days. There are still many workmen around and it could be dangerous for you to be seen here too frequently. Do you understand?"

"Of course, I do. Then I shall spend next weekend with you. No one will be here then," she said demurely.

"That's best," I said unconvincingly and added, "They say that absence makes the heart grow fonder."

XIII

Dr. Bremer arranged for a meeting with his daughter on the following day. We all met in his office. I was introduced to Serena, his daughter. She extended her hand, which I took and immediately felt the softness of her skin with a conglutinate feeling of our two hands. I let her hand go with great reluctance. We both smiled at each other. Then we all sat down and I began to inspect her in depth. She was smiling as I looked at her. She was a tall woman with long blonde hair which flowed down over her shoulders and down her back. She had an hour-glass figure which emphasized the narrowness of her waist. Her face was imbued with a milky-cream complexion daubed with touches of peach color at her cheeks. Her lips were pink and puckered. Her nose was aquiline but not long and her eyes were a sparkling bluish-green. Sitting she was able to show her long silky legs which she crossed in a provocative manner. Her voice was strong but agreeable to the ear when she spoke. She wore very little jewelry and her dress which had floriated ornaments was form fitting easily showing off her shapely figure to great advantage. The aroma of her perfume permeated the room making me very aware of her presence.

Dr. Bremer with his usual commanding presence began to speak, "OK, where do we stand? First, let me say that I have been able to get the Mayor Richard Fokachi and Senator Billy Boggs, I mean William Boggs as speakers. How about you Nakahara-san have you approached Reverend Yoshio Fujioka to bless the temple?"

"Yes, not only did he agree to come but he insisted on donating and bringing a small Buddha about three feet high for our services table. He will conduct an eye-opening ceremony on the Buddha and will invoke blessings on the temple." Serena was obviously entranced with wonder and asked, "What is an eye-opening ceremony?"

"Well let me try to explain. Buddhas are made with closed eyes. To bring them to life one places a small dot of black paint in each eye-socket area and simultaneously calls for aid and protection by prayer and an appeal for support through incantation. It is a beautiful and moving ceremony."

"Sounds great," exclaimed Dr. Bremer.

"It sounds lovely," said Serena.

"Yes, it can affect one spiritually," I added.

Dr. Bremer continued speaking, "We will rent chairs and a platform to be installed on the large lawn between the temple and the house. Also, we will need a large tent in case of fowl weather. Nakahara-san have you made up your guest list?"

"Yes, I have. I am afraid I have a small list of people."

"That's OK we will add your list to ours. Thank you," he said as he reached over to receive the list of names that I gave him. My list contained the names and addresses of Mr. Chigesu and his son Koichi, Ichiko and Michiko Fujimori, Yuko Aoyama, Mrs. Kangetsu and Myoko Yamaguchi. I was startled to see that I had very few friends who have entered my life since I left the monastery.

"I am told by the Senior Purchasing Agent that the big Buddha and the other materials you ordered from Japan will arrive on the ship Umi Maru next week in Port Elizabeth, New Jersey. He will arrange for a rigger to pick it up and bring it here."

My ears picked up, "Did you say Umi Maru?"

"That's what I am told. Why?"

"Oh, it's just that coincidentally I traveled from Yokohama to Honolulu on that ship?" I mused. Suddenly thoughts of Mrs. Kangetsu entered my mind. *I wonder how she is. I can remember fondly the wonderful evenings we had together.* I shook my head to dispel such thoughts and returned to the conversation. Dr. Bremer was speaking, "As soon as the big Buddha is installed we will announce the opening date, OK?" We all nodded in assent. Dr. Bremer continued as he looked at me," I hope you can start teaching Serena the practices of Zen before that time."

"Of course, we can start immediately," I said as I turned to her. "Is that alright with you?" I motioned to Serena. "Yes, yes. I am anxious to get started. Where shall we practice?" I hesitated for a moment but explained, "The temple is filled with workmen. Would it be alright if we met in my study in the house?" She looked at me and nodded as she spoke in her strong voice, "Of course, that would be very convenient." Her father was following this exchange and then looked at me with the impatient comment, "OK then why don't you get started."

"Well then let's meet every morning at 10:00 o'clock for an hour starting tomorrow, "I said. "I'll be there," Serena replied. The meeting broke up and I left the two of them to their own devices. I thought this teaching of Serena is going to be a burden but it must be done. One of the things I will have to learn in life is to reciprocate the kindness of a sponsor. I walked to the temple to inspect the work and made arrangements for one of the workmen to complete the work in my study. Tomorrow will be a busy day.

The next morning I arose at my usual hour of 5:00 am showered, shaved and sat on my cushion in zazen for one hour. This was followed by a small breakfast of toast and tea. I then busied myself in straightening up in the study in anticipation of Serena's visit in about two hours.

I was surprised to find that she arrived early. I led her to my study. She was dressed in shorts and walked on high heels which showed off the smoothness and sleekness of her long legs. She stood over me as I sat in my chair. I could detect the distinct aroma of her perfume. Serena was the embodiment of sensual, sexual attraction. Her long blonde hair and small petite face with puckered lips and green eyes in a field of white spoke volumes. She said in a melodious tone," I am very interested in Zen. I want you to teach me the ways of Zen." I was astonished at these words but hesitantly answered, "I would be glad to help you." She answered forcefully as she leaned over me exposing the cleavage of her breasts, "I want private lessons from you. I want to start now." I answered, "That's what we arranged."

I started to rise from the chair but she pushed me back with a gentle shove of her hand. Then without a word she sat in my lap and grabbed my head in her hands and began kissing me on the mouth with her tongue darting in and around my mouth. I was speechless but did not reject her gestures. Indeed, I placed my arms about her back and pulled her towards me. I felt an immediate arousal of my member and began to lift her in my arms as I rose from the chair. She was somewhat heavy but I was so excited I didn't notice. I placed her on the floor and we both began removing our clothes. She spread her legs and grabbed my member which she inserted in her vagina. The back and forth movements caused a secretion of her vaginal glands lubricating the movements to a high degree until finally I ejaculated as we reached coitus. We were both panting and sweating as I rolled off her and stood up. She coiled into a fetal position and began humming a lyrical tune.

From that moment I began giving her spiritual instruction. I taught her how to meditate by sitting zazen. She was a tall girl and very strong from her many hours at playing tennis. Getting her to sit in a lotus or half-lotus position was not easy but eventually she got the hang of it. I also explained the Four Noble Truths which reveal the suffering of human beings and how to overcome suffering by invoking the Eightfold Path. She came to my study almost daily for instruction. I continued to instruct her frequently. I recognized her state and initiated her with instruction in spiritual practice and training and thus a very seminal relationship had begun. She was an avid student and a gracious paramour. We practiced almost daily; first instruction followed by sex. To show her my appreciation for her ability to separate Buddhist learning from sexual activity I gave her an *o-mamori* (an amulet) which she proceeded to wear around her neck much like a piece of jewelry. "This is my talisman," she said.

As time went by she became reckless and at times would not be cautious when we were engaged in sexual activity. I became concerned that others might be gossiping. I was most concerned that her father might become aware. The thought frightened me. I decided to put an end to the daily individual instruction and told her so at our last meeting. "We cannot continue this way. I am worried that we will be found out."

"I understand, "she said. "Perhaps we can meet at my house. Would you like that?" I looked at her pensively, "I don't know. Do you mean to receive instruction?"

"Of course," she quickly answered. "What else did you think I meant?"

"In that case I shall come next week."

In the meantime, I was still seeing Myoko Yamaguchi. She came to me for overnight visits on weekends. I particularly enjoyed these moments because we carried on as if we were married even though the subject of marriage never came up. We were both deeply in love and I worried constantly that Myoko would find out about my carnal relationship with Serena. I thought it best to inform Myoko that I was giving private spiritual instruction to Serena. I thought in that way Myoko would not become suspicious.

The following week it came time for me to visit Serena at her home to continue her spiritual instruction. As I approached her house I noticed the four large columns in the front. I was to learn later that this is known as Greek revival architecture. With a certain amount of foreboding I knocked on the massive door with the provided brass door knocker in the shape of a lion. In a moment it was opened by a house-maid servant dressed in a black uniform and a white apron. She had short, wiry black hair topped by a white, lace tiara and a good-humored, almost perfectly round face. Her lips were very full, the lower one slightly droopy, as though dragged down by the big, dark mole just below the lower lip line. "May I help you?" she asked.

"I am here at the invitation of Miss Serena," I said in a forthright manner. At my words her face lit up as if in recognition, "Of course, you are Reverend Nakahara. I was told by Miss Serena to expect you. She is swimming in the pool. You may go directly there." I was led through a maze of rooms, some with high frescoed ceilings, through a long parlor which led to the French doors leading to the patio inside an indoor pool. The maid stopped at the doorway and said with a simper, "Please go in. She is waiting for you." I hesitated and said cautiously, "Wouldn't it be better if I waited for her here until she is finished swimming?" She looked at me with a broad grin, "She is finished now. Just go in and she'll be ready for you. "I was uncertain as to my next move. I paused undecidedly until the maid exclaimed, "Go in!" My vacillation came to an end as I reached for the door knob.

I entered the swimming pool area to discover Serena lolling in the water in an indolent manner. She had silky pale skin and full breasts. I looked on as she bathed herself, using every suggestive gesture she could find. Her hands were delicate and the way she touched herself only faintly hinted at lewdness. She emerged from the pool and I noticed that her Venus mound was completely shaven free of hair and she was as naked as a Greek statue. She turned revealing her backside and bent over to retrieve a robe establishing a disreputable position and hence its intense eroticism – a symbol of all that is delightfully naughty. She draped herself with a gossamer robe that showed her naked body in the light. She then knelt submissively before me.

I who came from a monastery and used to the conventional morality of Japan have always been swept off my feet by the freedom of American women.

I retreated slightly exclaiming in fright, "No. no, please, we mustn't." I looked about quickly in terror excited by sudden danger. She rose and moved deliberately toward me with outstretched arms. Her robe opened revealing her nudity underneath. I was overcome by intense sexual desire and submitted to my emotions. I fell into her arms and placed my arms around her drawing her to me tightly until my member flattened against her small protruding belly. She began pushing me and so I started to retreat. She reached out to my robe and tore it open revealing my naked torso. I slinked away frightened at her advance. Next she pulled the drawstring on my trousers which allowed them to slip down revealing my genitals. I became frightened at her erratic behavior. I tried to push her away to no avail. She grabbed my member and I fell backwards. At the same time she fell on top of me. I could sense her still moist skin against me. I shouted, "Please stop. Please get off me." She acted as if not to hear. She pushed me down forcefully and pummeled my chest with her fists. The blows hurt and I winced. I tried but could not push her off me; she was unusually strong and insistent. With one hand holding me down she then slithered down my body and I was startled to suddenly feel her wet lips on my member. When she finished fellating my member I could feel it stiffen. I had no control as she then straddled me and inserted it into her vagina. With that she began a vigorous pumping movement up and down while holding both her arms straight out against my chest. I uttered in a strained and unnatural manner, "Please don't. This will not do." She did not heed my pleas and continued the rhythmical motion of her body. I began to feel her soft thighs with my fingers as she was astride me. But I did not move even though there was an emotional sensation. Something happened to me over which I had no restraint. It just happened; I ejaculated. She squealed with a somewhat prolonged cry. I became queasy for the next few minutes as she continued her movements until she reached coitus with a sudden and loud outcry. She then rolled off me with panting and heaving laughter. I got up and adjusted my clothes. Turning to look at her shaking and trembling body, I left with a silent confused and dismayed feeling.

Without saying a word, I went through the French doors and trampled through the long parlor and the maze of rooms until I reached the front door. It was then I heard a voice behind me. It was the maid, "Are you leaving so soon, Reverend?" I detected a bitter taunt in her voice. I left without acknowledging her sarcasm and took the long walk back to the house. I stumbled most of the way with a heartfelt pain in my head. When I got home I was so upset I decided to relax in a hot bath. I remained there until the water turned cold. Strange thoughts went through my mind as I noticed an abatement of the severity of the incident. *Why did she have to rape me if we already had a good sexual relation during Zen practice?* I began to feel lax and weak as my mind mollified the moment. *What will happen next? It was an accident. Wasn't it? Ah, but accidents determine our lives more than we think.*

I climbed out of the tub and toweled myself dry. I dressed and went to the kitchen to make tea. It suddenly occurred to me that the weekend was approaching. *Myoko will be coming. Oh dear!*

XIV

It was late Saturday afternoon when Myoko arrived. I heard her car entering the garage and then she came up the stairs humming a tune. She came into the kitchen carrying a bag of groceries. "Hi," she said exuberantly in her American way. "What's doing?"

"You're a little late. I was worried that you were not coming," I said with a querulous voice. "Not coming. Why not? I was late because I had to take my mother to the doctor," she responded with some vexation. "Is she alright? Is there a problem?" I queried hastily. "No, it was just a routine visit. Since I am the only one with a car it's my duty to help her."

"Of course, I am sorry. I did not mean to make an inquest." She put her bundle down on the counter and then strolled over to me with outstretched arms. We embraced with a long hug and a kiss. "Do you still love me?" she said with a pout of her lips and a sullen look on her face. "You know I do," I answered with a peck on her lips repeatedly and quickly. "Shall I make a little bite to eat? I bought some delicious things for us to eat." She then began emptying the bag and put some things in the refrigerator. I watched her and thought how nice it would be to have her here permanently. My reverie was broken by her voice. "Why are you standing there staring at me? You look like you have something to tell me."

"No, I just like to look at you."

"Is everything alright? Is there a problem? You seem so pensive."

"Yes, everything is alright. It's just that the things I ordered from Japan are coming next week including the big Buddha for the zendo. I promised Dr. Bremer that we can have the opening the week after the Buddha is installed. That means we must have the rental agency set up the tent, the speakers platform and the chairs for the guests. Also, Dr. Bremer would have to alert the guest speakers. It's just a lot to do. After all I am a priest not a handyman."

"Never fear, it will all work out," she said with some optimism. We then had tea at the table while sipping and talking. It was getting late for me since I rise so early. We decided to turn in for the night. Each of us took care of our ablutions and then got into bed. She reached across to me and started soothing my chest with her right hand and then my thighs until she arrived at my member. Using dexterous motions with her fingers she could not cause an erection of my member. It remained flaccid. She stopped and said in an angry way, "You are too preoccupied and show no affection for me." In saying that she turned away from me in a huff leaving me to stare at the black ceiling thinking about the rape forced on me by Serena. I stared up into the darkness and even when I slept, I never rested. My dreams that night were filled with wild colors and violence and loud noises. I remember being in pain and crying for help and finding no one to rescue me. I dreamed that it was time for me to wake up, but I still did not awaken. If I woke Myoko, I knew she would resume last night's questions. I didn't want to get mired in any discussion. Eventually we both fell asleep.

In the morning, I sat my usual zazen at which time I heard her showering. My mind was racing and my whole body felt jittery. In time I became calm and finished zazen. We ate our meager breakfast of toast, marmalade and tea in near silence. She got up from the table saying, "I think I'll stay away until the day of the opening; by that time you should be back to normal. "That might be best," I agreed.

XV

The eight wheeled rigging truck brought the big Buddha to the temple site and a team of burly riggers brought the big Buddha into the temple with a heavy duty gantry crane equipped with chains and ropes and installed it at the far wall of the zendo. After the riggers left with their equipment, I went into the dark zendo and prostrated myself on the floor before the Buddha and asked to be made worthy of his compassion. I then rose with a gassho and deep bow and called Dr. Bremer. I told him that with the Buddha installed it would now be possible to have the "grand opening" in a week. He grunted to me on the telephone, "Good, good, I will inform the guest speakers. Would you call Reverend Yoshio Fujioka of the North American Soto Zen Administration? He is our principal speaker you know."

I agreed and proceeded to call Fujioka-san. He was happy to hear from me. "I will be honored to be there and participate, Nakahara-san. I shall arrange immediately for the small Buddha to precede me by air freight," he said.

"Thank you," I replied. "I look forward to seeing you." The conversation reminded me that the Stupa with the small Buddha inside, recently arrived from Japan with the big Buddha, had to be completed and installed outside of the front entrance to the temple.

Finally the day of the "grand opening" arrived. The tent was in place and the speaker's platform with a dais and public address system was included. There were one hundred folding chairs laid out in a regimental pattern with reserved seats on a gracious lawn between the temple and the house that sweeps down to the road. The front rows were reserved for special guests and the remainder for the public. The maintenance people did a magnificent job of finishing the gardens with specimen plantings and seasonal flowers. Even the Stupa was finished which had a beehive-like look but was in an important place for people to bow before entering the temple. Now all is ready.

Dr. Bremer was hobnobbing with the two political celebrities, the mayor and senator Boggs. I was saddled with Reverend Fujioka with whom I had much in common. It felt good to speak with him in Japanese instead of struggling with English. I suggested that we go to the entrance of the temple to admire the recently installed Stupa with its Buddha inside. On going up the pathway approaching the Stupa, we both bowed deeply with a gassho. Fujioka-san looked at it for a long time. Then with another deep bow and gassho I heard him say, "This is a fascinating instance of an ongoing creative process whereby a global religion is made locally meaningful through the construction of a Buddhist sacred place. A small religious structure, a Stupa, in rural Narack to explore larger issues related to the contemporary surge in interest in Buddhism"

I then added, "It has become increasingly clear that the rational and ethical religion that is Buddhism is as much a product of the late nineteenth, twentieth, and early twenty-first centuries as it is of the time of the Buddha, more than two millennia ago."

A stream of people began entering the compound and sitting inside the tent. The press and other media people arrived with two TV cameras and took their places in the reserved area. Also local educators, some clerics and business leaders joined them in the reserved area. Dr Bremer brought the two political persons up to the platform and I brought up Reverend Fujioka. We all sat on a line of provided chairs facing the audience. A team of men had brought up the small Buddha previously and it now rested on a pedestal next to the dais.

While waiting and looking out at the sea of faces all seemed in readiness. People in the audience were fidgeting and busy talking to each other in a loud murmur. As I surveyed the crowd musing about the various people attending the opening it struck me that I could not find Serena anywhere. I suddenly became anxious. Why is she not here? I became disquieted over a possible pending bad omen. Is she ill? I then recovered as my consciousness was restored. If her absence was anything serious Dr. Bremer would have told me. As it is he never posed the subject so my fears were somewhat abated. Actually, I am glad she is not here. It avoids embarrassment and many possible complications. I wiped it out of my mind. Off to the side, Fujioka-san's assistant began playing a somber melody in a minor key on a shakuhachi, a Japanese end-blown bamboo flute. The music wafted on the wind throughout the tent and seemed to quiet the crowd. When he finished playing there was no applause and Dr. Bremer got up, approached the dais and began to speak.

"We gather here today to dedicate the opening of the Narack Zen Center." He paused and then continued, "This temple will be available for the practice of Zen Buddhism for people regardless of religious affiliation." He then paused again, this time a little longer as he looked about the audience. "It is our belief that Zen offers a place in an integrated life with freedom from dogma and liberation to make choices. Now let me introduce Reverend Yoshio Fujioka who will bless this temple and perform the eye-opening ceremony on the small Buddha." He pointed to the Buddha on the pedestal. Dr. Bremer stepped back and Fujioka-san got up and slowly walked to the podium. He had a broad smile on his face and his bald head was bobbing to the crowd in multiple bows. He spoke in a low, endless sing-song voice to the crowd in Japanese and turned to his right toward the temple and shook his fly-whisk vigorously several times. No one understood him but somehow all knew this was a solemn moment. He then put down the fly-whisk while still muttering in his sing-song fashion. He picked up a small badger hair brush which he dipped carefully into a plate of black sumi paint. Reaching across the face of the Buddha he placed a small eyespot of black paint into each orbital area with a loud shout *Okosu! Okosu!* (Awake! Awake!). All present looked on in fascination. He put the brush down and assumed a gassho position while facing the Buddha and mumbled a prayer. Then he faced the audience and bowed with a gassho and retreated slowly back to his seat. A quiet hush spread over the audience for a few minutes. On looking at the Buddha, one could believe that it came alive. Its eyes were now seemingly wide open.

Dr. Bremer came back to the podium and introduced the politicians in turn, the mayor and the senator. Both gave a canned speech of short duration which seemed to bore the audience. At the conclusion of the talks, Dr. Bremer invited all present to inspect the temple with the admonition that they remove their shoes if they go into the zendo.

It was at this time that I spotted Myoko. She was seated at a table in the anteroom taking names and addresses of interested people. She also directed people who went into the temple. I was very pleased to see her and grateful for her unsolicited help. I was busy answering questions posed by people of the audience surrounding me and so I had no opportunity to greet her properly.

Dr. Bremer came over to me and said with a flourish of his hand, "It was a wonderful opening ceremony and Reverend Fujioka was great. Now the ball is in you court. Make a success of this temple." Then with his usual panache and flamboyant style said, "Let me know if there is anything I can do to help." I never can get used to Dr. Bremer's use of the vernacular but I understood very well that the responsibility of the temple was handed to me. The political celebrities rushed off with a handshake and eventually people dissipated. I was left with Fujioka-san who will be staying overnight in my house. I noticed Myoko walking towards us with a stack of papers in her hand. She bowed to Fujioka-san with a greeting, *konnichiwa* (good day). I introduced her and she began chatting in Japanese to Fujioka-san to his surprise and delight. She turned to me with the papers in her outthrust hand saying in Japanese for Fujioka-san's benefit, "These are names and addresses of interested persons. If you like I can review them with you next weekend."

"Yes, that would be fine. We have much work to do in returning the rentals and preparing the temple for services." She left with a smile and a low bow to both of us. By the end of the day the rentals were gone and the maintenance people had cleaned up the area and polished the floor in the zendo. I had them mount a table and place the small Buddha on it in front of the large Buddha. They also made a platform with a book rest next to the table for me to sit on during zazen services. I invited Fujioka-san to assist me in adding a plate of fruit on the table as well as a censor with a tube of incense sticks. He said in his low voice, "You are now ready to transmit the Dharma to the world."

That night Fujioka-san told me that he made application with the Sotoshu Shumucho in Tokyo for full recognition of the temple. He said, "Recognition will take some time and may involve a visit from someone to authenticate your activities but in the meantime you may call yourself Roshi (Zen Master) since you are the abbot of this temple. I was pleased beyond belief to have the title, Nakahara Jiun - Roshi. It sounded wonderful.

XVI

The following day an ad appeared in the local paper, The Narack Day:

A FREE BEGINNERS TUTORIAL IN ZEN
MEDITATION WILL BEGIN.
EVERY MONDAY AT 10:00 A.M. AT THE NARACK ZEN CENTER,
110 WILLIAMS AVENUE. PLEASE DRESS IN SLACKS OR PANTS.

This ad drew a large response. A contingent arrived the first day and I found myself very busy with instruction to novices and dilettantes. Most of the attendees were young girls. There were some middle aged women and an occasional teenage boy. After rooting out the curiosity seekers, I got down to the rubrics of zazen. Most of the young people seemed eager to learn even with the difficulty of sitting properly with folded legs and a straight back. Some of the middle aged women thought zazen was a form of exercise like yoga and had no interest in the piety and devotion of the practice. Still. It was a good start.

I had arranged for a car to take Fujioka-san and his assistant to the airport for their flight back to San Francisco. We said a tearful goodbye with multiple bowing. In a way I was very sorry to see him go. I certainly could use his wise counsel for the start up of the temple. But I was glad, on the other hand, since I knew that Myoko was returning to me this weekend. On Friday night Myoko returned for a long weekend stay. I was so happy I could not contain myself. "I am absolutely delighted," I said as I held her close to me. "I missed you and I want to make up for my inconsiderate attitude to you. I love you very much and I want you to be with me always." I hurriedly exclaimed in flustered haste. She leaned her head on my chest and quietly repined, "There is no need for recriminations. I really understand what troubled you. Now it is all in the past. From now on we shall lead a caring and graceful life together." She raised her head and I kissed her full on the lips. Having her in my arms made me feel like I possessed an object which I regarded with special affection. I have never known such bliss as when I held her close this way.

We did not speak we just stood together holding each other and feeling the current flowing between our bodies like a stream of water. It was such exalted happiness. Nothing else mattered to me. All my worldly cares were thrust aside as I entered this feeling of lighthearted blithesomeness. She kissed me again as she said, "I love you, Jiun." I answered in a hoarse voice, "I love you too, Myoko." I could see now we were meant for each other. It was as if our karma was the same. From the moment I saw her in the Mitsuwa Marketplace I knew we were destined to be together. *I have to find a way to keep her with me always.*

"What are you thinking," she said.

"Oh, wouldn't it be wonderful if we could be like this forever?"

"Well maybe someday we will."

"I hope so, but first I must make a success of the temple."

"Yes, of course," she hastily remarked.

We started to make dinner. Myoko made the rice in the rice cooker while I chopped the vegetables into small bite size pieces for a stir fry with egg. Dinner was delicious. "You shouldn't supply the food when you come. I have an allowance for food supplies," I said in a forceful manner. "There is always enough food left over for my needs midweek. I have yet to buy any food. The refrigerator and pantry were stocked before I came here."

"I enjoy shopping for us for the weekends. It makes me feel married and anyway it is not that expensive. All I bought were some fresh vegetables and eggs," she demurred.

After dinner we had our tea in the spare bedroom where we chatted for many hours until retirement. I watched her as she removed her clothes. She had a lovely well-formed body. Her breasts were small and firm like little mounds. Her hips were narrow making her derriere seem to stand out in a round protrusion. She had smooth inner thighs and the floss at her Venus mound was silky like the styles on an ear of Indian corn. We got under the covers and began to explore each other. My member began swelling as I continued feeling the smoothness of her thighs and the cheeks of her buttocks. We hugged and kissed and rubbed our bodies until she gently inserted my member into her vagina. It was heavenly. We did not move allowing our genitals to pulsate and throb. It lasted a long time until I felt it was time to move slowly and rhythmically in unison with Myoko. We both reached coitus at the same time in a vibratory tremor unlike anything I had ever experienced. She came over to me and began kissing me on the lips, on my face, and on my body saying breathlessly, "I love you, Jiun. You will be my lover forever. I love you. I love you." I returned the kisses on her mouth and on her little breasts and said, "I love you, Myoko. You belong to me forever." We then rolled over to sleep in a heavy slumber.

In the morning, at breakfast, we had an irenic account designed to produce peace and harmony by being conciliatory. "I am sorry for the way I treated you the last time you were here," I said in a remorseful tone.

"I guess I shouldn't have stomped out. I should have been more understanding at that time," she rejoined tending to make peace.

"It's all over, let's forget it. I love you now, more than ever," I said.

"You're right. I love you too, Jiun. Let's forget it."

And so we carried on our life as lovers with no idea where we were heading in the future.

I reviewed the names on the papers which Myoko had accumulated at the opening. We agreed to send invitations to most of the names after weeding out some. I said I would have the secretary at the Bremer Chemical Company send the invitations together with a copy of the newspaper ad to the list of names. On Sunday late afternoon, after doing the laundry, Myoko went home. I prepared myself for the Zen tutorial on Monday and then went to sleep in my futon in the office/den room dreaming of Myoko.

XVII

There were fifteen novices eager to learn zazen and the ways of Zen. These new students appeared at the zendo three-days-a-week on Monday, Wednesday, and Friday. (On the weekends I spent my days with Myoko.) They all seemed committed to learn and except for a few minor mishaps were progressing very well. Two outstanding students were Ed Green and Bill Stevens who took to zazen like a duck to water. I could foresee them being lay ordained in the Jukai ceremony in about a year. This thought brought to mind the need for in-house residence for those who would seek ordination as monks and receive transmission of the dharma.

The basement of the temple was now being used as a storeroom. It could be converted into living quarters for monks by constructing individual cells around the inner periphery and a central kitchen. I was excited at this plan but knew I had to consult with Dr. Bremer in order to bring it about. Several weeks went by, while the novices were training, before I approached Dr. Bremer for an appointment.

"Good morning, dear Sir," I said on the telephone, using the special number he gave me. "How are you? I would like to visit with you to discuss a plan which I have."

"I am very well, Nakahara-san. It is good to hear your voice. A special plan, eh? Would tomorrow morning at 10 o'clock in my office be okay?"

"Yes, indeed! I shall be there."

The next day I arrived at his office and when I entered he rose from behind his massive desk and greeted me with an outstretched hand. I grabbed it warmly as he said, "It's good to see you. Come let us sit here." He pointed to the couch on which we made ourselves comfortable. "Would you care for some tea?"

"No thank you," I said.

"Alright then what is your plan?"

I began to relate my plan of renovating the temple basement into living quarters for monks. I told him of Ed Green and Bill Stevens progress and their desire to become monks. He quickly responded, "It sounds like a workable plan but first we must apply for permission to have a residential component in the temple from the proper authorities. I will make the inquiries. In the meantime, you must discuss this plan with the maintenance department so that we can get cost figures and construction procedures."

"Yes, I shall do that," I said as I started to get up to leave.

"Wait, please sit down. I want to discuss something with you," he said with a scowl on his face. I was fearful about what would come next.

I apprehensively responded, "What is it?"

He looked very sullen, with a wrinkled brow as he slowly spoke, "You may have heard my wife and I are separated. She lives in our apartment in New York City. My daughter Serena lives with me but occasionally visits with her mother. They go shopping together and spend a lot of money. My wife wanted to travel in Europe and talked Serena into accompanying her. Serena felt obligated and now the two of them are touring Europe."

"I wondered why I haven't seen her at the opening and since that time," I deliberated.

"Yes, they will be gone at least another month," he added. "I want to request a special favor of you," he said after a moment of silence.

"What is it?" How may I help?" I weighed in my mind not knowing the nature of what would be requested.

He procrastinated but continued in a dilatory way. "Serena doesn't have sound judgment or a serious purpose in her life. She flitters from one thing to another and has no solid ground to alight on. That's why I thought she might become devoted to Buddhism." He stopped and looked at me with his piercing eyes. I stared back with a fixed gaze in wonder. Nothing was said as he gathered his thoughts. "I hope I can count on you to continue Buddhist instruction for Serena."

With a great sense of relief, I quickly said, "Of course, I shall continue with her instruction."

He answered, "That's swell. I really believe that studying Buddhist ways will give her a sense of purpose."

After saying farewell to Dr. Bremer with a hardy handshake, I wondered what the future might bring. For weeks on end, Zen instruction continued with the novices. Some progressed, others faltered. I wondered about these people. *Who are they? What do they want?* As best I could tell most came from alcoholic families or families with drug abuse problems. What one could call dysfunctional families or social dropouts? Some are disillusioned with their birth religion and some are discontented with life to the point of exhibiting despair and hopelessness. To my mind they are all ripe for a spiritual revolution. It was my intent to show them that salvation lay in self-reliance and to apply one-self vigorously. I explained that entreaty with some unseen superior being would not bring succor. One must finally decide to be the master of one's own fate.

Myoko continued to visit every weekend. It was my heartfelt delight to be with her as an imitation married couple. One day I asked her if she knew a seamstress who could instruct the novices in making a *rakusu*, the small imitation Buddhist robe worn around the neck by ordained lay monks. She said she did know someone who was a friend of her mother, a Mrs. Toshiko Yamanata. She volunteered to contact her. It would be several weeks before I could gather the participants together and explain the sewing of the rakusu with Mrs. Yamanata's help. All seemed to be going well.

Then one day it happened. I was sitting in the front office of the temple trying to decipher the workings of the computer when she arrived. She was tall and stately like a lily with her blonde hair. She said, "Good morning, Jiun"

I looked up somewhat startled at seeing her unexpectedly after such a long time. "Good morning, Serena. How are you? I heard you were vacationing in Europe. Did you have a nice time?"

"Yes, it was very nice, indeed. But I am glad to be home. I got tired of crawling through cathedrals and museums."

"I see."

Then there was silence for a considerable time as we examined each other. Suddenly with her big, liquid eyes she uttered almost incoherently, "I am very sorry for the way I acted with you in my house when we last met. Please forgive me and accept my apology. "She seemed very humble and thoroughly penitent. I felt sorry for her when I heard this sincere contrition.

"Of course, there is no need for an apology. Let us just forget it, "I said with a bit of bravado in a trifle of speech.

She extended her hand and said, "Well then we are still friends."

"Yes, we shall always be friends," I said as I grabbed her hand and held it for a little while. After another moment of awkward silence she asked, "May I continue my zazen practice?"

I let her hand go as I said deliberately, "Things have changed somewhat. We now have fifteen practitioners who meet in the zendo on Monday, Wednesday and Friday. Would you like to join us?"

"Yes, I would." She exclaimed in a forthright manner with a sparkle in her eyes.

I looked into her eyes as I said pedantically, "Zen practice offers opportunities to develop and deepen a steadfast practice of the Buddha's path in the Soto Zen tradition. Right now we provide non-residential practice in the form of practice periods three-days-a-week. You must learn how to sit still for long periods of time. You must fearlessly face hours and hours of sitting silently not twitching a single muscle. To venture courageously into this realm with full conscious awareness is the other side of silent relinquishment of consciousness while sitting zazen. This is finding completeness, wholeness, and true intimacy." I waited a moment then continued, "Would you like to join our *Sangha* (community)."

"I would like to try," she answered.

"The daily routine is vigorous. We start at 6:00 am and sit three periods of zazen and kinhin followed by a morning service of sutra chanting. Then we have a meager, vegetarian breakfast about 9:30 am. After breakfast, we have *chosen* (a formal tea). After *chosen* participants will have some time for activities of their choice such as communal discussion or studying."

She covered her forehead with the back of her hand as she exclaimed, "Oh my, it sounds very daunting."

"Yes, it is difficult but eventually you will succeed and learn to enjoy it. Remember that famous saying, *there is but one cause of human failure. And that is man's lack of faith in his true self.*"

She looked at me with limpid eyes as she said sarcastically, "you are full of bright sayings."

"I only wish to give you encouragement. The task is up to you."

"I shall do my best."

With that we parted. I could not help wondering what the future might bring. I shook it off quickly because I was grateful that I was able to fulfill Dr. Bremer's request.

XVIII

Mrs. Toshiko Yamanata, the seamstress, came to the temple the following week with a large bolt of black, cotton cloth and a basket of sewing utensils such as needles, thread, and scissors. In addition, she brought a pattern template for the participants to use in cutting and sewing the cloth strips for the rakusu. Everyone was given a large cloth piece. The first thing was to cut the provided cloth into many strips for the neck strap, the sides of the square and the little pieces that made up the center of the square. This was all to be sewn together to finally make the rakusu. Mrs. Yamanata came frequently to assist those in need but the participants usually did their actual sewing at home.

Meanwhile the students continued their thrice weekly practice of zazen which will continue until they are ready to accept the Five Precepts. At that time the completed rakusu is given in a lay ordination ceremony called *Jukai* where the Five Precepts are invoked.

The Five Precepts for lay people, in the rule of training, is to abstain from (1) harming any living being, (2) taking anything not given, (3) misconduct involving sense-pleasure, (4) false speech, (5) losing control of mind through alcohol or drugs. These are understood not so much as commandments, as promises that Buddhists make to themselves at the start of each day.

Serena came to the thrice weekly zazen practice. She seemed to be diligent in an earnest endeavor to learn. I found her punctiliously exacting in her attendance. She did not socialize with the other students. She came without fanfare as a committed student and sat at her prescribed place. When finished she left at her discretion. She would bow and gassho to me as did the other students but she did not speak. This continued for some time until one day as I was leaving the zendo after everyone was gone I discovered her waiting for me at the entrance hall.

"Hello, Jiun," she said coyly.

"Hello, Serena," I responded as I put on my shoes without looking up.

"I wanted to invite you to dinner at my house this evening," she quickly interjected in the greeting.

I hesitated for a while and after a moments thought replied, "I think not. It is not a good idea. I would rather not go to your house."

"My father has gone away for a few days. I am very lonely and would appreciate your companionship. I promise to behave civilly," she hastily replied.

"Serena, I still haven't gotten over the last incident in your house. Besides, I think it is too dangerous for us to be seen intimately."

"But no one will know. I told you my father is away," she beseeched me.

"Still, I am worried."

"What harm can come from an evening at dinner?" she implored.

"People will talk."

"Please, Jiun, I am so lonely, I just want to be with you for a little while," she said with increased fervor.

Finally, I relented and said, "Oh, alright, I'll be there at seven o'clock."

She left with a smile on her face and I had an ominous feeling that I made a mistake by agreeing to the tryst.

That night I walked the distance to her house arriving a little after seven o'clock. I was surprised to be greeted at the door by the maid-servant.

"Good evening, Reverend Nakahara," she said with a slight smirk on her face.

I was stunned by the affected smile but responded, "I am here to see Miss Serena."

"Yes, I was told to expect you," she simpered.

I was then led into the dining room.

The table was set in an elegant manner with linen napkins, crystal stemware, and silver tableware. I sat down on a side chair and waited for Serena to appear. It took a little while but she finally made her entrance with a flourish.

"Thank you for coming, Jiun. Have you been waiting long?" she exclaimed with an outstretched hand.

I rose slowly and stared at her in amazement. She wore a tight fitting lavender gown which exposed the cleavage of her breasts at the bodice. The gown contained lace and sequins which sparkled and showed off her tall, shapely body to great effect. Her long blonde hair was now coiffed and built up to a crown-like structure on top of her head. I was duly impressed with her appearance as I took her hand in acknowledgement.

"I didn't expect such a fancy dinner. I am a simple man with simple needs," I stated matter-of-factly.

She immediately took up the claim as she imparted, "That's what I like about you. You are always honest with me. Other men are usually out to get what they can from me. Please sit down. Would you care for some wine?"

She reached for the decanter, but I replied, "No wine, please. I'll just have some mineral water. I am thirsty after the long walk here."

She poured the ruby red liquid into her glass and then filled my glass with the bubbling mineral water. We raised our glasses in a toast. I said, "Here's to a pleasant evening Serena." Our glasses touched with a slight ting as she said, "Yes, Jiun, to a pleasant evening."

I hesitated for a moment but then continued, "I must tell you, Serena that I am delighted with the way you have taken to the Zen practice."

"Thank you, I really enjoy the practice and I hope to continue it for some time."

Just then our conversation was interrupted by the maid who brought in two plates of appetizer containing pieces of pickled vegetables garnished with olives and tiny jalapeno peppers. I was famished and began to eat rapidly until I bit into one of the peppers which immediately burned my mouth and tongue with a fiery irritation. I reached for the mineral water to quench the fire in my mouth but it did not help. Tears came to my eyes as I noticed Serena laughing at my distress. "I had no idea that food could be so spicy," I exclaimed in a choking and coughing manner.

Serena laughed as she handed me a piece of bread, "This will help remove the heat in your mouth. Chew it well."

I did as I was told and found to my pleasure that the heat did subside. "You know, of course, that Japanese food is very bland and depends very much on subtle flavor," I said by way of an explanation.

She continued the jocosity of the moment and offered a mild apology. "I'm sorry. I should have realized that you are not used to many varieties of Western cuisine. I am sure you will enjoy the rest of the meal." As she said that, the maid came in with two small bowls of thick potato-leek soup which restored my mouth to normalcy. We continued our conversation for a time while consuming the soup. I must admit it was very pleasant being here with Serena under these relaxed conditions. I almost forgot the terrible occurrence the last time I was here. But remnants of it in my memory prevented me from letting my guard down. The maid then came in with a platter containing, what I was told, was a pheasant decorated with vegetables and bits of fruit. Serena dished out pieces into my plate and after eating the meat of the pheasant I found it to be unusually delicious.

And so went the dinner meal. I was very relaxed and enjoyed the various dishes and the conversation with Serena. The maid brought in tea for me and coffee for Serena which concluded the meal. At this point the maid exclaimed, "Miss Serena if that will be all I shall leave and return early tomorrow. Please leave everything, I shall clean up tomorrow. Goodnight. Goodnight Reverend Nakahara" She left and we continued talking and sipping our beverages.

We went into the comfort of the living room and continued our conversation. She told me about her life as a child growing up with a workaholic father and a distant mother. "My father and mother were never around," she said. My mother spent hours primping and trying to suppress her inevitable aging. She went to many rejuvenating clinics that professed to arrest or at least limit the aging process, all to no avail. She was embarrassed to be seen with a little kid like me. My father, on the other hand, was very devoted to me. He gave me whatever I wanted. He sent me to private schools and I always had a "nanny". He never had time for me since he was always busy making money."

I listened to her with great interest. It was only now that I understood her hedonism. It reflected a relaxed, playful attitude toward life. She was very much involved with herself. She liked to espouse a form of extreme solipsism. I felt it was important, since she was baring her soul, that I tell her something of my own life. "I was a mediocre student in High School. When I graduated I decided to enter a monastery and study to become a Buddhist priest. My father and mother both approved of this and supported me. I was eighteen years old when I began and twenty-four when I was ordained as a Buddhist priest. In the six years that I endured my time in the monastery I never participated in youthful activities. It was constant work maintaining the monastery building and spending endless hours in farming the fields. It was hard, difficult work from early morning until late at night with only one day off per week. I had very few friends and never spent any time with women. I was beginning to lose the vigor of my youth. My only ambition was to get away from my burdens and try and see something of the world. My father located a spot for me. He wanted me to become the head priest of a small suburban temple which was worn out and weakened by an ancient community. But, I would have none of it. I decided to recover my life by going to America and through a series of good fortunes I arrived here in Narack."

She looked at me with sympathetic eyes and then kissed me on the lips. I said, "It's getting late. I must go now."

"No, please, Jiun, don't go. Stay with me tonight," she begged while holding both my hands firmly.

"That would be unwise, Serena. Someone might find out. Even though I would enjoy being with you I must refuse."

"Jiun, please, I need you very much. You must know that I love you."

After much repartee I threw caution to the wind, let my guard down and agreed to stay the night with the proviso that I leave at five o'clock in the morning when no one is about. After our intimate confessions we decided to go to bed. It was a long day. On entering her bedroom I wondered what I would do for bed clothes since I brought nothing. She noticed my dilemma. "Would you like a pair of my father's pajamas?" she offered.

"Oh, no, I could never do that. Would you mind if I slept in the nude?"

She clapped her hands in childish delight and said, "Oh what a great idea. I would love to sleep in the nude with you."

We undressed and I observed Serena's lovely, slim body before she got under the covers. We hugged and explored each other's bodies. It was pure magic as my member stiffened. We then had sex with breathtaking finality. After coitus I moved up to her back and held her tight with my hands on her breasts and my member at her rump until we both fell asleep. I had a fitful night and don't think I got more than three hours of sleep. Serena was dead to the world. I could hear her heavy breathing as she slept. I turned over on my back and stared at the dark ceiling until it was time to rise. A tremulous excitement surged up in me at the thought of the sex with Serena. I had all I could do to prevent myself from repeating last night's performance.

The next day at five o'clock in the morning I quietly slipped out of the house. I do not believe anyone saw me. It was still somewhat dark but I saw the beginnings of first light. I was able to make my way down the driveway to the road and thence walked back to the temple. When I arrived at the temple I let myself into the zendo and adopted a full lotus position and began sitting zazen. At first I found it difficult to empty my mind because the images of Serena in sexual posture kept appearing. I finally was able to rid these images by not dwelling on them. I sat zazen for one hour at the conclusion of which I felt very refreshed. I then went to my house and made a small breakfast of toast and tea. After breakfast I bathed and donned fresh clothing. I next went into my den and pondered the events of the day.

What have I done? Didn't I vow not to get sexually involved with Serena? What is wrong with me? What if her father or more importantly Myoko found out? The thought is too horrendous to contemplate. I must change. I must refuse Serena's advances. I must insist. I must. I must.

Before I knew it the weekend was upon me. After garaging her car, Myoko came in carrying a bundle of groceries which she placed on the kitchen table. We hugged and kissed and then she began distributing the food to the refrigerator and the cupboard, while prattling on about her day. "Would you like some tea," she asked.

"Yes, that would be nice," I answered.

She made the tea and we quietly sat and sipped. "You seem so preoccupied. Is everything alright? Is anything wrong?" she questioned.

I realized my silence might alert her to a problem so I tried to change the subject. "Oh, I'm sorry. Everything is really fine. I was just thinking about my students and wondering how they will do making their rakusu." I quickly acted to deceive her to prevent further probing.

"Has Mrs. Yamanata been able to help?"

"Yes, she is wonderful. I guess I am unnecessarily concerned," I deflected the subject. I now felt that I had to change my demeanor and get into a more pleasant mood or she will become unduly suspicious with more questions.

I breathed deeply and smiled as I said, "Shall I prepare the rice for a light lunch?"

"Why are you so solicitous?"

"I am so happy to have you with me that I don't know what to do to express my feelings," I felicitously exclaimed as I grabbed her at the waist.

"Oh, you are so nice," she said as she turned and kissed me. We then began chatting about the events of the past week as we sat at the table. "How long do you think it would be before I can join you here full time without hiding?"

I was stunned by the statement more like a question. I had not thought this problem would ever come up. What a kettle of fish this is. I had no way to give her an honest answer. I just assumed we would go on this way forever. What a fool I am. I love Myoko and I should think more about her feelings and needs. What Am I to do? "It will be soon my dear. I just have to be sure of a few things before I approach Dr. Bremer with the suggestion. Please be patient. It won't be too long," I acquiesced.

Having said that I felt I was fraudulent in giving such an immoral and unchaste answer. I had no idea how to reveal Myoko's presence without causing problems with Dr. Bremer, especially in view of the fact that Serena might cause trouble if Myoko was revealed. As it turned out, I did not need to call Dr. Bremer. He called me. He wanted to have a meeting with me concerning the renovation of the temple basement into residential cells for the lay monks.

XIX

I was shown into Dr. Bremer's office by his secretary. "Come in Nakahara-san. How are you?" exclaimed Dr. Bremer. His enthusiasm put my mind at ease. He rose from his massive leather chair and came over to me with an outstretched hand. We shook hands and made our way to the two overstuffed chairs which faced each other. As we sat he asked, "How are things going?"

"Well, sir, I can report that all is going well. We now have about fifteen practitioners who come on a sporadic basis. Some come frequently; some come infrequently. But only two come on a regular basis. I am most concerned for the two practitioners, Ed Green and Bill Stevens who are both dedicated and committed and could be our first ordained lay monks. When that time approaches I would like to be in a position to offer them residential status to continue their studies into full monk ordination."

"Yes, yes, that's exactly why I asked to meet with you. We've received official permission from the town council to run a residential capability as a Buddhist school in the temple. I, also, had our maintenance department file for a building permit so that they may begin renovating the temple basement into living quarters."

"That's wonderful," I said. "I, also, spoke with the maintenance people and suggested that they build about six cells, a bathroom and a kitchen in the basement. In addition, I requested that they install a raised platform in the zendo for six zazen positions. These positions will be reserved for the lay monks pursuing full ordination. Also, I asked them to build overhead cabinets at the platform sites for storage of futons because the platforms will be used as sleeping quarters at night, whereas the cells will only be used for study purposes and as retreats or sinecures for their personal needs."

"I see. You really have been busy with this matter," he remarked in an astonished way.

"We have both been busy. I had no idea you were able to get permission to establish a Buddhist learning center for the temple so quickly. I am truly amazed at the speed with which things are happening."

"Well it will have the same status as a boarding school," he added.

Then there was a long silence until Dr. Bremer suggested, "Would you care for some tea?"

"Yes, that would be nice," I answered.

He got up and went to the desk and ordered the tea over the intercom then he returned to his seat. "Tell me, Nakahara-san, how is your personal life?"

I was shocked at the question as the secretary brought in the tea service and placed it on the coffee-table. I needed time to think of an answer and so said, "Please call me Jiun. I want us to be friends."

"Of course, we are friends. I just wanted to maintain the respect for your position," he explained as he began pouring the tea into the cups.

I raised the teacup to my lips as I expiated, "Respect is earned by the good deeds we do, much like karma accumulation."

"Alright, Jiun, tell me about your personal life. Have you been getting around the community? Have you made friends?"

I found the questioning very daunting. What would I say? What should I say? "I have been too busy with the temple to do much else," I freely commented.

"I see. May I suggest that you get interested in civic matters, possibly meeting other clerics? It is important to make other contacts and not be parochial. It would not be good for our reputation to be perceived as standoffish. We must be cordial to other local religions," he espoused.

Suddenly a flash came over me. *Is this a good time to tell him about Myoko? Can this be the opportunity that I have been waiting for?*

"I do have one friend," I blurted out.

"Good, who is it?"

"I met a young Japanese girl when I lived in Fort Lee, New Jersey. She visits me occasionally."

"Did you say a Japanese girl?"

"Well actually she is Nisei; she was born in America."

"And she comes here from New Jersey/" he wondered.

"No, no, she lives in Fairfield and only visits me on weekends."

"I see. Is it serious between the two of you?" he questioned intensively.

"Yes, it is very serious," I admitted with great courage.

His face bore a frown as he questioned me. Looking at his gray eyebrows was like looking at two caterpillars charging each other every time he frowned.

"Then I am happy for you. I would like to meet her some day soon."

"It would be my honor to introduce you to her."

I now felt my personal demons were completely extinguished. We parted with a handshake. I was inwardly delighted at the outcome and relieved of the burden I carried for so long. I couldn't wait to tell Myoko. She would be so happy. On my way back to the temple, I could hardly contain myself. My worst fears were abated and now I no longer have to secrete Myoko. I am in love with her and it would be my greatest pleasure to let the world know this. *But what about Serena, would she understand?* I am uncertain but I have to rely on hope. I can hardly wait until this coming weekend to tell Myoko the good news. Meanwhile, I spent most of my time and the next few days in giving instruction to the participants, in particular to the two advanced students, Ed Green and Bill Stevens. I found it strange that Serena did not show up for any of the sessions but I didn't give it much more than a passing thought.

On Saturday, Myoko arrived with the usual bundle of groceries. I held her in my arms for a long time and kissed her several times on the lips.

"What's this all about," she said joyously. "Did something important happen?"

"Yes, I have some wonderful news," I replied in gleeful gaiety.

"What is it?"

I then related the entire story of my meeting with Dr. Bremer including the revelation of Myoko as an important person in my life. "And he wants to meet you," I hurriedly added.

"Really, Oh my, isn't that wonderful. I no longer have to sneak here and keep out of sight. I am so happy. You have no idea what this means to me. Thank you, Jiun. I am grateful and happy. Now we can have a beautiful life." She held me close as she spoke and kissed my mouth repeatedly.

A beautiful life, I heard that from Mrs. Tomoko Kangetsu a long time ago. Those words are still haunting me.

I shook my head and returned my thoughts to the instant moment.

XX

We spent the weekend together in near-wedded bliss and for the first time walked together around the property without fear or caution inspecting the plantings and making plans for the future. Suddenly, she turned to me and said, "Jiun, would it be alright if I moved in with you. I could then commute to my job in Fairfield from here."

I was stunned not having an immediate answer, "I have no notion what Dr. Bremer would think of that idea. Let's wait a while until I find out." We continued walking and talking but my thoughts were always on her suggestion. Finally, after the weekend tryst, I decided to call Dr. Bremer at the private number to seek his approval.

"Good morning, Dr. Bremer, how are you?"

"I am fine, Nakahara-san, how are you?"

"I am well, sir. I need your advice about a personal matter."

"What is it, Nakahara-san? I am at your service."

After some stammering, I blurted out, "Well, sir, you might recall that I told you about a woman I befriended who visits me on weekends."

"Yes, I remember."

I was silent for a moment as I hesitated, "Well, sir, she would like to move in with me. So I am seeking your approval."

"Is that all, Nakahara-san? I see nothing wrong with that arrangement. You have my approval."

My mouth was dry as dust and my temple veins were pulsing in anticipation as I spoke to Dr. Bremer. He cleared his throat as he continued speaking, "Do you intend marrying this woman, Nakahara-san?"

After some thought I responded, "Myoko and I talked about it but have not made definite plans yet."

"Is her name Myoko?"

"Yes, her name is Myoko."

"Well, you go right ahead with her moving in with you. Let me know when you have finalized your plans for marriage."

He hung up and I dangled the phone in my fingers in wonderment as I placed the phone down on the cradle. This is the most wonderful turn of events. Myoko will be absolutely delighted. *I must think about this more before I tell her. How would Serena take this news? I must think. I must think.*

For the next few days, I spent my time in intensive teaching of the novices through lectures, leading in zazen, and *dokusan* (individual discussion). I particularly focused on Ed Green and Bill Stevens. They were both progressing very nicely and I could imagine them being lay ordained in several months so I paid particular attention with them on the Five Precepts, the basic obligations undertaken by Buddhists:

1. Abstain from harming any living being.
2. Abstain from taking anything not given.
3. Abstain from misconduct involving sense pleasure.
4. Abstain from false speech.
5. Abstain from losing control of mind through alcohol or drugs.

I do not employ the Zen Buddhist teaching technique known as *Bokatsu*. This is an ancient technique which uses blows from a stick *(kyosaku)* or a shout *(ho)* not as a punishment, but – at exactly the right moment – to help the breakthrough to enlightenment. I feel this technique is too harsh and could possibly be abused. Instead, I prefer the intellectual method of reasoning known as critical thinking.

Myoko came on Saturday as usual carrying a bundle of groceries. She came into the house and immediately could read the expression on my face. "What?" What is it, Jiun?"

I could not contain myself I let out a shout, "I spoke with Dr. Bremer and he has given his approval for you to move in with me.

She dropped the bag of groceries on the table and turned to me with open, outstretched arms. We hugged tightly as she began crying, "Oh, Jiun, I am so happy."

"Don't cry, Myoko, now we can live a beautiful life."

"When should I move in?"

I hastily answered, "Right now, if you like."

With wide eyes she questioned, "Right now?"

"Yes, go home and get your things."

"No, no, Jiun that would not be fair to my mother."

"Yes, I understand. Would next weekend be alright?"

"Yes, next weekend would be better. That would give me time to make arrangements with my mother." With that she gave me a long wet kiss on my lips, "I love you, Jiun."

"Incidentally, Dr. Bremer asked when we will be married."

"She looked up at me and said, "I leave that to you, Jiun. I shall live with you with or without marriage. All I want is to love you."

"Okay, we shall see. We don't have to make that decision now."

I took my arms away from around her waist and as I released her she began distributing the groceries in her household way. I could see a broad grin on her face. She looked up and turned to me, "I am so happy, Jiun."

I took her in my arms and said, "I love you very much, Myoko and I am sure this will be the beginning of a perfect and devoted life."

Myoko returned with her belongings the following week. We made room for her clothes in the closet of the spare bedroom. When she finished, she turned and stated matter-of-factly, "I am not sleeping on the floor in a futon."

I laughed and replied, "It might be fun. Ha! Ha! Of course we'll use the bed."

We finally settled in and began our new life together. Myoko had arranged to visit with her mother everyday at lunch time. This would enable her to maintain contact with her mother now that she no longer lives with her. It was a most suitable arrangement particularly since it did not involve me. Myoko left every morning for work while I was still sitting zazen. I made my own breakfast and was busy all day until her return in the evening. She sometimes arrived with a bag of groceries causing me to comment, "You don't have to use your money for food. I have a food allowance provided by Dr. Bremer."

"But I want to do it, Jiun. It makes me feel I am contributing to our life together. After all I don't pay rent while living with you."

"If you feel better about doing it then I concur, "I said reluctantly.

And so our life took a very domestic turn. We were very happy building a life that provided love and companionship. Every day has been a gift. We sometimes spoke Japanese but most of our conversation was in English. I enjoyed learning more English expressions. Weeks went by and it felt like we were never apart. We had each other and it seemed that was all that mattered. I never knew any of her friends and she never spoke of her work. I continued with my work in the temple, supervising the conversion of the basement into living quarters for future monks as well as teaching the rudiments of Buddhism and zazen to the novices.

One day while leading a group in zazen, I saw, out of the corner of my eye, that Serena was standing by the entrance to the zendo. I was shocked to see her having driven her out of my mind since Myoko took up living with me. I did not know what to think and was completely unprepared. She waved to me with a "come hither" gesture so I rose from my sitting position and met her in the anteroom. "Hello, Serena, where have you been? You have not come to Zen practice for a long time."

"I am sorry about that, Jiun, but I have been living in a Spa with my mother. She has not been feeling well and needed my help. I am back now and want to get together with you."

"Get together, what do you mean? Your father wants you to practice zazen."

"I don't care what my father wants. It's my life and I want you."

I was dismayed because I knew, in my mind; this situation would have a bad ending. I tried in a calm voice to offer an explanation. "Serena, I have a fiancé who is now living with me. You and I cannot have intimate relations any more."

I saw her face turning gray as she produced an animal-like snarl, "Fiancé! Living with you? How dare you. You belong to me."

"Now, Serena, be reasonable. You know we can't continue as we have in the past."

"We can't? We'll see about that."

"Serena, please try to understand. We have never been in love. Our involvement was simply a convenience. I now have someone I love and I want to sever all my old ties." Sweat droplets appeared on my bald skull. I looked at her with pleading eyes as I spoke. But, I knew it sounded inadequate.

She seemed to be a completely different person. Her face was flaming red. Her blonde hair was tussled as she shook her head palsy-like. Her eyes were fiery and moist and her lips were covered with spittle as she spoke. "You cannot do this to me. I won't allow it. I will not be rejected like some worn out shoe. You took advantage of me."

"Serena, please don't be angry. You are acting like a child. We were nothing more than love-making partners. We never meant anything to each other. We shall always be friends." She turned quickly and walked out of the anteroom in a huff.

I spent several days in a worrisome state. Even Myoko noticed my ennui. However, I slowly recovered from my undue vexation and zestfully returned to my everyday life. I was alone one day in the zendo sitting zazen when I spotted a uniformed security guard entering the zendo without removing his shoes. I was alarmed at this heretic act and started to rise to take issue with the offender when he spoke with a grin, "Are you the priest Nakahara?" There was a sneer in his voice when he said this. His teeth were very white in his dark face, their edges sharp and serrated. His hair was kinky and unruly as it protruded from under his cap.

"Yes my name is Nakahara."

"I have been sent here by Dr. Bremer to accompany you to his office."

"I see. Just a minute and I'll go with you." I readied myself as best I could and accompanied the security guard to Dr. Bremer's office.

On entering Dr. Bremer did not greet me as he usually did. Instead he turned to the security guard and said, "Thank you, Bill that will be all. Please wait outside." Then he turned to me and said, "Sit down Jiun," while pointing to a chair with his liver-spotted hands. The air was heavy with tension. I felt dispirited as I sat facing him. He hovered over me and he slowly tottered towards me in a draconic way. "I'll get right to the point, Jiun. Have you been having an affair with my daughter Serena?" His bushy eyebrows were attacking each other as his face bore a scowl. He was on the point of rage. I could see the fire in his eyes and the tremble of his lips as he spoke. His face was becoming blotchy red with anger. I was too distraught to answer. His arms quivered as he impatiently shouted loudly, "Well, answer me."

I hung my head and continued my silence except for a faint whimper, "I don't know what to say."

He shouted again forcefully, "Did you have an affair with my daughter?"

I winced and shrunk back as from a blow then looked up to say, "Yes."

There was silence as he slumped in the chair facing me. He muttered, "You have committed a grievous and sinful act unbecoming a priest." Then he looked straight at me and shouted, "You lecher, you are addicted to lust and lewdness. " He continued in his strident way, "You are an embarrassment to me and my family. You have sullied our family name with your vacuous antics. Is this the way you repay me for all I have done for you?"

I could not answer, nor do I think he expected an answer. My throat was choked up. I could only whisper, "I am sorry. I did not mean to harm anyone."

He looked at me with a more placid tone to his face as I spoke those words and in a calmer voice said, "Is that what you call remorse?"

"Yes, I am truly sorry." I could see he did not accept my contrition.

"You have vilified the temple by your presents. I want you off this property in twenty-four hours. You must return the passbook I gave you and remove all your personal possessions from the house. I hope you have an easier time explaining this disaster to your girlfriend. Now, get out and leave me alone."

I left his office and was accompanied by Bill, the security guard, in silence to the house. I started to pack my meager possessions in my travel bag and spent the remainder of the day waiting for Myoko to come home. In the meantime, I decided to write a letter to Dr. Bremer and leave it with the passbook on the kitchen table.

Dear Dr. Bremer,

I am leaving the passbook with this letter. I have never used it nor have I used any of the provided funds. I am truly sorry for this outcome. It was a great opportunity which I botched up. I want to wish you luck in the future. You have been very kind to me and I hope that someday you will find it in your heart to forgive me.

Gassho, Nakahara Jiun.

At 6:00 pm, Myoko arrived with her usual bright enthusiasm. She noticed immediately from my demeanor that something was wrong. "What's wrong, Jiun?"

I rallied my courage and forthrightly said, "I have been dismissed from the temple."

She was nonplussed as she asked, "Dismissed, what do you mean? I don't understand."

With uneasiness, I tried to answer, "It's a long story but the core essence is that Dr. Bremer found out that I was having an affair with his daughter Serena."

She covered her mouth with her hand in abject horror while the words squeezed through her fingers, "How could you?"

I said nothing and shook my shoulders.

"You mean you were sleeping with her while we were in love?"

I hung my head and did not answer. She had a newspaper in her hand which she immediately used as a weapon. She struck me on the head several times as she shouted, "You louse. You worm. Why? You never loved me. You are only interested in sex."

"Please, Myoko let me explain."

"There is no explanation. You had sex with her and sex with me. You are a pervert. I never want to see you again." She ran out of the house with a loud bang of the door.

I sat in an oneiric state without moving for a long time. *Is this all happening to me? What will I do now? I know. I know. I'll go back to Japan and try and start over. But how, I have no money. I don't know anyone who can help me. Wait. I could call Mr. Chigesu. Yes, he may be able to help me.* I got up and looked for my address book in my travel bag. When I found it I placed a collect call to Mr. Chigesu's phone number. I heard his voice, "Hello". The operator interrupted, "Will you accept a collect call from Mr. Nakahara?" He answered, "Of course." She said, "Go ahead Mr. Nakahara."

"Hello. Mr. Chigesu."

"Yes"

"Forgive me for calling you collect but I am short of funds and must ask a big favor of you."

"What is it?"

"I have been recently dismissed from my position in the temple in Narack and have decided to return to Japan."

"I see. How can I help you?"

"I was wondering if you could secure a berth for me on one of your freighters going to Japan."

"I see. *Chotto matta* (just a minute) let me look at the shipping schedule."

There was a rather long delay before he came back on the line. "There is a small vessel leaving from Brooklyn, New York tomorrow at 8:00 pm. It is called the Saga Maru. Would that be alright?"

"Oh, yes, yes. That would be ideal."

"Okay, the Saga Maru is leaving from the 53rd Street pier on the Brooklyn docks. I shall call the captain to expect you and arrange a berth for you. Do not be late or the ship will leave without you. The ship is going through the Panama Canal and will make a stop for three days in Honolulu before continuing to Kobe."

"Mr. Chigesu, how can I thank you? I cannot thank you enough. I really appreciate it very much."

"There is one way you can thank me."

"What is it?"

"You must write me a letter with the whole story and also I want to know where you wind up. I may come to visit you since I shall be traveling to Japan in a month or so."

"I would be most happy to write you all the details. Thank you once again."

After that I went to the kitchen table where I found the letter I had written to Dr. Bremer and added a postscript.

P.S. Please allow Miss Myoko to return to the house to retrieve her clothing. Thank you. I will be on my way back to Japan. Goodbye.

I decided to sit zazen all night in supplication until I leave in the morning for the freighter Saga Maru to take me back to Japan.

XXI

"Good evening, Captain. My name is Nakahara Jiun," I said with a bow.

"Yes, yes, good evening. I was told to expect you. We are leaving in an hour. Let me show you to your stateroom."

The Captain was a stout, short man with a full salt and pepper beard covering his face. He had mere slits for his eyes but he smiled incessantly with nicotine-yellowed teeth. He seemed full of spirits and jovial while talking rather rapidly as he led me to my room dragging one foot as he walked. "This room was formerly used for storage but we removed most of the items to give you some livable space. This ship does not take on passengers so you will be traveling alone. We did the best we could to fulfill Mr. Chigesu's instructions. We shall provide two meals a day for you. The first meal is in mid-morning and the second in late evening. The meals are simple fare, usually rice and vegetables. Is there anything else I can do for you? I am expected on the bridge so I must hurry."

"No, Captain, this will be fine. Please don't fret about me. I shall not be a burden to you."

He stared at me a long time before saying, "I wish you much luck as we set out to sea for we know not what destiny awaits us, what storms we may encounter, what dangers we may have to undergo."

"I am prepared for any eventuality Captain. Thank you for all your help."

I entered the room after the Captain left with a salute. It was nothing more than a cubicle with wooden boxes lining some of the walls. There was a small cot placed to one side with a mattress and some blankets. There was also a chair but nothing else. The room had no porthole and only a naked bulb hanging from the ceiling. It was all very depressing. *Yes, this will be fine. It is here I shall do my penance.* I placed my bag on the floor and wrestled one of the boxes over to the cot to use as a table. I then sat down to relax and survey my surroundings. I was tired having been awake while sitting zazen all night. I was jolted out of my slumber by a knock on the door. On opening the door I discovered a small unshaven, unkempt, red-haired man holding a tray containing a plate of food. I took the tray and said, "Thank you." He did not respond but turned and left. Using the wooden box as a table, I began eating the meal. I was famished not having eaten since breakfast yesterday. The rice and mixed vegetable stir fry tasted good. I was so hungry that I found myself wolfing down the food with the provided chopsticks. When finished I placed the tray and empty plate on the floor and lay down on the cot completely exhausted. I soon fell asleep with my clothes on and had the most awful dream of being chased by Dr. Bremer with a cleaver. I felt as if I was on a moving sidewalk going the wrong way, running but getting no closer. When I awoke at one o'clock in the morning I found the ship had already left the harbor and was now plying through the Atlantic Ocean. I went out on deck to look at the wide expanse of watery desert with awe and wonder. There was an air of mystery about the far distances of sky and ocean. The stars seemed embedded like jewels in the dark sky and all I could hear was the steady ripple of the ship's wake and a soft swish-swish of the waves.

After observing the sea for a few minutes I went back to my room and undressed for bed. Laying there I found the steady rhythm of the ship's engines lulling me off to sleep. In the morning dawn I opened the door to look out. The moon had long since disappeared and one by one the stars had left the sky until only the morning star remained. My eyes ached for sleep; my fingers were numb from dampness and fatigue, my heart heavy with despair. *I have committed a sin that was uglier than all the sins I have ever made. This sin is huge and shapeless it is like a great rock leaning on my back. Will I be able to shake off this sin when I get to Japan?* Now, I must sit zazen and so I went back into my barren room and sat on the floor for one hour. Then there was another knock on the door. I opened it and there stood the little man who brought me my evening meal yesterday, "Mr. Priest" – his English was very bad, but he told me in faulty Japanese – "if you want a shower follow me." Small and ugly and pock-marked and hollow-eyed was this man, although his knotted shoulders were wide enough for two and he had fiery red hair. I since learned his name was Sati. "Yes, I shall follow you, Sati."

He picked up the tray and the plate and led me to the galley where the shower was located. I removed my clothes and attended to my ablution with warm brackish water which could not lather the soap. Having finished, I felt restored and refreshed and proceeded to the deck. Sati brought me the late breakfast which I ate while sitting on deck. When I finished I took up a book and began reading all afternoon. Meanwhile, the sky threw the sun over its shoulder, and the water began to grow darker and darker. The stars gave light and then were hidden, but others came and took up their posts. But on the bed of the sea the waters began grumbling, and the wind began slapping at the ship. At last a great storm arose with rain and snow and the ship rocked this way and that, sometimes to the right and sometimes to the left, sometimes sinking and sometimes rising and rearing up, the waves wrestling angrily with the ship, ready, to swallow the ship and all who dwelt therein.

All day into the night the eyes of the crew were deprived of sleep and their bodies of rest. All my bedding was soaked with salt water. All those on board were thrown against the sides of the ship, and screamed and wept and wailed. A chill salt sweat appeared on my face, drops of salt dripped from my head and rolled down into my mouth. At midnight the storm grew worse, and breached the walls of the ship. The noise grew even greater. No one could be heard above the sound of the waters.

Then as suddenly as it started the storm ended. We had sailed through a squall into calmer waters. The sea is our foe and could have been our deaths, but it is over now. In the morning, the sun was reddening the East; the sea, awakening from slumber, breathed almost inaudibly, exhaling lazily and inhaling dreamily; somewhere in the azure, white wings fluttered and cried – then again quiet – here and there quiet iridescences flitted over the sea, golden spots skimmed the rolling waves. I was glad to be alive. I busied myself draping my bedding and mattress over the railing to dry out. I also swept out my room and dried the floor with a mop. I then sat on my chair to rest while reading my *Shobogenzo*. I was grateful that it did not get wet. It was a good idea to have it in a plastic bag since everything else in my bag got soaking wet. All had to be dried out. For the next few days all was quiet and back to routine living. The weather got warmer as we sailed into the Caribbean Sea. There was always a refreshing breeze and I found myself spending most of my time on deck from early morning light until nightfall. Finally, we reached the Panama Canal. We had to line up behind other vessels ahead of us. Some ships were immense. I think our ship was one of the smallest. We entered at Colon and went through the locks to Gatun Lake then once again the ships lined up to go through the locks and exit at Balboa, a total distance of about 50 miles. We were now in the Gulf of Panama sailing into the Pacific Ocean and on our way to Hawaii. We picked up the wind-driven North Pacific Current in free run to the west and eventually the coast of Japan which is approximately eleven thousand miles away. Honolulu on the island of Oahu is about half way to Japan and it is estimated that it would take three more days to arrive going in a continuous north-westerly direction.

The weather was ideal. Every day I spent on deck I experienced sunny warm air which was clear and cloudless. I even spent warm evenings sleeping on deck by bringing out my mattress. Every once in a while I spotted dolphins riding along our bow wake. Once up in the distance I saw a whale slamming its fluke on the surface of the water. There were schools of fish swimming in unison in the clear, blue waters and many birds of different varieties accompanied us with their shrieks as they dived into the azure water for a meal.

On the third day out of Panama I could see Mt. Maunakei on Hawaii Island rising out of the mist. There was a trembling below my heart as if the blood was draining from it. I guessed we would be landing soon in Honolulu on the island of Oahu where Tomoko Kangetsu lives. I actually thought I felt the beginning sensation of nausea and wiped my hand across my forehead. *I must not think of such things, they only contribute to my bad karma.* It took a while for the Saga Maru to tie up after which some of the crew began debarking. I remained at my spot at the railing watching the busy activity of the harbor. Some stevedores began unloading the cargo in a huge net conveyed by a winch-windlass and a crane. While watching this activity I was silently approached by Sati who said, "Mr. Priest are you going ashore?"

"No, I shall remain on board, Sati, until we leave Hawaii."

"We are scheduled to be here three days to take on new cargo and get refueled."

"Still, I shall remain on board."

"In that case may I suggest that I take all of your clothes with me? I am going to a laundry which will wash our clothes fast. Yours must be salty from the storm."

"Oh, what a good idea, but I do not have any money."

"Not to worry, the Captain said he will pay. Take off your clothes and give me your travel bag filled with everything. You do not have to be embarrassed waiting for me in your underwear. There is no one about except stevedores and besides the weather is warm."

I immediately picked up my travel bag and unloaded the few trinkets it contained. I then undressed and removed my *samu-e* (everyday clothes) placing it in the travel bag with my three robes, all my underwear, the kimono and the hippari. All the clothes needed cleaning since they were beginning to smell and were very much afoul. I handed the filled travel bag with a kind word of encouragement, "I am very grateful, Sati."

"I am happy to oblige, Mr. Priest."

He hobbled off carrying two bags of dirty laundry. I then sat on the chair near the railing observing the scurrying world at work and attended on Sati's return. I was reading my *Shobogenzo*. After about an hour or more of waiting I was not aware that Sati was walking up the gangplank carrying the bags on his shoulder. He approached me with the cleaned laundry and put the travel bag down on the deck. He handed me a small paper bag saying, "All done, Mr. Priest. I brought you a submarine sandwich for lunch. The cook is off today and there will be no meal until late this evening. The crew will eat on shore. I hope you like Genoa salami and Provolone cheese."

This simple man with the ugly, disfigured face expressed a beauty rarely known to me before. I was dumbstruck by his kindness. I thanked him profusely and I could see the blush of color rising in his face. He hung his head and said, "No problem, Mr. Priest." He then turned and left me. I was hurrying to dress in my samu-e and then sat down to enjoy the sandwich.

The taste was very unusual and unknown to me. The bread made my mouth water. I have rarely eaten bread while in America since I spent most of my time among Japanese people who only ate rice.

After three days of outfitting and provisioning the ship we left Honolulu and were on our way to the port of Kobe on the south coast of Japan. The weather continued to be warm and peaceful as we plodded through the unruffled sea. It would take another three or perhaps four days to reach our final destination depending on whether the North Pacific Current cooperates and helps us along. Meanwhile, life went on as before except that I now was satisfied with my newly made personal cleanliness. The long range weather prediction is that there are no storms awaiting us and should be clear sailing to Kobe. As we approached Japanese waters, I noticed many fishing boats of different nations trying to catch the fish that were teeming in these waters. The weather became warmer as we entered the Kuro Shio Current. I was excited at the prospect of being so close to home and perhaps a new life. The Kuro Shio is a warm benevolent current which hugs the coast of Japan. This will enable us to steam into Kobe harbor quickly after coming into contact with the North Pacific Current which we have ridden from Hawaii. Kobe has a beautiful natural harbor surrounded and protected from the cold winds by high mountains. It has had its troubles in the distant past when a large earthquake and a subsequent tidal wave hit the town badly but not long after a new city was built. The port is a deep fjord with a narrow entrance, so that it is protected from rough seas as well as from inclement weather.

The Saga Maru docked in an easy way allowing for an immediate placement of the gangplank. The crew began unloading the cargo as before in Honolulu and some excess crew members left the ship and hurried down the gangplank. I changed into my priestly robe and began to gather my possessions. After cleaning up my room I went looking for Sati. I found him working in the galley. "I came to say goodbye, Sati, and to thank you for all your help." I bowed with a gassho and then put an item in his hand. "This is my *O-mamori* (talisman). I hope it brings you much deserved luck." He looked at the O-mamori in his palm and began to sniffle as his eyes watered. He then closed his hand to a fist and placed it against his chest saying only, "Thank you, Mr. Priest." Finally, I went to the bridge in search of the Captain. He was busy commanding people and using his instruments. He saw me with a questioning eye and approached me. "Nakahara-san are you leaving?"

"Yes, Captain, I came to say goodbye and to thank you for everything."

"It was my pleasure, Nakahara-san. I am sorry that we could not see much of each other during the voyage but the storm and other things kept me busy."

"I understand, Captain."

"Well, good bye and good luck, I must get back to my work." He extended his hand in an American handshake. We parted so I made my way down the gangplank. I asked directions to the Inariji temple from a well-dressed gentleman standing on the dock and watching all the activity. He pointed and told me where it was in detail, so I proceeded to walk in that direction. When I finally reached Inariji, I was exhausted from the long walk but there it was in front of me. It was a poor, very old, weathered and shabby wooden temple obviously not known for its beauty. Inariji did become known as a temple to practice Zen without distractions. Most temples in Japan cater to parishioner's needs such as funerals, memorial services, religious holidays, and in some cases weddings. At Inariji, the resident monks took care of the temple grounds, practiced zazen, and engaged in *takuhatsu* (begging). I knocked on the wooden door and was greeted by a small, craggy faced, smiling monk who introduced himself as Ikegami Akira. I bowed very low with a gassho and said, "My name is Nakahara Jiun, honorable Akira-roshi, I am destitute. I have been the victim of a sexual affair."

He laughed, "Ha, ha," He seemed to be amused by this confession. "The Japanese are very discreet about matters sexual. Public display of affection is rare, pornography and suggestive ads or clothing are non-existent, and inquiries about premarital sex and out-of-wedlock births are generally met with polite, even terse, 'It does not happen here,' so you see we do not condemn. Ha. Ha. You are welcome. Come in, come in."

"I need a place to seek *kensho* (awakening), can you help me?"

He looked at me up and down and saw my priestly robe. "We always provide a place for traveling Zen monks. Come inside and rest yourself. Have you eaten?"

"I am hungry, Akira-roshi, but I do not wish to bother you."

"Nonsense, make yourself comfortable in the zendo and I shall bring you a bowl of *gohan* (cooked rice). You may sleep in the zendo tonight. I'll see that you get a fresh futon."

He left me and I brought my travel bag into the zendo which I deposited on the floor by the door. Then I removed my robe and put on my nightshirt. In a few minutes, the Roshi returned with a bowl of cooked rice and a pair of *hashi* (chopsticks). Eat well, Nakahara-san. The futon is on its way. Sleep well and we shall talk in the morning. With that he left to be followed in a few minutes by a monk carrying a futon. He placed it on the zendo floor and I lost no time getting inside and looking up at the dark ceiling. I could smell the residual incense odor and knew this familiarity claimed me completely. I fell asleep immediately. Towards morning, I felt a loud thump that shook the building. Not as much a sound as a vibration, an impact, like the first jolt of an earthquake. Then there was following vibrations and things began falling and suddenly the roof collapsed and fell in hitting me on the head and knocking me unconscious for a time. When I came to it felt like I had been out for hours, but I quickly realized it was only a few seconds. I also realized that my right hand was numb. I could not feel it. The roof had hit me full on the shoulder and my arm hummed with dull pain from the point of impact down to the dead hand. There was rubble covering my whole body. I could feel the blood running under my nightshirt and down my chest and arm. I now could smell the sharp, acrid smoke of a fire. I was gasping for air and tried to regulate the intake. I was going into shock and I knew it. There was nothing I could do. I was pinned down and unable to move. I became weak and tired. The humming pain in my arm moved up a notch to a throb. My right hand was useless and my left hand was nothing but torn flesh. I was shaking badly now, my body in shock, and I knew I would soon pass into unconsciousness and not wake up. I tried to yell but my voice was only a grunt. A vision of Myoko passed before my glazed eyes. I dropped my head until my chin was on my chest. My eyes were rolling up into my lids. I wanted to sleep now but I was fighting it. I groaned and then nothing. Then I saw, Myoko's face floating out of focus and then it sank away into inky blackness.

Nakahara Jiun – roshi died at 5:46 a.m. on Tuesday, January 17, 1995 in the Hyogo Ken Nanbu (Kobe) Earthquake. He was twenty-nine years old.

THE ROSHI

The Adventures of a Wayward
Zen Buddhist Priest
Part 2

"WHAT IF?"

INTRODUCTION

In Part 1 of the Roshi we learned that Tomoko Kangetsu was anxious to have Jiun Nakahara join her in her home after her husband's death and cremation. Jiun Nakahara refused and went on with his ill-fated life until his untimely demise at a very young age.

What if Jiun Nakahara had taken up Tomoko Kangetsu's offer? What would his life have been like and what would have been the outcome? Could his destiny have changed? Could his weak character have been strengthened?

In Part 2 of The Roshi we shall explore Jiun Nakahara's scene of life and individual experience which takes place in this alternate route to reveal the ultimate denouement of this complex situation. The story begins in a taxicab in Part 1 where Tomoko Kangetsu asks Jiun Nakahara, "Well then can I expect you one evening? I would like to see you again." The story continues: She suddenly and without warning or provocation reached across the seat and grabbed my head while planting a long steady kiss on my lips.

"If you will wait for me, I will go in the monastery and retrieve my travel bag and say a fond farewell to Koichi Kagaguchi."

"Yes, I will wait for you. Please hurry. I am anxious to start our beautiful life together."

PART 2

I

I ran into the monastery and packed my few possessions in my travel bag. I next went in search of Kagaguchi Koichi-roshi and found him in the monastery office 'hunt and pecking' on a typewriter. "Kagaguchi-san I am leaving the monastery to take up residence with Mrs. Kangetsu. She is lonely and frightened after her husband's death and offered me free room and board if I would provide security and safety for her."

"I see."

"I shall come every day in time for morning zazen and services."

"I see."

"I intend to fully honor my commitment to the monastery. I will not fail you.

"In that case, I wish you much luck in this venture."

I left the monastery and entered the waiting taxicab which took us to Tomoko's house. She spoke in a low sibilant tone while holding my hands, "I want to make you happy" I will see to it that you never regret making this decision."

In response, I leaned over and kissed her many times on the mouth. We then hugged as I said, "I shall make you happy as well." The taxicab drew up to her small simple house. When I stepped into the house the first thing I noticed was the plethora of plants and flowers in pots and vases everywhere. There were bonsai plants on every windowsill and Ikebana flower-arrangements in unusually shaped vases on furniture tops everywhere. I examined many of them before I turned to Tomoko questioningly,

"They are all very beautiful. Do you engage in bonsai?" She continued, "A good bonsai has beautiful form, grace, and character, and should always be healthy. My husband treated them with great care as if they were his children. Bonsai techniques such as wiring, trimming, and root pruning are all meant to enhance the beauty of the tree. My husband was an expert in the art of bonsai," she said proudly.

"How many bonsai plants do you have?"

She pointed as she spoke, "Well let me see, the varieties include: Japanese Maple, Flowered Apricot, Shimpaku Juniper, Japanese Black and Japanese White Pine, Satsuki Azalea, Korean Hornbeam, Fujian Tea, Ginkgo, Wisteria,

Bamboo and others. They have all been presented at contests and many have won prizes. Now they are part of my legacy."

"How wonderful it must have been for Mr. Kangetsu to have such a beautiful hobby."

"My husband had a workshop in the basement and was a highly-skilled artist. He had a rare glimpse into Japanese bonsai tradition as well as Ikebana Flower-arrangement. I truly believe it was a spiritual endeavor for him."

"Yes, I can appreciate the relationship to contemplation. Ikebana is also known as *kado* (the way of flowers)."

"My husband told me that the art of Flower-arranging has been influenced by all the religions of Japan."

"Yes, it has become an important part of a Japanese religio-aesthetic tradition in which the artistic disciplines and creativity carry important religious meaning as 'ways' of spiritual fulfillment."

She looked at me wide-eyed as if studying me. "Naturally, you would know about that. Yes, they are beautiful. They were left to me by my late husband. He did both bonsai and Ikebana as a hobby. He learned Ikebana at the Sogetsu Ikebana School in Tokyo and studied bonsai at the Hawaiian Bonsai Gardens here in Honolulu. He was very proficient at it and many of his specimens were prize winners."

"I see. Exactly what is bonsai; they seem like very unusual plants."

"Bonsai is a marriage of art and horticulture with a rich history. The Japanese word, bonsai, simply means plant in a shallow container."

"Yes, yes, I've noticed the small almost flat containers."

"Oh well, let me show you around."

With that we proceeded to go from room to room with a constant commentary by Tomoko. The place was small but comfortable and I could easily see me spending much happy time here. I decided to tell Tomoko of my commitment to the monastery and my schedule. "Tomoko, I am required to perform my clerical duties as a visiting priest at the monastery every day except Sunday. Therefore, I shall leave every day at four o'clock in the morning to be present in the monastery in time for zazen by four-thirty. Of course, I will return at five o'clock in the evening on completion of my daily tasks."

"I understand, that will work out well. I will arrange for a limo service to take you both ways at the appointed times every day."

"No, no, that would be too expensive."

"Be not alarmed, Jiun, my husband left me a lot of money; I am a rich widow. It would be my greatest pleasure to make this simple contribution. I know you are making a sacrifice to be with me. It's probably not easy for you."

I relented and finally after much hesitation agreed to her largesse. "Thank you, I shall do my best to make me worthy of your generosity."

It was by now late afternoon. Tomoko took my hands and said, "Make yourself comfortable while I prepare dinner. Every day when you come home from the monastery there will be a wonderful dinner waiting for you. I am an excellent Japanese cook.

"Oh, how nice, of course, you should know that I intend eating breakfast and lunch in the monastery. It is expected of me but I think it should all work out."

After getting myself settled in the bedroom, I began exploring around the house. I noticed a shelf containing many books on horticulture and a few books on Buddhism. They were all written in Japanese except some popular novels which were written in English. I examined, in detail, the bonsai plants which appeared to me to be miniature old trees. I found this ability to be quite remarkable. After a while Tomoko joined me in the living room to say that dinner was ready. I turned and grabbed her gently around her waist and planted a kiss on her full lips. She giggled and returned the amorous gesture, "I have loved you, Jiun, since we first met on the boat. I am very grateful that you decided to live with me."

"I enjoy being with you. It is so long since I have had a family life."

"This is your home and I am your family now."

She withdrew from my embrace and said, "Alright, now, let us have dinner."

The meal was amazing. I have never tasted food like this before. It started with clear soup with flower-shaped prawns, followed by white meat fish roasted in foil as an appetizer. The main dish was boiled chicken meatballs with turnips plus a crab and cucumber salad with *kimi-zu* dressing along with the inevitable cooked rice with green peas. For dessert we had *kuroiso* (steamed ginger cake) and *nihon cha* (Japanese tea). "*Oishi* (delicious)," I exclaimed.

After dinner we sat in the living room with a pot of tea. We chatted and sipped tea for hours. She revealed much of her life with her husband which seemed to be a marriage in name only and did not provide her with the intimacy she cherished. Finally, I found myself stifling a yawn. Obviously, getting up so early in the morning required me to go to sleep early in the evening. She noticed my sleepy discomfort and suggested that we go to bed. "I must adjust myself to a new schedule," she said. "Come, Jiun, my dear, you're half-asleep. Let us retire. Tomorrow is another day when we shall adjust our schedule. She then explained the workings of the bathroom and the various places that I could occupy.

We both undressed and slipped under the covers. The feeling of the sheets was very luxurious. She immediately reached out and pulled me close to her warm body. I could smell the sweet scent of her skin and her hair. I felt a dizzying flash quickly move through my mind reminding me of our past encounters on the ship Umi Maru. I enjoyed holding her close and running my hands over her soft skin. I felt an immediate strong yearning to place my body between her legs as we held each other. She seemed to acknowledge this and moved over on top of me. She then slowly rubbed my stiff member against her pubic hair before placing it into her vagina. In a low voice I heard her say, "Don't move, my love, let me feel you inside." I willingly complied and could feel the pulsation of her labia. We remained unmoving like this for some minutes until she began a gyration causing my member to move back and forth in her vagina. After coitus, she rolled off me, put her arms around my body and held me close until I fell asleep.

The alarm clock woke me up at four o'clock. Tomoko stirred but did not rise. I got up and immediately went into the bathroom to shave, brush my teeth, and shower. I dressed in my robes and was outside to meet the limo in fifteen minutes. I carried my *samu-e* (every day work clothes) in a small bag provided by Tomoko.

"Good morning," I greeted the driver.

"Good morning," he replied in a sullen way.

"Take me to the Emerald Sangha, please."

"Of course, I know where it is."

We sped through town and arrived at the entrance to the zendo by four-thirty. I sat in my place on the platform just as the *rin* (bell) was struck. Zazen was forty minutes followed by *kinhin* (walking meditation) for twenty minutes. Then it was all repeated for a second time and concluded by six-thirty. The group then moved into the *hatto* (services hall) for morning service sitting in *seiza* position (on the knees). At the conclusion of services a *teisho* (sermon) was given by Koichi-roshi. It was now seven o'clock and time for breakfast which consisted of *congee* (rice gruel) flavored with a sprinkling of ground sesame seeds. The usual meal *gatha* (prayer) was recited before eating and was consumed in total silence.

After breakfast, I changed into my samu-e and prepared for work practice. The monastery had an adjoining two acre parcel of land which was tilled and on which grew several varieties of vegetables such as mustard greens, egg plants, and cabbages. The monastery was not self-sufficient but this farm did produce much of the food for the residents. The remaining food was acquired by *takuhatsu* (begging rounds) and contributions by local merchants. My job was to hoe the furrows of the growing vegetables. I did this for two hours until ten o'clock. I then went to the meeting room to deliver a *sutra* (a scripture) lecture to the novices until lunch time. Meals in the monastery are sparing and simple; its purpose being to avoid luxurious indulgence and to foster an abstemious life. For lunch we had a piece of grilled salmon over a bowl of steamed rice.

At one o'clock I held a class on calligraphy and Japanese written language recognition. The Japanese writing system consists of two types, Kanji and Kana. Kanji makes use of Chinese characters and requires memorizing about 2000 characters for one to be proficient. Kana is a phonetic system that consists of two syllabaries, Hiragana and Katakana. Kanji is a classical system which is being replaced gradually by Kana as Japan enters the modern western world and encounters many foreign words, particularly English. I taught this group for two hours and then spent the remainder of the day with Koichi-roshi reviewing and discussing monastery matters. At five o'clock I left the monastery and took the waiting limo home. When I arrived Tomoko was waiting for me. "Konnichiwa, Nakahara-san" (Hello, Reverend Nakahara), she exclaimed with a gassho and a bow.

"Konnichiwa, Tomoko, please do not kowtow and please call me, Jiun."

"Yes, yes, how was your day?"

"It was a good day but uneventful."

"Come let us have a hot bath together," she said rather coyly.

I came into the house and began removing my clothes. Tomoko was already nude when I entered the bathroom. We soaped up with wash cloths in the shower each helping the other. I could feel her smooth skin as I ran my hands over her body. After rinsing off the lather we entered the special tub together and began relaxing supinely. The tub maintained a constant temperature permitting us to soak for a long time. We played with each other by touching and feeling our bodies. At the conclusion of the bath we dried each other with large bath sheets.

"Would you mind using my husband's kimono? I had it cleaned for you." She questioned.

"Not at all, it is a fine silk garment," I said as I put it on.

"I bought you a present today," she said in a mysterious tone.

"Did you say a present?"

"Yes, I bought you another samu-e."

"What for, I have one."

"I know but this way I will be able to wash all your clothes daily while you are in the monastery; In that way you will have fresh clothes to wear every day."

"Thank you, you are very good to me."

She grabbed my hand and led me to the dinner table. This was the first time that I noticed her hands were frail, veiny, the color of skim milk as if they had already died and were patiently waiting for the rest of her body. I put these thoughts out of my mind and sat down at the table. The dinner was superb and I complimented her on her culinary expertise. After dinner we sat in the living room chatting and sipping tea. I told her of my ambition to eventually become a Roshi (Zen Master) and be an abbot of a temple. "I must work hard and study well before I can reach such a height."

"I will help you all I am able. I have faith in you and know that you will one day realize your ambition."

We then were off to bed.

II

I became used to the routine and adopted the habitual course of a commuter, going to the monastery every day and coming home to a superb dinner followed by a kindred relationship with Tomoko. I did not love Tomoko. I mean not in a romantic way. I did enjoy being with her much like a family man and we did enjoy sex together. For me it was the best of all worlds. For her it fulfilled a need which she always wanted for the many years of her past empty marriage. I became her affectionate paramour. She became my tender and passionate sex nymph. We continued this mode of living for many months.

Late in the month of May I was informed by Koichi-roshi that the monastery will be holding a sesshin period in the first week of June. Sesshin which means 'collecting the heart-mind' in Japanese is a period of particularly concentrated zazen practice consisting of long periods of zazen interrupted only by brief interludes for meals. Sesshin at the Emerald Sangha Monastery starts at four-thirty in the morning with forty minutes of zazen followed by twenty minutes of kinhin repeated over and over again until five-thirty in the evening every day for one week. This results in a total of thirteen relatively exhausting hours per day for seven days. I was told that a crew of laymen, monks and nuns were assembled and assigned the task of preparing for the coming participants. Apparently, thirty people are coming from the outside in addition to the residents of the monastery. I was placed in charge of this crew. We had to prepare futons for those who will be sleeping over night for the seven days and also prepare *oryoki* bowls for their meals. Oryoki bowls are three concentric nested bowls which come equipped with chopsticks, a sponge tipped dauber, and are all wrapped inside a folded cloth napkin. At meal time the participant separates the bowls and places them in a line in front of his/her folded feet. A monk goes from person to person with a bucket of food ladling food into the individual bowls. The meals are usually simple consisting of cooked rice in one bowl, steamed vegetables in a second bowl and tea in the third bowl in decreasing order. After finishing eating, hot water is poured into the large empty bowl. The dauber is used to rub down the sides of the bowl to rid it of residual food. This is repeated by pouring the water from the first bowl into the next bowl and finally into the last bowl. The water is then drunk down. The bowls are wiped dry with the napkin, put in a nest and wrapped together as a kit with the folded napkin. The oryoki kit is placed behind the participant and zazen is continued.

I had to make sure when I got home to have Tomoko adjust my pick-up time by the limo for that week. On May 31st, I brought my crew to the warehouse which contained the futons. The futons were heaped together in piles. They had to be carried individually together with a fresh sheet to a suitable spot in the hatto and some other empty rooms which were designated as sleeping quarters for the visitors. One of my assistants, a nun named Mitsuko Kalapa, did all the place names for the zazen spots. Mitsuko Kalapa is the product of a native Hawaiian father and a Nisei Japanese mother. Mitsuko is very proud of her hybrid heritage. She has assisted me in my calligraphy classes and we have become good friends. Since she is American born she does not speak much Japanese, so we converse in English. She was ordained the same as a monk even though she is referred to as a nun. I have noticed on occasion she had an amorous trifle and a definite flirty nature towards me. I tried very hard to avoid all such intimacy, but I believe it has not been successful.

Every evening after sesshin I came home physically tired and mentally exhausted. One evening I fell asleep in the limo, "we are here, sir," exclaimed the driver.

"What, what, oh yes, thank you."

I got out of the limo and made my way to the house where I was received by Tomoko with open arms.

"Oh you poor dear," Tomoko cried. "Come, let me help you. A nice warm bath and a good meal should restore you."

After our bath together and the pleasant meal we went to bed and had sex. When sesshin was finally finished we continued to carry on our life together for several more months in this manner. I found myself steeped in monastery matters, acting as a visiting priest at services, teaching and even delivering a teisho (sermon) occasionally. One day I was in a discussion with Koichi-roshi. "Tell me Nakahara-san what are your future intentions."

"What do you mean?"

"I mean, how do you see your life developing? Do you have any plans?"

I hesitated in a moment's thought then answered slowly, "I would like to continue in the Emerald Sangha until I can be offered a position as a Roshi in a temple."

"I see. The reason I am asking is because I have a serious matter to propose to you." His face looked ashen as he spoke. I immediately knew that something important was about to happen.

"What is it?"

"I am thinking of stepping down as the Roshi here in the Emerald Sangha." He looked white as a ghost as he held back his breath.

"What is it, Koichi-roshi? Why are you telling me this?"

He took a deep breath and continued, "The truth is that I have pancreatic cancer and I am told I do not have more than six months to live."

I was dumbstruck at his words. I had no way to respond. I just looked at him wide-eyed and mumbled something like, "I am sorry."

He took out a handkerchief from his sleeve and blew his nose, and wiped his face. He then straightened up and declared, "Well, I would like to propose your name as my replacement, if you want it." There was a thick silence. I said nothing. I was too distraught by all that was said. I looked at him with a frowned forehead, "Are you sure Koichi-roshi?"

"Yes, I am sure; now tell me do you want to be Roshi of the Emerald Sangha Monastery?"

"Yes, yes, indeed. I am sorry; this is all happening so quickly."

"I propose to submit your name to the Board but first there is one condition."

"What is the condition?"

He was silent for a minute but then continued, "You must move back to your room in the monastery and be a full time resident."

"You mean for me to give up my abode at the house of Tomoko Kangetsu?"

"Yes, that is a necessary requirement before I submit your name to the Board."

"I see, well that would not be a problem."

"If you move back this week, I shall submit your name next week and then you will be interviewed by the Board, a mere formality, and possibly be confirmed shortly after that."

I looked at him in dismay not knowing what to say. He could tell I was perplexed by the look on my face. "Do not be concerned about me. I am not afraid of death." I was shocked to hear this but could only stare at him in silence. He continued," I have been dying since the day I was born. You must know, of course, that in early Buddhism, it was accepted that there is continuing reappearance, but no self or soul being reborn. There is only the production of one aggregated moment of appearance caused, or brought into being, by the immediately preceding moment." I looked at him with great interest as he continued, "*Yogacara* (school of idealism) recognizes that there must nevertheless be a sufficient nature of appearance, even though devoid of characteristics, opening the way to the Buddha-nature of all appearance."

Not knowing what to say, I reiterated, "I shall go to Tomoko Kangetsu today and tell her of my decision to move back to the monastery."

"Very good," he said with a mirthful grin.

I left him with a deep bow and went to my old room to see if it needed any optimizing. I cleaned it up as best as I could and went to the warehouse for a fresh futon and bed linens and returned to make up the room in a receptive mode. It was now time to meet the limo to take me back to Tomoko. On entering Tomoko's house she could sense that something was amiss. "What is it, Jiun? Has anything happened?"

I was startled by her uncanny intuition, "Yes, Koichi-roshi told me he is dying of pancreatic cancer."

"What did you say? Is that true?"

"Yes, it is true and in addition he offered me his position as Roshi of the Emerald Sangha Monastery."

She hesitated for a moment looking off in the distance and finally said in a soft sibilant tone, "I am happy for you, Jiun, but I am sad for Koichi-roshi."

"Yes it would seem that this is the opportunity I have been waiting for. There is, however, one condition."

"One condition, what is it?"

"I must move back to the monastery and be a full time resident there."

She held the back of her hand to her mouth and meekly said, "So it has come. I have been wāiting and expecting this, I dreaded the day it would come."

"You knew this day would come?"

"Yes, I always knew. You see, Jiun my dear, I am thirty years older than you and I always knew as I got older that you would one day become dissatisfied with me. But, I did not think it would happen so soon. Believe me I am truly happy for you."

She hung her head and sniffled.

"I am sorry, Tomoko. It is not really over; I shall come to see you on Sundays."

She looked up with a glint in her eyes, "Really?" She perked up at this suggestion and held my hands, "come let us bathe and eat dinner." That night we had very meaningful sex. Tomoko performed in a special and momentous way as if it would be her last time.

In the morning I picked up my travel bag and the few extra possessions that Tomoko bought me. She awoke, kissed me and said, "Good luck, Jiun. I shall always love you." I then met the limo which took me back to the monastery. While sitting in the racing limo I reflected: *Tomoko and I have been together about a year since her husband's death.*

III

The head of the Board was a short rotund man with wild bunches of gray frizzy hair protruding from all parts of his head. Half of his face was covered with an unkempt gray beard that began fairly high up the cheekbones and sprang in all directions. Most of his nose was visible as was part of his mouth. The wild frizzy whiskers were allowed to run free and apparently go unwashed. Because so many of his features were masked, his eyes got all the attention. They were dark green and projected rays that, from under a set of thick sagging eyebrows, took in everything. He spoke with a deep heroic bravura, "Tell me about your unexpected inheritance."

I was shocked by these words but answered quickly, "As you say it was unexpected. I would give it up in an eye blink if it would cure Koichi-roshi."

He dismissed my remark with a shake of his hand and repeated, "What I mean is, what makes you think you are qualified for the position of abbot and Roshi?"

I hesitated but then gathered my wits and answered without humility, "Firstly, I was ordained as a Zen priest in the Soto Zen Tradition at Eiheiji Betsuin in Tokyo. I trained there for six years. For the past year I have worked and taught at the Emerald Sangha, I am also bilingual which I believe is an advantage in Hawaii. But most importantly I want the position with every fiber in my body and I know I can perform the duties of Roshi with great vigor, confidence and deep intellectual understanding."

He seemed to be taken aback as he commented, "Well, well, you certainly have unusual self-confidence."

I looked around at the participants. The Board consisted of two monks and one nun whom I recognized. In addition, there was one female civilian, one male civilian, the Roshi and the head of the Board They all seemed sycophantically in agreement with the head of the Board as he spoke. I felt uneasy with my answers and squirmed in my seat, Then the head of the Board addressed me, "Nakahara-san, would you please wait outside while we discuss this matter."

I rose and walked out of the room. Looking back before closing the door I spotted Koichi-roshi blinking his merry eyes in a show of approval. I closed the door believing the vote would be in my favor. In about ten minutes, the door opened and the head of the Board standing on the threshold shouted, "Come in Nakahara-roshi." On hearing this salutation I was happy beyond belief. I went back in the room and was given the good news by a unanimous show of hands by the entire board. "Thank you, my friends; I hope to justify your faith in me by pursuing this appointment with wisdom and compassion." I bowed to the entire ensemble and they responded with a loud clapping of hands. After all the members dispersed I approached Koichi-roshi who remained and said to him in a heartfelt way, "I am grateful for your confidence in me and all that you have done for me. I will not let you down."

"I wish you much luck, Nakahara-roshi; remember to accept the back-biting with the benefit. You can accomplish by kindness what you cannot do by force."

"Yes, indeed, I shall remember."

"One more thing, I shall be going into the hospital soon when I do please occupy my rooms. All that is in them will belong to you. I no longer have any need for them and I shall not return."

I found the sorrow whelming up in my body/mind and tears forming in my eyes. I looked at Koichi-roshi and saw only a broad smile on his face.

IV

I became very deeply involved in my clerical duties. I led zazen every morning and officiated at morning services every day with a *teisho* (sermon). I held *dokusan* (interview with Zen Master) for aspiring monks and nuns and some times I gave a select few koans (a conundrum) to solve. A koan is fundamental practice in Zen training, challenging the pupil through a question, or a phrase, which presents a paradox or puzzle. A koan cannot be understood or answered in conventional terms; it requires a pupil to abandon reliance on ordinary ways of understanding in order to move towards enlightenment. The answer to a koan lies outside logic and enables the pupil to break down mundane ways of seeing. I now have four pupils who have been given koans to solve. I have been so busy in the past two weeks since taking up the position of abbot and becoming a Roshi that I was not able to visit Tomoko. But on the following Sunday I did take a taxicab to her house for the promised visit.

"Oh, Jiun, it is so good to see you. How is your new position in the monastery?"

"I am fine, Tomoko. It is good to see you. I am doing well and I enjoy the work."

"Jiun, I am glad you have come. I have something very important to tell you. I have sold my house and I am moving into a senior retirement center."

"What did you say? Why are you doing this?"

"Jiun, I cannot be alone. I find the thought of being alone depressing and even dreadful. I am very grateful for the time we had together but since you left I seem to wander around with no purpose in life. I have no one to cook for and no one with whom to share daily events. At the retirement center I have already made friends with some other single women who are anxious for my arrival. I have given my husband's books and bonsai plants to the Hawaiian Bonsai Gardens. They promised me they would take care of them and place them in their museum.

I was speechless but as I examined her eyes and face I saw a definite commitment to the ineffable future, "I wish you luck and a happy life, Tomoko. It was you who gave me the impetus to gain my present position. For that I am truly grateful to you."

She handed me an envelope as she spoke, "I was going to mail this but now that you are here you may take it with you."

"What is it?"

"It is a donation to the Emerald Sangha."

I opened the envelope and found a check in the amount of one hundred thousand dollars. I was disconcerted. I spoke hesitantly, "Tomoko isn't this too much? Will you have enough money to live on?"

She laughed and embraced me, "Jiun, I have money from the sale of the house and money my husband left me. It will be quite sufficient."

"When are you planning to go to the retirement center?"

I am moving next week. I promised the new owners, a young couple, they could have occupancy next week.

I breathed deeply and said in exasperation, "Well as soon as you are settled I will come visit you."

"That would be nice, Jiun."

We both knew with the passage of time that would never happen. It is just as well. For my part I would prefer to remember her as a dynamic, vivacious, woman with a youthful soul rather than a decaying old woman.

I returned to the monastery and gave the check to one of the nuns who took care of financial matters. I then returned to my room and flung myself on the futon with tears in my eyes. My chest was heaving as I cried out, "Goodbye, Tomoko."

The next day I went to visit Koichi-roshi. He looked terrible. His face was emaciated, gaunt and reddened from the chemotherapy. I knew he was in pain but all I could do was be upbeat. "How are you, Koichi-roshi?"

"Not well, Nakahara-roshi. I am due to go into the hospital today. I was told about the large donation from Mrs. Tomoko Kangetsu. Would you thank her for me?"

"I already have."

"Yes, I am sure." Then there was a long period of silence before he began speaking again. "I am a little tired. Would you please leave me now so I may rest?"

That was the last time I saw him. He made a spiritual journey along a Buddhist path, shedding all worldly belongings and casting fate to the winds. He died in the hospital two days after entering. He was seventy-one years old. I received his body at the crematory where I presided over Mr. Kangetsu's cremation. A very beautiful memorial service was performed in the hatto in the monastery. The entire congregation and some local friends were in attendance. His ashes were buried in a special memorial grave at the side of the pathway to the farm enabling all passersby the opportunity to gassho and bow. After forty years service to the monastery he became a legend.

I began to move my possessions into his rooms and collect those things of his which I did not want. The apartment consisted of two rooms and a bathroom, one room is a bedroom where I placed my futon and laid out my *zabuton* (mat) and *zafu* (sitting pillow). There was a small shrine in the room which has a small Buddha, a candlestick, and a censor for incense sticks. There were several sepia-toned pictures of people on the walls. Not recognizing any of them, I removed them for storage with several other extraneous items. The second room was a library with many books on Buddhism, in particular the complete fifty volume set of the Pali Canon. There were six zafus on the floor. This room was obviously used for teaching seminars. I knew that this room would be very useful in the future.

I brought the discarded items in a box for storage in the warehouse. As I went inside I heard a female voice singing.

"Who's there," I shouted. Then I heard a lyrical voice say, "It's only me, Nakahara-roshi." With that Mitsuko Kalapa appeared from behind a pile of futons.

"What are you doing here?"

"I am taking inventory of the futon sheets for our next sesshin on *Rohatsu* (commemoration of the Buddha's enlightenment – the eighth day of the twelfth month).

"Yes, yes, of course."

I looked at her intently as she walked towards me and noticed her peach-colored skin and light green eyes. Her facial features seemed to be chiseled by some unknown sculptor. She had a completely shaved head and I could not help wondering what she would look like with a full head of hair. Buddhist monks and nuns shave their heads to overcome insidious vanity which is empty pride. Pride is known as one of the one- hundred and five negative passions. Pride is related to conceit and self-esteem. To me she appeared very beautiful even with her shaved head.

Not knowing what to say I offered her an invitation, "I am holding a seminar on the Pali Canon in my library next Wednesday after breakfast. Would you like to join us? There will probably be six participants whom I shall select."

"Yes, I would like it very much but what will we discuss about the Pali Canon?"

"Well as you know, the Pali Canon is recognized as a scriptural source for all Buddhist traditions even though it is most closely associated with the *Theravada* sect (teachings of the elders). The Pali language is a close relative to Sanskrit spoken by the every day people of the time hence the name Pali Canon. Buddhist scholars refer to the canon as the *Tipitika* (three baskets). The Discipline Basket *(Vinaya Pitika)* covers the rules and historical events related to the Buddhist *Sangha* (monastic community). The Discourse Basket *(Sutta Pitika)* preserves the sermons and teachings of the Buddha and his earliest disciples. The Higher Teachings Basket *(Abbidharma Pitika)* offers a systematic and detailed analysis of the Buddha's doctrines, concepts and philosophy. I intend to carry on discussions of all three baskets by examining one basket on each weekly Wednesday. If this seminar is successful I expect to have seminars on other Buddhist concepts such as *Shunyata* (emptiness), *Dukkha* (suffering), *Anatman* (no self) and *Anicca* (impermanence).

"It sounds very formidable."

"Do you still want to come?"

"Yes, indeed, I'll be there. Thank you for inviting me."

On Wednesday a group of my selection gathered in my library for the seminar on the *Vinaya Pitika*. There were three monks, two nuns and myself. The method consisted of my reading a passage followed by an open floor discussion as to its meaning and purport as well as its significance. All the participants became actively engaged in the discussion and at times the interaction became agitated and even sometimes exasperating. But all the participants seemed to enjoy the conduct of the class. In my view, this was stimulated by the fact that since Zen monasteries are a silent order this gave the monks, who rarely speak, an opportunity to sound off. At its conclusion all of them came up to me and bowed with a gassho and expressed kindly, positive feelings. They were still talking on the way into the hallway. We had agreed to meet the following Wednesday. Then they left in a single file; that is all but Mitsuko Kalapa who stayed behind to have a word with me. "It was a good discussion and I look forward to continuing next week."

"Thank you."

"Do we have to wait a week to be together to enjoy each other?"

"What do you mean?"

"I mean I like you very much and would like to be with you."

"I like you too, Mitsuko, how do you suggest we accomplish being together more often?"

"I could come in the evening and leave in the morning in time for zazen."

"I see, are you sure about this?"

"I've thought about it and my plan is to come to you for our bath together in your room and then be with you all night until wake up time in the morning."

"Don't you think someone will see you? Remember wagging tongues could be injurious."

"I don't think anyone will see me because the monks and nuns will be busy in their separate baths. If we both have our bath together in your room no one will notice because they will be busy at their own baths."

"I see, well let me think about it."

"Shall we try it tonight?" she insisted.

I was silent for a long time deep in my thoughts. She kept staring at me wide-eyed in anticipation. The prospect of being with her was very intriguing. I did like her and we were both about the same age. *Why shouldn't we enjoy each other? What harm would result if we try it once?* "Alright, I'll meet you here in my rooms tonight for the bath. But I insist that if it doesn't work out that we end it without any recriminations. Do you agree?"

"Yes, yes, I agree." She turned to face me with a smile on her face and kissed my lips. She then turned and left hurriedly.

I stood for a moment stymied but the sweet taste of her kiss on my lips fortified my resolve to meet this situation with prowess and gallantry.

V

All day long I could think of nothing else except the prospect of being with Mitsuko. I began to straighten up my bedroom and even plumped up my futon in anticipation of our forthcoming tryst. That night I heard a soft knock on my door. On opening it I found Mitsuko standing on the threshold with a broad impish grin on her face. "Good evening, Roshi."

"Come in Mitsuko. Please call me, Jiun," I said as I held the door open for her. She slinked into the room in a furtive way and stood before me. "Yes, of course. How are you, Jiun?" she breathed in a whisper.

"I am fine, Mitsuko. Please come in and make yourself comfortable." I was completely startled when I saw her begin to remove her robes. She was like a young goddess wearing practically nothing below the waist and was barely covering her breasts with her folded arms. I noticed that her breasts which were nothing more than small mounds had two centered pink dots. She had a slim body which was well proportioned. Its secrets were mostly hidden by the flowing, bulky robes she wore. I was fascinated by her aqua eyes, high cheekbones and her peach-colored skin. She moved towards me with outstretched arms. My kimono, which was given to me by Tomoko, fell off my shoulders to the floor. I could feel her smooth arms around my torso and I responded with a close hug and a kiss on her warm lips. I could feel my member stiffening. Because of our proximity she could feel my member against her flat, round belly. Suddenly she reached down and held my member in her hand. "Let us take our bath then we can go to sleep together," I said in supplication.

"Yes, yes," she agreed hastily.

We walked into the bathroom completely nude enjoying each others naked bodies. I turned on the shower and at the proper temperature we wetted our bodies so that we could soap up each others body with a soapy washcloth. As I soaped and scrubbed Mitsuko I could feel her lubricious skin under my fingers. I experienced a blissful emotion which gave me much pleasure. We hugged and moved our hands up and down each others body moving the soapy lather and exploring the mysterious clefts and apertures. Finally, we rinsed the soapy lather off our skin by a warm shower. We then proceeded to enter the special tub which I had prepared before Mitsuko arrived. We soaked in the warm water and frolicked for a long time like two children.

At the conclusion of our bath we dried off with large bath sheets and then got into my futon together. That night we had sex. This activity continued only on every Wednesday for many months. By then I was beginning to seriously need the amorous emotion in unbridled anticipation. We did not see or recognize each other during the week in fear of being identified as lovers. The once-a-week liaison satisfied the both of us. We had no alternative life. We carried on as usual with our monastic life. All we had from each other was bathing and sex.

One day as I was working in my library I heard a soft knock on my door. On opening the door I discovered a young novice standing at the threshold. "Nakahara-roshi there is a gentleman in the monastery office waiting to see you."

"A gentleman, you say. Who is it?"

"I do not know."

I went downstairs to the office where I encountered a middle-aged man wearing civilian mufti. I bowed with a gassho.

"Yes, may I help you?" I inquired.

"Are you Nakahara-roshi?"

"Yes, I am."

"I am happy to meet you, Nakahara-roshi. My name is Clayton Ridley. I am the attorney for the Happy Valley Senior Center in Honolulu."

"Yes, I am glad to meet you," I said with trepidation as I shook his extended hand.

"I am sorry to be the bearer of sad news but I am here to tell you that Tomoko Kangetsu died of a heart attack last night."

I was shocked beyond reason at hearing this terrible news and began to sob tears of grief uncontrollably. My knees weakened and I almost toppled over. I sunk to the floor weeping loudly. Mr. Ridley helped me rise to my shaky feet. I took out a handkerchief from my sleeve and wiped my eyes. "Are you alright?" he said.

"Yes, please forgive me for my emotional outburst."

"Think nothing of it. Is there anything I can do for you?" He was silent for a moment but then continued," I found your name in her will. Apparently, you are her only beneficiary."

I interrupted him and muttered, "Where is she now?"

"She is in the crematory awaiting your presence."

"Shall we go there now?"

"In a moment, but first I must tell you the contents of her will." He hesitated for a moment but then continued after swallowing hard. "She left you all her possessions which consist mostly of furniture and clothing. In addition, she left you the sum of $50,000, which is presently in a bank account in trust for you.

I was stunned on hearing this but could only say, "Shall we go to the crematory."

"Yes, of course. I have a taxi waiting."

On the way to the crematory I told the attorney that the Happy Valley Senior Center could sell all her clothing and furniture and keep the proceeds from the sale as a donation. We agreed to this disposition and I signed a document to that effect. At the crematory I recited the Heart Sutra, as I did for her husband, while she was being cremated. I arranged with attorney Ridley for her ashes to be buried next to the gravesite of her husband. I was too distraught to attend the ceremony. Thus, Tomoko Kangetsu left this world unattended and unheralded. I shall never forget her kindness and love for me.

Finally, I went to the bank to receive the money bequeathed to me by Tomoko. I opened an account in my name and deposited $10.000. I then withdrew the remaining $40,000 in a cashier's check. I returned to the Emerald Sangha and gave the $40,000 check to the nun in charge of finances.

"Thank you, Nakahara-roshi, this is a wonderful donation."

"Please list it in the name of Tomoko Kangetsu."

"Yes, she gave $100,000 sometime ago. Please thank her."

"She died last night."

"Oh, I am so sorry. I did not know. Please forgive my stupidity."

"Of course, you could not know. I just found out myself."

I left to return to my room where I sat down on my zafu and reflected on my life with Tomoko. *Somehow, I thought she would always be there.* I broke out crying once again.

The following Wednesday Mitsuko came to me. She saw immediately that I was preoccupied with thought.

"What's wrong, Jiun? Has something happened?"

"Yes, I recently lost a very dear friend."

"What do you mean?"

"I mean a very dear friend of mine died this week. It has affected me so much I can't get the thought out of my mind."

"Who is this friend?"

"Her name is Tomoko Kangetsu and we lived together for a long time."

"Were you in love with her?"

"Not in a romantic way but in my own way, I suppose I did love her. She was very kind to me and made my life happy and secure. The truth is I shall miss her."

"Well, maybe I can help you forget."

"Yes, yes, that is certainly possible."

We then went through the bath ritual and slept together until rising at four o'clock in the morning. We left my rooms at staggered times to avoid anyone seeing us together. But we never failed to have our illicit intimacy on Wednesday nights. We were never without our lustful desires even though we had to wait from week to week.

For the next few months I threw myself into my work. A new project came into being. It was decided, with the approval of the Board, to build an addition to the monastery. It was planned to be a large 10,000 square foot building for the practice of sesshin. The intent is to have sesshin on the first week of April, May, and June in the spring and October, November, and December in the fall. The auditorium will have closets to contain futons, zafus, and zabutons thus freeing up the warehouse. Also, a separate kitchen and bathrooms will be installed. After a long arguing session with the Board I got my way to name the building the Tomoko Kangetsu Auditorium. Those objecting wanted to name it after the late Koichi Kagaguchi-roshi. But I reminded them that a new dormitory will be added in the future and we could name that building after Koichi-roshi. They finally agreed.

In the meantime, I tried to convince Mitsuko to keep herself busy during the week with a meaningful hobby. Some nuns and monks practice calligraphy but I suggested that Mitsuko try mandala workings for inner self-development. I told her, "Personal mandalas protect and adorn. They express your subconscious and bring you back to your center."

"What is a mandala?"

"The theme of the mandala – the square within the circle, containment within the infinite – can be found in nature as well as throughout history in cultures all over the world. It can be fun once you explore and learn the making methods. It will inspire you to make your own mandala – a symbol of your journey toward wholeness."

"How do you make a mandala?"

"You can embroider one using the cross-stitch method. You can also make a mandala out of tissue paper and hang it in front of a window, or you can make a mandala quilt out of cloth. You may even devise significant symbolism by using different shapes, colors, and numbers or picking images you want to work with."

"Oh, it sounds so difficult."

"No, no, you will enjoy it once you get started."

"Well, I shall try."

I continued, "You should know that mandalas are a pictorial representation of the universe especially prominent in Tibetan Buddhism. Although mandalas are commercially found on scrolls or as wall paintings, for important rituals the practice is to trace the mandalas onto consecrated ground using colored powders which may be erased upon termination of the ritual. This is commonly but erroneously called a sand painting." I waited for a moment but then continued, "All mandalas follow a precise symbolic format. Their circular shape indicates an all-including pervasion which consists first of an outer ring of flames. This lends the area a protective nature, and as the *yogin* (monk or nun) visualizes his entry into the mandala, his impurities are symbolically burned. A second circle consists of a ring symbolizing the indestructible quality of enlightenment. You should remember this description Mitsuko when you do mandala makings."

"I will remember, Jiun. Thank you for the information."

"Yes, indeed, they can be religious tokens."

After a moment she changed the subject, "Jiun on Sunday my father is coming to visit me. Would you like to meet him?"

"Oh, I am not sure. How would it look to others who are about?"

"Well, I thought of that. You see I am meeting him in the dining room at noon. You can just be strolling through unaware of our presence. I then will call you and you can come over to us. I will then introduce you and after a minute or two you may leave."

"Well, I don't know. I am not sure."

"Alright, think about it. I am sure it will work out."

"We'll see."

On Sunday I found myself occasionally shivering with fear. I decided to surreptitiously encounter Mitsuko's father who was scheduled to visit her at noon in the dining room. I had no appetite for this meeting but I must admit I was mildly curious and so I agreed with the plan proposed by Mitsuko. Having spent the morning straightening up and cleaning my rooms, I showered and dressed in my best robes. I went about the grounds inspecting things and greeting people until the critical hour of the meeting with Mitsuko's father. I walked slowly through the dining room greeting people with a bow and gassho when I heard the sibilant voice of Mitsuko, "Nakahara-roshi, over here." I looked up and saw Mitsuko waving at me. I just waved back but as I hesitated I saw her signaling for me to come over. I finished greeting the people around me and began walking over to Mitsuko.

"Hello, Roshi, I would like you to meet my father."

She pointed to the man who had risen as I approached. He was uncertain whether to extend his hand and so it dangled. I bowed with a gassho and said," I am honored to meet you, dear sir."

"My name is John Kalapa and the honor is mine. My daughter was telling me about your accomplishments here," he bowed as he spoke. He was in his mid-forties, dark wavy hair, dark mustache, dark everything, black denim jeans, black T-shirt, black pointed-toe boots. He was glib and seemed at ease talking about anything. He obviously was a serious weight lifter who wanted folks to know it. His shirt stuck to his chest and arms and he liked to pick at his mustache. Whenever he did so, his biceps flecked and bulged. "My daughter, Mitsuko, was telling me about your plans to build a new auditorium. I would like to contribute this check of $1000 towards your efforts." He handed me the check with great bravado. I received it with both hands and a slight bow. "Thank you very much for your generosity. I hope you enjoy this lovely afternoon with your daughter. Goodbye *Kalapa-kun* (Mr. Kalapa). Goodbye Mitsuko." I then turned to leave but not before seeing Mitsuko beaming. I assumed this meeting was important to her. I spent the rest of the day preparing for the seminar on *emptiness* to take place on Wednesday. Emptiness is the most important concept in Buddhism.

The Madhyamika or Middle Way, a school of Buddhist thought that originated in India in the second or third century, was a decisive influence in the subsequent development of Mahayana Buddhism. Emptiness considered the central doctrine shows that the Madhyamika critique of all philosophical views is both subtler and more radical than most Western interpretations.

The doctrine of emptiness (Shunyata) received its fullest elaboration at the hands of Nagarjuna, who wielded it skillfully to destroy the substantialist conceptions of the *Abbidharma School* (Tipitika) of the Hinayana. The latter considered the emptiness of phenomena to lie in their impermanency, and maintained that while entities are subject to a process of almost instantaneous change, they are none the less substantial and possessed of a true 'self nature' (svabhava) in their moment of being. Nagarjuna took the doctrine of emptiness to its logical conclusion and argued that this notion of a 'self nature' was at variance with the Buddha's teachings of no-self. The true nature of phenomena, he concluded, was to be empty of a self or self essence of any kind.

Our seminar on Wednesday produced much fever-pitched discussion. Most of the participants found the subject very difficult to understand. There were many unanswered questions. As a result we decided to continue, or more accurately to repeat the seminar on emptiness the following Wednesday. In particular, Mitsuko was having a problem understanding the material. We discussed this while lying down together in my futon. I was not in a mood to sacrifice sex for an academic dissertation but I tried very hard to enlighten her.

It was more than six months since I became the Roshi of the Emerald Sangha. I found myself busily engaged in administration matters, fund raising and clerical duties. I continued the Wednesday afternoon seminars on the great Buddhist concepts and I now began a *Shobogenzo* studies class, open to all, in the hatto on Saturday afternoons. The *Shobogenzo* is the Zen Buddhist equivalent of the Bible for Jews and Christians and the Qur'an for Muslims.

The *Shobogenzo* (Treasure of the Eye of the True Dharma) is said to have been a major work of Dogen Kigen, Zenji (1200-1253) founder of the Soto Zen School in Japan. It's a vast and difficult work, written during the last decade of his life. It contains 75 unrevised chapters and 15 revised chapters much of which was translated as paraphrases in English. The translation we are using is by Kosen Nishiyama.

The first chapter, *Genjokoan* (the actualization of enlightenment), is used as an introduction to Zen Buddhist practice. It was developed from a letter which the Buddha wrote to his disciples. It begins, "When all things are the Buddha-dharma, there is enlightenment, illusion, practice, life, death, Buddhas, and sentient beings. When all things are seen not to have any substance, there is no illusion or enlightenment, no Buddhas or sentient beings, no birth or destruction." And so it goes on and on to be read, contemplated and studied. *Shobogenzo* is a collection of discourses and essays given or written in Japanese by Dogen Zenji during the years from 1231 until his death in 1253. It is truly a monumental work based on Dogen's unsurpassed religious experience and his unique interpretation of the Buddhist Dharma. Our group will study one chapter a week. At this rate it should take us almost two years to complete, a most challenging task. Many of our participants accepted this challenge with enthusiasm. I found these academic sessions not only to my personal enjoyment but also a boon to the monks and nuns who attended. Life continued this way for many weeks, leading daily morning service, being part of the retinue at the weekly Buddhist concept seminars and supervising weekly *Shobogenzo* studies. In addition, I had the administrative duties as the abbot of the monastery and the interviews (dokusan) with prospective monks and nuns as the Roshi. All of this was a heavy burden in which I delighted and accepted with ardent zeal. My only form of relaxation was the weekly meeting with Myoko in my room where we could talk, bathe and have sex. I could not foresee a change in this activity. I would soon be proved wrong.

VI

One day I received a letter from the Head of the Board requesting a meeting in the monastery office. When I got there I found only two men waiting for me. After the usual pleasantries, the Head of the Board introduced himself to me. "We have never really met formally, my name is Brent Callaway. You may call me Brent." We shook hands feebly in American style and he turned pointing to the other man. "This is Professor Curtis Stewart of the Board." I reached out to shake Curtis's hand. He was a short man with a tiny waist, very light brown skin, a small slick head missing most of the hair except for a few strands he kept smoothly oiled and combed back. His eyes were black and bunched with wrinkles, the result of many years of smoking. After shaking hands and moving towards chairs I said, "I know we met at my interview some months ago but I am happy to renew our acquaintance. How can I help you gentlemen?"

Brent cleared his throat and wiped the beard covering his mouth with a handkerchief. "We are here to discuss a sensitive matter which involves you." His voice was not friendly. Both Brent and Curtis looked at me with wide eyes waiting for my response. But I said nothing. The scene was frightening but I remained cool. Finally, after a prolonged silence Brent continued, "It has come to our attention that you are engaged in sexual activity with one of the nuns."

I could not believe my ears. "Are you accusing me of unnatural behavior?"

He immediately exclaimed, "No, no, of course not. We are just trying to verify a rumor."

"Rumors are common talk of notoriety. Has the rumor been authenticated?"

"Well, that's why we are here."

Not knowing what to say I shouted, "The rumor is false."

"Are you telling us that you are not involved sexually with a nun?"

"I am telling you that my private life is none of your business."

"Are you then denying the allegation?"

"I am neither admitting nor denying it. I do not like the way this meeting is going."

"Why are you stonewalling the question?"

"I am not stonewalling. You have no right to question my private activities.

I have not engaged in any criminal actions and I do not recognize your authority to question me."

Brent immediately puffed up his chest and reddened his face as he spoke, "We certainly do have the right to learn if you have acted in an immoral manner."

"I do not wish to discuss this any longer. I must get back to my work. Please excuse me." I left in a huff with both of them standing in unrelenting wonderment. But I was very disturbed by the implication of the meeting. This could lead to dire consequences. The following Wednesday after our seminar I took Mitsuko aside and explained to her, "We shall have to delay our clandestine meetings for a while. It seems that a rumor about our liaison is floating on the air. I do not want to see you get into trouble."

She held the back of her hand to her mouth as if to hold back tears, "Jiun, how awful. When do you think we will be able to pick up our meetings again?"

"I do not know but let's stop for a month."

VII

The six month hiatus from Mitsuko seemed to be working with no repercussions from the Board. She did not come to my seminar class on Wednesdays any longer but we did see each other at morning services where we acknowledged each other with a bow and a blinking of the eyes. It probably appeared to onlookers as a simple courtesy. As the months went by I found myself steeped in my work but I could not forget the good times with Mitsuko. I dreamed about her and experienced strange visions of sexual encounters. I could not erase her from my mind, she was with me constantly. One day I was in the garden puttering among the flowers when I heard her approaching from behind, "Good day, Jiun. How are you?"

I turned surprisingly and saw her bowing with a gassho, "Good day, Mitsuko, I am well, thank you. How are you?" For a moment on seeing her I wanted to lunge at her, to feel her body again, to smell the natural scent on her neck, to run my hands along her legs. But I controlled myself. I wondered if there was anyone about spying on us. I had this ominous feeling that we should not be seen together. Our conversation was polite and stilted. It was reserved in tone and manner and I became frustrated with a need to satisfy my dreamy imaginative mind with its ardent affection for Mitsuko. I spoke softly in a whisper under my breath, "I miss you, Mitsuko."

"I miss you too, Jiun," she responded in a low sibilant, rustling sound.

I looked about to see if our utterances had alerted anyone. No one was near and I felt foolish being so fearful.

She resumed with a question, "When may we meet again?"

"I don't know."

"I am anxious to be with you."

"I feel the same but we must be careful."

"Please make it soon, Jiun."

"Yes, yes, I shall try."

She then left hurriedly and I continued with the gardening. During my busyness I kept thinking about her peach-colored skin, her sparkling aqua eyes, and smiling mouth. I resolved to recommence our romantic intimacy knowing full well that this could be a risky affair. But I threw caution to the wind and approached Mitsuko at the next morning service and said hurriedly, "Please meet me Wednesday night after the seminar."

She looked at me wide-eyed and said in a low voice, "I shall be there."

I could hardly concentrate on the subject matter being discussed in the

Wednesday seminar. My mind was intently focused on the coming evening with Mitsuko.

The seminar consisted of the Buddhist Path often referred to as "The Middle Way". It is focused on the practical task of finding balance between the negating behaviors of asceticism and desire. Shakyamuni Buddha was the founder of this tradition. His primary teachings are outlined in the "Four Noble Truths". The First Noble Truth is that there is suffering. This is an observation, not a condemnation or prediction. The Second Noble Truth explains the cause of the problem: desire resulting from ignorance of the ultimate nature of reality, which is impermanent and interconnected. In other words, suffering occurs when a person becomes attached to things that cannot create happiness or rejects things out of fear that they will create unhappiness. Decisions and actions made on the basis of the "Three Poisons" of delusion, greed, and aversion will inevitably result in suffering. According to The Third Noble Truth, it is possible to cease suffering. Delusion, greed, and aversion can be extinguished. The Fourth Noble Truth which contains the "Eightfold Path" tells one how to cure this problem. The eight guidelines are to live in accord with the view, intention, speech, action, livelihood, effort, mindfulness, and concentration that derive from wisdom and compassion. Each participant seemed to engage himself in these teachings with a consenting mind and a favorable approval.

Once again, Mitsuko did not attend the seminar. I did not know what to make of this being fearful of the possibility she would not come this evening. But my fears were of no account and finally abated when I heard the faint knock on my door. I opened the door to find Mitsuko with her peach-colored skin standing before me wide-eyed and smiling. *Konbonwa, Jiun.* (Good evening, Jiun).

"Come in," I said. "You look wonderful, Mitsuko." I took her hands and led her into the room.

"Jiun, I've missed you very much."

"I missed you too, Mitsuko." I then embraced her and we kissed with an enduring passion and intense emotion. I could feel the love and joy of this emotional excitement surging up within me. I was being deeply affected by my feelings for her and I was reluctant to release her. She turned to me and looked up into my eyes and said, "I love you, Jiun. I know you don't have the same feelings for me but I don't care. I love you any how."

I was stunned by this remark. "What do you mean? Of course, I love you."

"Oh yes, you love me in your way but I think it's more about lust. You satisfy your sexual appetite but my desires are stronger. I want us to be a couple with a longing for sensuous desire not only a sexual eagerness."

"I don't know what you mean. I thought you enjoyed having sex with me."

"I do but I do not enjoy sneaking in and out, afraid to be seen. It degrades the passion for me. I want to be with you always."

"Well, that cannot be."

"Why not, can't we get married?"

I was daunted by this bold request. "Well let me think about it." Although my attention was aroused, I knew marriage was something that was not part of my life scheme. I was only interested in sharing our sexual encounters. We later went through the usual ritual of bathing and sleeping together with a promise to continue in this manner until I could reach a resolution.

Several months passed as we renewed our liaison. The subject of marriage came up occasionally but I was able to deflect it with many inane excuses. Mitsuko was not careful about being seen any longer. She did not attempt to hide her comings and goings. Her audacity was unbelievable. No matter how I would caution her she continued to be impudent and venturesome. I was very troubled by this behavior. More so, I was afraid of the outcome. Then it happened. One day I received a letter form the Head of the Board. It indicated a Board meeting would take place the following Tuesday. Although it was not stated I knew exactly what the purpose of the meeting would entail. I worried about their worst possible decision and I forewarned Mitsuko of my fears. We ended our liaison immediately until the day of the meeting.

The six members of the Board gathered in the monastery office. There were the usual expected greetings and pleasantries. The Head of the Board, Brent Callaway, began the session. "Nakahara-roshi it is good to see you once again. Do you remember our last meeting?"

"Yes, I remember."

"At that meeting we cautioned you about having an illicit liaison with one of our nuns. Do you remember that?"

"Yes, I remember."

"Well, it has come to our attention that you are continuing this affair with the same nun. Is that true?"

I noticed him smoothing his beard with his hand as he spoke – an obvious sign of nervousness. I did not respond. I was caught in the trammels of my own thought. After a few minutes of silence he continued, "Nakahara-roshi this is not easy for me. I do not enjoy this but I feel we must elicit the truth by an appropriate discussion befitting our common nature. Do you agree?"

"Yes, I agree but I don't appreciate this type of quizzing by a formal examination. This appears to me to be nothing more than a trial."

"I am sorry you feel that way but very serious charges of sexual misconduct have been levied against you. This Board is entrusted with the responsibility of determining the veracity of the charges."

"The charges, as you say, are not true. I did not engage in sexual misconduct."

"Do you deny having an affair with a nun?"

"I did not say that. I said I did not engage in sexual misconduct."

"Are you quibbling? You do admit having an affair with a nun. Is that not so?"

"Yes, I admit the affair. But I hasten to add that it was consensual. Indeed, we even spoke of marriage."

"Did you say marriage?"

"Yes, we spoke of it."

"Ah, that's different. If that is so you must certainly cease your liaison immediately and prepare for your forthcoming marriage. Of course, you must realize that the nun will be terminated from the union with the monastery upon your marriage to her. That is the rule, monks and nuns may not be married while members of a monastery."

Small beads of sweat appeared on my brow and my throat felt parched as I spoke, "We are still in discussion. Nothing definite has been determined." Then, I was very surprised to hear Professor Curtis Stewart lean forward and say, "This is your last chance to resolve this issue."

"That remark is uncalled for and is not productive, dear professor. I was under the impression that this meeting was a discussion. There is no need for threats. Did I surmise wrongly?"

Just then Brent Callaway interjected, "Gentlemen, gentlemen let us not indulge in remonstrations." The other members of the Board looked on with gasping, throaty sounds and some were frowning. Nothing more was said until Brent Callaway continued, "Nakahara-roshi, this Board is very appreciative of the wonderful work you have accomplished since your take over. Frankly, your academic programs included in the monastery clerical life are noteworthy as is the funding efforts for the building of the new auditorium and the new dormitory. All we are doing in this meeting is pointing out the error of your way with the hope of prevention and so to mend your way and become an example of virtue and piety to the other members of this monastery."

I left the meeting with the distinct feeling that I was reprimanded. For a while I thought about ending the love affair with Mitsuko but somehow I could not bring myself to give her up. I did stop seeing her for a while with the excuse that I was mulling over the possibility of marriage. She seemed very hopeful at this prospect even after I explained that marriage would mean that she would of necessity have to sever her ties to the monastery and perhaps seek practice elsewhere. She was not frightened by this possible outcome. Her only question was, "Would I be able to live with you in your rooms as a wife and not be a nun?"

"I am not sure. I would have to find out if that is possible."

"Please look into it, Jiun. I am very anxious to get on with our married life."

I felt much pressured. The truth is that I was not really interested in marriage. It is too confining for me and would put constraints on my life. I enjoy my freedom and would prefer continuing as we have in the past as sometime lovers.

VIII

We kept up our illicit love affair for several months with little concern about the ultimate consequences. Mitsuko kept badgering me about marriage but I found a myriad of excuses to deflect her constant nagging. She finally gave up insisting on marriage and settled into being a paramour. Eventually, I forgot about the concerns of the Board believing erroneously that the matter was closed. I felt no anxiety as I arrogantly assumed that I was secure from the threat of dismissal. Living in this fanciful world I was soon to learn that my sinecure would be exposed to danger by the Board working behind the scene. The Edict and a letter came to me by a messenger.

Dear Nakahara-roshi,

The attached announcement is self-explanatory. You have been sexually reckless. Your carnal lust and appetite has done you in. I have tried to warn you but you did not see fit to heed my advice. You are seen as a dangerous liability by the Board for this monastery. I have the deepest respect for you. I am sorry I have to do this. It is not easy for me. Please understand I am just trying to correct an impropriety. Goodbye and good luck.

Brent Callaway, Head
Board of Trustees
Emerald Sangha Monastery

EMERALD SANGHA MONASTERY
AN EDICT

The Board of Trustees of the Emerald Sangha Monastery announce that having long known of the evil acts of Nakahara Jiun, they have endeavored by various means and promises to turn him from his evil ways. But having failed to make him mend the abominable acts and deeds which he practiced, they became convinced of his refusal to comply with suggestions and orders to cease and desist, they have therefore decided that the said Nakahara Jiun should be expelled from the Emerald Sangha Monastery forthwith and with forfeiture of all pay.

Signed by the Board of Trustees below.

BRENT CALLAWAY

Reading the Edict was nothing short of shocking. It was like a hammer taking aim on a nail. The blow hurt. It was very painful. Was it necessary to be so unkind? Am I really as evil as pronounced in the Edict? After finally achieving my life's goal I have destroyed all I have attained. There is no one else to blame. It was my arrogance and unmitigated gall that prevented me from doing the right thing. I threw the letter and Edict down on the floor and began to cry and shake uncontrollably. I then stepped on the cursed letter and Edict and ground it into small pieces with my slippers. I was angry and troubled. I was foaming with displeasure. What am I to do now? I thought about this problem for a while. What shall I do? I know. I know. I'll go to Japan and visit my aged parents. Yes, I'll go to Japan.

So for the next two days I stayed in my room and did not attend any rituals allowing my vexation and resentment to subside. Needless to say, I was also ashamed to appear in public. On the third day I heard a soft knock on my door. I opened it to see Mitsuko standing there with tears in her eyes. Suddenly she reached out with both arms and hugged me closely as she heaved with sobbing.

"Jiun, I am so sorry. The Edict was so cruel. What are we to do now?"

I looked at her moist eyes as I said pensively, "I don't know. I am thinking of going to Japan to visit my parents,"

"Well, can we get married now?"

I hesitated but said forcefully with a little anger in my voice, "No, I don't want to be married."

She burst out with a terrible crying jag, "I love you, Jiun. I want to marry you. We can find another position for you somewhere."

I looked at her with an incredulous expression and hung my head as I exclaimed, "No there is nothing else for me. This Edict will follow me for the rest of my life. I am done for. I must go to Japan to revive myself."

After I said that, I led Mitsuko to the door and bade her goodbye. I could hear her sobbing as she walked down the hallway. *Poor thing, I am to blame for her sorrow. Maybe, I am evil.*

The next day I withdrew my money from the bank and bought a one way airplane ticket to Tokyo.

IX

After the long flight from Honolulu I arrived in Narita Airport where I took the bus to the Tokyo railroad station and thence the train to Omiya to the home of my parents, father Noriko and mother Yukio Nakahara. I entered the house with a strange feeling of foreboding.

"Hello mother. Hello father," I said as I bowed deeply to both. "I am home to visit. How are you both?"

"Hello Jiun. You look wonderful, all grown up," my mother said.

"Yes, yes, you look wonderful," my father said. My father had shingles of crinkly hair springing up from his head like broken lyre strings. His long, translucent fingers plied the air, as white as communion candles, embellishing a point of doctrine. "I am glad to see you. What will you do now?" he asked. His brown eyes roamed restlessly.

"I don't know," I answered reluctantly. Across the room my pink-cheeked mother had returned and said aloud, "Give the boy a chance to settle down," Her eyes didn't leave my face. I noticed she had a thatch of course brown hair beginning to gray. My mother and father looked on in growing bewilderment. They stood looking at me reprovingly. Suddenly, my father said, "Why have you come home? Is there a problem?"

I looked down as I moved to a chair. While seated I said, "As a matter-of-fact there is a problem."

My father looked at me with his piercing brown eyes, "What did you say? What kind of problem?"

My mother moved closer, "What is it Jiun? What is wrong?"

I could not speak. I didn't know how to begin. I was too embarrassed to broach the subject. "I have been expelled from the Emerald Sangha Monastery."

My father stared at me silently, trying to guess the meaning of the words. "Please tell me what happened, Jiun."

Again I waited. My lips seemed to move but I caught myself. Beads of perspiration stood out on my forehead. My father watched my face silently. It was an important moment. Again I caught the movement of my lips. I hesitated uncomfortably but finally I slowly replied, "I was caught having a sexual affair with a young nun." I could see my mother's hand cover her mouth as she gasped, "Oh Jiun."

My father said nothing as he deliberated. He turned toward the dark windows. Night had fallen. The mist was in the trees. He turned around and looked at me. "Please explain what you mean," he said in a stern voice.

I stood up and faced him with renewed courage. "There is nothing to explain. I had an affair with a nun while I was the abbot of the monastery. It was a stupid thing to do and as a result I have fallen from grace and brought dishonor on me and my family." I then sat down again.

I could hear my mother emit a cry. My father slumped into a chair and held his head in his hands. My mother came over to where I was sitting, placed her hands on my shoulders as if to give me solace and comfort. "It is getting late, Jiun. You must be tired from your trip. Go upstairs to bed. We will talk about this in the morning."

It was late, getting close to midnight, as I rose to go upstairs. The room had grown chilly. My father pulled on his coat and lit the fire in the grate, then squatted on the stone hearth and watched the flames sweep through the bark and dry tinder in the fireplace, exploding its dry, fragrant heat into the cool mustiness of the room. The old house was silent. The wind stirred through the tall pine trees at the edge of the woods. The misty rain had stopped. For a moment I'd forgotten where I was. Something in the room reminded me of my youth and I stood up slowly looking around as I tried to remember. But I couldn't find it and so I stood silently for a moment then picked up my travel bag and made my way upstairs. In a little while I was asleep in my small bedroom on the second floor. I went to sleep depressed and uneasy.

In the morning I came downstairs to a delicious breakfast of congee and a piece of blue fin tuna. No one said anything while eating. It was obvious that they discussed this matter last night in their room. My mother greeted me politely as if I was a visiting stranger. After a while my father asked, "What are your plans?"

"I shall visit my mentor at Eiheiji Betsuin in Tokyo today. In that way I shall find out what my options are."

"I see. When will you go?"

"I will go right after breakfast."

"I see. Do you need any money?"

"No, thank you, father. I have enough money."

Then my mother spoke, "Jiun we will not pry into your private life. You may tell us what you wish. Please believe that we are here to help you." With that she hugged me and smoothed my bare skull with her soft hand.

"Thank you, mother," I said with a lump in my throat. After breakfast I went to the Omiya railroad station and took the train to Tokyo. I arrived at the Eiheiji Betsuin Tokyo Monastery in late morning after a ten-minute walk from Roppongi station on the Hibiya subway line. When I got there it was after zazen and morning services. The monks were busy with their daily chores. I was led to the office of the abbot, Sasaki Kenishi.

"Good morning, Nakahara-san. It is good to see you. How have you been? I have learned you are now a Roshi in the Emerald Sangha Monastery in Honolulu."

I bowed with a gassho, "Good morning, Kenishi-san. I am well, thank you. I am no longer a Roshi at the Emerald Sangha. That is why I am here. I would like to seek your advice."

"I see. Tell me what happened."

I showed him the copy of the Edict which I obtained from Mitsuko and explained my aberrant sexual behavior to him taking full responsibility.

He looked at the Edict and shook his head. "Tsk, tsk, I will probably get a copy of this from the Soto Zen Administrative Headquarters. Because it is an Edict you will have difficulty finding employment. It is a shame that Americans are so prudish."

"What shall I do? What do you advise me?"

"Well there is one possibility. There is a small temple, Kawaki-an, which is part of the Daitoku-ji complex in Kyoto. They are known for taking in wayward monks. If you like I can arrange for an interview with the head monk Hiroshi Kihara."

"Yes indeed, Kenishi-san, I would be most grateful."

"Remember, Nakahara-san, life recovery is nothing but a series of small steps and small victories."

"Is it too much to ask that you call him now?'

"Of course not I will be right back."

He went to the next room to telephone Hiroshi Kihara and I anxiously waited for him. He returned with a broad smile on his face. "It is all arranged you may visit him tomorrow afternoon. Is that alright?"

"Oh yes indeed. Thank you very much Kenishi-san. I am most grateful."

I left after more pleasantries and returned home to confront my parents. "I am going to Kyoto to see if I can enter the temple Kawaki-an in the Daitoku-ji complex in Kyoto."

"Is that true, Jiun? When will you leave?"

"I am going tomorrow morning. In that way the neighbors will not know of my presence and you will not have to lose face."

I left the next morning from the Omiya station to Tokyo and there took the Shikansen (bullet train) to Kyoto. When I arrived I took the number 206 bus from Kyoto station to the last stop Daitoku-ji and walked all through the temple complex looking for Kawaki-an.

Daitoku-ji is known as the Great Virtue Temple and was started in 1319 with the first building erected and dedicated to the Zen sect. It was officially sanctioned in 1342 and was declared a place of worship for the imperial court. The temple prospered until 1453, when it was damaged by fire. Then in 1468 it was completely destroyed in the Onin War. It was restored in the 1470's with backing from the Emperor. During the 16th century Daitoku-ji was patronized by the prominent warriors of the time. It was in this period that most of its numerous sub-temples were founded. At present Daitoku-ji have more than twenty sub-temples on its grounds. The monastery possesses one of the finest collections of art treasures in Japan. It is, without doubt, one of the great Zen monasteries.

When I found Kawaki-an, I was told to wait outside until the head monk Hiroshi Kihara would arrive to greet me. He was an affable, average size man wearing black robes. I was invited into the anteroom and we sat on cushions while sipping tea. I inquired about the possibility of taking up residence here. We then had an interesting conversation. I told him about my experiences in America. He told me that Kawaki-an accepted wayward monk without question. It also was a center for foreign scholars interested in Zen practice and learning the Japanese language.

"Would you be willing to be a teacher of Japanese language to American students?"

I readily agreed to this, "Yes, of course."

"If you are willing then there will be no charge for room and board."

"Thank you, Oh, how wonderful, this can be my penance." I then deemed it important to show him my copy of the Edict. He took it and glanced at it with great interest.

"This is a very harsh Edict. There was no need to issue this kind of condemnation. I am sure things could have been worked out."

"That is very kind of you to say, Kihara-san, but they did try to divert me from my deviation from moral standards. They were unsuccessful because of my arrogance and obstinacy. You see I have had an easy time of life during my youth and have not experienced the value of virtue. I promise you that I will not stray again."

"Alright then, I would like to introduce you to your first student. He will arrive tomorrow morning in time for zazen after which time you may begin with rudimentary Japanese language studies."

"Who is he?"

"He is a professor of Asian history at St. Michael College in New York and he lives in a ryokan in downtown Kyoto."

"You mean he doesn't live here"

"No, we do not have enough room to take in students. They must live outside the temple."

"I see. Well then until tomorrow." I left him to find my sleeping quarters.

X

The next morning after zazen and breakfast I met my student, Dr. David Keene in the hatto of the temple. He was a man with carefully disarranged hair. His face was a mask of lines around bright dark eyes. His voice was deep and melodious. He had a friendly smile and a slight stoop when he walked into the hatto. "Good morning, dear sir," I said. "My name is Nakahara Jiun."

"Good morning my name is David Keene. You may call me David. What shall I call you?" He reached his hand out to shake in the American way but I did not take it instead I bowed with a gassho.

"The proper way to address me is Nakahara-san since I am a Buddhist priest. The san on the end of my name is like calling me Reverend."

"Are you a priest here in Kawaki-an?"

"No, I am here as a Japanese language teacher."

"Then where do you perform as a priest?"

"I used to be a Roshi in a monastery in Honolulu but I left there recently."

"Really, why was that?"

"Oh, it's a long story. Someday I'll tell you all about it. Right now we should get on with our lesson. By the way, may I ask how long you intend coming to Kawaki-an?"

"I am on sabbatical leave from St. Michael College so I plan to come here everyday, except Sundays, for one month. Do you think I will be able to speak Japanese by then?"

"If you study hard you probably will be able to speak reasonably well by then."

So we began our first lesson with the rudiments of the Japanese language. This went on every day for a week in which time we became socially friendly. He told me much about his college life as a teacher of Asian history, his personal life in New York and his goals and aspirations. I learned he was a bachelor and his age was fifty-two years, although he looked older due to his wrinkled face. He sometimes probed for me to reveal my life story. I felt it would do me good to confess the incident of the Edict. The opportunity arose one day when he asked me an exploratory question.

"What made you leave the monastery in Honolulu?"

"Actually I was dismissed."

"Wow, what happened?"

I withdrew inwardly and hesitated to answer since I was not of a probative mind, but he insisted. "Come now, tell me what happened. Get it off your chest. I do not mean to embarrass you. My only motive is to help if I can. I've noticed in these last few days you seem to be very morose."

I was taken aback by his statement. "I am sorry if my temper is sullen or gloomy. I do not mean to be that way."

"Nothing of the kind, you sometimes are off somewhere else, that's all."

"I see. Well, if you choose, I shall tell you my tale of woe." I cleared my throat and leaned back to sort out my thoughts. I began slowly trying to muster enough courage. "I became the Roshi of the Emerald Sangha Monastery in Honolulu after the demise of the previous Roshi. Considering my age, I was only twenty-five; it was a great and unexpected opportunity. I had just been ordained as a Buddhist priest the year before and did not dream that I would attain such a high status so quickly. It was the culmination of all my boyhood dreams. But, I made a serious and probably unforgivable mistake. I became sexually involved with a young nun." I stopped speaking and waited for a response from David. It came quicker than I thought.

"What, is that all? Did you say sexually involved with a nun? So what, was it consensual? Is that any reason to engage in self-flagellation?"

"Wait, you don't understand. I am mandated by two of the precepts which I accepted at my ordination; Do no harm and do not engage in sexual misconduct."

"Who did you harm? Having sex with a consenting partner is not misconduct."

"But you see as a Roshi and the abbot of a monastery I am supposed to be a paragon of virtue and set a proper example for others.

"What nonsense, no one is a paragon of virtue."

"More importantly, I was given every opportunity to cease my impropriety and I refused. For this I have been expelled from the monastery and am now marked as a pariah."

"Well, I am sorry to hear that but I am sure all will turn out well in the end. Life is just a series of events. You will see it will balance out in the future."

"Thank you for your kind thoughts. I hope you are right David."

As if it was prescient, I was approached not long after by Kihara-san with a totally unexpected request. "Nakahara-san, I need your help. Would you do me a favor and take over the priestly duties of the morning service? I find I am too busy to continue the task."

"Of course I will. But I don't understand is this only for tomorrow?"

"No, no, I need you to be the guiding priest in our morning service from now on."

I looked at him in disbelief. *Can this be the road to my revival after indifference and decline? Is it possible my languor and depression are over?* "Thank you Kihara-san. I am willing and delighted to perform the morning services as the guiding priest." I was all choked up as I looked at Kihara-san's angelic face. I then knew he was giving me a second chance. This is the perfect way to start a life – at the bottom.

I continued the Japanese language lessons with David every day after morning services. He saw the change in me immediately. "Nakahara-san you are doing what you have trained for. Your life will now take a new turn. Next week my lessons will be completed and I shall return to New York."

"Thank you for your understanding, David. Our friendship has meant a lot to me. If you ever need my help please contact me here at Kawaki-an." I bade goodbye to David.

At the end of the month of Japanese language lessons I approached Kihara-san with a request. "I feel the need to engage in a solitary retreat. Thanks to you I believe I am on the road to recovery."

"Do you have a place to go, Nakahara-san?"

"Not yet, but I shall make inquiries."

"It happens that I have a small cabin on Kyushu, near Shimabara at the foot of Mt. Unzen which I use for fishing in the Ariake Sea. If you would like it you may stay there for your retreat. It is an ideal place for such a purpose."

I was stunned, "Thank you Kihara-san. You are so good to me. I shall always be grateful to you for your kindness and faith in me."

He continued, "To get there you must take the Shikansen from Kyoto to Fukuoka then take a JNR train to Omuta and finally a boat to Shimabara. It is really out of the way and will provide the silence you require you require for proper introspection."

"Thank you once again, I shall make arrangements."

"The cabin has a wooden bed and a small wooden desk. There is a cabinet in which there are some blankets and sheets. Please bring home whatever sheets are to be washed. You will have all you need otherwise it is very Spartan living."

"That sounds perfect for my retreat. Thank you again. I shall leave tomorrow."

I decided to write a letter to my parents before leaving for the cabin.

Dear Father and Mother,

I hope all is well with you. Please forgive me for leaving in such a hurry. I am writing this letter to tell you that I am well and that my work is very stimulating. I have become the guiding priest at the Kawaki-an temple in Kyoto. I am truly happy and I am sure I will eventually overcome my adversity.

I am enclosing with this letter a check in the amount of $5000 for your use. I don't need much money since my room and board is given me gratis as the guiding priest. I have enough money to live on otherwise.

Tomorrow, I am going to Shimabara for a solitary retreat for a few days. I was graciously given the cabin of Kihara-san to occupy. I shall write again when I return to Kyoto.

With respect and deep Gassho,

Jiun.

I felt good about sending the letter. I was sure it would help overcome the shame I brought on them.

After a difficult and long trip the boat docked at the Shimabara pier. I was given directions by some local fisherman hanging around the pier. I was told where the cabin was and how to get there. They were very friendly people and offered to help me get set up but I politely refused. I suppose being a Buddhist priest brought forth this largesse. When I got to the cabin I opened the rusty lock on the front door with the key given to me by Kihara-san. I was so tired from the long trip that I just sunk down on the wooden bed and fell asleep with my clothes on. I woke very early in the morning while it was still dark and decided to sit zazen before acclimating myself to my surroundings.

I bought enough food for five days from the local market. There was a wood burning kitchen stove with pots and pans. I was not surprised to find no electricity but I made use of the candles which I found in the cabinet. The bed was a wooden platform with a thin mattress. I was used to this since I slept most of my life on a futon on the floor. There was some fishing tackle in the cabinet and I was very proud of myself when I caught a small sea bass. I skewered it and roasted it over the open fire of the stove. It was delicious when eaten with the boiled rice I made on the top of the stove.

I brought nothing to read except my Shobogenzo. I studied it for many hours everyday. Most of the time I just sat in the doorway looking at the rolling sea and thinking: *What have I done with my life? Can I change and be the person society expects of me?* After a long day of doing nothing but thinking, I went to bed at dusk hoping that tomorrow will bring joy to my spirit.

I was fast asleep on my bed when for some unknown reason I became fitful and my eyes fluttered. There was a loud explosion. I woke and it was dark. There was a large cloud of ash and gas developing. I tried to say something, just a small drink of water. But my voice was gone due to the toxic fumes, speaking required effort and movement, especially when trying to yell over the rumble of the rushing lava. My joints pulled me tightly into a knot. A river of fire streamed down the mountainside. I was welded to the board on which

I lay. The air had no oxygen left and I choked repeatedly. Then it happened, flames broke out all around me and finally consumed me as the little cabin crushed and slid with the pyroclastic flow and fragments of rock. All was incinerated by the immense temperature.

The volcano on Mt. Unzen, 4462 feet high, erupted in June 1994 after being dormant for two hundred years. It killed Nakahara Jiun and forty-two other people.

Jiun was twenty-nine years old.

This same volcano killed 14,000 people when it erupted in 1792.

Author's Comment

This is a fictive saga which is completely a product of my imagination. There is no real character named Nakahara Jiun and indeed all other characters named in this story are fictional and do not exist, to find one would be coincidental. Some of the described localities are based on real places but the names have been changed to protect the guileless and the innocent. An attempt has been made to be true to Zen Buddhist practice and Japanese culture. I ask for forgiveness if I have failed in that endeavor. I personally have never known any Roshi or other Buddhist official involved in scandal or misdoing, although I must admit some incidences have come to my attention.

The purpose of this writing was to investigate and analyze the character of a man, particularly one trained in the ethical principles of right and wrong. It begs the question: Is it possible for a man to escape his nature? In this story we have seen a bifurcation of the activity of Nakahara Jiun making for two stories with an alternate route to the same ending. As will be seen he never really harmed anyone but the society in which he was immersed demanded a greater propriety from him. Unfortunately, he had no indication how to accomplish this considering the customs and manners of the alien society which he entered.

In Part 1, Nakahara Jiun becomes dazzled by the easy sex he experiences with a woman aboard a tramp steamer but exercises good judgment by refusing a continuation of this illicit romance with the widow Kangetsu. He eventually becomes an integral part of a new temple in Connecticut where he is beguiled by the sponsor's free living daughter ending in his ultimate reproach and degradation.

We next examine his possible choice made in Part 1 by the widow Kangetsu. In Part 2 having been caught in a dilemma he chooses to live with the widow Kangetsu. It is evident after examining both stories that Nakahara Jiun ends up in each life in a tragic death. Is it unfair to ask why this is so? This story forces us to ask ourselves uncomfortable questions, chiefly: What would we do in this situation? I, as the author, do not presume to judge but I hope this tale of cunning, compromise and survival is a mirror-image of man's nature.

Albert Shansky, Norwalk, CT

The Japanese Castaway

The Adventures of a Shipwrecked Japanese Sailor

ONE

The officer of the Hudson Bay Company stood there asking questions. He was a large burly man with a bushy handlebar mustache and a curly flowing length of hair down his back and a bald pate on top of his head. He constantly cleared his throat with loud harrumphs before he spoke to me.

"I would like to tell you my story, my name is Sueki Fumihiko. You may call me Sweki. I am a castaway from Japan. After more than a year of drifting on the Pacific Ocean Kuroshio Current I finally washed up on the shores of America at Cape Flattery where I was captured and enslaved by the Makah Indians."

"Yes, I know," said the officer. "I had to barter for your release. It cost me ten large machete knives for your freedom. Please continue with your story."

"Oh yes, yes, thank you. Well in 1863 I was on the Kojun-maru a junk which left the Port of Tobu on the Japanese Island of Honshu bound for Edo laden with a cargo of rice and ceramics intended as annual tribute for the Shogun up the coast. I knew it was a foolhardy venture to set sail after the autumn rice harvest but the Shogun was anxious for his annual tribute." I stopped speaking and looked up to the officer. "May I please have a drink of water? I am awfully thirsty."

"Yes, of course," he said and handed me a leather flask.

I coifed the water from the flask spout and handed it back saying, "Thank you very much."

"Please continue," said the officer somewhat impatiently.

"Suddenly the wind caught our high stern and snapped the side-rudder. There was a great storm brewing. In order to reduce the risk of foundering in the storm, the crew cut down the mast. This turned our vessel into a hulk, at the mercy of the wind and waves. The wind grew in intensity and the waves which washed over our deck became monstrous as if intending to swallow us whole."

"Wait a minute. Are you saying that cutting down the mast stabilized your boat?"

"Yes, you see with the mast up we could have been blown over. As it was it became nothing more than a floating platform."

"I see, quite right. Please continue."

"There was no way to escape the rain. It beat down on us in a steady pelting. The hulk heaved up with a wave and crashed down into the valley in the sea. It was a frightening and sickening ride, up and down. I held on to the railing until my hands became bloody from rubbing the wood. I found my breath failing and my spine cold as ice. The wind lifted the hair from my head. I held my breath, my heart beating rapidly, the blood beginning to pound at my temples. Darkness was falling. It had begun to snow, at first a dry flutter, stinging my cold face and covering my body with fine dry pellets, then more heavily as the wind eased." Once again, I stopped speaking. "I am sorry to trouble you, but may I have another drink of water?"

"Oh, indeed. Here you may keep the flask, he said as he handed me the leather pouch.

"The night was silent; the snow flakes clung to my hair and cheeks. Then the wind picked up again and swirled the snow like a sirocco. After a time the snow stopped as quickly as it started but was replaced with a steady rain which had fallen continuously. The wind and rain began sweeping across the hulk. I had all I could do to hold myself down from being blown overboard. Suddenly a gigantic lurch lifted the hulk high up in the air and fell down to crash in the agitated sea splintering the hulk into many pieces. I was swept overboard into the churning sea and sunk deep into the water. I was kicking fiercely trying to surface but the debris of the shattered hulk surrounded me preventing me from moving. I reached the surface with a burst of air entering my open mouth. My lungs ached from the rush of air and my lips sputtered the salt water which accompanied the air in my mouth. I flailed my arms trying to keep afloat when my hand slapped a large floating board." I stopped to catch my breath and looked up at the officer. He seemed anxious for me to continue. So I took another swig of water and picked up where I left off.

"I climbed on top of the board and stretched out thoroughly exhausted. All night I rode the rolling waves surrounded by darkness and the detritus of the broken hulk. The rain continued to fall. At night a freeze came. I was shivering and shaking with my teeth chattering as I lay on the board waiting until morning. At first light, I could make out the forms of floating objects such as barrels, crates and pieces of broken wood. I could even hear the faint cries of some other men in the dark night and surrounding mess." I needed a rest but I knew the officer wanted my whole story. I reflected on my past and continued.

"The wind and rain stopped as the sun began to rise into view. The orange and yellow sky overhead became brighter as the red, fiery ball lifted high overhead. I rose halfway on my knees to look about me. The entire area in my sight was covered with lumber floating all around and items bobbing up and down in unison with the gentle waves. I shouted and in a little while heard a faint response. I was heartened by the thought that others are accompanying me on this fateful voyage. After a while I fell forward into a prone position on the board and felt the warm sun on my back. It lulled me off to sleep. I awoke in late afternoon, not having slept all night. I could feel us drifting in an easterly direction rather swiftly. I had heard of the Kuroshio Current and assumed that I must be in it. I had hoped we would be picked up by a whaling ship or a Russian fishing vessel, both plied the waters between Japan and Hawaii. The terror of being lost at sea began to creep into my mind. Foreign ships do not come this close to the shore of Japan so I knew we could not be rescued until we floated a little further east. That night I fell asleep hungry and thirsty and a little cold. This was to be the pattern for the remainder of my time at sea. I began to dream about my home."

TWO

I looked across the frozen fields, the stubbled rice rows, and the fencerows beyond. It was autumn in the Echigo region, quail and dove weather still, and the recollection brought a familiar ache to my bones. I could see my mother and sister each swathed in a bonnet, as protection from the sun, bending over and tending the rice rows, pulling out unwanted weeds. My father and older half-brother were tilling the soil with hand tools. My father's first wife died leaving him to care for their child, my older half-brother, and then he married my mother who bore two children, me and my younger sister.

A crack of sunshine broke through the clouds and bathed the wintry countryside. The clouds were beginning to clear; patches of blue sky were visible. At dinner that night I told my father and mother, "I am thinking of going to sea." They both cried out, "Why?"

"Elder brother will inherit the farm one day. Sister will probably get married. I have to make my own life. I shall become a sailor and go to sea."

Suddenly, I heard a deep voice. "Mr. Sweki, Mr. Sweki," said a voice nearby. I turned to see a tall man in a dark coat holding a glass towards me. His eyes were cool, as colorless as sea water. He had high cheekbones, like a Slav, and dark blond hair. The officer standing next to the Slavic man said, "It's hot tea, the glass still extended. "Your preference to water, I believe."

"Thank you very much. Yes, I enjoy tea." I took the glass and drank from it in small loud sips.

"Would you please continue with your story," said the officer impatiently. In the meantime, the Slavic man squatted on his haunches to listen.

"Where was I," I said coming out of my oneiric state.

"You were telling us about falling asleep on the board while drifting along."

"Oh yes." I drank the tea and put the glass aside. "Before I continue my story I feel very dirty and clammy. May I have a hot bath? I am chilled to the bone and have not washed for days,"

"Yes indeed, come with me and I will show you the tub which we have already prepared for you."

I followed him to the next room where I found a metal tub filled with steaming water. I got into the tub and took a hot bath and soaped up and scrubbed the dirt off my skin with a wash cloth. I sat in the tub for a long time, letting the hot water bring the life back to my bones. I dressed in my buckskin clothes and returned to the room where I found the officer and the Slavic man. An old iron stove stood on a piece of tin plate inside the door. I went over to it with outstretched hands to warm myself. The ancient pine floors of the room were scoured to an almost pale color. I turned toward the two men and picked up my story where I left off after sitting on the floor in cross legged position.

"For days I had nothing to eat or drink and all the time the blistering hot sun beat down on me. I was miserable and musing at the endless water when one day I spotted a fish swimming near the board. I became instantly excited at the prospect of catching it, but how? I found a piece of wood floating nearby and carefully picked it up. I raised it like a club overhead and slammed it into the water with all my strength. The fish turned belly up. It was dead. I reached into the water and retrieved it. I looked at it with wide eyed disbelief. How to eat it? I grabbed the tail in my left hand and the head in my right hand and brought it to my mouth. I bit down hard on the soft underbelly, all sorts of strange things plus blood came oozing out splattering on my chin and cheeks. But I swallowed the warm liquid without a care. The drinking of the body fluids was soothing to my parched throat. Then I began systematically eating the raw flesh and spitting out the scales which lodged on my lips. My hunger was somewhat sated. Afterwards I munched on the backbone discarding it when I was finished and washed my face with seawater. I vowed that I would soon try fishing again.

I looked around at the floating debris and noticed several square boxes floating along and bobbing up and down in the water. What's in those boxes? I decided to retrieve one of the boxes out of curiosity. I eased into the cold water and swam over to one nearby box. I pushed it back to my board and with some difficulty lifted it on top of the board. I did nothing while I rested from the exertion. I shook my head back and forth to rid myself of the water dripping from my hair. I turned and stared at the box. *I wonder what's inside.* I turned on to my knees and grabbed my makeshift club. Swinging it up and down, I finally broke through the paper-thin wood of the case. Lo and behold! I discovered the contents to be rice kernels. I could not believe my good fortune. Now I have food to eat. I grabbed a handful with unusual gluttony and stuffed it into my mouth. I chewed and swallowed. It was hard with no taste but I didn't care. I swallowed a lump made pasty with my saliva. I then grabbed another handful and repeated the mastication. I leaned back against the box to savor my delight. Suddenly I felt cramps in my stomach. I tried breathing deeply to relieve my stress to no avail. The cramps increased. I tasted a bitter acid taste growing in my mouth and with very little warning I leaned over and vomited into the sea. My eyes were tearing from the retching as I spit into the sea. While I peered into the murky water I noticed several fish feasting on my vomitus. I quickly grabbed my club and began beating the water. I was able to pick up three dead fish. If the rice attracted the fish then I had a goodly supply to use. *But what caused my stomach to heave, I wondered? Could it have been the large amount of uncooked rice I stuffed into my mouth?* From now on I shall eat the rice in minute amounts and chew it thoroughly until it is ground down.

I now paid attention to the three dead fish. I managed to make a sort of knife from a sliver of thin wood from the rice box. With this I began to scrub off the scales and eviscerate the fish bodies. I threw all the entrails into the sea which brought a large number of fish to the side of my board. Ah, yes I was beginning to learn how to attract the fish. Using the wooden sliver I cut the fish bodies into small pieces of flesh and consumed them slowly with thorough chewing. As I chewed and sucked I swallowed the fluid expressed by my chomping teeth. Although this satisfied me I was still extremely thirsty.

I leaned back and relaxed while the sun beat down on my head. I noticed we were still drifting in an easterly direction. While lazily musing on my plight I spotted a small round cask or barrel bobbing up and down in the water. Thinking of my past good fortune I decided to retrieve it. Once again, I felt myself dip easily into the cold water. Indeed, I felt I needed a bath after consuming the smelly fish. I hastily swam over to the small cask and began to push it back to my board. As I swam I noticed that the board had drifted far ahead of me. I panicked and began to swim faster. I suppose I could have forsaken the small cask and concentrated on swimming back to safety but somehow I was convinced the cask contained water; cool, clear water. After much effort I managed to reach the board with the cask in tow. I got the cask on to the board and lay in supine position breathing heavily. I was thoroughly exhausted and my arms ached all over from the constant swimming motion. I rested for a long time and began internal conversation with myself. *Was it worth risking my safety for a cask of I don't know what? But if it contains water then wasn't it worth the risk?* I sat up and held the cask between my knees. Using the club, I was able to pull the bung which sealed the contents.

I put my nose to the hole and whiffed a familiar odor. It was sake, Japanese rice wine. I threw my head back and laughed so loud it echoed through the endless sky. Raising the small cask to my lips I drank heartily from the opening. The taste was smooth and pleasant. I kept drinking in great gulps until I was full. I then put down the cask and lay back. In minutes I was in a drunken stupor, rolling back and forth and spouting nonsense from my mouth. Eventually I fell asleep and dreamed of incoherent things. In a few hours I awoke to a dark sky with a cold, white, moon shining down, leaving a silvery trail on the rippling water. I felt good and was grateful for the respite of unconsciousness.

I looked about me and felt the crush of loneliness. *Where am I? What is happening to me?* I thought if I come out of this disaster alive I will cut off my hair and become a Buddhist. I eventually fell asleep again and dreamed of home.

My father spoke to me. "What is the use of being a sailor? You have a good job here on the farm."

"No father, farm work is not for me. You work terribly hard all year long and at harvest time you have very little to show for it. This farm is rarely able to keep this family alive. Also the annual tithe to the Shogun depletes any profit we could have realized."

"You may be right but we are able to grow our own food and keep ourselves alive until better times."

"No father I am off to sea."

I awoke the next morning to a mild but steady downpour. I took off my shirt and caught as much rain as possible. I then knotted it to make a bag-like receptacle. I then held my head back to catch as much rain-water as possible in my mouth. The rivulets of rain-water going down my parched throat relieved the hoarseness of my throat. I licked my lips with every mouthful of rain water to relieve the pain of my cracked lips. The rain did not last long. At its conclusion I spied a rainbow in the sky and quickly assumed that it was a sign of divine intervention.

THREE

I hardly slept at all at night. The board was uncomfortable and I had no blanket or bedclothes to ward off the cold. I slept in fits and starts. At first light I sat up to begin my day. I noticed a strange phenomenon occurring within my body; I felt the need to urinate. This was probably due to my consumption of the sake and fish. *What should I do?* I decided to drink my urine. *I wondered how to do this?* I got on my knees once again and held my penis with my left hand while urinating in spurts into my cupped right hand. I then brought the cupped hand carefully to my mouth and swallowed the warm liquid. I repeated this several times until I ran out of urine. The urine had a salty, organic taste which was not unpleasant. It definitely soothed my parched throat. I vowed to continue this in the future.

I looked around and surveyed my field of vision. With the rising sun I calculated that we were veering to the left in a more northerly direction. This is probably the reason that the weather seems to be getting colder I also saw that we are not drifting as fast as before. The shipwreck debris seemed to be accumulating closer together. I also observed additional strange objects such as logs, tree branches and some vegetation amongst the debris up ahead. This stagnant state remained for a whole day then by evening suddenly the debris began expanding and our drifting movement began floating again. The buoyancy of the debris in the water amazed me with its power of support while the waves jostled the items up and down. Since the debris was closer to me I decided to call out to see if anyone else was in the water. Halloo, I shouted. But I received no answer. I repeated this shouting intermittently several times, still no answer. What I heard the first day was either my imagination playing tricks or the other party was too weak to respond. *Maybe, the other party died.* This was a very gruesome thought since it portended to be my fate. I immediately cast it out of my mind since I believe my resourcefulness would eventually save me." I stopped speaking and looked up. "May I have another glass of tea? My throat is very dry."

"Of course, "said the officer and he motioned to the Slavic man who turned to get the tea. "How long had you been floating in the water by this time?" he asked.

I became very pensive. "It is hard to say. I had no way to keep a calendar. But I would estimate about two weeks."

"Really, two weeks, what were your thoughts and concerns at that time/"

"I always hoped I would be picked up by a whaler or a fishing vessel but neither came to pass and the weather was getting fiercely cold. I only had my underclothes and a pair of trousers on. I thought I would surely succumb to exposure."

The Slavic man returned with a steaming glass of tea, which I took in both hands gratefully. "Thank you very much," I said as I looked up into his bright eyes. He waved me off with a motion of his hand.

The officer picked up the conversation again while I was slurping the tea. "How large was the field of debris in which you were lodged?"

"Well it depends. Sometimes it would expand and other times it would contract. I would say at its maximum it covered about one hundred meters in each direction while the current was moving at its swiftest. Then again as the current slowed the field of debris would contract to about fifty meters but that didn't happen very often."

"I see. You say you were moving in a northerly direction."

"Well at first we were drifting to the East but after several weeks I noticed the current was veering slightly to the North."

"Did this disturb you?"

"Of course, I was afraid we would reach Arctic waters before I was rescued and I did not think I would survive the cold."

"Alright then what happened next on your journey?" he asked as he looked at me with a sympathetic frown on his forehead.

I continued, "After several months of drifting, everyday became weary and tedious. I had no way to keep myself occupied other than sprinkling some rice kernels into the sea to attract fish which I slew with my club. Every day was filled with the same dullness. Boredom overtook me until one day I looked ahead and saw a mist rising from the sea like steam from a boiling pot of water. At first I thought nothing of it until I found that the closer we drifted the darker and more opaque it became. We were drifting into a murky condition of the atmosphere; a dense fog. I knew enough about the sea to assume that our relatively warm water current was meeting the northern cold water. The fog eventually became so thick that I couldn't make out any forms or positions about me. I became blind to my surroundings. In addition, the weather turned colder and I began to shiver and shake." I stopped speaking again. The thought of that experience sent a chill up my spine.

The officer looked at me and slowly said, "Would you like to rest now?"

"No, no I'm alright. I just wanted to collect my thoughts."

"How long were you in the fog?"

"What did you say?"

"I mean how long did the fog last?"

"It lasted all day and night into the next morning. Then the rising sun began to burn it off leaving wisps like cob webs hanging from the sky. My fright was somewhat abated when I saw my familiar surroundings. To me it was most unusual to feel safe amongst the debris. It was like the closeness of a home. But you must understand that being blanketed by the fog with no vision and only the noise of the waves slapping at my board was very frightening. The fog was so dense that I couldn't even see the water surrounding me."

"Just a minute." The officer cried. "You keep calling your raft a board. What was it really? Can you describe it to me?"

"Well first of all it was not a raft; it had no keel and no mast. It was nothing more than three-twenty-five-centimeter boards in width by about three meters in length held together by cross beams. I assumed it was part of the deckhouse. It was always wet with the sea flowing over it as we bobbed up and down to the rhythm of the waves; thus I was always wet. Whenever the waves became unruly the water would wash over me. There were many times I could see the rolling waves approaching and I would steel myself to prevent being thrown overboard."

I then took another sip of the tea which by now was getting colder but I continued, "I did have one unusual experience."

"You did? What was it?"

"Well after we reached what I thought were Arctic waters I spotted a forced fountain of water spouting from a whale's blow hole. Then I saw others, at least three whales. I must have drifted into the feeding grounds of the whales. One whale was swimming close to the current apparently lost for the moment. His fluke slapped the water with a loud sound and produced a fast moving wave which washed over me. Then without warning he dove under and came up to tumble the board and me into the sea. When I surfaced I was gasping for air and I felt the searing, pricking of the icy waters. The board righted itself and I clambered aboard shivering uncontrollably. I noticed my rice box and cask of sake had fallen overboard and was now bobbing in the sea. I was sad to have lost my club and wooden sliver which I used as a knife as well as my knotted shirt containing the rain water. All I could think about was getting warm and so I was constantly rubbing my arms and chest for relief from the cold. Finally, I stopped shaking but my teeth were still chattering. I mused about my situation and tried assessing what to do. I had no food, beverage or tools and minimal clothing. The only way to retrieve them was to go into the cursed icy water. The thought of it was anathema. *I'd rather starve.* Then, I saw the rice box and the sake cask were nearby. They were within a close enough distance if I could row the board over to them, but how? I had no paddle and not even an implement to push the water. While on my knees, I used my hands over one side to paddle the board. I splashed a lot but I was able to come within reaching distance. I pulled up the rice box with great effort and then paddled some more until I reached the sake cask. I was almost totally exhausted but with one last great effort I pulled up the sake cask. My hands were numb and blue. They looked like mummy's hands without life. They were very stiff and frozen but I kept rubbing them together to increase the blood circulation. This eventually worked and my fingers felt like a million pins were sticking me.

I examined the rice box and found a little sea water mixed with the rice kernels. The sake cask's bung hole fortunately was plugged and upright while floating. I surmised it was not tainted with sea water. I felt good about this retrieval but my real concern was getting warm. My hair was matted with filthy seaweed and I now was bearded, filthy and half starved. I also was blind as a bat as the sun climbed into the bright sky. High cirrus clouds moved in a thin herringbone overhead. I bent over and removed the bung from the sake cask. I swung my head back, raised the cask overhead and allowed a trickle to enter my mouth. I was surprised to find the sake had a mulled wine taste. *Was it my imagination?*

FOUR

By now I had been drifting about six months and it seemed that we reached the apex of the current since I noticed that we were now drifting to the right of the sun. This could only mean we were heading in a southerly direction. I was overjoyed by this new discovery because it could mean that we are leaving the cold climate. I would be very glad to leave the awful cold climate and the presence of the threatening ice floes I see all about me. My skin was beginning to pucker into folds and wrinkles. The only way I could warm my hands was to hold them in my armpits. I was almost reaching suicidal despair about my future when I saw the triple mast of a whaler way off in the distance. I began to jump up and down crazily waving my arms and shouting at the top of my lungs. All for naught, the ship was too far away and started to disappear in the distance. I was very disappointed and became frightened at the way the board was shaking as I jumped up and down. *All I need now is to topple over.* A few snowflakes drifted down from the gray skies. I sat down on the wet board completely dejected with a feeling of weariness and hopelessness. The tedium and boredom pierced my mind with psychic forces. *What good is living like this? Maybe I should end it all?* Despite my feelings I had an obsessive need to live by scorning death and pain. I somehow knew in the inner recesses of my mind that I would be rescued.

We are going southerly now and the weather will almost certainly turn warmer. *Oh what I would give for a warm jacket to cover my naked body.* Scabs and scurf were appearing on my chest and back forcing me to scratch and rub my skin where ever they appeared. A crust would appear over the sore wound after I scratched and the only relief I had from the irritation was to splash icy sea water on the crust like spots. But I hated doing this because it would cause me to shiver.

Then something wonderful happened. I spotted a tree limb floating by the side of the board. I carefully grabbed it and began to break off the twigs shaping it like a club. I thrust it against the top of the rice box, again and again, and broke off another sliver of thin wood which I fashioned into a knife. For the last few weeks, after the whale upset of the board, all I ate by chewing was a few kernels of salted rice each day. Now I had the means to catch and eat fish again.

Despite the cold weather I began to feel warmth creeping up to my head. Obviously I was developing a fever and was getting very sick. Sitting on the wet board with my arms across my raised knees, I noticed that my arms were very thin and that the image of my ribs was evident on my chest. I had lost a considerable amount of weight and my stamina was slipping away. I became nothing more than a living skeleton. I was so weak I couldn't hold myself in a sitting position any longer so I lay back on the wet board and awaited my fate.

I must have dozed off because I could not remember past events. I awoke because of the warm sunlight shining in my eyes. I waved my hands quickly in front of my eyes to shoo away the intense sunlight. I rose slowly to find the sun baking on my body. Oh joy, the first thing I thought of was that we entered a southerly climate. I checked our drift pattern against the sun's position and indeed we were now drifting in a south-easterly direction. I was very encouraged by this but perhaps too soon since the nights were still bitterly cold. As soon as the sun dipped beyond the horizon I began shivering. My nights were unbearable but I looked forward to the days which would be warm and sunny. Since the cold kept me from sleeping at night I relegated a certain amount of sleep time during the warm mid-days, usually after I fished and had a meager meal. I would sprinkle a few rice kernels in the water by the side of the board. When this attracted a fish I would swing my new club down on the fish's head and grab him after he went belly up. By this method I would eat fish almost every day. Of course, there were days when there was no fish so I resorted to eating only the salted rice."

"Wait a minute, "said the officer, "Were the fish of only one variety?"

"No, no, there were many different types and they all tasted differently."

"Really, I didn't think that one could taste the difference between raw fish."

"Oh yes, there is a considerable difference. Some types tasted awful but I was so hungry and thirsty it didn't matter to me."

"Well, please continue."

"Oh yes, a cold steady rain had been falling most of the day but I was moving along through the wind swept current. I lay myself down on my back and opened my mouth to catch as much rain as possible. My hair and body became saturated with the rain but I didn't care. I was enjoying the pure, sweet water being caught in my mouth. The wind brought the cold rain to my face still I lay there catching the rain in my open mouth. My thirst stiffened my determination to drink as much as I could while the rain continued to fall. After a while my neck and back became stiff from muscular strain. Still I continued.

Icy draughts swirled across the board. I was in a most uncomfortable position. At last I stood up and stretched my neck by twirling my head back and forth. My breath showed on the chill air of the surrounding environment.

Eventually a warmer mist blanketed the surrounding area, hiding the debris and the few ice floes accompanying me. I realized immediately that I was entering a warmer climate. As the mist cleared I looked up to see the gunmetal sky. I found myself quite fatigued and sat on the board holding my head in my hands. It was mid-afternoon and a pale sunshine was beginning to lie over the rippling water; the sky now turned a pale blue; the wind was bitterly cold but was diminishing. Yes, yes the weather was getting warmer, but it would not last long as the dusk gathered. In a while, I looked up at the dark racing clouds. The day was ending. I lay on my side with my head on my arm and tried to sleep but all I could do was think about home.

In my dreamlike state I could hear my mother calling, "Sueki, Sueki, get up. It's time to work in the vegetable patch. "I arose, washed my face, dressed and went into the kitchen for breakfast. My mother was spooning steaming congee into a bowl for me. I greeted my mother, "Good morning, mother. Where is father?"

"He is working in the rice field with elder brother. He told me to tell you to cultivate the furrows of our vegetable garden today," she said.

"Alright, as soon as I finish breakfast." I had two bowls of congee and a plate of pickled vegetables followed by a pot of green tea. After breakfast I made my way to the vegetable patch with a hoe to remove any weeds from the furrows. These weeds were collected and placed in a compost bin together with kitchen garbage to form black humus which is a decomposition of vegetable matter added to the soil as an organic portion.

The vegetable patch had snow peas, lima beans, egg plants and soy beans. This together with rice was our family's sustenance. I worked for several hours until the sun raised high in the sky. It was a very hot day and the sun beat down on me with a fierce temper. I began sweating profusely so I removed my jacket and shirt and continued working with a bare upper torso. The sun seared my back puce causing a tawny glow to appear on my skin. I was glad that I was wearing my floppy hat otherwise the heat would have made me dizzy. My body seemed to be rising in temperature. The sweat on my brow was dripping into my eyes causing me to stop several times to wipe my face with a cloth. The heat gave me an intense feeling as if I was working in a forge or a furnace. My body seemed to be inflamed as I bent over to do my hoeing work.

After a while my sister came by with a pail of cool water from which she dispensed a ladle portion for me to drink, then she went to the rice field to attend to my father and brother. Finally, I dozed off thinking about the wonderful days I spent at home. *Will I ever see those wonderful times again?*

I slept fitfully all night finding myself going into and out of a somnolent state. At first light I sat up awake but remained with torpor and quiescence. *Where am I? I must have been dreaming.* I looked around me and saw that the debris had expanded into a larger field and the ice floes had disappeared. Yes, it was getting warmer. I felt good. Better yet, I felt grateful that I was not shivering any more. You can't imagine how dreadful it is to shake constantly like a palsied person for hours at a time. Yes, it was getting warmer. According to my reckoning I had by now drifted for almost nine months. I left Japan in the fall and went through a winter and now it is spring.

Then a wonderful thing happened I saw a small flock of birds flying towards me. Most began landing on the broken lumber in the debris, others landed on the branches and vegetation. I thought this could only mean that I was nearing or approaching land. I was cautiously encouraged at the prospect of reaching land so soon. But that was not to be. My hopes were dashed again. I now speculate that these were migrating birds on their way to the North Country. The afternoon sun was low in the sky, but over the next two hours I became completely absorbed in the actions of the birds before me – flocks of plump birds feeding on the small fish caught in the debris, noisy birds pacing from lumber to lumber and twittering and dashing here and there looking for a meal. Given my inexperience, these small birds were maddeningly difficult to identify. But above all, I remember being overwhelmed by the mystery of these birds, which in their calls and movements seemed to share some higher form of site-specific communication. Then all of the birds would burst into flight with an unusual singularity of purpose and then proceed to give a stunning demonstration of synchronized evasive flying. Then they were gone and I was alone once again. I tried to make sense of the behavioral intricacies of the birds without dulling the romance and wonder they inspired in me for watching them. A feeling of loneliness came over me. I was conscious of, and depressed by, my solitude. This was very much pronounced by the departure of the birds.

By now the sun was beginning to set and I was prepared for another cold, sleepless night. The horizon was fiery red as the last rays of the sun reached skyward. I began to shiver and could only stave off the cold by beating my arms against my body. As I did this I looked up to see a full moon. It was silvery and shone its light on the water leaving a trail of sparkling diamonds. I sat down on the wet board and circled my knees with my arms. I looked up to watch the moon. Moon viewing is a particularly unique activity among the Japanese people. Whenever a full moon occurs, multitudes of people go outside to view the moon. They bring chairs and seat themselves in a space unobstructed by trees and buildings. It is a time for people to interact and discuss the images they make out on the moon surface. As I sat viewing the moon I could not help wishing I was home to partake in this activity.

FIVE

The next day at first light I saw the sun rising in the East. Its rays projected yellow, orange, and red coloration to the morning mist which hung like a gossamer curtain from the sky. I was so weak from a lack of proper food I said to myself; *I would gladly trade all this beauty for a good meal.* I have not caught a fish in days and I only had uncooked rice kernels to munch on. My lethargy even prevented me from chewing and eating these hard kernels of rice, *What for? I will probably die soon.* I shook my head back and forth to ward off dejecting thoughts. I know there is land up ahead even a tiny speck of an island. I heard many stories about little islands in the Pacific Ocean used by whalers to provision their ships. While thinking about these matters I lifted the sake cask to my lips in order to imbibe. That's when I received more sorry news. The cask was empty. I was so mad and disheartened that I tossed the cask overboard to find to my surprise that the cask hit a very large fish which I quickly scooped out of the water. He was still wiggling so I bashed his head with my club. He stopped moving. I then began to scrape off the scales and eviscerate the entrails with my thin wooden knife. It was a very large fish with enough flesh for several days. I delighted in my good luck."

"What kind of fish was it, Sweki?" the officer said in a questioning tone.

"I am not sure but since the flesh was pink in color I assumed it to be a salmon."

"I see. Never mind Sweki, continue your story."

"Well, the weather suddenly turned churlish and foul. The temperature hovered several degrees above freezing. I believe this often happens in the spring. It drizzled every day and the decaying debris caused a feculence which followed me licking its sour breath everywhere. The mornings dawned without sunlight, and the afternoons dissolved sullenly into evening, vanishing in the thick yellow gloom of sunset. I was hidden beneath the mist; fog seemed to bury me and even obscured the water. The debauch of fog and mist had crept everywhere. This went on for many days until I suddenly drifted out of the fog like leaving a tunnel into a warm, sunlit climate. I was so happy I could barely contain myself. I began shouting knowing that no one would hear me. I was like the Lord and majesty of this empty world. I realized I was all alone. Sitting back on the wet board tears came to my eyes. *How long must I endure this plight? Yes, I am alive. But it is almost like a living death.* I lie back on the board and fell asleep with warm sun baking me. And so the days followed into weeks with the weather becoming more tolerable with every distance that I traveled every passing day.

As summer approached quietly, a monsoon season came across the Pacific – smothering heat followed by pounding rain – this constitutes the miserable reality of my summer experience. This frantic existence is still better than the unendurable, harsh cold climate that I just went through. I am not complaining, in a way I enjoyed the hot, scorching sun beating down on me. After many days the sea became tranquil again. I actually started to enjoy the lazy drifting beneath the sun. Even the evenings were tolerable as I began escaping the interminable cold. Then after many weeks of placidity the sea began to churn and my movement was speeding up by repetitive lurching forward. The sea was torn white by massive over falls. There were tidal rips as I approached land that could overwhelm even a well-founded vessel much less my flimsy board. Because of the sea's vicious caprices I very nearly drowned. Tons of watery green waves suddenly pounded me and my board. I was so shattered that I thought I had reached my end. As I returned to reality I noticed my skin turned to prune while I lay flat hugging my board at its triangular corner. I sensed the presence of land ahead. Then the sea water settled to a bobbing up and down. I now was stranded and marooned in a totally exhausted state. I was too weak to move or care. But somehow I was exhilarated by the knowledge that I was safe and made land fall. It was the longest and most arduous journey imaginable. I did not forget my promise to the Buddha and renewed it once again; if he saved me I would cut off my hair and enter a monastery. But this had to wait a while longer. Meanwhile, a heavy rip tide pulled and pushed my board. The rip tide extended for miles along the coast and even more so to seaward. When the wind is strong and opposed to the tidal stream, the over falls are overwhelming and very dangerous. On shore winds, I was afraid, could cause me to wreck and topple overboard. This threat abated, however, and I lay on the board in a semi-unconscious state bobbing up and down."

"Wait, wait Sweki, how long did the whole journey take?" the captain questioned.

I stopped talking for a while as I pensively pondered the question. "I am not sure but I have reckoned that I was drifting at sea for more than a year."

"My, my, that's incredible. What happened next?"

I thought for a moment then after taking a swig of water, I continued. "I was in a semi-conscious state while bobbing up and down on the board in the water. But I was awake enough to hear shouts. Lifting my head slightly I could see people running into the surf to retrieve various items from the shipwreck. They took boxes, casks and some of the lumber. I was too weak to call out. All I could do is lifting my arm. It was not long before two men approached me speaking loudly in a language I could not understand. They both reached down and lifting me under my arm pits dragged me on to the warm sand of the beach. I lay on the beach draining the water off my body into the warm sand for about a half hour. It was the first time in all this terrible duration that I felt totally dry. I did not move for fear of disturbing my tranquility. It seemed so wonderful not to be wet. My eyes kept closing as if searching for sleep. Sleep did come in fragments but I was aware that my present circumstances were different.

I kept hearing shouts on the beach but eventually I dozed off into a deep sleep. I do not know how long I slept but I was awakened by someone pulling me up by the hair and shouting into my face. I could not understand what was being said to me but through bleary eyes I saw that it was a bronzed-face individual with a broad flat nose and long, braided black hair. He shouted at me again with some gestures. I felt his hot breath on my face as he spoke. I did not understand anything being conveyed to me and so I slumped back on the ground. In a few minutes another man came over noisily and the two of them lifted me bodily and carried me off the beach to a grassy knoll. I now could see that we were entering a little village made up of small huts with people milling about and some very busy at their tasks. They threw me into one of the huts on top of some animal skins and covered my naked body with a furry pelt which felt very warm and luxurious instead of cold, wet and exposed as I experienced previously. Suddenly I felt someone poking me. I turned over to discover a woman stroking my hair with one hand while she held a steaming bowl in her other hand. She spoke to me in a kind, soft voice which I did not understand. She had a small round bronze face with deep black eyes and a small pug nose. Her hair was long, black and shoulder length. She pointed to my mouth and then pointed to the bowl. I understood immediately that she had brought me something to eat. I sat up eagerly since I was famished from lack of food. I took the hot bowl in my two hands and began rapidly swallowing what seemed to be a rich broth. The hot liquid passing through my mouth into my stomach felt good and for the first time in a long while warmed my insides. I handed the bowl back to her and tried to speak but found it difficult so I merely grunted. She giggled like a child and left through the opening of the hut. I lay back somewhat sated and soon fell asleep again."

"Sweki, let me interrupt you," said the officer. "You should know that you landed on Cape Flattery on the coast of the Oregon territory near the border of Canada. You fell into the hands of the Makah Indians who enslaved you. They are a part of a large group of Indians along the Oregon coast from Canada to California who speak a language called Salish."

"I now know that but it surprises me that you are able to speak Japanese."

"Yes, well let me introduce me to you. My name is Captain Nigel Macgregor of her majesty's Royal Navy. I was a liaison officer in Nagasaki where I lived for three years and learned the Japanese language. Then I was attached to the Hudson's Bay Company assisting in the fur trade. It was here that I learned to speak Salish. I travel up and down the coast into Canada and easterly inland to Lake Cushman. I have contact with all the Salish speaking tribes but I headquarter here with the Makah and the Ozette tribe just south of here." He leaned back in an erect and exalted manner stroking his handlebar moustache and looking proud as a peacock in his blue uniform with gold braid and gold buttons.

"I am sorry to interrupt you Sweki. Please go on."

"Alright, as I said I was kept for a few days in the hut until I regained my strength. I found myself able to get up and move around on wobbly legs. The hut was nothing more than a skeleton of tree branches accumulated and tied at the top like a bird cage, over which were laid animal skins of various kinds. All cooking was done outside at a pit in the ground. The Indians were semi-naked and wore only loin clothes made of buckskin. The hut was occupied by two women in addition to me. I was to later learn that they were the chief's wives. They treated me like a pet, always feeding me the once-a-day meal and stroking my hair. I am grateful for their care.

As I said I was fed a bowl of rich broth which contained some kind of vegetables and meat of unknown source. The broth was more like a stew because it contained solid pieces of food. It was cooked in a large iron pot which bubbled over the open fire for about six hours every day. I believe all members of the tribe partook of this food. We always ate in the late afternoon after work.

I was beginning to enjoy my respite when one day the chief came in the hut shouting at me loudly and pointing to the outside. I did not move because I could not understand him. He then grabbed my arm and pulled me to my knees. I tried to stand but found my legs shaky. He pushed me gruffly outside the hut with loud shouts and commands. I found myself becoming steadier as I walked in front of him. He kept pushing me along until we came to a field where other people were digging in the ground with sticks. He gave me a stick and pointed to the people working, then to the ground indicating that I was to do the same work. In all that time he was shouting in a commanding voice without let up. The work consisted of digging for tubers. After breaking the ground and lifting the root-like tuber out of the ground they were brought by some people to the shore for washing in the sea water.

As I worked at this task I wondered in amusement, *I went to sea because*

I didn't want to work on a farm. I was actually grateful for the work after spending a year or more in relatively inactive boredom hanging on to a wet board. In addition, to digging for tubers I worked at cultivating the plants in what seemed to be a sort of cabbage field. Some times I would go into the forest with the women to collect berries but this was dangerous work since the berry bushes attracted bears. It was an opportunity for me to sneak berries into my mouth unseen to supplement my diet. I worked at these tasks from morning until night for almost six months. I was given one bowl of stew once-a-day to eat and I slept in the hut with the two women. One night I saw some of the men dancing around a fire in a drunken stupor. Apparently they found the casks of sake and thinking it was water imbibed. I found it very comical to watch.

I noticed after several weeks that the scabs and sores on my body were disappearing. I exchanged my torn and tattered trousers for a buckskin pair of trousers and a buckskin shirt given to me by one of the women. She came over to me one day and took down my trousers, laughing all the while, staring and pointing at my genitalia and my nudity. She covered her mouth with one hand as she laughed while pointing with the other hand. I was not embarrassed and laughed along with her in good humor. I was glad to have the new trousers which gave me a modicum of dignity."

"Yes, yes when we found you, you didn't look much different than the Indians," the captain interjected. "You know, of course, I released you from bondage by bartering for your freedom with ten large machetes."

"Yes, and I am very grateful to you."

"Think nothing of it. The first thing we did was to prepare a hot bath for you. You were really dirty. I surmise the Indians didn't expect you to wash your self. What would you like to do now? I mean do you have an ultimate goal?"

"Well, I would like to return to Japan."

"That may take some time to arrange. Ships are always coming into our harbor to transport furs for us and to provision their ships. It is rare to find one going near the coast of Japan. But, I shall keep my eyes and ears open. You know, of course, that once you leave Japan you are not permitted to return."

"Yes, I know. But I will sneak in. It is my intention to secure myself in a Buddhist monastery."

"Did you say in a Buddhist monastery? That could be a very difficult life. Are you sure you want to do that?

"Yes, Captain. I promised the Buddha that if I came out alive from my ordeal that I would serve the Buddha the rest of my life. By the way have there been any other survivors?"

The captain thought for a moment then slowly spoke, "There were two other men picked up. One was dead and apparently a victim of the fish chewing on his face. There was very little left of him. The other was brought ashore in terrible condition. He was barely alive and died a short time later. We gave them both a Christian burial and interned them on the mountainside. Did you know them?"

"Not really, but after the shipwreck I called out and thought I heard a response. They must have been the ones who called back to me."

"Well, you are here and alive. Now it is time for you to carry on."

SIX

The officer looked at me with a slight frown, "If you want to you can work here at the trading post for your keep until your ship arrives."

"Yes. Thank you that would be wonderful."

"I must tell you it may take months before you can get a suitable berth."

"That's alright, I can wait."

"In that case you can work with Sven Ronaldson." He pointed to the Slavic man. "This is Sven Ronaldson. He's from Sweden. He doesn't speak very much Japanese, but he does speak Salish and a few other Indian dialects. He will show you what to do."

I found it difficult to pronounce his name so I called him Suen. I bowed to him, "I am happy to know you, Suen." He bowed and said something in turn which I assumed was an acknowledgement. Then we walked away together taking a two-wheeled cart with us. He led me to the warehouse where he showed me the piles of animal pelts, mostly fox and wolf skins but I saw many bear and bison skins as well. He pointed to the cart and then to the animal pelts and then gestured towards the Indian camp while grunting *Makah, Makah*. I understood we were going to the Indian camp to pick up more animal skins.

I was glad to be going to the Indian camp because I felt a close kinship to them; after all they saved my life and provided me with buckskin garments and sustenance. As we came into the camp the Chief approached us and held up his hand in a greeting. Sven and he spoke at length with many gestures and hand signals. Finally, Sven told me in his faulty Japanese, *ke-gawa* (pelts) while pointing to a hut in the distance. I understood that was where we would pick up the pelts. I took this opportunity to confront the Chief with some trepidation. I bowed low with palms together and said in a distinctive voice, "Thank you, great chief for saving my life. I now consider us brothers." As I rose erect I noticed a smile on his face. I half expected a severe shout. But Sven came over and translated. The chief let out a loud explosive chuckling sound and then, with a cheerful expression on his face, came over and placed his strong hand on my shoulder, saying something I did not understand. I was touched by this gesture of friendliness and camaraderie. Before leaving I noticed some women skinning the dead animals and placing the pelts on poles to dry. Obviously the remaining meat was used for the boiling pot. We then rolled the two-wheeled cart to the hut and began loading up the animal pelts which we brought back to the warehouse.

At the warehouse I helped Sven sort the pelts by species, size, and condition. In addition, I was required to keep the cabins swept and clean up the kitchen after meals. I was allowed two meals a day, breakfast and a late lunch. There was a cook who made interesting but simple fare for the men of the post. He was a short, rotund Chinese man who wore a perpetual smile and spoke in short choppy words. The meals consisted mostly of the meat of various animals which was obtained from the Indians. I was also provided with a bed in a room with three other occupants, the bedding consisted of bear skins which were very warm in the cold nights. Bathing was done in the ocean surf where I often came upon Indian men and women bathing in the nude.

Some days Sven and I went to the Ozette people to trade their animal skins for various paraphernalia such as implements and finery. I began to use a few words in Salish which with Sven's help became useful during the intercourse with the Indians. The Indians were very happy with the intimacy I showed during my visits and were always ready to laugh and jocose at my limited speech. This work went on for six or more months into the late fall approaching winter rather rapidly. The weather became colder every day. One day the captain approached me with a jacket made of mountain sheepskin. "Here, Sueki, you'll need this jacket for the cold winter months. It is a gift from the Chief of the Makah Indians."

I thanked him profusely and put it over my buckskin shirt. Yes, it was very warm. I was most grateful and asked that he thank the chief for me. But he spoke over my words, "There is no need to thank me Sueki." He stopped speaking then started again. "I have some good news to tell you. We are expecting a trawler from Brighton, Massachusetts in the next day or so depending on weather. They will be trawling for the large fish near the coast of Russian Sakhalin Island. The captain may be willing to take you with him. But, of course, you will have to work out with him the possible arrangements for dropping you off anywhere near Japan. Since you don't have any money to offer you must try and arrange a work passage with the captain. They will only remain here for a few days until they provision."

I was so excited at this news that I could hardly think straight. Many thoughts were racing around in my mind. *Can it be that providence has come to my aid once more?* Two days later I saw the three masts of the ship-rigged trawler with its square sails off in the distance. I was aroused emotionally and began frantic activity so that I would not dwell on this exciting news. I was trying not to count on it too much in the event the captain of the trawler refused to take me. The ship came in closer to the harbor. I could clearly see her bowsprit and the three masts, foremast, main mast and mizzenmast. She remained just outside the harbor entrance and eventually lowered a skiff to bring some passengers ashore.

By the end of the day Captain Macgregor called me into the office and introduced me to the skipper of the trawler. "Sweki, this is Captain John Boling of the trawler U.S.S. Salem." Captain John was a man of medium height with full, nicotine stained beard on his face. He had deep, penetrating blue eyes. Whatever facial skin was visible was bright red. He was smoking a pipe clasped between his yellow teeth which never left his mouth. There was an occasional drool onto his beard as he spoke. He wore a blue naval cap with an eagle emblem on the front. As he spoke he extended his hand in an American style handshake saying something in English which I did not understand. I took his hand and bowed my head in addition.

Captain Macgregor looked at me with a bright facial expression. He began speaking excitedly and hastily causing me to squint at his words, "I took the liberty of arranging everything for you Sweki. I thought it best because of the difficulty with language. Captain John is willing to take you if you are willing to work your passage as a deckhand. He is apparently short handed and I told him you are an experienced sailor. He says he can let you off at the coast of Hokkaido, known as Ezo."

"I don't know what to say Captain Macgregor, I am so happy I am speechless. I am truly grateful and in your debt for all your help and I cannot begin to thank you enough."

SEVEN

I had mixed feelings about leaving the trading post at Cape Flattery. On the one hand, I had deep feelings of attachment to Captain Macgregor. He liberated me from slavery and gave me back my dignity. On the other hand, I was uncomfortable in this strange culture and had a strong desire to return to my native land. In addition, I was anxious to spend my last days in a Buddhist monastery among my own people. The day finally came when I was to leave. I stood before Captain Macgregor to say goodbye. I put my palms together and bowed deeply, "Goodbye Captain Macgregor. Thank you for your many kindnesses to me. I hope your life will be long and pleasant. I shall hold you in my memory forever."

"Goodbye, Sweki, good fortune to you. Have an easy and pleasant trip."

I said goodbye to Sven and turned to board the skiff. While rowing out to the ship I tried to etch the sight of Cape Flattery into my mind. The day was bright but cold and I fingered my new mountain sheepskin jacket lovingly. When we approached the ship I grabbed the hanging rope ladder and hastily climbed up until I reached the railing. I clambered aboard by catching hold of the railing with hands and feet. With great exasperation, I stood before a tall, young man in a blue uniform and wearing a blue naval cap over his long yellow hair. He had a ruddy complexion, blue eyes, and a small fuzzy beard at the end of his chin. He seemed very young to me, no more than twenty years old. "Welcome aboard, my name is Lieutenant Jack Beale. I am the first mate on this ship. I take orders from the captain and give orders to the crew." I did not understand a word he spoke. But suddenly a little Asian man standing next to him translated and repeated his words in Japanese to me in a high pitched, squeaky voice. He was small – not just short. He looked like a young child standing next to the Lieutenant but his face was tawny and hairless. The wrinkles around his eyes belied his age. His eyes were slanted and thus gave away his ethnicity. He continued, "My name is Shibata Mori. Everyone calls me Shib. I am requested by Lieutenant Jack to translate his orders for you when I am able. Please allow me to show you the sleeping quarters and the galley."

I followed him below and he showed me my sleeping hammock hanging from the rafters. Then he showed me the galley and the place at the long table where I would sit. These were obviously inferior accommodations but I could not complain, after all it was my way back home. Suddenly, I heard shouting above deck. "C'mon lads, weigh anchor!" Shib told me to go on deck where the first mate was shouting orders and words of encouragement at a half-dozen men who were pushing a windlass to hoist the anchor out of the water.

I was told by Shib to climb up the ratline and release the sails from their spars. It was a full-rigged ship and other men were releasing sails from spars all along the three masts. I worked my way down the foremast from the fore-skysail to the fore royal and then the fore-top gallant sail, upper fore top sail and lower fore top sail and finally the fore sail. I came down the ratline and jumped on the deck. I looked up to see the extent of canvas fully open to the wind to propel the vessel through the water. The ship was moving with loud creeks. I was excited to feel the craft being propelled by the wind. I could see the captain on the poopdeck at the after section of the vessel. The poop was above the upper deck abaft the mizzen. He was speaking calmly to the boatswain mate while he was at the binnacle steering the ship. The first mate was running about the main deck giving orders to the men who were scurrying hither and thither at his commands.

I was surprised when he grabbed my shirt and pulled me towards a pile of unsightly cordage which he wanted me to wind up with loud orders and gestures. I understood his meaning but I felt his martinet demeanor was unnecessary. I was to later learn that shouting and uncivil ordering by the mate is the way of life on board ship. He could be contemptible and ill-tempered in his desire to get the shipboard tasks accomplished.

So the days went on with constant work from morning until night. My work consisted of working the sails and spars of the foremast when needed by orders from the first mate. I also had to scrub the deck and regularly keep the ship trim, tidy and orderly. This often seemed to me to be a make-work condition since I often repeated clean up on the same spot. But I continued this unnecessary work without objection. Our two-meals-a-day consisted of stews with hardtack known as ship biscuits. In addition, we were given a dram of rum once-a-week to avoid scurvy. This was dispensed under supervision of the first mate from a barrel into our tin cups.

As we sailed in a northerly direction the weather became colder and so I was grateful to have my mountain sheepskin jacket. It took a month or more to reach the outer bank of the island of Hokkaido. Hokkaido, the northern most island of the Japanese archipelago, is a land of natural wonders and, being sparsely populated, abounds in mysterious areas where men have never set foot. It is a forlorn area inhabited mainly by the Ainu people except for fishing colonies of Japanese people on the southern coast. Hakodate is a city situated on the south coast of the island of Hokkaido and on an inlet of the Tsugaru Strait. Hakodate constitutes a good harbor, completely land locked, easily accessible and spacious, with deep water almost up to the shore. This is where I would be left off.

After the ship found a suitable place for anchoring, the anchor was then cast into the sea and thus secured the ship. In the meantime, the skiff was made ready with a rowing crew of four men to take me closer into the inlet. I said goodbye to Captain John Boling and to Lieutenant Jack Beale who stood together with me at the railing, "Good luck to you Sweki," they both said.

"Thank you for all your help," I said in return. Then I turned to Shibata Mori and bowed with a gassho without saying anything. I next crawled over the railing onto the rope ladder and at the lowest rung jumped into the skiff. The oars were held aloft until I could get into the skiff then they were secured in the oar locks and the rowers began the arduous task of propelling me close to the shore all the while avoiding rocks and other impediments as we got closer. It was dark at dusk but I could make out the outline of the shore. No one said anything but as we got closer I could see them rowing slower and more carefully.

As the men rowed I could see the ship receding into the distance. I felt a pang of sorrow mixed with joy as we approached the sacred land of Japan. Waves were breaking against the rocky shore in constant movement. As we approached the men stopped rowing and told me in unintelligible language and gestures to wade ashore. I said goodbye in whispers to the four rowers with American handshakes and waved to them as I stepped into the cool water and silently waded with some difficulty across large boulders made slippery with seaweed, until I came to the flat ground of the shore. I sat on the ground and rested for a few minutes. I could see the skiff returning to the ship which was somewhere off in the dark night.

No one was around. For the month that I was on board the USS Salem I made no friends with anyone unless my limited conversations with Shibata Mori count as friendship. I spent the month on board in back-breaking labor but now that I am here all alone in this strange land I am looking forward to my new life among my own people. But first I must find sustenance and shelter. I decide to avoid the Japanese colony since they may return me to officialdom. I must find an Ainu village.

EIGHT

I picked myself up and started trudging inland in search of some friendly Ainu people all the while avoiding the Japanese colony. The Ainu, the native aborigine population of the Hokkaido, are believed to be descendants of early Caucasian type peoples. Their numbers have been decreasing through intermarriage with the Japanese. The Ainu people are an ethnic group indigenous to Hokkaido, the Kuril Islands, and much of Sakhalin. The area is habitat of brown bears and I must be very careful not to encounter them. They roam in the Hideka Mountain range, in the forest of Mt. Daisetsuzan so I don't think I will have any problems with them.

Most Ainu are proficient in speaking the Japanese language so I don't expect any trouble in communicating with them. Their economic life is based on farming as well as hunting, fishing, and gathering. Ainu men generally have dense hair development with full beards and moustaches whereas Japanese men have minimal body and facial hair. The Ainu women tattoo their mouths and forearms. In walking inland it was my hope to come across a village with their reed-thatched huts. Because of intermarriage many Ainu are indistinguishable from their Japanese neighbors. I thought perhaps I could blend in with my long hair and wispy beard; they may even take me for an Ainu speaking Japanese.

It was so dark that I had much difficulty in making my way. There were no stars in the sky and moving clouds hid the moon. I stumbled a few times. I bumped into trees and was caught by a thistle bush. I stopped and rested in order to make a decision about continuing. That night I slept on the ground feeling warm enough wearing my mountain sheepskin jacket despite the cold climate. I hoped to continue my quest for an Ainu village at first light. I wanted to avoid the Japanese colony at all costs since I could be turned over to some official as an illegal immigrant. During the Tokugawa Shogunate there was a law that anyone who leaves Japan is not allowed to return. This was done in order to prevent bringing back modern influence from the outside world.

I continued on stealthily. There was darkness ahead of me, the total darkness of the countryside. I managed to walk along, dragging my feet through the wooded area. At first I wasn't aware of the smell; my mouth was a sewer, my nose filled with sweat and dirt. I stopped and looked about. Then I noticed it: dung - dung just ahead. I walked along, into the darkness, hoping for the best. I came upon the dung heap, apparently used for fertilizing the fields. I began running away and walking hastily away to avoid the dung heap.

I walked faster, swathed in the stink of dung, until finally my legs gave in. I fell down exhausted until dawn lying in a ditch. I drank muddy water and collapsed into the darkness. As the sun rose the sky was aflame. Every corner of my body was on fire; encrusted with mud and dung. At least I am alive. I got up and looked about but all I could see were fields, forest and the edge of a wood a few miles ahead. I had to get on. But I'll have to wait for the darkness again. My bag seems to have doubled in weight.

I am very weak and very hungry. I've got to eat something. A few meters away I saw green ears of corn growing. I grabbed them by the handful and chewed them and swallowed them down with difficulty. I must look for a refuge, far from here, somewhere safe. I wonder what I must look like. I must find an Ainu village, but I must travel and search at night to avoid discovery. I heard of shipwrecked sailors being executed on capture. It is too dangerous during the daytime. I am too close to the shoreline where the Japanese fishing colony has been established. I found a sinecure in a field of tall wild grass and waited there until evening. At dusk I started out again in search of the Ainu village. Indeed, I am not sure they will accept me or possibly they would turn me over to the Japanese authorities. I must risk that possibility. For two nights I had been walking in the forest, all my senses alert, jumping at the slightest sound, the wing-beats of birds, the distant howling of wolves that runs down the spine and loosens the bowels. Heading north until my legs wouldn't hold me and I fell to the ground. I've devoured whatever I could get hold of, acorns, wild berries to ease the pangs, when hunger bites.

Wait, wait, and then I saw the embers of a fire appearing through the bushes. I went closer creeping up behind an oak tree. Yes, yes, it was a campfire surrounded by a group of hairy, bushy men sitting on their haunches and eating the flesh of a roasted animal. It was a frightening sight because of the unknown and unfamiliarity of the men. At the same time I was comforted by the awareness of humanity. My mouth watered at the thought and sight of the roasted meat. I was sure they were not Japanese and hoped they might be friendly Ainu. I slowly slithered out of the wood and approached the men with hand waving greetings. They were startled at the sight of me and began rising in slow, careful, defensive backward movements.

"Who are you?" one man said in Japanese.

I was amazed and grateful at the sound of the Japanese language and carefully responded, "My name is Sueki and I have been put ashore here by a fishing boat that rescued me."

The men relaxed and the one who spoke in Japanese said, "You look terrible. You must be hungry. Come join us and partake of this juicy badger meat."

I was very relieved at hearing this. I nearly collapsed at the campfire and began tearing at the roasted meat, stuffing pieces in my mouth. "Thank you. Thank you," I exclaimed while chewing the meat and swallowing large morsels.

As I was eating the large man who spoke Japanese approached me and sat nearby,. "My name is Hodka and these men are my brothers. We are Ainu people on a hunting trip. You don't look Japanese but you don't look Ainu either. Who are you, may I ask?"

With my mouth full and the fat running down my chin I answered, "I am a Japanese sailor. My junk capsized in a storm more than a year ago and I drifted on the current to America where I was rescued by the English Hudson Bay Company and eventually was provided with a berth on a fishing vessel that dropped me off here."

"I see. But your hair length makes you look like an Ainu. Are you disguised to avoid the Japanese authorities?"

"Well when I was floating on the current I vowed to the Buddha that if he rescued me I would let my hair grow until I was rescued and then I would cut my hair off and enter a monastery."

"There are no monasteries around here," Hodka exclaimed forthrightly.

"Yes, I know. I hope to sail across to the Honshu mainland disguised as an Ainu. Do you think that is possible?"

Hodka looked at me pensively with his deep set eyes, "Maybe, but first come back with us to our village where you can bathe in the river. You smell awful. What happened to you?"

"I am sorry for my condition," I answered, "I was traveling at night to avoid detection and without knowing it I crossed over a dung heap."

"Ha! Ha!" Hodka began laughing loudly, "I now understand. When you first appeared the smell on you and your appearance made me think you were a bear."

The brothers also picked up the humor and began laughing as well. *A good sense of humor is the first sign of friendliness.*

After I finished eating I joined the troupe on the return journey to their village. They brought with them two large badgers which were eviscerated and slung on poles to be carried on their shoulders back to the village. Two of the brothers went off into the depths of the bushes to urinate. I could hear them splashing into the grass. After walking some considerable distance we arrived at the village. Hodka immediately came up to me and showed me the river where I was to bathe. I took off my mountain sheepskin jacket and entered the river fully clothed in my buckskin trouser and shirt. I scrubbed myself as best I could and scrubbed my buckskins knowing they would dry rapidly. My mountain sheepskin jacket seemed to be free of odor so I put it over my shoulders until I could dry.

Hodka was waiting for me by the riverside. He showed me to his hut. The hut was reed-thatched about six meters square without partitions and a fireplace in the center. There was no chimney, but only a hole at the angle of the roof; there was only one window on the eastern side and there were two doors.

Hodka was a rather tall man, about two meters in height. He had a large head which was covered completely with black hair. This dense head of hair mingled with a bushy long beard. His whole face seemed to be covered with hair. His mouth was not visible and one could barely make out his nose and deep set eyes. He wore a long sleeved caftan of indiscriminate color, which was belted at the waist and leggings made of deerskin. He spoke with a deep, mellow voice, "Come inside and sit." He provided a fur-skin mat for me to sit on. "Sit and rest by the fire to dry off," he said. There was a woman inside who had long hair but no facial hair. Her forearms and top lip was tattooed with a black ink of sorts and she sported a necklace, which I learned was called a *tamasay*. She looked down and averted my eyes.

"This place which is called Hokkaido by the Japanese is known to us as *Ezo*. Our people came here from Sakhalin Island in Russia and there are many Ainu people in Northern Honshu as well. Most Ainu people speak Russian or Japanese in addition to our traditional language. The Ainu lived in this place a hundred thousand years before the Children of the Sun came. We are farmers as well as hunters and fishermen. The Japanese moved north to Hokkaido to take control of Ainu lands. We offered no resistance and the Japanese established fishing posts along the shoreline. We are considered Japanese citizens but we retain much of our own culture."

"I see. That is very interesting," I said thinking how this could help me get to Northern Honshu. I went inside the hut at Hodka's beckoning and squatted down on my heels on the thick fur-skin floor covering. We began a conversation in which I related my tribulations and adventures to Hodka since the shipwreck more than a year ago. He could not believe my good fortune in surviving such distress and suffering. "Well, you are with us now. We shall make you comfortable until you are ready to leave," he said.

"Thank you, Hodka. I am most grateful."

Hodka seemed to be interested in life on mainland Japan and eventually his questions turned to the Shogun. "Why did the Shogun allow your junk to travel up the coast during that time of the year? Even here in Ezo we get the brunt of the Autumn storms."

I hesitated for a minute but then blurted out, "He is a selfish, avaricious man with no regard for the sanctity of human life. He was so anxious to receive his tribute that he risked the lives of some sailors to get it sooner rather than wait until spring when there would be no storms. Now the tribute is gone, some of it eaten by the fish and some unfortunate sailors drowned. I was the only one who survived."

"Will he request a replacement tribute?"

"Of course," I readily added. I had no words to soothe the remorse I felt for my powerlessness and the guilt of being alive.

"You look tired why not sleep by the fire," Hodka remarked after patting my shoulder in sympathy.

"Yes, thank you. I am tired," I replied.

"You will have much work to do starting in the morning, if that is agreeable. We will keep you with us and provide for your needs until you leave us, but you must work to stay with us."

"I see. Yes, certainly. Hodka, thank you for your kindness," I remarked with a yawn.

"Alright then, I will see you at first light. Goodnight."

I dozed off instantly under the cover of a large bearskin.

NINE

The business of earning your daily bread is really sad and wearisome. People come up with the most pious lies about work. It is just another abominable form of idolatry, a dog licking the rod that beats it – work.

In the morning, Hodka requested that I chop wood. I was at the axe and chopping block from daybreak. I chopped firewood in the area separating the orchard from the vegetable garden. I've only been here two days and I've got to earn my hospitality. Well, I have a place to sleep and a plate of soup. I'm still alive, I don't know how. I won't be setting off again for a while. These were long, unbearable days; cleaning the hut, stacking wood, mulching, hoeing and weeding the vegetable rows, picking the fruit in the little orchard and mending the worn-out tools. The work consisted of repetitive tasks, movements imposed on the limbs, for the equivalent of a bowl of dog food. It is ironic that I went off to sea because I didn't want to work on a farm. Yet I found myself farming with the Makah Indians and now with the Ainu. You could say farming saved my life.

My brother approached me in the wet rice paddy where I was planting the seed rice. It was back-breaking work and the weather didn't help my situation. It was damnable hot.

"Sueki, when I inherit the farm from father, I would expect you to work for me. I shall treat you well and give you a portion of the profit we make," he exclaimed in an officious and authoritative manner.

I looked up and stretched my back by leaning back as my eyes looked to the blazing sky. I wiped my sweating brow with my forearm, "No, thank you I am not interested in farming. I am going to sea, if they will have me."

One of the few pleasant things about the day was chatting with Salina, Hodka's wife, a slow-witted woman who tends to all of Hodka's needs. She actually does almost all the talking, while axe blows fall on the logs of wood. She smiles, her mouth half toothless and her hands have calluses from a lifetime of menial labor. She talks about the times at night she has sex with Hodka. For people like Salina it's the most sacred of pleasures. She laughs like a mad woman, spitting and spluttering all over the place. Her Japanese is very faulty but I was able to follow her. For Hodka, on the other hand, there isn't much talking to be done. He's a fine enough man and I really like him. He says that fate and the supreme will of the gods decreed the burden of our lives, as something that must take place, that the unfathomable supreme power of the gods exhorts us to understand through his signs, even signs that are tragic or gloomy, that the will of the just and meritorious men is not enough to bring about a change. What a crock! I don't believe any of it for a moment. But I must stay in the good graces of Hodka. To disagree would be enough to invite disaster. That is why I shook my head up and down in agreement. Anyway, as a child I was told by my mother about the Kami, the gods of the Shinto religion of Japan. So we aren't much different in our beliefs.

After a week of living with Hodka and Salina in there hut I was invited by Hodka and his brothers to go with them on a hunt. We trekked up into the mountain area in search of deer. The men all spread out holding bows and arrows at the ready. They were creeping and crawling like reptiles, very quiet out of sight. It was deathly silent. I was behind Hodka carrying the necessary utensils and implements for eviscerating and preparing the carcass. I tried not to make any noise and was intent on following Hodka.

Suddenly, I was astonished at the sound of breaking tree limbs behind me, a sound growing louder and closer. There it was. I saw a large brown bear charging through the forest at breakneck speed with loud grunts and growls; a deep threatening sound made by the surly bear. He leaped at me and we fell down together. I could feel the hot breath of his mouth as he snapped at me. In the next instant the bear collapsed with blood spurting from his head like a fountain all over me. I could see an axe protruding from his skull with the blood spewing and Hodka standing behind the bear grinning like a spoiled child. The weight of the bear was crushing me and I had all I could do to topple it over, the vomit rising to my throat taking my breath away. Hodka was laughing, "Ha! Ha! You make good bait, Sueki."

I didn't think it was funny and said so with vehemence, "Not funny, Hodka, I was frightened out of my wits."

"Ha! Ha! Now you will have to clean yourself in the river again."

I noticed, in addition to being covered with the bear's blood I had released my bowels and my buckskin pants were feculent. I smelled of blood and feces, damn it. I sat on the ground in a total state of discomfit as I was abashed in the presence of the men. I just sat there glad to be alive and grateful for Hodka's quick action. I watched the men as they skinned the bear and removed his hide with singular deftness. They cut the carcass into smaller pieces for easier transportability.

Hodka spoke softly, "I am sorry to laugh at your problem but I must tell you that we love to eat bear meat. We don't often get it, bears avoid humans. Thanks to you we shall feast for days to come."

At the village I bathed in the river once again. I removed my buckskins and scrubbed them clean; then I dressed in the wet buckskins and sat by the fire in the hut until I dried sufficiently to be comfortable. Salina was outside by the campfire roasting large pieces of the bear meat on wooden skewers. The aroma of the grilled bear meat was mouth watering. I found I was salivating at the thought of eating such a delicious morsel. She called me to come out and partake in the festivities. I saw her offering me a roasted piece of meat on a stick. I grabbed it willingly and consumed it by taking great bites on the shank of meat with loud chewing noises. The meat was stringy and fatty which ran down my beard but I did not care. I was ravenously hungry from my near-death experience. My mouth dribbled but I wiped it with my hand and let out a large burp.

The men were drinking and passing around a gourd containing fermented fruit juice which had a high alcoholic content. I was later told that imbibing was not a passion of the Ainu except on special occasions such as an unusual kill. As the day went on into evening some of the men including Hodka became very inebriated. I decide to retire being very upset with the day's events. I went into the hut, took off my damp buckskins and covered my nude body with the furry bearskin and went to sleep at my end of the hut. The warm fire embers gave off a comforting spicy and pungent aroma. Soon I was fast asleep. Sometime during the night I felt someone touching my penis. Could it be a succubus? There was a body next to me. Then I heard the chimerical giggle of Salina in my ear as she began nibbling and licking my ear lobe. My penis became hard and swollen. Then without speaking she straddled me with her legs wide apart and sat astride me. She next grabbed my stiff penis and slid my penis smoothly into her vagina. She began gyration movements which within minutes caused me to reach coitus. When she was finished she left me to go I know not where. In the meantime I thought about this event for a long time before falling asleep. Why did she do this? Wasn't her sexual hunger sated by Hodka? I, of course, was satisfied to the fullest. I have not had sex with a woman for a long time. But the danger was obviously manifest. What if Hodka found out? What recourse would I have? After all I did not pursue Salina, she came onto me. I never solicited sex from her. She and I only had work relations. I must be careful. This could become a very precarious situation. I fell into a troubled sleep causing me to fidget under the bearskin. I noticed the embers of the fire were smoldering in their ashes. A cold wind was blowing through the hut which caused me to shiver. Is this an omen of some future disaster?

In the morning, Hodka approached me, "Sueki, my brothers and I are going fishing. Would you like to come along and help?"

I looked at him and saw no sign of suspicion in his eyes, "Yes, yes, indeed, I would like to help very much." Once again the men had me carry things such as the huge bundle of nets which was placed on my shoulders as we trudged along to a steep escarpment overlooking the sea. I placed the bundled net on the ground. Hodka spoke to me in a restraint way, "we must make our way down by the trail to the left. Pick up the nets and follow us, we are going to the small inlet below us." He pointed to the shore below which had a beach. I looked but was worried. "Wouldn't the Japanese fishermen spot us?" I inquired with much trepidation.

"Nonsense, we are Ainu. This is our country. If they are there they will not bother us."

"What about me?" I questioned directly at him.

He looked at me with compelling eyes and coercion in his voice, "Didn't you say you were Ainu too? Now is the time to test it, besides there are no Japanese fishermen in this inlet."

Yes, it is true. I felt like an Ainu. I even look like an Ainu. I have even adopted some of their habits and mannerisms including words and phrases of their native language. Hodka's confidence in me helped me overcome my fear of the Japanese authorities.

I shouldered the large bundle of nets with renewed vigor and followed the men down the trail until we reached the shore. It was rough going and several times I almost tripped. The bundle on my shoulders became heavier as we walked cautiously down. Finally, we reached the shore and I deposited the bundle on the sand. The men came and took it apart. The bundle actually consisted of several smaller nets. These smaller nets were tossed deftly by the men into the sea to snare fish in their meshes. As I watched the men in their netting movements I was impressed by their expertise. I couldn't help thinking of a dancing ritual. But they did catch fish. When they retrieved the nets they would bring them to the beach and I would pick out the squirming fish and place them in a pail of sea water *I could not help thinking about my fishing prowess when I was on the board in the current.* After several hours our fishing duties were completed. I was requested to carry the pail with the fish whilst the men carried the individual nets. The pail was very heavy and the handle dug into the skin on my hands. The trail going up was arduous and difficult and several times I felt my feet slipping backwards but after a time we reached the top of the escarpment where I sat and rested. I was sweating profusely and was totally exhausted from the climb.

Hodka came over to me and suggested that we make a pole from a tree limb and sling it through the pail handle; then it can be carried between two men on their shoulders. When we returned to the village Salina and some of the other women began the drudgery of scaling and eviscerating the fish. I was told by Salina to bury the entrails in the vegetable patch as a fertilizer. After completing this task I returned to the open area in front of the huts where I found Salina and some of the other women chopping the fish meat into small pieces on a smoothly shaved log. They were comminuting and making a fish-force meat in which the fish is chopped very finely and highly seasoned with lemongrass and green onions. It is served with some cooked esculent vegetables such as beans or lentils.

That evening we all sat around the camp fire in a circle partaking of the fish-force meat. It was in a bowl which was passed around from person to person. Each person ladled out a mouthful with a cupped hand after which the fingers were licked clean. This occurred several times until the bowl was empty. Then the cooked vegetables were served. Afterwards the gourd containing the fermented fruit juice was passed from person to person. I was grateful for the drink since I found my throat parched from the piquant tartness of the fish. The acrid taste was pleasant but it did whet my mouth for copious quantities of the fermented fruit drink. The result was that I became dizzy and decided to go off to sleep in the hut before I got into a drunken stupor. I removed my buckskins and shoved my nude body under the bearskin covering. I fell asleep immediately with strange dreams running through my mind.

I was being chased by a group of Japanese policemen. I knew they were Japanese policemen by their blue uniforms and brass buttons. They were waving their batons in the air in a threatening manner and shouting obscene epithets at me. I was running as fast as my legs would carry me but the police-mob was gaining on me. Then I spotted a tram running on street tracks just ahead. I quickly reached out while running to grab the rear escutcheon on which the name *seppuku* (suicide by disembowelment) was emblazoned. I lifted myself up only to find that the tram reversed itself just at that moment and was now heading back toward the police-mob. They pulled me off the tram and pummeled me soundly with their batons until I woke up screaming.

"What is it?" shouted Hodka from across the room.

I was bleary-eyed but answered immediately, "It's nothing, I just had a bad dream." Then we both were silent. I was lying under the bearskin in the darkness with my eyes open for a long time and pondered the meaning of this dream. Is this the fate awaiting me if I return to mainland Japan? What is the significance of the name on the tram medallion? I have struggled for more than two years to stay alive under the most arduous conditions. My suffering cannot be for naught. I could certainly stay here amongst the Ainu forever. I am getting to be so much like them. But I am obligated to honor my promise to the Buddha to eventually enter a Buddhist monastery. If I was able to float thousands of kilometers on the Kuroshio Current across the Pacific Ocean half frozen and dying of thirst and hunger then I will be able to reach my destination and complete my destiny.

The next morning we had a breakfast consisting of cooked millet laced with sliced apples. I ate in silence thinking about my bad dream last night. Then I heard Hodka's voice, "Do not dwell on your dream, Sueki. It means nothing. Bad dreams come from thoughts of hate and worry. Good dreams come from things you love and enjoy. You should go to sleep with good thoughts from now on."

"Yes, yes, you are right but I suspect it has more to do with the fermented fruit juice that I drank."

"Ha, ha, you were drunk alright."

"Yes, once when I was home on the farm I drank a lot of sake which made me very drunk."

"Elder brother I have finished tilling the soil so I am leaving for the farmhouse now. The weather is stifling hot and I need a rest," I said as I wiped the sweat off my brow.

"Yes, you are right. It is very hot and we can use the shade of the farmhouse. Let's go."

We walked together until we reached the shade which the farmhouse cast on the ground. "Come inside," my brother said. "I have a treat for you."

I followed him into the house and saw him remove a bottle of sake from the kitchen shelf. He poured two glasses of sake and offered one to me. I never had sake before and I found it smooth and restful. "Thank you," I said as I continued drinking the pale liquid but I quickly found myself getting very dizzy and thoroughly drum bled. My brother took me into my room and put me to sleep.

"Alright," said Hodka impatiently, "You will work on the farm today with Salina. My brothers and I will go into the hills to collect wild vegetables."

"Are the men really your brothers?" I asked with cautious curiosity.

Hodka hesitated then explained, "The word for brother in the Ainu language is the same for friend and neighbor."

"I see, and then am I a brother?"

"Well, if you stay with us we will help you build a hut and provide you with a woman. Then we shall call you brother and you will become part of our community."

"I really appreciate your offer and am honored that you would include me in your community but I must think about it. In some ways I am anxious to get back to my people and, of course, there is my promise to the Buddha who spared my life."

"I understand. We can talk about it later, if you like." He hurried off to catch up with the men to search for wild vegetables. I was left with Salina.

We shouldered our hoes and went to work to cultivate the vegetable patch. We worked independent of each other in utter silence along the uniform rows of growing vegetables. My back was aching from bending over and I was sweating from exposure to the scorching sun which was beating down on me mercilessly. After a few hours of dogged work Salina approached me and spoke to me in an officious and impudent manner, "Take this pail and go to the beach and fill it with sea water. Be careful not to pick up any seaweed or other rubbish." She handed me the pail then started to turn and walk away.

"Wait, May I ask what the sea water is for?"

She hesitated for a moment but turned as if in a quandary, "The men will return soon from gathering the wild cabbage palm. I must prepare the camp fire and boil the sea water which you will bring back to make a stew of the cabbage. Now, do you understand?"

I was repulsed by her manner but answered, "Yes, yes, I only wanted the information." I took the pail in a huff and made my way down the trail which reminded me of the time when I first arrived after being let off by the sailors and I happened on the campfire of Hodka and his brothers. I now knew to avoid the dung heap. The thought of it sent a shiver through my body. At the beach I walked into the surf and dipped the pail into the sea taking up a large quantity of sea water. At the shoreline I put down the pail and after inspection removed some seaweed, pieces of wood splinters and a few small sea shells. When the water appeared clean I picked up the pail by its handle and began trudging back to our village site. Just then I heard a loud voice calling, "Halloo!"

I turned to see a Japanese gentleman dressed in the conventional Japanese clothing of a long black coat with balloon sleeves and a split skirt trouser that I remembered. He came nearer speaking in faultless Japanese, "Hello, do you speak Japanese?"

I immediately surmised that he thought I was an Ainu native. I decided to continue the ruse and answered in the dialect used by Hodka, "Yes, I speak a little Japanese."

He bowed and said in a staccato voice, "My name is Kondo Harumi. I work as a surveyor for the Japanese Fishing Colony. I just arrived yesterday and I am happy to meet you."

I returned the bow somewhat hesitantly and decided to continue the artifice by using Hodka's name, "Good afternoon and welcome to Ezo. My name is Hodka. I live on top of this hill with my brothers and their families."

"I see. What will you do with that pail of sea water?" he asked with some forbearance.

"Oh, this pail of sea water will be used for cooking vegetables," I quickly answered patiently.

"Cooking vegetables isn't that interesting."

He looked at me in a curious way so I said, "Well, I must go now. It was very nice meeting you."

He continued looking at me and then quizzically and slowly asked, "Can we meet again one day soon?"

I hesitated for a minute but then quickly recovered my thoughts and responded, "I think not. I almost never come down to the shoreline. Besides I am very busy with my daily chores and would not have the time."

"Alright, then, goodbye," he said mildly annoyed.

We parted company and I trudged back up to the Ainu village. I was struck by the ease with which I "passed" as an Ainu person. It seemed that the trick was to believe in oneself with confidence. Using Honda's Japanese accent was a fortuitous stroke of luck. I may look like an Ainu but the purity of my Japanese speech would certainly give me away. I must remember that and practice colloquial speech more often when I speak with Hodka.

Towards dusk, the men returned with the wild cabbage palms. They were tossed on the ground and separated into several equal piles. Salina began removing the badly spoiled leaves from the green leafy cabbage and then placing them into the boiling sea water which was already prepared on the fire when I returned. In the boiling water the palm buds began opening and releasing the leafy cabbages to the water where they softened into a heap of leafy vegetation. The cooked leaves were placed in a bowl and passed around to be eaten with the hands. The cooked cabbage leaves had a sour, salty taste which gave off a delicious vinegary taste and aroma. Picking up the hot cabbage with the fingers was difficult but worth the taste. The cabbage was accompanied with cooked soy beans adding to the repast. The juice of the cooked cabbage had a somewhat fermented, briny taste which I enjoyed slurping as I drank from the edge of the bowl. At the conclusion of our meal I spoke with Hodka about my experience with the Japanese gentleman.

In his pontificating style, Hodka said, "I am glad this meeting occurred. It means that the Japanese will accept you as an Ainu. The longer you stay with us the better it will be for you."

Little did Hodka realize that the incident with the Japanese gentleman gave me the increased courage to leave for the mainland? I went to sleep that night feeling pleasantly satisfied. Sometime during the night when all was dark and everyone was sleeping I felt someone creeping beneath my bear skin. As I feared, it was Salina who curled her arms around my naked body and began rubbing up against me with her legs. She did not speak and I was too frightened to speak knowing that Hodka was only a stone's throw away. I had no choice but to have sex with her. On completion she moved stealthily and furtively away to Hodka, I assumed.

The next morning I decided to speak with Hodka about making arrangements for my departure.

"Hodka, I must talk with you about my leaving."

"You have really decided to leave?"

"Yes, I think I am ready. I want you to know that I am grateful for all your help."

"And despite that you want to leave?"

"Yes, yes, I think I am ready."

"Well, I tried to keep you with us by making your life pleasant and productive including giving you Salina for your pleasure."

On hearing this I was taken aback with astonishment and disbelief of his words. "Do you mean to tell me that you arranged for Salina to have sex with me?"

"Yes, of course, she didn't mind and I had to think of ways to keep you with us."

I was aghast. "But why, to what purpose, I sputtered.

"The reason was very simple. I wanted you to appreciate our life so that you will agree to stay with us. Many Japanese people have intermarried with the Ainu. I thought that by allowing you to work and enjoy a family life you might stay with us."

I was annoyed and petulant at his last statement, "Allowed me to work? I felt like an indentured servant."

He looked at me with large eyes in amazement, "Not so, we took you in when you were lost. We fed you and gave you a place to sleep. We asked you to work in order to pay for your keep. We taught you our ways and methods of survival. If you did not work then you would have lost all self-worth. Work gave you dignity and a sense of accomplishment. You were not a servant or a slave. You were treated as a member of our family. You could have left at anytime without recriminations. We offered you a place to live after your many trials and tribulations. Now you want to leave and I can understand that but, please, do not bite the hand that feeds you."

"I am very sorry, Hodka. I spoke without thinking. I am truly grateful to you and the other members of your family. Without you I might have perished in the forest. You saved my life when the bear attacked me. I shall never forget your kindness to me. Please forgive me."

"Yes, enough said. Tomorrow I shall discuss with you the way to get to Honshu."

TEN

Can our actions change our destiny? Or are they like sand piled up against the breakage in a dam, merely delaying the inevitable? I chopped wood all morning long waiting for Hodka to meet with me for a discussion regarding my leaving. But he never came. I kept on working until lunchtime when finally I saw Hodka who gave me a sign of recognition but otherwise was silent. For lunch we had corn soup more like chowder which was thickened with May apples of mawkish flavor. The men seemed sullen and disinterested as they slurped their soup emitting loud noises. I was becoming impatient. I had to have Hodka's help before I left.

After eating I rose and slowly approached Hodka who was seated with a group of his "brothers" huddled in conversation. For a moment I stopped just before them then sat on my haunches to listen uninvited. I could not understand their speech because they were speaking in their native Ainu language. Hodka noticed me and nodded his head. They were having a mildly heated discussion and every once in a while Hodka would raise his head and jut his chin forward as if to recognize my presence. I was able to catch a word here and there which was familiar to me but in reality I had no idea of the subject under discussion.

Some of the men began rising as the discussion came to an end. Hodka walked over to me as I got up. He clasped my shoulder with one hand and spoke as I straightened up, "Good day, Sueki. I was just discussing with my brothers the best way to help you with your departure."

I was startled. "Really, how wonderful. I had no idea of the reason for the congregation of the men."

Hodka continued uninterrupted, "We think it best if you go to my cousin in northern Honshu. In that way you will have a destination to disclose to the ferry man should it come up and so avoid suspicion. You will not have to speak with him since I will accompany you and be present as you board the ferry. The ferry man is Japanese and you will have to "pass" the same way you did with the Japanese gentleman you encountered on the beach. Remember he is the checkpoint for entering mainland Japan."

"Oh, that's great," I said with a deep breath and a long exhale. "I'm sure it will work out. I have every confidence in my ability."

"I am going to provide you with a map which will get you from the landing place of the ferry to the place where my cousin lives. He is married to a Japanese woman and lives in a regular house. You might say he is civilized or better yet Japonified. Ha! Ha!"

We both laughed at this remark after which Hodka continued, "I must forewarn you that I haven't seen my cousin in many years. I am not able to give you a worthwhile description of him or any hint of recognition; He may not even accept you. But I am sure you will be able to manage. At least you will be in a safe area where the Japanese authorities do not patrol and have no presence. Once you cut off your hair no one will care about you because you will just be like every other Japanese citizen."

"I don't know how to thank you, Hodka. I shall remember your kindness forever."

Hodka hung his head in embarrassment and as his face reddened slowly said, "If you like we can go to the ferry slip after the morning meal tomorrow. The trip across will take several hours and you should be in northern Honshu by late afternoon."

"That's wonderful, Hodka. Thank you."

I spent the rest of the day working on the farm. As I was bending over while hoeing the furrows I noticed Salina coming towards me. She had an expressionless look on her face as she said, "Would you take out enough soy beans to fill this basket?" She handed me a rough hewn basket and left. I was slightly miffed at her standoffish attitude but complied with her request, nay her demand. Perhaps I shouldn't blame her having been a pawn in Hodka's plan to persuade me to remain in the village. Still, we had work in common and decency requires some kind of acknowledgement. *"Oh well," I said to myself "I'll be gone soon enough."* These petty problems meant nothing at this point. Actually we were very friendly before the sexual encounters. Her present demeanor is understandable but her quarrel should be with Hodka not me.

I don't know what came over me. I was in a high state of anxiety. At the evening meal that night, I made a speech to the gathering crowd, "Tomorrow I shall be leaving you. I want to thank all of you for treating me like a brother. I shall never forget you. If I successfully return to my people I shall always be for equal rights for the Ainu people. Know that there will now be a voice in Japan on behalf of the Ainu people." There were loud favorable comments and murmurs from the group. Some men came over to me with backslapping encouraging words. Then the crowd dissipated into their individual huts while others continued sitting around small campfires.

The next morning Hodka and I trekked to the escarpment and followed along a winding trail on its edge until we came to the bottom. We walked along the beach to a weathered-wooden ferry slip along which was docked a sloop. It was a fore-and-aft rigged vessel with one mast and a single headsail jib. I was amazed at its size and knew that such a sea-worthy vessel was needed to brave the channel between Hokkaido and Honshu. There were several people on board already and I noticed a sprinkling of Ainu among the passengers. I could make them out by their full beards and hair.

We approached the ferry man who sat with feigned indifference at a small wooden table. He wore a blue uniform with brass buttons and sported a visor cap on his head. He looked up at me with severely slanted eyes and said, "Are you going to Hokkaido?"

"Yes," I answered.

"Then that will be ten Sen.," he quickly remarked.

Hodka placed the coins on the table without speaking.

As the ferry man retrieved the coins with his thumb and fingers and turned his head I noticed he had a scar that furrowed his left cheek and ran down to his neck. His grey inexpressive eyes told of someone who had seen a great battle. His voice echoes as though from a cave, "You may get aboard. We shall be leaving in about an hour."

I took a deep breath to quell the panic. I overcame the first hurdle. Hodka took me aside to give me the promised map and last minute instructions. I stammered with my mouth dry and my breath trapped in my chest, "Hodka, I want to thank you for all you have done for me. Without you I might have been a lost soul." I removed my mountain sheepskin jacket and handed it to Hodka. "This is my most valuable possession. I want you to have it, as a token of my appreciation." The jacket worn and filthy was draped over Hodka's shoulders. Gratitude was written in the expression on his face.

"Goodbye, Sueki. Do not forget us. If you ever come back you will always have a home with us."

With bleary eyes I said, "Goodbye Hodka. I shall never forget you." I shouldered my bag and boarded the sloop as I waved my hand to Hodka. I saw him turn and trudge up the trail to his Ainu home with the mountain sheepskin jacket bouncing up and down on his back.

ELEVEN

The weather was warm and sunny and the movement of the sloop stirred the wind to create a pleasant breeze. The balloon sail was full and dragged us along with speed. I was sitting cross-legged in the center of the boat amongst other passengers, some were eating, and most were chatting. I was preoccupied thinking about my future. A young well-dressed Japanese gentleman suddenly roused me from my reverie by coming up to me speaking in Japanese. I decided for safety's sake not to enter into conversation with him so I faked answers to his questions with the few Ainu words and expressions I knew. He was startled but bowed and said in Japanese, "I am sorry I do not speak Ainu." I smiled secretly to myself at his surprise as he walked away. I now knew that I would not be bothered by the Japanese passengers any more on this voyage.

After about an hour of sailing a dark cloud appeared above us blocking out the sun. Then the rain began. At first it was falling in small drops but in time it became a steady downpour. People about me tried covering themselves to avoid getting wet, to no avail. I was soaked and blue with cold from the pelting rain. I thought of my mountain sheepskin jacket, *it is now on the back of Hodka*. Suddenly the rain stopped almost as soon as it started and a great shout was emitted from the passengers. The sun came out once again and my buckskins dried out rather quickly. We continued racing to the peninsula Shinokita of Honshu unimpeded by the sea. I feel something happening getting closer to Honshu with each passing minute – something is struggling to get out. But I choke it back down again to the pit of my stomach with all my strength. *I'll be home soon.*

After another hour someone shouted, "Land, land ahead." I got up and squinted at the horizon where I could make out a long chain of purple mountains appearing like a smudge at the end of the sea. I felt the excitement of the passengers, some were shouting, others were dancing. Could that really be Honshu? I felt my heart pounding loudly in my chest. Can this be a turning point in my life?

It took some time for the sloop to approach landfall and dock at the pier where it was finally tied up. People who had been standing began debarking hurriedly across the narrow gangplank. I buried myself within a group of Ainu to avoid detection. We shuffled along almost like a single organism. No one stopped us although I noticed some uniformed men on shore watching us and curiously examining us from a distance. My heart was in my throat as I moved along in a dragging gait with the Ainu crowd. Some of the Ainu attempted speaking to me in a friendly manner but all I could do is smile and respond by shaking my head to statements I did not understand. It seemed to work because as we reached the strand everyone dissipated to find their own way.

I kept walking until I reached the streets of the small village of Oma. There was an aggregation of small wooden houses facing the streets. My first impression was that it was a primitive organized agricultural community. I saw a few villagers walking on the streets and some walking in and out of the local merchants. The merchants or traders had signs written in Kanji on cloth banners in front of their establishments. I realized to my astonishment that this was the first time in over three years that I walked on a real city street. I decide to get directions to Hodka's cousin's house by making inquiry in one of the small stores. I approached the shopkeeper with deference and held out the map which was given to me by Hodka. I spoke to him in a courteous and complaisant way, "Kind sir, are you able to help me? I am looking for the proper direction to take to find this house." I pointed to a spot on the map. He looked at me in disbelief but withheld comment. I spoke again, "Please do not be disturbed by my appearance. I am Japanese. I just returned from working in Hokkaido. Can you help me?"

As if by magic he overcame his disquietude and took the map in his hand and began studying it. "Ah, yes, I see, you must take the main road to your right." He went to the door and pointed. "Walk out of town until you come to a rice paddy field. Walk along the dike across the paddy until you come to a road on the other side. Then you should follow your map towards the city of Omate." He returned the map to me after gently folding it. I said in an obsequious tone, "Thank you, kind sir, I am most grateful." I bowed and left the premises to continue my journey to Hodka's cousin.

By this time the sun had set and it was getting dark. I found the road beyond the rice paddy and made my way, according to the map, along the road which had houses stretched along either side for about a kilometer. Walking on the road I now began passing an occasional house. It is a curious fact that one may walk long distances in the country without passing a single dwelling and then abruptly enter a village. There were many houses on each side but there was a dearth of pedestrians outside. Each house that I passed had almost the same architectural design – wooden sides and thatched roofs. Some of the houses had gardens and were surrounded by trees. By referring to my map I eventually came upon a house which seemed to fit the description and location on the map. I stood before the only two-story house in the neighborhood. I was in a quandary. What do I do now? Should I make my presence known?

The first sight of a Japanese house is disappointing; it is unsubstantial in appearance, and there is a meagerness of color being unpainted. It suggests poverty, and this absence of paint, with gray and rain stained color of the boards, leads one to compare it to a barn or shed. I walked up to the front entrance and shook the bell hanging from the door lintel. In a moment the door slid open on tracks revealing a tall gentleman who looked at me slowly up and down with great curiosity before speaking. "What is it? How may I help you?"

"Forgive me, kind sir, I am searching for the cousin of Hodka the Ainu. Are you he?"

On hearing this he was stunned speechless for a moment but quickly recovered and responded, "I have a cousin named Hodka who lives in Hokkaido. Is he alright? Is anything wrong?"

"Yes, he is alright. I am here at his suggestion. He thought you might be able to help me. I just arrived on a boat from Hokkaido."

He looked at me with a frown on his face. "What do you mean? How can I help you?"

"Well if I may come inside, I will explain everything."

"Yes, of course, come in," he said cautiously as he stepped aside to allow me entry.

Suddenly, from inside the room I heard a shrill female voice, "Who is it, Sangaku?"

"It's alright, dear. It's only a friend," he shouted back over his shoulder. With that a medium sized, rather pretty woman appeared. "Yes, this is my wife, Teruyo Mayeda," he pointed. "What is your name, sir?"

"My name is Sueki Fumihiko," I bowed as I spoke.

"My name is Sangaku Mayeda," he responded with a bow. "Come in and sit by the fire."

In the front room there was a *tokonoma,* an alcove with a hanging scroll of a waterfall rolling down the side of a mountain. I was led to the center of the room which had a charcoal burner. We sat cross-legged on the matted floor. I began speaking hastily about my adventures from the time of the shipwreck to the drifting and landing in America and the subsequent freedom from the Makah Indians and the berth on the American fishing vessel which brought me to the Ainu people. He was particularly interested in my life with the Ainu people.

"I see, I see, very interesting," he said. "I suppose you re-entered Japan disguised as an Ainu with long hair and strange clothes,"

"Hodka told me it would not be possible to enter anywhere else since northern Honshu has many Ainu and I would not seem out of place. It has been over three years since I left during which time I did not cut my hair or beard as a promise to Buddha that if he saved me I would then cut my hair and enter a monastery."

"Well the first thing we must do is remove your disguise by cutting off your hair and beard and change your clothes so you will look Japanese. After that you will blend in with no trouble."

His wife, Teruyo, came in with a platter of rice cookies and a pot of tea, "You must be hungry, please eat." She set the tray of comestibles down on the floor.

"Thank you, you may call me Sweki."

"And you may call me Teri."

Sangaku watching these activities added," Tonight you may take a hot bath and stay the night. Tomorrow I shall cut your hair and give you a change of clothes."

"Thank you, Sangaku, you are most kind."

"You may call me Gaku."

"Thank you," I said as I munched a morsel of cookie and sipped a bit of tea. "It is my intent to enter a Buddhist monastery when I leave here. Can you help me with that endeavor?"

"Yes, there is a monastery at Osorezan on the Shinokita peninsula near the town of Mutsu. We can talk about this tomorrow. Please take your bath and please take off those dirty, ugly, torn buckskins."

I exclaimed, "These buckskins were made for me by the Makah Indians and have a story to tell."

"I'm certain of that but they are a sure give away. Now is the time to give up being an Ainu and becoming a Japanese gentleman. I gave up being an Ainu when I married Teri. She and I have lived here happily for many years by adopting Japanese customs. My Ainu name was Sabatka but I changed it to Sangaku which means "mountain learning" and I adopted Teri's family name, Mayeda. Now, I am Japanese."

"I see." That night after the bath I went to sleep in a provided, heavily wadded futon placed on the floor. It was pure luxury sleeping on a soft, clean sheet with a warm blanket cover. I reflected on my life in the Ainu village where I slept on a bear skin that smelled of an animal odor. Life for me has changed abruptly and unexpectedly.

I slept fitfully all night besieged by strange dreams and wondering what is to become of me in the future. In the morning I was woken by Sangaku who said, "Wake up Sweki. It is time for your haircut and shave." I bestrew the bed cover and bounded out of the futon. Sangaku sat me on a small stool and began cutting my hair close to the scalp. He left my hair with a close-cropped, shorn look, barely bald. He then shaved the wispy beard off my face with a sharp razor blade close to the skin. When finished I touched my face with my fingertips and found it bare and smooth. He provided me with a looking-glass and I was immediately astonished at the reflected image. "Is that me?" I muttered.

"Yes, Sweki, that is you. The best disguise is being you. Now you can go out into the world without fear." He next took me to his closet and gave me underpants, a split-skirt, striped trouser and a long black coat. "These are a gift for you. I shall dispose of your buckskins," he asserted in a brotherly manner."

"I don't know what to say, Gaku. I have lived as someone else for so long that I find it difficult to recognize me in my new finery. Thank you again."

"I am happy to help. Now let us eat breakfast," he maintained as we left to enter the kitchen.

The interior of a Japanese house is very simple in its constitution. The first thing I noticed when I entered the house was the small size and low stud of the rooms. The ceilings are so low that I felt I could easily touch them and going into the kitchen I almost struck my head against the lintel. Each room is divided by sliding screens and the floors are covered with *tatami* (straw) mats precisely measured and fitted together. This house was composed of a suite of three rooms in a line separated by movable screens. There was a second floor which I have not seen. I noticed that a peculiarly agreeable odor of the wood used in the structure of this house seemed to fill the air of the rooms with a delicate perfume. The kitchen was located in one corner of the third room. It had a fireplace for cooking and a large urn containing fresh water.

We all assumed a kneeling position at a small, low table. The food was served in lacquer and porcelain dishes on lacquer trays placed upon the low table in front of the kneeling person. We ate *congee* (rice gruel) and pickled vegetables. At the conclusion of our repast, Sangaku took me aside to discuss the nearby monastery.

We went into the middle room and sat on the matted floor in cross-legged position. There were several interesting pictures on the walls otherwise the room maintained the sparseness of the rest of the house. Sangaku began speaking slowly but with great enthusiasm, "The Osorezan Mountain is about ninety kilometers from here, just outside the city of Mutsu. Fortunately, there is a horse drawn tram from here to Mutsu, but from Mutsu you will have to walk the remaining distance to the monastery. I have here, in my hand, some coins for the tram and I made a small map giving directions to the monastery." He handed me these items to me, which I anxiously received.

He continued pontificating, "Osorezan, "dreadful mountain" is a volcanic area on the Shinokita peninsula, full of sulfur hot springs bubbling from rocks and blood-red pools of scalding water, as a *reijo*, a place where departed souls linger, it is a point of contact between this world and the next. The temple at Osorezan is called Entsuji and is a Soto temple in which *itako*; blind female mediums make contact with the dead and predict the future for parishioners. The goings-on at Osorezan represent the immemorial traditions of folk religion and shamanism but once you are accepted as a monk trainee you will be only involved in the Soto tradition of Zen."

"You make it sound forbidding."

"No, no, I do not mean to frighten you but there are certain obstacles you will have to overcome before they will accept you. It is not easy. This is done to test your mettle and seriousness of purpose."

We rose from our sitting position and went into the front room where Teruyo was waiting for us. I bowed deeply to both of them while trying to express my gratitude, "Thank you very much. I shall never forget your kindness." They remained in bowed position as I left the house. Once in the street I felt like a different person, much like one who is reborn. I walked along with my head held high until I reached the tram stop. While waiting at the tram stop, I acknowledged other people with friendly greetings. The feeling was like a new or second birth. I felt I had sprung back from the depths of despair.

TWELVE

I felt uneasy as I walked up to the stone steps to the massive gate. The door of the gate was closed but I saw a wooden mallet hanging in front of a wooden plate that had a gouged out concavity in the center. I hesitated. *What should I do?* I grabbed the mallet and with great force struck the wooden plate several times producing a harsh, sharp, cracking tone like a thunderclap. It took several minutes before anyone responded. The door was partially opened slowly and a clean shaven head appeared with severely slanted eyes which examined me from top to bottom before speaking. After scrutiny he said, with a hissing sound emanating from his clenched teeth, "What is it?"

"I am here to see the abbot. I would like to enter the monastery to train as a monk."

There was silence. The monk opened the door fully and stood still continuing to look at me. He sidled as he came out to speak, "The abbot is busy right now. You must wait if you want to see him." Then he abruptly turned to re-enter the doorway which was left ajar. I felt the abuse of his coarse, insulting speech. The door closed and I was left to contemplate this mistreatment. But, despite this gruff offense, I decided to wait. After waiting for a half-hour without receiving compliance, I decided to knock again. This time I struck the mallet against the wooden plate with even greater force. It was obvious from the sound that I was in a state of quandary. This time it took even longer for the monk to come and open the door. The massive wooden door creaked with an ear-piercing vibration sound as it opened ever so slightly to allow the monk to view me before he spoke, "What is it?"

"I am wondering if you forgot me. I would like to have an audience with the abbot. I've been waiting here for one half-hour?"

He sneered as he spoke through clenched teeth, "I have not forgotten you. If you want to see the abbot, you must wait." He turned in a huff to re-enter the doorway. The massive door closed with a loud timbre leaving me standing in wonderment. I decided if I had to wait I might as well sit down on the stone steps. More than an hour had passed by with no response and I became irritable and peevish. *Why is this taking so long?*

I began wondering about the unmannerly conduct of the monk. Why was he so hostile? It seems to me such deportment is uncalled for. Is this a customary way for Buddhist monks to act? The prevalent customs in Japan require a modicum of intimacy in mode of behavior. *Oh well, I'll just wait.* Several hours went by and I was not only getting bored but by now I was getting increasingly angry. It was late afternoon when I realized that I was hungry. I had not eaten anything since breakfast this morning with Sangaku. If I am not called in by evening then I will have to leave to find something to eat. But, if I do, I might miss my appointment with the abbot. *What shall I do?* I see that I have no choice but to remain here until I am called in. Late afternoon became evening. I was increasingly surrounded by dusk as nightfall crept in. I started to get up. The abbot will not see me in the nighttime. Ah but, I thought he might have evening hours. I was really very tired of waiting. I began stretching my arms and rose to relieve the pain in my back. I found myself yawning and stamping my feet for the want of something to do. I began pacing back and forth in front of the massive door. My fatigue now changed to drowsiness and dullness and I had all I could do to keep myself alert. But nothing helped. I sat down with my back against the door and began dozing. Eventually, I fell into a deep slumber with my legs splayed outward and ungainly. I slept all through the night in this position until I was woken by mist like drops of water splashing on my face. It was raining or better yet it was drizzling in the early part of the morning when the blackness of the sky changes to a gunmetal gray. I picked myself up and huddled under the canopy over the doorway and thus avoided getting drenched.

I have waited here all day and all night with no response to my request to see the abbot. I was becoming mentally distressed and perturbed. Is this waiting part of a plan to see if I am capable of becoming a monk? Yes, yes, that must be it. I suddenly realized that I am being given the preliminary preparatory training. Now that I thought about it I felt a lot better – if I could do this – then I had the capacity to absorb more difficult chores.

Suddenly, I heard the door jostle and begin to open on its heavy iron hinges. There in front of me stood the monk with a broad grin on his face. For a while he said nothing. He just stood there with his lips drawn back so as to show his teeth. I did not know what to make of his demeanor until I heard him say, "Would you like some breakfast?"

"Yes, indeed," I replied anxiously.

"Well then come in and follow me."

I was stupefied by his action as we walked rather quickly to an open-sided wooden pavilion with all the sides opened by sliding walls. I could see monks sitting on the floor in front of low tables eating their meal. He turned to me and said in an agreeable, sweetly manner, "Please remove your shoes and come in. I shall show you your place."

"Yes, of course," We entered the large room which had a low table running down its middle at which sat about thirty monks. They were sitting on their knees in what is known as seiza position. I noticed they were eating from bowls in a prescribed manner. The monk indicated a vacant spot for me to occupy.

He sat next to me with instructions, "You may take the boiled rice from the wooden bucket and the cabbage-bean mixture from the large plate." He pointed to the two items with his long index finger. I filled the bowl in front of me with the cooked rice and while holding it in my left hand began shoveling and stuffing the rice quickly into my mouth with a pair of provided bamboo chopsticks in my right hand. After consuming the rice I took a helping of the cabbage-bean mixture. I experienced a high degree of gratification while eating and extreme satisfaction when I finished. After washing it all down with a coif of green tea I turned to look at my companion as I meekly stated, "Thank you for the wonderful meal. May I see the abbot now?"

"Yes, of course. But first you must help with the clean-up."

All the monks began chanting in unison at the conclusion of the meal. Everything was then put away and the floor swept. We both finished clean-up. I followed him to another house across a central plaza which was planted with many groups of flowers consisting mainly of multicolored lilies. There were several houses on the periphery of this plaza and I could only guess as to their use. At the door to one of the houses we removed our shoes once again and walked into a dark interior. I could barely make out the image of someone sitting inside. It took a moment before my eyes got used to the dark. I saw a small rotund man sitting at a table. There was a large Buddha statue behind him. I heard a deep, booming voice, "Please sit." I sat where the monk indicated. After making myself comfortable I heard some rapid fire questions. "What is your name?"

"My name is Fumihiko Sueki."

"My name is Matsu-roshi. Where do you come from?"

I then responded unwinding the entire story of my adventures since my shipwreck more than three years ago.

"So you promised Buddha that you would enter a monastery if he saved you?"

"Yes, I am here to fulfill that promise."

"Do you wish to train as a monk?"

"Yes, if you will have me."

"Well considering the difficulty you had in getting here, we will certainly keep you. But remember training as a monk is not easy." He pointed to the monk sitting behind me. "Shigeru-san will help you. He will be your *Taiban* (personal helper)." With a movement of his hand the interview ended.

Shigeru and I got up with a bow and a gassho. We left the room and spoke outside. Shigeru turned to face me as he said, "My name is Tanaka Shigeru. Everyone calls me Shig."

I looked at him as I responded, "You may call me Sweki."

"I would like to apologize for my behavior as you waited outside the gate." He bowed deeply with his palms together in gassho.

"I understand. I have no grievance against you. I would like us to be friends." I returned the bow and gassho.

"Well, I am glad of that. Come I'll show you where you sleep. "We walked across the plaza once again to another house. It was a two-story dormitory style building which housed the monks and novices. We climbed the stairs to the second level where Shig showed me my sleeping spot. It was a paillasse, nothing more than an under bed of straw. On the wall were hooks from which were hanging clothes. The room was Spartan and bare except for a small incense burner and Buddha on a shelf in one corner. Shig pointed to the clothes hanging and said, "This is your *samu-e* or work clothes. Please change into them and I shall meet you in the office room downstairs." He then left and I began to change my clothes. The samu-e gave me a feeling of belonging. Wearing the samu-e I had the feeling of being of the same form as the others. I was now in the dress of a particular Buddhist style wearing the same fashion being worn by the monks in the same service. After redressing I went downstairs to receive instructions from Shig.

"You may have the remainder of the day to yourself," he said. "Lunch will be served at eleven o'clock this morning. Walk around and familiarize yourself with the surroundings. Look into all the buildings, especially the kitchen, locate the outdoor latrine and certainly view the farm. We are self-sufficient here since we grow all our own food. Tomorrow we rise at four o'clock in the morning by bell and meet in the *Zendo* (place of meditation) for morning *zazen* (meditation). After zazen there will be a period of cleaning up. You will be a sweeper. Then there is breakfast after which you will work on the farm until lunch time. Do you have any questions?"

I shook my head negatively knowing that the future will certainly bring some questions. We parted company and I watched Shig trudge off in a toilsome way. I decided to walk around to learn the lay of the land. As I passed monks we would gassho each other but not a word was spoken. Most everyone walked with a hurried gait; no one stopped to exchange greetings or pleasantries. I developed a plan of the monastery layout in my mind as I walked about.

Lunch, like breakfast, was eaten in the same place and in the same manner. We all sat on our knees in seiza position and used the bowls and utensils in a prescribed manner called *oryoki*. The oryoki style of eating consists of three nested, concentric bowls which are placed before you in a line and used for eating one's food. For lunch we had seafood miso soup, followed by vegetable tempura with soba noodles and steamed white rice. I have not had such typical Japanese fare in so long I almost forgot the taste. I knew now that I was home and I hoped it would help me forget the hurtful times of my pernicious past. After lunch I went back to my room to rest and perchance to sleep. Lying down on my paillasse, I began to dream of home.

"Mother, mother, I am home!"

"Yes, Sueki, you're home."

"How is everyone? I miss all of you."

"Are you finished being a sailor?"

"Yes, mother, I went to sea and became shipwrecked. It took me three years to return to Japan."

"Will you now stay in Japan?"

"Yes, mother, I am living in a Buddhist Monastery. I am studying to become a monk."

"When will you come home to visit?"

"I don't know, mother, I hope to visit soon."

"Well don't make it too long. We are all getting older. I would like to see you before I die."

"I will come as soon as I am able, mother. The rules in the monastery are very strict. How is father?"

"We are all getting older."

"I shall try to make it soon, mother, I promise."

After a therapeutic rest on my paillasse, a small monk came into the room and stood before me. He was not much taller than a child wearing an apron over his *samu-e* (work clothes). His round shoulders were stooped forward over his chest; he was pointy-headed, which was neatly shaven and his face was completely hairless. He had doe-shaped eyes and a small pug nose. He bowed before speaking, *"Sumimasen* (excuse me), I am sorry to disturb your *wa* (tranquility) but would you like to help us in the kitchen? We are short-handed today since one of our helpers left the monastery for personal reasons. The *Tenzo-san* (chief cook) sent me to request your help."

"Yes, yes, of course," I said as I jumped to my feet. "What kind of work shall I do?"

"Oh, thank you. It isn't much. You will wash and chop the vegetables which come from the farm. We need them in time for *yuhan* (dinner)."

I followed him as he waddled out of the room at which point he stopped and spoke as he turned, "By the way, my name is Akamatsu Akira. You may call me Aki, all the others do." He bowed and I returned the gesture.

"My name is Fumihiko Sueki. You may call me Sweki."

We kept walking silently until we reached the kitchen. The kitchen was behind the dining pavilion and as I walked in I could hear the distinctive din of pots and pans clattering and the Tenzo-san spouting orders in a pompous manner to the scurrying monks. He approached me with a kindly sparkle in his eyes. "Thank you for coming. We really need your help." Pointing to a table laden with vegetables he said, "These need washing and chopping."

I got a large pan filled with water and began scrubbing the vegetables and removed all excess greens. I next peeled the tubers and carrots. I was amazed to find that the carrots were all of different sizes. After that chore I picked up all the shavings and excess greens and placed them in a pail containing matter for the humus compost bin. I placed the cleaned and chopped vegetables in a separate pan and brought them to the large cauldron on the stove.

"Thank you, Sweki," said the Tenzo-san. "Now would you please wash all those dishes," pointing to the sink containing dirty dishes.

"Yes, indeed." I said with enthusiasm. I went to the sink and one by one began washing the dishes with a soft cloth. Suddenly, one of the dishes slipped out of my hand and crashed to the floor with a loud noise. It seemed that all activity in the kitchen came to a stop. I was very embarrassed as I looked down to see the dish in a million pieces. The Tenzo-san came bolting over to me shouting at the top of his voice. He treated me with blows and insults and chided me with loud words. The chastising continued, "I am a bee to a sluggish horse which needs a bit of stinging for its own good." He told me to pick up the pieces and take them outside and bury them in the soft earth. "The dish was made from ingredients of the earth and must be returned to the earth." he said in a philosophical manner. With a blushing face I did as I was told.

Next to the Roshi, the Tenzo is the most important person in the monastery. It was Dogen (1200-1253), the patriarch of the Soto Zen tradition who designated this official position in his writings. The Tenzo, the chief cook, is responsible for the nourishment of the monks while the Roshi, the abbot and Zen master, is responsible for the nurture of the monks.

I went outside carrying the shards of the earthenware plate in my cupped hands. Having found a suitable place in back of the kitchen I proceeded to dig a small trench in the earth with a large shard. I then buried all the pieces. Upon completion of this task and not knowing what to do I looked around and then I bowed with a gassho (palms together) to the spot where I buried the shards. I heard a giggle behind me and turned to find Shigeru laughing at me. "Ha! Ha! Why did you bow to the ground?"

"I bowed out of respect and to express my sorrow for destroying the plate."

"Well that is commendable but unnecessary. I really came out here to find you so that I may give you the daily schedule." Shigeru handed me a slip of paper containing the daily schedule.

4:00   Wake up
4:15-5:00   Zazen
5:00-6:15   Morning sutra chant
6:15-7:45   Cleaning
7:45-8:15   Morning meal
8:15-9:30   Individual study time
9:30-12:00   Class (sewing Buddha robes, sewing kimono, lecture on a
Zen text, flower arranging, chanting practice, or calligraphy)
12:00-12:30   Midday meal
12:30-13:30   Free time
13:30-15:00   Work period
15:00-15:30   Tea
15:30-16:00   Free time
16:00-16:30   Evening sutra chanting
16:30-17:30   Individual study time
17:30-18:00   Evening meal
18:00-20:15   Bath
20:15-21:00   Zazen
21:00   Lights out

While examining the schedule I heard Shig explain, "Wake up is made with a bell ringing in the hallway. Training in the monastery is regulated by bells and drums, not clocks. You will be seldom aware of the clock time and you may not be able to tell what might constitute a typical day."

"I see. Please tell me what is *Individual study time* that I see written here?"

"I will join you at that time. We shall study the *Shobogenzo* (Dogen's treatise) during the first period then you will study on your own during the second period."

"I see. What about *Work period*. What is that?"

"During work period you will work on the farm."

"Aha, I thought so. It is ironic that I left home because I didn't want to work on a farm." This statement brought much shared laughter.

"Sweki, don't get discouraged it takes sometime to get used to life in the monastery. There is an old saying: *You can measure your cloth ten times but you can only cut it once.* The real effort comes after being given a koan (conundrum) by the Roshi to solve. Also, your ability to accept the five precepts will be required before you can be accepted as a monk trainee."

"What are the five precepts?"

"The five precepts are called *sila* in Sanskrit. They are the basic obligations which Buddhists undertake, five for lay people, in the rule of training. They are to abstain, from harming any living being, taking anything not given, misconduct involving sense pleasure, false speech, and losing control of mind through alcohol or drugs. These are understood as promises that Buddhists make to themselves at the start of each day."

"Well, that seems simple enough."

"The receiving and granting of these five precepts will take place in a formal initiation ceremony (*Jukai*) into the Zen Buddhist way by the Roshi sometime after you have been here a while."

"Thank you for explaining it to me, Shig."

"Alright, now it's time to return to the kitchen to help out."

I turned and left Shig behind me. On entering the kitchen, I noticed someone else washing the dishes. The Tenzo approached me and pointing to the metal pots and pans in the second sink said, "You may scrub these utensils. Please use the sand as an abrasive to remove all the encrusted particles."

I began the cleaning by first sprinkling sand on the metal surface then with soap laden brush scrubbed all the pots and pans. On completion, I saw a sparkling, shining, reflection in the metal. I found the result very gratifying. All of the workers in the kitchen began leaving and since I didn't see the Tenzo I too walked outside to the central plaza. There I saw a most unusual sight. At first I wasn't sure but as I came closer I realized it was a woman. Since her hair was closely cropped she did not have a feminine appearance. She was rather small with a flat, broad face, severely slanted eyes and a small sharp, pug nose. I approached her and said, "Hello, my name is Sueki."

She looked up from her labors and smiled, "My name is Noguchi Ichi." She began rising and bowed to me which I quickly returned.

"What are you making?"

"I am making brooms by attaching short twigs to a bamboo rod with a cord."

"I had no idea there were any females in the monastery."

"Yes there are six of us training to be monks. We live on the other side of the compound. I am only here today to make the brooms. We have our own quarters and facilities but we do come here for interaction with the Roshi."

"What do you mean interaction?"

"We attend zazen in the Zendo (place of zazen), services in the Hatto (place of religious services), *dokusan* (interview with the Roshi), and listen to *teisho* (sermon) by the Roshi. Otherwise, we carry on our life separate from the men."

"Please forgive my surprise. I had no idea that women would be interested in becoming monks."

"Yes, many of us follow the teachings of the Buddha. Have you been here long?"

"No. no, I just arrived today."

"I see. Well, come visit us for tea during your free time."

"Is it allowed?"

"Yes, during free time. You may come to our compound only if invited."

"Thank you. I shall come tomorrow."

I wanted to continue speaking with her but knowing that idle conversation is discouraged except at designated times, I backed away with a bow and gassho and made my way to my room. Lying supinely on the floor I kept thinking about Ichi. She was not beautiful but her face was pleasant and smooth as a peach. The sibilant tones of her voice captivated me. Since it was rare for me to hear a feminine voice, I became emotionally intrigued by the sound of her voice. Soto Zen as practiced in the monastery is a silent order. There is no speaking allowed except during free time and tea time. It is assumed that necessary conversation is performed by hand and body gestures. Greetings are performed with the usual bow and gassho. Greetings are also accomplished by head movements and eye blinking.

THIRTEEN

The next morning I was awakened by the rapid ringing of a bell and a scurrying of feet along the hallway. The sound of the bell was like the *doppelganger* effect of a passing train. I scrambled out of my paillasse and headed for the zendo for morning zazen. A bell (*rin*) is rung once signaling the beginning of zazen.

Sitting motionless on the wooden platform in the cold zendo was mind boggling. Posture, breathing and mind are the basis of zazen. There are three ways to harmonize breathing in zazen depending on the teachings of one's Zen master: breath counting, watching the breath, and neither counting nor watching the breath. Since I am a new disciple in this monastery my own instruction is based on *neither counting nor watching the breath*.

I must concentrate my entire body and mind on the whole process of sitting in zazen. I don't set my mind on any particular object, visualization, mantra, or even my breath itself. I just sit, my mind is nowhere. My body and mind is concentrated in just sitting. Sitting mindfully, whenever I deviate from upright posture, deep and smooth breathing, awakening and letting go of thought, I just return to the point. I sit on my zafu (cushion) in half-lotus position by simply placing my left foot on my right thigh, with my knees and the base of my spine forming an equilateral triangle. These three points support the weight of my body. I place my right hand, palm-up, on my left palm, and my left hand palm-up on my right palm with the tips of my thumbs lightly touching each other.

I sat like this for forty-five minutes and every once-in-a-while I was struck on the shoulder muscle with a long stick, rounded at one end and flat at the other to relieve my drowsiness and relax my back muscles. The blow sometimes hurt but it did relax my back muscles. This stick is called a *kyosaku* and is carried by a monk (*jikido*) who constantly patrols around the zendo seeking out victims during zazen. Sometimes the *jikido* would strike a seated practitioner with a blow for no reason. At such a moment it is not the physical pain which hurts the most; it is the mental agony caused by the unreasonableness of it.

By way of explanation, I must state that practices that involve specific actions of the body are central to Zen. The assumption is that the mind-body is an organic and dynamic unit. Therefore, entering practice through disciplining the actions of the body is understood to be effective on the mind as well, and every activity in daily life can be an opportunity to practice. No action is too menial for Zen practice, from how to fold a towel to how to wash one's face, from how to sweep the floor to how to place one's slippers. Each act can be done with respect for all involved, whether that be another person, oneself, a utensil, a morsel of food, or even dust. For example, learning the proper form required to wash one's face is in itself treating the water and one's body with the respect accorded a Buddha. Sitting still is simple in form, and it is held as the paradigm for how to learn to act as a Buddha. A hallmark of Zen-style sitting (zazen) is the focus on body posture, especially a straight spine. The two most common rituals are bowing and chanting the Heart Sutra.

The bell *(rin)* is rung once again to signal the end of zazen. I got up and bowed with a gassho. It was very painful for me to sit on a cushion on the wooden platform. My leg muscles ached but I immediately assumed the *shashu* position while standing by putting the thumb of my left hand in the middle of the palm and made a fist around it, put my right hand around it and placed it in front of my chest and left the zendo for the *hatto* (religious services room) and morning sutra chanting. Sutra chanting is one of the most important aspects of Zen and the most popular sutra to monks and laity alike is the Heart Sutra.

The Heart Sutra (*Prajna Paramita-Hrdaya- Sutra*), a Buddhist classic and the most popular sutra in Japan, comprises only two hundred and sixty-two words. It is said that the essence of the Heart Sutra known as the Prajna Paramita Sutra (Perfection of Wisdom Sutra), and even that the entire Mahayana teaching, is contained within it.

Following is the complete text of the Heart Sutra that I chanted in which *Kannon* (the Bodhisattva of compassion) is speaking to a monk disciple, Sariputra.

Kannon (Avalokitesvara), the Bodhisattva of all seeing and all hearing, practicing deep prajna paramita, perceives the five skandas (material composition, sensing, perception, mental formations, and consciousness) *in their self-nature to be empty.*

O Sariputra, form is emptiness, emptiness is form, form is nothing but emptiness, emptiness is nothing but form; that which is form is emptiness, and that which is emptiness is form. The same is true for sensation, perception, volition, and consciousness.

O Sariputra, all things are by nature empty. They are not born, they are not extinguished; they are not tainted, they are not pure; they do not increase; they do not decrease. Within emptiness there is no form, and therefore no sensation, perception, volition, or consciousness; no eye, ear, nose, tongue, body, or mind; no form, sound, scent, taste, touch, or thought.

It extends from no vision to no discernment, from no ignorance to no end to ignorance, from no old age and death to no extinction of old age and death.

There is no suffering, origination, annihilation, or path; there is no cognition, no attainment, and no realization.

Because there is no attainment in the mind of the Bodhisattva who dwells in prajna paramita there are no obstacles and therefore no fear or delusion. Nirvana is attained; all Buddhas of the past, present, and future, through prajna paramita, reach the highest all-embracing enlightenment.

Therefore know that prajna paramita holds the great Mantra, the Mantra of great clarity, the unequaled Mantra that allays all pain through truth without falsehood. This is the Mantra proclaimed in prajna paramita, saying:

Gate gate paragate parasamgate bodhi svaha

Gone, gone, gone beyond, gone altogether beyond, awake all hail!

The Heart Sutra concisely elucidates the philosophy of *sunyata* (emptiness) which teaches that not only the self (*atman*) but also all dharmas – the elements that make up our world – are empty and ultimately nonexistent. The fact that all things in the phenomenal world are constantly changing indicates that they are devoid of inherent self-nature (*svabhava*). The reason that they are without selfhood is because they arise in dependence on causes and conditions. Insight into the empty nature of everything leads to the perfection of wisdom. This is the message the Heart Sutra is conveying. The soteriological significance of *sunyata* lies in the fact with the realization of emptiness one is able to eradicate attachments to the supposed reality of the self and dharmas. As a result one can undertake spiritual endeavors egolessly.

After chanting I left the hatto with the others to return to my room for one and a half hours of clean-up. In addition to cleaning my portion of the room I was assigned the job of sweeping the plaza walkways. Interestingly, I used one of the brooms made by Ichi. Pleasant thoughts of her came to my mind as I swept. Finally, I put away the broom and followed the others into the dining hall for the morning meal.

My seat was at the far end of the table. This was the furthest point from the Roshi. After all were seated we chanted a meal *gatha* (Buddhist verses) then large buckets of rice gruel (porridge) were laid out. The buckets were passed around and each diner spooned out large helpings into one's bowl. I added pickled cherries to my gruel and sprinkled powdered sesame seeds on top. I had two bowlfuls followed by a bowl of green tea. The meal was eaten in silence according to the regimented method of *oryoki*. At the conclusion of the meal we chanted another closing meal *gatha*. Then all of us retreated to our abodes leaving behind a small clean-up crew.

It was now individual study time. I met Shig in my room. He was carrying a book. It was the *Shobogenzo*, the most important writing of Dogen, the patriarch of Soto Zen.

He looked at me with a broad smile on his face. "Today we shall read and discuss *Butsudo* (The Buddhist Way), the Eye and Treasure of the True Law or the Great Way of the Buddhas and Patriarchs. Once you understand the Eye and Treasure of the True Law we shall move on to other chapters in the *Shobogenzo* in the future." We were sitting on the floor with the book spread out between us. Shig was reading and commenting as he proceeded from line to line. I found the reading and discussion very interesting and I could understand it as an important training feature. I was almost sorry to see the session end. Needless to say I was lonely and it was good to hear a human voice. Truly, I was intrigued by the philosophy in the *Shobogenzo*. But, I had to attend a class where I was to make and sew a robe and kimono for my use as a monk. In this class I was given instruction by an elderly monk in the method of cutting the fabric and sewing the parts together with a needle and thread. He was a very patient gentleman who understood my grossness at this task. I spent all of my time in the class preparing the parts of the robe for final assembly. I noticed that other monks were learning *Ikebana* (flower arrangement) and still others were learning calligraphy. Then it was time for the midday meal.

We all gathered in the dining room and were seated in the usual assigned order. The midday meal is the largest meal of the day in the temple. It consisted of first a crab and cucumber salad with kimizu dressing (*kami to kyuri no kimizu-ae*); second Japanese chicken (*yakitori*) together with rice with green peas (*aomame gohan*). I had second helpings of chicken and rice.

After lunch it was free time, I decided to go to the women's quarters during free time with the wild anticipation of seeing Ichi once again. I must admit that I was thinking about her all day. I secured a bag of apples from the Tenzo in the kitchen and brought it along to be used as a gift. When I arrived in the women's quarters I immediately noticed the six women seated in a circle around a burning brazier gabbing away. I hesitated for a moment but suddenly the talking stopped and Ichi rose to greet me heartily, "Sweki, so good of you to come and visit us." She bowed low with a gassho as she approached me. I returned the gesture and handed her the bag of apples that I procured from the kitchen.

"Thank you for inviting me," I said nervously as I bent my body deeply with my palms together.

"Thank you for the apples. Come Sweki sit here next to me." The others moved to make a place for me as she spoke. Some giggled while covering their mouths with their hands. Nevertheless I sat in the circle and looked at each member of the group with a nod of my head. Ichi sat next to me and introduced each member by name. I acknowledged each introduction with a nod of my head. Ichi made an offering gesture with one hand.

"Would you care for a cup of tea?"

"Oh, yes, indeed, that would be nice."

Ichi poured the tea into a small earthenware cup and offered it to me with both hands. The cup felt warm to the touch and I enjoyed holding it in my calloused palms. Then Ichi held up a plate of rice cookies.

"Have a sweet treat, Sweki. These are cookies we made ourselves."

"Yes, how wonderful, thank you," I blurted out as I reached for the shiny, round morsel. I began munching the cookie and sipping the tea as I looked at the women surrounding me. They all had close-cropped hair which removed all vestiges of femininity. Still, I could see their girlish faces which were smooth and ruddy. As a matter of fact, their eyes which were doe-shaped were always smiling. They covered their mouths with a hand when they spoke to prevent revealing their teeth. They all wore the typical black Buddhist robes which covered their bodies completely. I turned to Ichi and spoke in a soft voice, "How long have you been in the monastery?"

"I have been here six years. I came when I was fifteen years old. My parents were both killed in an accident, so my uncle placed me here as an indentured servant. But the Roshi thought I had the makings of a monk so I studied and practiced for three years and was finally ordained three years ago."

"I see. How wonderful. I am hoping to become a monk as well but I believe it is very hard work to train."

"It is hard in the beginning but it becomes easier as you get used to the routine."

"Oh, I am not afraid of hard work. My life has been nothing but hard work and survival. I am glad to be here. I have not spoken to a woman in a very long time and I enjoy speaking with you." I felt somewhat embarrassed by these words since the others could hear my conversation. I looked around with my eyes darting from one to the other but all dropped their eyes in a shy manner and did not meet my gaze. At this time I felt I was staying too long and interfering with their free time so I got up to leave.

"Where are you going, Sweki," she said with a fretful tone in her voice.

"I do not wish to intrude any longer. I feel I am taking up your free time."

"Not at all, the women are glad to have you here. They never get to speak to a man. This is a real treat for them. Please stay a little longer."

"Well, I shall return soon, perhaps in a few days."

"In that case, thank you for the apples. There is no need to bring gifts in the future. We are friends and you are always welcome here."

"Thank you. I enjoyed being here and I promise I shall return."

I stood up straight and then bowed low which she returned. I was about to turn to go when I saw the other women rise from their places and bow repeatedly with goodbyes emitted in shrill sibilant voices. I laughed at their good spirits and move away from the compound. I next walked to the center of the plaza trying to orient my direction. I knew I had to go to the farm to work and sought the best route to get there. I finally spotted a path leading past the recycle bins and thence to the farm. The farm had different rows of vegetables. It reminded me of home and I suddenly had a feeling of homesickness whelming up in me. Well, the conclusion of free time meant it was time for the work period.

I met Shig on the farm. He was carrying two hoes. "Take one of these and begin digging in the furrows of the soy beans over there," he said, pointing to a long row of sprouting vegetation. "Be sure to remove all the weeds, then gather them up and place them in the compost bin."

I took the hoe from him and began cultivating the furrows. The work was hard and boring but in time I could see the straight, clean edge of my work. I was overcome with an existential feeling of triumph. *The work was producing something of value.* Shig was working opposite of me on the parallel side. We did not speak as we worked. I found my back aching and my brow sweating as I increased my labor.

Then it happened. A boom, the earth trembling somewhere, its bowels opening up to swallow us, the earth trembles, cracks, breaks open, thunders, erupts with the power of a God. It was my first experience of an earthquake. "Shig, Shig!" There were crazed shouts, mostly mine. I could see chasms of panic all around. There was a flight of people from the monastery. I see him ahead of me, kneeling, flat on the ground, frozen like a statue. Above him, I hear my voice shouting over the rumble that is approaching us, "Shig, Shig!"

His eyes empty, elsewhere, a prayer mumbles slowly on his lips.

"Shig, for heaven's sake, get up!"

I try to lift him, but it's like trying to uproot a tree or resuscitate a dead man. I kneel down and manage to turn his shoulders round; he falls into my lap. There's nothing more to be done. It's over. I support his head, my chest torn apart with weeping and my final cry, spewing blood and despair to the heavens.

FOURTEEN

The noise abated and there was an eerie silence except for an occasional rumbling of the earth. I looked about me to discover a long fissure in the earth beginning at the farm and traveling all the way down to the central plaza. The farm was strewn with rocks and boulders which came down from the mountain. It was this detritus that hit Shig, killing him. Shig! I must see to him. He was lying down in a supine position with his legs splayed and his arms thrown askew. I went over to him and straightened his legs and then placed his arms across his chest. He looked like he was sleeping. I had an urge to kiss his cheek but thought better of it. Instead, I straightened up and bowed low with a gassho in the Japanese way of respect.

I turned and followed along the fissure down to the central plaza. When I got there I couldn't believe my eyes. The Zendo and Hatto collapsed and were totally destroyed. They looked like two piles of massive rubble. The monk's quarters was broken down but still standing precariously. The most miraculous sight was the dining hall/kitchen; it was completely untouched as if the earthquake simply by-passed it. I saw people scurrying hither and yon aimlessly but then I thought of the women's compound. I ran over to it to find it totally destroyed. The six women were safely sifting through the rubble. I cautiously approached Ichi.

"Are you alright?"

"Yes, we are all alright."

Just then loud shouts came from the plaza causing us all to run over to see what was happening. There we saw a large crowd of acolytes surrounding the Roshi. We joined the throng, pressing together. All were shouting, "Roshi, Roshi, Roshi." He raised his arms for silence and looked skyward. Then in a low, deep voice began stoically speaking, "This devastation is a gift from heaven. Divine logic cannot be understood by humans. We must submit to this ordeal to determine our worthiness. Please accept it without complaint." He hesitated for a moment as if to gather his thoughts then continued, "We must retrieve the Buddha and the Kannon from the Hatto to properly express our gratitude. But first we must care for the injured and prepare a funeral pyre for Shigeru." Once again he stopped speaking to gather his thoughts then he continued, "I was told by the Tenzo-san that we have sufficient food in storage but he suggests that we should only eat one meal a day for a while until we know exactly what our status is. Now, with great care, go into the shattered monk's quarters, two at a time, to search for your bedding and bring it out and place it on the flat ground of the plaza facing east."

The women returned to their compound and small groups entered the monk's quarters bringing out their bedding and some possessions. At my turn, I quickly found my palliasse and blankets and some clothing which I brought out and placed in an orderly established spot according to rank.

I then began to gather wood and tree limbs which were felled by the earthquake. I placed these items in a criss-cross pattern on a suitable place on the farm. This funeral pyre was to be Shigeru's final abode so I was conscious of placing the wood in a carefully thought out manner. Some men came over with a white kimono. They removed his clothing and dressed him in the white kimono. Next we all lifted him up and placed him on top of the funeral pyre. He would be cremated the next day. I was given his clothing which eventually became a spare *samu-e* (work clothes) for me. I cleaned and collected the detritus away from around the area and threw it all into the cleaved earth. I felt a shadow of ennui come over me so I returned to the plaza in a dejected mood.

Dusk was approaching and most of us were exhausted and tired from the day's events. I lay down on my paillasse and pulled a cover over me. In seconds I was fast asleep. In my oneiric state I thought I heard Ichi's voice. "Sweki, Sweki, may I join you?"

"Who is it/"

"It's me, Sweki. I have no place to sleep and I am frightened. May I join you?"

"Yes, yes, of course."

She removed her robe and slipped beneath me before I could breathe, before I could collect my thoughts. She was thin with angular elbows, long straight legs, little breasts pointing up at me. I struggled to control my breathing, more intense by the minute and stared into her dark eyes. She made herself smaller, her face pressed against my chest, one leg gently wrapped around my hips. I dissolved days, months of tension and desire inside her, gasping at every touch, every smooth caress. Her quiet moans asking neither words nor promises. I bent over, my mouth sought her breast, first brushing, and then pressing her nipple with my lips. I held her face and her head between my hands, and I stayed inside her for a long time, longer than I can remember, until she went to sleep, still holding me in a tight embrace.

As I dozed off, I couldn't help thinking that I entered the monastery only twenty-four hours ago and a lifetime of events has already happened to me. I chuckled a little at this realization. It was fortunate that my place on the plaza ground was last place according to the "pecking" order of the monks. Because of this, the tryst with Ichi was not visible to the rest of the people. Still, I told Ichi to leave in the morning at the ringing of the bell.

In the morning, the bell rang to wake us up. Ichi quickly and carefully removed the cover, put on her robe and disappeared into the women's compound. I was grateful that she was unseen. The others began stretching, yawning, and harrumphing. Then as if by an obscure command we all sat in our places and began zazen. After forty minutes, we all stood up at the sound of the bell. We bowed to each other and then straightened up our bedding on the ground before leaving for the farm to attend the cremation of Shigeru.

The Roshi was standing in front of the funeral pyre; while all the monks gathered about him. He began speaking in his characteristic low, deep voice,

"*Mujo jin jin mi myo no ho wa* (An unsurpassed, penetrating and perfect Dharma)

Hyaku sen man go ni mo al-o koto katashi (Is rarely met with even in a hundred thousand million kalpas)

Ware ima ken-mon shi ju-ji suru koto o etari (Having it to see and listen to, remember and accept)

Negawakuwa nyorai no shin-jitsu-gi o Geshi tatematsuran (I vow to taste the truth of the Tathagata's words)."

While the Roshi delivered his sermon he lit the dry tinder of wood at the base of the funeral pyre with a torch given to him by one of the monks. In a few minutes the flames of the burning wood rose to great heights engulfing Shigeru's body. It took more than forty-five minutes for the immolation to be complete. The Roshi then said in a loud voice, "May our intention equally extend to every being and place with the true merit of Buddha's way." After that, while we were watching the flames, a great chant went up from the crowd of monks:

Shu-jo mu-hen sei-gan-do (Beings are numberless, I vow to save them)

Bon-no mu-jin sei-gan-dan (Delusions are inexhaustible, I vow to end them)

Ho-mon mu-ryo sei-gan-gaku (Dharma gates are boundless, I vow to enter them)

Butsu-do mu-jo sei-gan-jo (Buddha's way is unsurpassable, I vow to become it)

The Roshi raised his arms to silence the crowd, and then began speaking slowly with his head raised skyward. "Shigeru has entered Nirvana. We should all take a handful of ashes after they cool and throw it to the wind. This ground will then become sacred with his elements. Now, let us all repeat the Five Precepts."

Once again a great chant went up from the monks:

"I vow not to do harm.

I vow not to take what is not given.

I vow not to use false speech.

I vow to avoid sexual misconduct.

I vow not to use mind altering drugs and alcohol."

Then the service concluded with the thrice repeated formula of the Theravadin faith spoken by all the monks in unison, "*Namo tasso bhagavata arahato samma sambuddhasse* (Homage, be to him who is arhat, the Enlightened One, the Buddha)

After the ceremony was over the Roshi established groups of three monks to clean up and repair the women's compound, the monk's quarters, and the Zendo and Hatto. He approached me and said, "Sueki you will now be in charge of the farm. I understand you were born on a farm"

"Yes, Master, I have considerable experience as a farmer. I will do my best."

"I know you will Sueki but I am having Akira help you. He also will be your *Taiban* (personal helper). I want you to keep up with your studies until ordination. We will not allow this disaster to interfere with our Buddhist studies"

"Thank you, Master, Aki will be very helpful."

One by one the monks grabbed a handful of Shigeru's ashes, despite the fact that they were still smoldering, and flung it to the wind in various places about the farm. The ashes settled as a dust on the ground and along the vegetable furrows to inevitably be ground under the soil as fertilizer.

Akamatsu Akira, known as Aki, came up to me with enthusiasm in his voice, "Where shall we start?" He tried straightening his small bent body to appear strong as he spoke.

"First, Aki, we must clean up the debris and detritus. Throw all the rocks and boulders lying out on the farm into the fissure in the earth. Then we will have to get a *korinsha* (wheelbarrow) from the tool shed and move earth from the mountain to fill up the cleavage of the fissure. We must retrieve the farm very soon in order to start planting. Before that, however, please remove any unburned logs and the remainder of ashes from the funeral pyre and deposit it into the fissure."

This work progressed for the remainder of the morning until the midday meal when we will enjoy our only meal of the day. The monks including the women assembled in the dining hall. It was an opportunity to see Ichi. She sat up front with the other women closer to the Roshi as guests of honor. Our eyes met in recognition but nothing else transpired between us. Then the wooden buckets were brought out containing *gohan* (cooked rice) and *yochai* (mustard greens). At the conclusion of our meal we went back to our labor. There was a steady murmur of voices as everyone proceeded to their assigned tasks.

Aki and I went back to the farm to continue cleaning up. The farm was two hectares (five acres) in size. It was surrounded by a natural fence of tea bushes on its periphery. On the eastern side was a stream meandering down from the mountain top feeding into a pond at the side of the kitchen. This was the monastery's source of fresh water; bamboo piping brought the water into the kitchen. The pond contained fish; mostly *koi* (carp). On the western side was a bamboo forest which furnished the monastery with building materials. Since the bath houses in the monk's quarters and the women's compound were both destroyed by the earthquake, the men and women had to bathe separately in the pond; women first followed by the men. Although communal bathing is not uncommon in Japan it was decided to separate bathing times to avoid unnecessary embarrassment.

A concentration of workers was assigned to rebuild the facilities of the women's compound. Meanwhile, Aki and I were laboring steadily to restore the farm. Some of the previously grown vegetables were ready to be picked. Such items as egg plants, cucumbers, soy beans, and snow peas were picked and brought to the kitchen. The rice in the one paddy was not ready for harvesting yet and neither was the field of lentils. After picking we continued to fill the fissure with dirt and stones culled from the mountain. It was getting dark by this time and so we laid down our tools and went to bathe and finally retire to sleep.

It took about a month for the monk's quarters to be repaired sufficiently to allow all of them to return with their paillasse to resume sleeping indoors. Zazen and services had to be continued on the outside at the plaza since the Zendo and Hatto were still not completely restored. I was concerned about Ichi. I think about her constantly and fall asleep dreaming of her lovely face. One day I decided to visit her to see how she was faring. I arranged with Aki that I would not meet him at the farm, using a lame excuse.

When I arrived at the women's compound I was startled to discover the progress made in recovering the sleeping quarters and facilities of the women. Ichi, coming out of the house at that moment spotted me immediately. "Oh, it is you Sweki, how wonderful of you to come."

"I was concerned about you. How are you? Is all going well?"

"Yes, yes, indeed. Our quarters have not only been restored but have been much improved. The Roshi came every day to supervise the construction crew."

"I can see the improvement, I am glad for you." I hesitated for a moment but then continued, "Are you busy now?"

"Not really. Would you like to go for a walk in the woods? The other women are working inside the house. I can take a short break."

"Alright, I would like that if it is not interfering with your work."

"No, it will be quite alright for a little while."

We started ambling along side by side out of the compound down a little flower strewn path leading through the wooded area all the time chatting away. Suddenly, Ichi pointed to an area of tall grass at the side of the path. "Shall we rest here for a little while?"

"Yes, that would be nice." I looked round to see only solitude.

We both sat down and I examined her face in admiration. She was a strange, witchlike woman with cropped hair, sharp, small nose, a face both hard and sensual. We couldn't pretend for long, passion took us by the hand; it drove us wild straight away. She crept over me, sinuous and silent as a wildcat, pressed her breast to my chest and then I noticed her desire. I exploded inside her, unable to contain the yell that mingles with hers. Pleasure shakes my body, twisting me round like a dry branch in a fire. She lowers herself unto me, white and amazing. I listen to her breath slowing. She takes my hand, in a gesture that I learned to indulge, and puts it between her thighs, to touch, in a single delicate gesture, her still contracting sex. I hear her say in a melancholy way, "I love you, Sweki."

I nod silently, hoping she will surprise me again. She smiles and repeats, "I love you, Sweki."

I respond pensively, "I love you, Ichi."

We rose, hitched up our clothing and walked back to the compound holding hands. No one was about and so I said goodbye to Ichi with a bow and a promise, "I shall return soon to see how you are progressing. Please give my regards to the other women and tell them that I am sorry to have missed them."

"I shall tell them, Sweki, and I shall hold you to your promise to return soon."

I made my way to the farm and greeted Aki, "I'm back, Aki. What are we doing now?"

"I believe it is time for your lesson in the *Shobogenzo*. Are you ready to proceed?"

There was no hint of question in his voice. I saw that he was holding the book under his arm and so answered him resolutely, "Yes, of course, let us begin.

FIFTEEN

Slowly, the farm became productive again. Aki and I had sewn the seeds of many different vegetables and took care of the rice paddy and the lentils field. The construction crews were finishing the resurrection of the Zendo and Hatto and there was a spirit of accomplishment and finality developing amongst all the monks. Soon life will return to normal and we shall take up and continue our practice as before.

The Roshi returned to having *dokusan* (interview with Roshi) with the monks. One evening a line gathered outside of the still incomplete Hatto. I got on line and waited my turn. No one spoke but I could see anxiety in the faces of the participants. When it came to my turn, I approached the Roshi with a gassho and a bow. He looked at me in his usual solemn manner, "Please sit Sueki."

I sat on the ground in a half-lotus position in front of him.

He said in a low voice, "I am glad to see you Sueki. I want to thank you for your hard labor in helping the monastery recover from the disaster."

I blushed but responded, "I only did my part, Roshi-san."

"Yes, well, I think you are ready for a koan."

"Yes, I am ready, Roshi-san."

"Well then, here it is. *A buffalo passes the window. His head, horns, and four legs all go past. But why can't the tail pass too?"* Think about this conundrum, and then give me your answer when you are ready. Do not tell anyone your koan and do not think about it during zazen."

I was taken aback by the koan. What does it all mean? The koan made no sense to me but I was told not to use logic to arrive at an answer. My mind was dazed from the koan knowing that it was an important preliminary task to ordination. I thanked the Roshi and left. Being tired from a long hard day's work on the farm I decided to bathe and retire. The rain was falling in a warm gentle drizzle when I went to bed at nine o'clock. It was very warm for mid-September but I thought to myself, *this rain will help the vegetables sprout."* I was too involved in getting settled in my paillasse to notice anything unusual.

I was awakened about midnight by the shaking of the floor upon which I slept. My consciousness gradually surfaced to a most horrifying roar, one which continued to mount in intensity. With the house shaking and rattling, the wind howling, and the rain pouring down in torrents, I was afraid, to say the least. Then I heard someone running in the hallway, ringing a bell and shouting *tai-fung, tai-fung* (typhoon, typhoon). It was a tropical cyclone with a great wind and flooding rain. It kept up all night.

The morning brought calm and a brilliant sun to greet me. I went outside and looked about to see more destruction everywhere. Roofs of some houses were torn off and some windows were blown out. I ran to the farm to assess the damage. I was shocked by what I saw. The farm was completely flooded and most of our plantings were washed away. The tool shed was blown away but the tools were salvageable. The only good sign was the rice paddy which was flooded but could be drained. The lentil field might also survive since it usually needs a lot of water to grow. I looked around me with moist eyes and wondered to myself, *all this work lost; all for nothing.* I began to despair; *it seems that all my life has been plagued by bad luck. Can it be that man is meant to suffer?*

Aki came up behind me stepping like a cat. I turned at the sound of his voice, "The Roshi is calling for everyone to meet in the plaza."

"Alright, I'll be there in a few minutes. I can't seem to make sense of all this destruction," I exclaimed with a shake of my head.

"Yes, it is a terrible blow, particularly after the earthquake."

"I wonder what's next," I said in an ironic way.

"Well, winter is coming and we could get a great blizzard," Aki said with a sardonic voice. The two of us joined in a walk back to the plaza. It seems that all the monks were gathered there. There was a slight hum wafting in the air from the whispers of the monks. I saw Ichi in the crowd and she noticed me as well. We nodded to each other. Then there was a hush of silence as the Roshi appeared in the center of the gathered fellowship. He looked from face to face; then began spouting words of encouragement in his deep resonant voice, "We are being tested by heaven. We shall overcome this double disaster. Most of our work has been spared. The structures are still sound but we need to replace a few roofs and windows; that is all. The real problem is the drenching our goods have received. Everyone must bring the bedding and clothing outside to dry in the hot sun." Then he looked at me intensively with fierce, piercing eyes, "Sueki how is the farm?"

Everyone turned, following his line of vision and looked at me while I responded forthrightly, "I am sorry to say, Roshi-san, that the farm is flooded. The rice paddy is flooded as well but we will open the dike and let the water drain out. This should save the rice shoots. The vegetable farm and the lentil field will have to wait until the water subsides into the ground. This unusually hot weather should hasten that."

The Roshi turned to the *Tenzo* (chief cook) with the next question, "Do we have enough food?"

"Yes, Roshi-san our, our frugality of meals has helped considerably in preserving our food stock."

"That is very good. We shall continue with one meal a day. You all know what to do. Let's go back to work. We shall skip zazen today. Tomorrow the ground should be dry enough to continue zazen and services."

The crowd began to split up into small groups and eventually dissipate. Aki and I went up to the farm, after consulting with the *Tenzo* (chief cook) as to which seeds to plant. On the way we noticed an unusual sight, amongst the upturned trees was a ginkgo tree about ten feet tall, standing alone healthy and hardy amidst the rubble of split trees and upturned trees. I stopped for a moment to admire this sacred tree of Asia, the symbol of long life and memory. Aki, who came up with me, stood next to me and admired the tree as well as he mused, "The survival of that tree, the progenitor of thousands of years, is a good omen. It means we too shall survive."

I looked at him and smiled, "Perhaps you are right, but to make it happen we must get back to work. You know, Aki, I passed that tree many times but never noticed it before," I pondered as we reached the rice paddy and began digging a small passageway in the dike. Suddenly, as we were digging, there was a rush of water through the passageway and down the hill to eventually meet the swollen stream in a confluence. I straightened up and spoke to Aki, "I believe the water will totally evacuate in about two hours and it seems to me that the rice shoots are unharmed and probably will produce a crop in a few weeks."

"I agree, just in time for a second fall planting."

I looked at Aki with newly gained respect, "Alright, now let us inspect the vegetable farm, and see what must be done. We trudged up to the farm at a snail's pace because of the muddiness of the trail causing us to slip and slide. On arriving we could see the farm was dotted with small puddles everywhere and the furrows were despoiled with some remaining vegetation rotting on the ground.

We set about marking a quadrant in the front half of the farm. Into each of these sections we would plant the vegetable seeds. Our stores of seeds were kept in an earthen cellar which was dug beneath the tool shed to keep them cool and safe from nocturnal rodents. Aki retrieved four kinds of vegetable seeds as determined by the *Tenzo*, cabbage, egg plant, mustard greens, and adzuki beans. I began furrowing the muddy soil with a hoe and Aki followed me dropping the seeds in the opened chamfer and patting it down with his foot.

The sun was oppressively hot beating down on us as we worked. The mist rising from the heated ground produced an almost jungle-like humidity. I seemed to be sweating from every pore of my body. I thought it best to remove my clothing to expose my upper torso for relief but this did little more than allow the sweat to roll down my body. There was no relief from the unbearable sun. We worked like this all morning until meal time. After we finished one of the four quadrants I blurted out, "At least we won't have to water the plantings."

Aki laughed saying, "The ground is so wet it may not have to be watered for weeks."

Then Aki and I bathed in the running stream. It was a real pleasure to have the cool water run across our bodies. The midday meal consisted of one bowl of *congee* (rice porridge) with some pickled vegetables. After our midday meal we returned to the farm to complete the second quadrant. By the end of the day we were both totally exhausted. Despite this we felt good about our accomplishment even knowing that we would spend the next day in another hot, steaming, back-breaking job to complete the last two quadrants. At the end of the day we bathed again and went off to bed on the paillasse.

As hot as it was during the day it was fiercely cold at night. Not having a roof contributed to this situation. But I paid it no attention; I slept. I was so weary and fatigued from the day's work that I was not conscious of falling asleep.

SIXTEEN

The lentil field was saved. Small bushes were rising out of the ground. It was a joy to behold. Life has come back to the lentil field. In a few weeks we will be able to gather the lentil seeds in buckets and these will provide the *Sangha* (Buddhist fellowship) with sustenance in the form of soup and vegetable pate (paste). The other plantings on the farm were thriving as well. The weather turned unusually mild for the end of September. The Roshi announced that we would celebrate the O-Bon ritual even though it was usually celebrated in mid-August. Anyhow, we did not have much food for a festival. I can still hear the Roshi say, *adversity should not prevent our responsibilities; it is important to remember our ancestors and pray for the departed.*

One of the most important events at the monastery is the annual O-Bon festival. O-Bon is a traditional holiday, which remembers and honors those who have passed away. The monastery residents will prepare a paper candle-lit lantern for the deceased. Also, the Tenzo will prepare a meal to be served later in the evening. After this evening meal the ceremony will begin with a Dharma talk given by the Roshi. O-Bon culminates with the candle-lit paper lanterns floating on the river and pond in the late evening.

The following excerpt is by Shundo Aoyama, a Soto Zen Roshi, and chief priest of a training temple for women in Japan:

"In relation to our ancestors, we are like the apex of a pyramid. The levels of a pyramid ever widening toward its base represent past generations of ancestors. Our present existence is the sum of all they did, and we are the starting point for our descendants. All that our ancestors did reflects on us, and all that we do reflect on both our ancestors and our descendants. One's life is not entirely one's own; it contains the past and conceives the future, and should therefore be lived with great care. This is the teaching of the O-Bon Festival".

That is the purpose of O-Bon in a nutshell. It is a very solemn occasion and yet is a happy celebration. Local residents are always invited to join the monastery residents on all aspects of the occasion. But, this year that will not happen due to the devastation by the earthquake and the typhoon.

Suddenly, I discovered Ichi approaching me. She made the comment, "Would you like me to show you how to make a paper lantern?"

I grabbed on this immediately. "Yes," I replied.

"Well then come to my area and we can work on it together after clean up time."

I was grateful for her offer since I had no idea how to make a paper lantern. I later found out that she was going to demonstrate the method of making a paper lantern to a group, but I didn't have the heart to cancel her individual offer to me. We worked most of the day on clean up including raking the fallen *shikiji* leaves all the way down the road to the entrance gate. Another group was busy weeding and straightening flowerbeds. After this spruce up we were ready for the O-Bon celebration.

I did not forget my promise to Ichi to visit with her in order to learn how to make a paper lantern. When I arrived I found the other women busily engaged in straightening up the outside area. When they saw me they began giggling and shyly bowing to me. Ichi came over to me smiling and indicated a place for me to sit. "I am glad that you came, Sweki. I would like to show you how to make a paper lantern."

I admired her smooth face and ruddy cheeks causing a wave of emotion to come over me. She was lovely and I had all I could do to refrain from grabbing her in a hug. Instead I sat down and watched her as she deftly folded the paper into a lantern. It was an amazing change of nothing into something. Then she spoke in her soft voice as she pointed to the portal in the lantern, "This is where you put the lighted candle."

"I see, thank you very much."

"Do you have a small candle?" she inquired.

"I can get one from Aki," I quickly replied.

"That's good. Now tell me about your family."

"There isn't much to tell. My mother, father, older brother and younger sister live on a farm in the Echigo district. I haven't seen them for over three years ever since I left home to be a sailor and then became shipwrecked."

"Do you intend visiting them soon?"

"Not until I become ordained as a monk. I must fulfill my promise to Buddha who saved me." I hesitated for a moment and then continued, "Then after my ordination I would like to visit them. I truly miss them and think about them all the time."

"Do you have any ancestors?"

"Yes, I remember the graves of my grandparents. They are buried on the farm in a distant corner under two large pipal trees. They are the parents of my father and the previous owners of the farm. I remember on O-Bon my father would go to the graveside with a brush and a pail of water and scrub the headstones until they were clean."

She looked at me intently and then began speaking very slowly with a slight pain in her voice, "I never knew my ancestors. They are all dead now and I do not know where they are buried." She stopped speaking then looked up to me with moist eyes, "I think of my life as beginning when I came to this monastery so O-Bon does not mean much to me, but I enjoy the festivities just the same."

"Yes, yes, I see."

"Sweki, do you know how O-Bon started?"

"No, I don't, please tell me."

"O-Bon is derived from the Sanskrit word *ullambana* meaning hanging down. The O-Bon ritual is performed to save deceased people from torments after death – such as being suspended upside down."

"Ha, ha, that sounds very funny."

"Yes it does but serious practitioners believe it." She waited a while and then continued, "In any event, the first performance of the ritual occurred in the third century."

"Really, I had no idea."

"Yes, it has been going on for a long time."

"All I remember is that I was told by my parents that it was a ritual of respect for the departed."

"That's true, but it is also a celebration for the living. The women monks will perform a dance and I shall play the *koto* (Japanese thirteen-stringed zither) tonight.

"Oh, how wonderful, I never heard a koto played before."

"Yes, I am lucky that the koto was not ruined in the earthquake or the typhoon."

"That's true; many people lost much of their belongings. Since I came with little I, of course, had nothing to lose."

That evening there was a gathering of all the monks in the plaza sitting in a circular fashion in the center of which the dancers performed with Ichi playing her koto. The music was wonderful wafting on the evening air and the dancers whirled on the toes of both feet in the style of a pirouette. They performed in a rhythmic and patterned succession of movements in unison with the music. It was a delight to watch them move nimbly and merrily. This was the first and only social meeting that I experienced at the monastery.

At the conclusion of the festivities we all gathered at the pond and floated our candle-lit paper lanterns. It was interesting to see the lanterns floating off as a message to the great unknown. Then the group broke up and went their separate ways. I went off to sleep after bidding Ichi a farewell by a wave of my hand. The Roshi had told us earlier that tomorrow there would be a *dokusan* (Roshi interview).

SEVENTEEN

During "free time" a waiting line of monks formed in front of the Hatto. I got on the queue and waited my turn. At the sound of the bell I entered the Hatto and went to the small room in the rear. The Roshi was already seated. We bowed to each other with a gassho. I sat on the floor in front of him. He looked at me strangely but then suddenly blurted out, "Why have you come?" His eyes had the steady piercing, fixed stare as through querulous wonder.

In a frightened voice I said, "I have come to give you my answer to the koan."

"What is your answer," he grumbled gruffly.

A buffalo passes by the window. His head, horns, and four legs all go past. But why can't the tail pass too? This koan means that the eightfold path will release you from *dukkha* (suffering) only if you include all eight. The tail can't pass because one of the eightfold path has not been completed. The path is not intended to be a series of sequential steps it must completely include the perfected ways of behavior; the eight summarize the necessary constituents in the process toward enlightenment."

The Roshi seemed dazed. He lowered his eyes and shook his head. His face grew red as he looked at me steadily before speaking. "What gibberish. You are caught in a logic trap with this sophistry. I do not accept your answer. It is all nonsense."

I was stunned speechless. He continued with sadistic pleasure in a most sardonic way, "You're a man of the world, Sueki, why did you not make use of your experiences in solving the koan?"

"Yes, I have traveled the world and suffered much. Indeed, I have had many near-death experiences. But will that help me solve the koan?

The Roshi pontificated," Don't you realize that when you sit zazen you must try to gain the Great Death? The activity of consciousness dies away in absolute *samadhi* (concentration)." He stopped speaking and held up both hands. "Go now and work hard so that your mind will reveal your needs. You are a simpleton and a farmer."

"Yes, I am a simple farmer but this talent has provided food and sustenance for my fellow man," I answered forthrightly and without regret. Having said that, I rose, bowed and turned to leave. My mind was racing with many different thoughts. What was the need for insult and abuse? If he did not like my answer couldn't he have told me so in a civil manner? In my dejection I thought – it will be a long time before I return.

On the outside of the Hatto I bumped into Aki. "How did you do Sweki," he said with mirth in his voice.

"I had a terrible session with the Roshi. He was very sarcastic to me and he did not accept my answer to the koan."

"That some times happens. He can be very gruff sometimes."

"Well, I'll try again sometime in the future."

I went back to my room to sulk. I began to realize that answering the Roshi back was not a good idea. I hope he will not hold it against me.

Weeks went by then months and finally the monastery was restored to its original appearance. The sleeping quarters for the men and women was fully restored as were the Hatto, Zendo, and dining hall. The farm was very productive and grew a great variety of vegetables. Normalcy seemed to be at hand.

One day after the Roshi's *teisho* (sermon) he announced that tomorrow a complement of monks would go outside for *takuhatsu* (begging round). He insisted that I accompany the monks assigned to this task.

EIGHTEEN

After zazen, sweeping, breakfast, and prayer service, we prepared for *takuhatsu*. There is a small anteroom in front of the dining hall, which has hooks on the wall containing the robes, hats, and straw fiber slippers used by the monks for *takuhatsu*. I took a complement of items to my room and changed. I immediately went downstairs to congregate with the others and get last minute instructions. We were told to put on our hats and pick up our wooden bowls and file out through the great wooden gate. A gauntlet of the remaining people was waiting in gassho position outside of the gate to wish us luck. We then moved into the neighboring residential area loudly chanting sutras. There were twelve monks and me making this excursion.

Takuhatsu literally means request *(taku)* with the eating bowl *(hatsu)*. In *takuhatsu* the monks generally go in groups of ten to fifteen, one behind the other, and recite sutras in front of the houses for the benefit of the residents. Believers and well-wishers, when they hear the sutras, make donations of cooked food, which they place in the monks' wooden bowl or sometimes uncooked rice which the monks collect in a sack. Recipient and giver then bow to one another in mutual gratitude with humility and respect. The frequent translation of *takuhatsu* as "begging round" is not accurate, since here both parties are "recipients." The notion on which *takuhatsu* is based is as follows: the monks, who are guardians of the dharma, offer it to the public by means of their own example; in exchange for this they are supported by those who trust in the truth of the dharma. In addition, from the traditional Buddhist point of view almsgiving is considered a virtue, which increases good karma. The monks through *takuhatsu* provide the public with an opportunity to practice virtue. According to Dogen, there are three types of "pure food" that which comes from trees and plants, that obtained from begging and that donated by supporters. Anything that is given is purified by the act of giving, provided it is pure giving, done with an open heart, with no strings attached. And so it is with all things. The purity of the thing is determined by its origins, how we come by it.

While walking around the neighborhood soliciting alms I was surprised to see the extent of repair of most of the houses affected by the earthquake and typhoon. Of course, there were still some houses in disrepair and some were shored up with timbers but, generally, the neighborhood survived and returned to a semblance of its regular life. I found after more than two hours that I had collected a full bowl of food and a half sack of uncooked rice.

I was affected emotionally by the generosity of the people which caused a tremulous excitement throughout my whole body. After all, these people had little enough for themselves and they also went through hard times after the earthquake and typhoon.

When we returned to the monastery the Roshi gave a blessing to each bowl, then the bowls were given to the *Tenzo* in the kitchen. One of the monks started to dance a jig with hand-clapping at our good fortune. All of us joined in. It was the first time I felt some camaraderie with the other monks. At the sight of this frivolity the Roshi began to foam with anger. "What is the meaning of this," he shouted. His strong passion of displeasure was evident in his loud voice as he continued the tirade, "Stop this unbecoming levity immediately and return to your serious duties. We are not finished with overcoming our disasters yet." His excess of rage caused all the monks to quickly disperse. We then returned our robes to the hooks on the wall in the small room in front of the dining hall and resumed our routine in utter silence.

Winter was approaching with the weather turning colder and increase intensityof the wind. It was time to harvest the tea leaves before they spoil. The farm was surrounded on three sides with a fencing of tea shrubs. During the growing season the shrubs produce a new growth of tiny leaf buds which have a lighter green color than the old leaves of the shrubs. These tiny leaf buds are harvested by picking and cured by steaming. From these cured leaf buds an aromatic beverage is prepared by infusion with boiling water. The tea is called *ocha*.

A large group of monks including some of the women were assigned the task of picking the tiny leaf buds and placing them in baskets carried on their backs. By midday the crew was finished and brought their gleanings to a place behind the kitchen where the tea leaves were dumped on a large silken mesh cloth. A cauldron containing water had already been fired up to produce steam.

The silken mesh cloth containing the tea leaf buds was stretched over the top of this steaming cauldron and left that way for an hour of curing with occasional mixing. At the end of this time the silken mesh cloth was removed and placed on the ground; the leaves were spread out to dry and cool. The leaves were then crushed in a stone mortar with a wooden pestle by the monks each taking turns at the pounding. A small quantity of crushed tea leaves was given to each monk for his personal use (some monks made tea in their rooms). The remainder of the crushed tea was held by the *Tenzo* for the daily comestible. With its mild climate and fertile soil this northern district is perfect for growing tea shrubs. Although the history of tea-making dates back to the Kamakura-Era (1192-1333) it is only recently that people started cultivating tea shrubs seriously.

After tea harvesting, Aki and I returned to the farm to reap whatever vegetable crops that remained on the ground. We brought these to the *Tenzo* in the kitchen. Now we earnestly returned to our routine duties. I had continued my study of the Shobogenzo with Aki's help and felt very confident that I was fully prepared.

The first snow fall came some weeks later. This was accompanied by a biting wind which caused snow drifts everywhere, especially on the tea shrubs making them look like snowberry bushes. The rooms in the sleeping quarters contained charcoal burners which gave off limited warmth requiring us to wear additional layers of clothing. Since my farm duties were suspended for the winter I was assigned the task of servicing the charcoal burners in the Zendo, Hatto, and dining hall by the Roshi. "Because you have worldly experience; I am assigning you the job of caring for the charcoal burners in The Zendo, Hatto, and dining hall," he said sarcastically with a bitter taunt.

"I shall do my best, master." I replied propitiously.

The Roshi turned and left in silence with his head high perhaps knowing that I had turned his wrath into bliss. I have decided henceforth not to let his sarcasm get the best of me. It is well known that all Roshi's everywhere rule with an iron hand, but the attitude of our Roshi to me flies in the face of one of the most important tenants of Buddhism – compassion. Could he not have some sympathy for my distress? His cruelty towards me was unfounded and unnecessary.

NINETEEN

The world turned white. It snowed unrelentingly for four days and four nights. When it finally stopped everything was a covered with a blanket of snow. In my estimate the snow reached about two and a half meters in height. We were actually snowed in unable to open the doors to the men's sleeping quarters, thus we were not able to attend zazen or morning services. But I had to get out and make pathways to the Zendo, Hatto, and dining hall.

The charcoal burners had to be started in order to provide warmth to these places. Three monks accompanied me in the task of shoveling snow. We had wooden shovels. These were nothing more than long-handled flat-faced implements which were used to lift and throw the snow. The amount of snow contained in such an implement was minimal adding to the tedium of the task. But, eventually we managed to make suitable pathways including one to the women's quarters. I thought about Ichi but immediately dismissed the thought since I was so busy with my labor.

Now, life in the monastery returned to its normal routine. Aki and I spent our leisure time studying and reviewing the *Shobogenzo*. By now I was confident that I understood the concepts of Dogen's teachings.

It was announced one day that the Roshi would hold a *dokusan* (interview). I was anxious to discuss my koan with the Roshi and so I attended his session. "Good day, Sueki, please sit," he calmly and indifferently said. "Are you ready to give me your answer to the koan?"

"Yes, master, I am ready," I retorted in a forthright manner.

He looked at me, eyeball to eyeball, without saying anything for a while. Then in a steady voice he grunted, "What is it?"

I slowly repeated the koan, "*a buffalo passes by the window. His head, horns, and four legs pass by but the tail does not pass by. Why can't you see the tail?*"

"Yes, yes," he said impatiently. "Get on with it. What is your answer?"

I slowly spoke with a steady, confident voice, "The body of the buffalo and the tail are just two aspects of the same reality. The tail and the body of the buffalo are together one Divine Being – impersonal-personal, transcendent-immanent, static-dynamic. You cannot see the tail because you are blind to the truth."

He looked at me with his dark, piercing eyes in silence. After what seemed like a lifetime he slowly spoke in a mollified voice, "I see you have escaped the logic trap." He stalled for a moment then continued, "That was a very unusual explanation." He stopped speaking and continued looking at me as if uncertain as to his words, but then looked down for a moment, raised his head again and said in a low voice, "I accept your answer."

I was overwhelmed by his statement. I feared the outcome of my answer but was greatly relieved at his words. "Thank you, master," is all I could say. I knew in my heart that I had accomplished something worthwhile.

"Continue your studies with Aki and do your work diligently." He hesitated for a moment but then said with earnest deliberation, "Sometime in the spring, if all goes well, you shall be ordained a monk."

I rose and bowed very low with a gassho, turned and left his presence. When I came out to the pathway I found Aki waiting for me. He was bent over in his usual stance shivering in the cold, blustery weather. "How did it go, Sweki?" He blubbered with quivering, swollen lips.

"It went very well, Aki. The Roshi accepted my answer to the koan," I said excitedly.

"How wonderful," he replied. "Now you will be on your way to ordination."

"Yes, that will occur sometime in the spring," I said.

We both started walking back through the mountains of snow packed on both sides of the pathway to the sleeping quarters and climbed the staircase to the second floor. The small charcoal burner barely warmed the nearest area but it was comforting nevertheless. I started to remove my clothing before getting under the blanket of my paillasse when I noticed white hoarfrost at the portico which made me quiver with a slight jerking, tremulous motion. But after a while, under the blanket, the shaking subsided and I dozed off to dream of home and the warm weather of the farm.

It seemed that the farm was shod with fire. All around the green sprouts the sun was ceaselessly beating down. As I walked toward my father, who was in the rice paddy, I could feel the sun following me and striking me on my back. "Hello, father, how are you?"

He looked up from his bent position replying in a startled voice, "Sueki, its good to see you. How are you? Are you a Buddhist monk yet?"

"Not yet, father, but I will be soon."

I jumped to my feet at the sound of the distant rumble, my eyes narrowed to slits. It's just the thunder. A sudden cold gust drags me from my sleep. At the window, a very strange, ferrous light beneath a low sky, filled with clouds and frost that awaits the courageous monks going to the Zendo. There goes a second thunderclap to make me shiver. The third thunderclap is a flicker that splits the horizon. It is coming quietly closer, as the sparrows cry out with hunger and the frustration of not being able to fly. It will crush us, an even blackness spread across the whole sky. That's the fourth, much closer. It's almost on top of us. Then there was a crash that shakes the earth and the sudden roar of rain bouncing off leaves and hammering down from the roof. I look at the road to the farm, already a channel of mud sliding down the low hill; only a madman would go out in weather like this. The monks ran to the Zendo, charging down the pathway, slipping on the rain-soaked grass, getting back to their feet and laughing like drunkards. Once inside the Zendo everyone took his place while the water ran down from their bald heads and faces, but in moments, all was still except for the constant rhythmic beating of the rain on the roof.

Finally, the rain stopped leaving mud, ice and flooding in its wake. But happily one could see significant depletion of the snow. It was time to assess the damage from the storm. It turns out that all the roofs of the several buildings had small but annoying leaks. These had to be repaired and so a crew was assigned to this task while the weather was still cold but dry. It was still winter and another rain storm or snow storm could erupt at any time.

Aki and I went from building to building mopping up puddles of water which resulted from the leaks in the roofs. We also cleaned out all the charcoal burners, removing ashes and supplying fresh fuel and then lighting them up again. It was the responsibility of an assigned person on each floor to keep the charcoal burners fed with fuel but inevitably this task was sometimes forgotten causing the fires to go out. Much of this work was performed during free time as well as the time we would have normally spent working on the farm. Otherwise our routine remained relatively the same.

On the second day after the rain storm, the sun came out fully bright and the temperature rose to a tolerable level. Mud was everywhere. The road to the farm was impassable. Walking on this road resulted in sinking ankle deep and slipping. The pathway was muddy as well and required the laying of tree limbs so the monks could get to and from the various buildings. Aki and I spent some time in removing the packed snow from the sides of the pathway. The work caused us to sweat but it was a good feeling after the shivering and shaking of the previous days.

Sitting in the Zendo during zazen was a trial. The temperature in the Zendo was extremely cold despite the charcoal burner which only provided warmth to a small area. Those of us in the lowest pecking order, especially me – a novice, were seated some distance from the charcoal burner where it was ineffective. I usually came to the Zendo with a blanket shawl to wrap myself cocoon-style and thus ward off the cold. I could see my breath freeze to a smoky trail as I exhaled and my nostrils would collect ice droplets which hung from my nose like stalactites. Interestingly, I found that by not thinking about my plight I was able to go on independent of this situation around me. After zazen, I returned to my sleeping quarters to clean up the area. I was glad to keep working at sweeping the floor and servicing the charcoal burner as this was the only way I could keep warm.

Eventually, the weather got increasingly warmer. It seems that the harsh winter was abating and I looked forward to life returning to the monastery. The mud began to dry up leaving a coating of dust which flew into the air as it was kicked up. Still it was better than the persistent mud. Aki and I had to go up to the farm in order to till the soil and fertilize with liquid human dung for early spring planting. All the feces in the outhouse was collected in buckets and used as fertilizer on the farm. Everyone took turns at this collecting. The tiller was a long-handled blade pulled by me as Aki held it straight. In doing this work I felt no different than a work-animal. After turning over the soil we went down the furrows with a large ladle pouring liquid dung into the furrows. The stench that pervaded the atmosphere was awful, but one could get used to it and after a few days the smell seemed to disappear. The prepared soil was allowed to lie fallow until the dung fertilizer mixed with the tilled soil by seeping into the turned over soil.

After two weeks, we obtained various vegetable seeds from the Tenzo who harbored the seeds all winter. These seeds were planted in the furrows by me as Aki followed with a hoe to cover the seeds with soil. We established a pattern of different vegetables in plots such as eggplants, carrots, mustard greens, and adzuki beans. By planting early we could harvest these vegetables in time to plant a second crop.

The next major job was to work on the rice paddy. After inspecting the rice paddy we discovered that the seed sprouts planted last fall were alive and ready for separation into rows in the paddy. This was back-breaking work putting a single sliver of a rice stalk into the ground in a regimental order. We worked at diverting the stream which by now was running rapidly due to the melting snow. This irrigation was made to flow into the paddy flooding it to a height of about twelve centimeters. After the paddy was flooded we repaired the opened dike to allow the stream to flow its normal course down to the pond next to the kitchen. No doubt about it, spring was coming and my heart filled with joy in anticipation of my ordination.

As the weather became warmer one could see life returning to the earth. Little shoots of grass were beginning to push there way to the surface and greet the sun. Tiny buds began to appear on the barren trees. It was like a resurrection from death. I decided to walk over to the women's quarters to visit with Ichi during free time. My duties on the farm only consisted of weeding the furrows at this time and so I was not that busy. When I arrived there no one was about. I went to the doorway of the sleeping quarters and called out, "Ichi, it is I, Sweki." In a moment I heard someone rustling and then followed by shuffling footsteps. Suddenly, Ichi appeared with a broad grin on her face.

"Oh Sweki, how nice it is to see you."

"I hope I am not disturbing you. I only came to tell you the good news about my pending ordination in the spring."

"Yes, I heard about it. I am glad for you."

"Of course, I shall have to undertake the ten precepts as a moral obligation but that will not be a problem for me."

"Sweki, you'll do fine."

"Well, how have you been? Are you alright?"

"Oh Sweki, it was a terrible winter and it is still very cold, but at least the snow is gradually going away."

"Yes and the earthquake and typhoon damage were not easy to overcome."

"That's right but the repairs have been made and life is finally becoming normal again."

"Is there anything I can do for you?"

"No, thank you, Sweki, we are all doing well. Would you like to come inside and sit by the fire?"

"Yes, yes, it's cold outside. Are you sure I am not interfering?"

"It's alright, Sweki, the other women would be glad to see you."

I followed Ichi inside to a small room with a very active charcoal burner. The women were all seated around it in a circular fashion with some sewing. On seeing me they all greeted me; some giggled. A place was made for Ichi and me in the circle.

I had an idea on seeing the sewing and asked Ichi, "I will need my new robe and the *rakusu* (miniature symbolic robe) for the ordination but I have not finished sewing them. I am not very good at sewing. Could you and the women help me?"

"Of course, Sweki, bring the material during your next visit and we shall complete them."

"Looking at the women she asked, "Is that alright, friends?"

They all nodded and said in unison, "Yes, yes, of course, bring the material, Sweki. We would be most happy to complete them."

I was very pleased to be relieved of this burden. This task weighed heavily on my mind. "I shall return tomorrow during free time with all the material. Thank you all very much." I then rose to depart.

Ichi accompanied me outside saying, "I am looking forward to the spring so that we can go for walks in the forest." This statement reminded me of our past experiences. "Yes, indeed, that would be very nice."

After bowing I trudged away to complete my clean-up work; all the time recollecting the intimate moments I had with Ichi.

So, the days passed with the weather getting warmer until the mountains of snow began disappearing. The melting snow produced more mud due to the water run-off. It was quite a feat avoiding the mud as one maneuvered the pathways to the various buildings. Eventually, the mud dried up leaving a coating of dust on the pathways, which was kicked up by walking forming a choking cloud. In order to overcome this problem it was planned and decided that planting rocks in the pathways as paving stones would be the prudent thing to do.

There were many suitable rocks which fell from the mountain during the earthquake. This was also an opportunity to continue filling the still open fissure with rocks which were too big for paving the pathways. A large crew of monks was assigned to this task. Aki and I busied ourselves removing unwanted residual rocks from the farm so that our future plantings could be increased on rock less earth.

Carrying rocks to the paving site of the pathways was incredibly arduous work. By the end of the day everyone was exhausted. But now that the pathways were paved properly this gave a renewed spirit of satisfaction to the monastery. Yes, slowly the monastery was rising from the destruction like a phoenix rising from the ashes.

One day, it was announced by the Roshi in the dining hall that my ordination would take place next week. I was very excited and I could see from the faces of the other monks seated at the table that everyone was pleased. I hastened back to the women's quarters to retrieve my finished robe and rakusu.

TWENTY

It was a bright sunny morning for the *Jukai ceremony* (the receiving and granting of the precepts, the formal initiation into the Zen Buddhist way). The day has arrived. After zazen I was led to a side room in the Hatto and dressed in a white gown. White is the color of death and symbolically this white gown is a sign of the death of my old life. Now, I am to be reborn as a Soto Zen monk. I was seated in *seiza position* (sitting on one's heels with knees touching the floor) facing the lectern in back of which the Roshi read from the scriptures.

I was nervously excited as I listened to the words expounded by the Roshi. Finally, he looked at me with his piercing eyes as he slowly questioned me, "Are you ready to receive the *Jujukai* (the ten main precepts of Mahayana Buddhism)?"

"Yes," I answered in a loud, clear voice.

He cleared his throat and began to recite in a very solemn way, "The exoteric precepts forbid taking of life, stealing, unchasteness, lying, trade in alcohol, gossip, praising self and deprecating others, reluctance in giving help to others, aggression, slandering the Three Jewels of Buddha, Dharma and Sangha." He rested for a moment then looked up to meet my eyes once again before continuing," Do you accept these precepts?"

I answered forcefully without hesitation, "*Hai*" (Yes).

He continued to look at me as if he had not heard me and once again he slowly spoke, "The ten esoteric precepts have been part of your training here in the monastery. Do you vow not to abandon dharma, not to abandon seeking enlightenment, not to covet, not to lack compassion, not to slander any Buddhist teachings, not to be attached to anything, not to entertain false views, to encourage all to seek enlightenment, to instruct adherents to *Hinayana* (lesser vehicle), to practice responsive charity to *Bodhisattvas* (one who delays Nirvana in order to help others). Once again he looked up to meet my eyes, "Do you so vow?"

I answered in a clear, loud voice, "I so vow."

"Well then, these are the promises you must make to yourself at the start of each day. The observance of these precepts has been ordered by the Buddha. You have taken these precepts upon yourself therefore I pronounce you a member of the *Sangha* (Buddhist fellowship). Your dharma name will be Kosan (Old Mountain). As your teacher I have been certified by another previous teacher in the long line of Mahayana lineage which can be traced back to the Buddha. You are now part of that lineage. As a monk you will be identified by the wearing of this *rakusu* (the miniature robe sewn by Ichi)."

He handed the rakusu to an assistant who placed it carefully around my neck. It hung in front of my chest like a badge of honor. I was very proud. I thought about the promise I made to the Buddha so long ago while drifting on the wet board on the ocean current; *Buddha, if you save me I shall cut my hair and enter a Buddhist monastery.*

I was then led by a small contingent back to the side room where I removed the white robe and redressed in the new robe made for me by Ichi and her friends. On leaving the Hatto all the monks crowded around me saying kind words and bowing profusely. Yes, I am now a monk. I really felt like I belonged. I was now one of them. Aki and Ichi both came up to me with congratulatory expressions of sympathetic pleasure. All I could say was, "I am grateful to the both of you for your support and faith in me. I shall never forget your help."

The crowd of monks began to disperse to various venues until we met again in the dining hall at breakfast. I could now notice a completely different attitude towards me. Yes, indeed, I was now one of them.

Spring brought with it much work on the farm. For one thing the rice paddy revealed mature shoots which must be harvested. This was accomplished by cutting bundles with a sickle. It was back-breaking work. The bundles were accumulated and then threshed to loosen the small rice kernels. When that's accomplished the kernel mixture is thrown up in the air for the wind to separate the seed from the chaff. The wind blows away the worthless chaff while the rice kernels fall back to the ground.

At this point the rice kernels contain some hard, immature, inedible kernels which must be removed. Large bags of this composite were brought to the kitchen where the hard, inedible kernels are removed by tediously picking them out one by one by the monks. For some of the monks doing this work became a form of meditation due to its steady mindless work. Meanwhile, a second crop was planted in the paddy to be harvested in early summer. Then a third planting will take place to be harvested in the fall.

TWENTY-ONE

By early summer, the daily routine of the monastery plodded on to an ultimate boredom. I always found working on the farm most gratifying especially when it was interspersed with occasional walks in the wooded area with Ichi during free time. I also continued my Zen literature studies with Aki as my *Taiban*. But I found these limited and the wanderlust kept whelming up within me. I could not help myself; I thought about my parents and home that I have not seen for about six years since I left home to become a sailor. But I am no longer the same person. I am now a Zen monk ready to help my fellow man. Shouldn't I go into the world to minister to people and spread the teachings of the Buddha? These thoughts plagued me constantly as I worked on the farm tilling the soil and harvesting vegetables.

I spoke of these concerns to Ichi, one day, during one of our walks. She looked at me strangely as she said, "You should be patient, Sweki. We of the monastery live in a communal society. You must learn to enjoy the benefit of a simple social life. We, here, are a small group with shared similar tastes and motives. It is not like this on the outside. We are the protectors of the Buddha's dharma."

"Yes, yes, Ichi, I know what you are saying is true but I have the distinct feeling within me that I should be doing more productive work as a monk."

These dubious queries continued to haunt me for sometime. One day, I decided to attend the Roshi's *dokusan*. I had not spoken with him since my ordination. We saw each other and passed each other with bows and other gestures of familiarity but we have not spoken. I needed to explore these feelings with him and seek his advice.

The little room to the side of the Hatto was darkened but I could make out the Roshi in the candlelight. His shadow was projected immensely on the wall behind him. As I entered the room I could detect the dank characteristic odor of human bodies from previous seekers. The acridity of the odor made my nostrils quiver.

"Please sit down *Kosan* (Sueki's dharma name). How can I help you?"

"Roshi-san, I have not seen my family for six years. I am troubled by this absence and I miss them very much."

"I see."

"What advice would you give me to overcome these troubling thoughts?"

"You should go to visit your parents."

"What, what did you say. I mean what did I hear?"

Without moving a muscle in his face he calmly repeated, "I said, you should go visit your parents."

"Do you mean, I should leave the monastery and travel to Echigo where they live?"

"Yes that is precisely what I mean," He said matter-of-factly.

"But how, where, I do not understand."

He then raised his right hand which contained a strand of mala beads twisted around his palm and slowly spoke, "There is a small temple I know of in Echigo which services the local farming community. Its name is Koetsu-ji. The *sensei* (teacher) of the temple died about a year ago and the temple has been without a leader since then. My suggestion to you is that you visit your parents first then take up residence at temple Koetsu-ji and serve the community as the new sensei.

I was stunned and speechless at his words. I couldn't believe that I was hearing them or only imagining them. I could only look at the Roshi in wonderment – *he is giving me an opportunity to find meaning in my life.*

The silence was broken by his next words," I must forewarn you that the temple Koetsu-ji is in grave disrepair. In the last year there was no one to act as a caretaker and so some of the building is in shambles and would require major fixing. In addition, the surrounding fields have lain fallow for the past year and would require maintenance to resuscitate them as a working farm."

"Yes, yes, I understand."

He continued, "Koetsu-ji is a temple with practitioners but no parish."

"Are you saying it has no support?"

"I am saying that Koetsu-ji, which you will inherit, needs a way to survive financially. As you know all temples in Japan are usually supported by the parish. In addition, you must take care of the parishioners needs such as funerals, memorial services, religious holidays and even weddings. As the resident monk you must take care of the temple grounds, practice zazen, and engage in takuhatsu. It is a formidable task. Are you ready and able?"

"Yes, Roshi-san, I look on this as an opportunity."

"Good, then be ready to leave in a week and I shall contact the village head."

I left his presence with a formal low bow. My mind was swimming with many heady thoughts as I stepped outside. *Where do I start? I must gather together my meager possessions and start saying goodbye to people.* The thought of leaving this "safe harbor" became a vexing problem. But looking forward to new adventures and seeing my family again was an exciting feeling of delight and happiness. How do I begin? First I must seek out Aki and tell him the news. I must also visit with Ichi to tell her of my plans – suddenly I stopped in my tracks and thought – *will that be a problem? I wonder how she will react to the news.*

I went up to my room where I found Aki. He was bent over sweeping the floor with a small hand broom made by Ichi.

"Aki, I have good news to share with you."

"Yes, yes, what is it?" he questioned as he straightened up as best he could.

I looked at this pitiful creature who was not only my very good friend but also my dedicated helper. I choked up before speaking but cleared my throat and said, "Aki, I shall be leaving the monastery next week."

"What, what, you are leaving?"

"Yes, I will visit my parents and then take over a small temple nearby."

"Why are you leaving? Aren't you happy here?"

"Yes, of course, I am happy here. But I miss my family and I have become restless with life in the monastery." I hesitated a moment then continued, "I shall miss you very much. We have been very good friends. You have been my true teacher. I shall always remember how you worked with me unflinchingly on the farm with such outgoing intensity."

"Yes, I shall miss you as well."

We bowed to each other and then I retreated to my area. Aki continued watching me until he turned and returned to his work.

During free time I left my room to bring the news of my departure to Ichi. On seeing her I requested that we go for a walk into the woods. She was overjoyed at this prospect being unaware of my true motives. After a little while I stopped and faced her. She looked at me with a moonstruck gaze. I could not speak. I was all choked up. I just stared at her as we faced each other.

"What is it, Sweki?"

"I have something important to tell you, Ichi," I stammered.

"What is it, Sweki?" she repeated.

"I am leaving the monastery and going home," I blurted out with obvious exertion.

She was silent and visibly morbid. "When are you leaving?"

"The end of the week," I uttered in a staccato fashion.

"Oh, oh, so soon, but why are you leaving so soon?"

I could not respond since the question was probably only rhetorical and had no real answer. Instead I said meaningless things to overcome the need for an authentic response. I was very sorry for her, but I saw in a flash that I could not help her; that was what made her so tragic.

"I shall miss you."

"I shall miss you too."

I turned and left her standing in the footpath. I was overcome with guilt for my naïve behavior and sought the solace of Aki.

Once again, I discovered him in the room. I approached him pensively and began relating my encounter with Ichi. He raised his head and became animated. "What did you expect? We all care for you very much. We have all been like family dealing with tremendous adversity. We need each other. We depend on each other. Now you are abandoning us."

"No, no, I am not abandoning anyone. I am simply going home. After six years I am entitled to that. Would you have me neglect my parents? I do not want to lose the remembrance of them."

"Yes, but you will not return. We shall never see you again."

I breathed out in exhausted impatience and then said convincingly, "Aki life moves on. I will be presiding over a small temple in the Echigo area. We will be able to visit each other in the future."

He seemed to accept my words as he wiped the tears from his eyes with a small handkerchief which he removed from his sleeve pocket. Then he did a very unusual thing. He reached out to me and drew me to his body in a hug. I was startled as I felt his bent body with my hands. We quickly withdrew with immediate alacrity and went our separate ways.

TWENTY-TWO

Every day was filled with painful anticipation. I was so anxious to be on my journey home that I could not concentrate on my daily chores. But, the day of departure finally came. I sat zazen, attended services, and left to clean up my room. I took my paillasse to the compost box and dumped the straw out of my paillasse. I then shook out the long cloth bag/container and hung it up at the laundry area to air out. I returned to my room to bid goodbye to Aki. "I shall be leaving after breakfast Aki and I just wanted to say goodbye."

He turned to face me, looking up into my eyes. He was silent for a moment before speaking, "Sweki, you have been my true friend. I enjoyed working with you and will always remember you." His eyes became moist as he reached out to me and touched my arm. I could see that no one could ever be less invidious than Aki. He was always at my side working without complaint despite his obvious infirmity. I shall miss him as a friend and a teacher. I turned and left to visit Ichi. When I arrived at her dwelling I called out, "Ichi, it is I, Sweki."

She came outside carrying something in her hand which she presented to me saying, "I refuse to believe this is the end." She hesitated before continuing, "I made you a pair of *hangtsu* (walking slippers) for your journey." Once again she hesitated then continued, "I am sure some day we shall see each other again. I wish you much happiness in your new position."

I accepted the *hangtsu* with outstretched hands and could only mutter, "Thank you." I hung my head and almost started to turn away when I saw her offering her hand. I quickly grabbed it and said, "I shall never forget you. I look forward to the time when we shall meet again." Realizing these words were empty, I left with a heavy heart and a moment of depression. Even so I rallied and made my way to the dining hall for breakfast. As I entered I spotted the Roshi about to sit down. I approached him deferentially and I spoke in an almost whisper with a small bow, "Roshi-san, may we meet after breakfast?"

He looked at me in surprise and whispered back, "That is a good idea, Kosan; let's meet in my dokusan room after breakfast."

I was thrilled at the prospect of discussing my travel plans with him. It turned out there was much to learn before leaving. Once again, I found myself in the small room off to the side of the Hatto seated in front of the Roshi. He adopted his usual officious demeanor with the statement, "Are you ready to leave today?"

"Yes Roshi-san, I am ready."

"Good, well then, I have prepared a small map for you to follow on your way to Niigata. Actually you will be following the trail blazed by Basho, the great poet, in 1689 on his way along the northern coast. "He stopped for a moment to clear his throat then continued, "When you leave the monastery you must head for the city of Mutsu; from there to Nohesi and then across to Hirosaki. There is a temple in the city of Hirosaki where you may be able to stay the night. From Hirosaki, in Aomori prefecture, you should proceed to the coast at Noshiro. From Noshiro there it is a continuous road along the coast to Niigata. You must follow the coast route until you reach Niigata in the Echigo area. The distance is about 450 kilometers which means with steady walking you should reach your destination in about twelve days depending on how many times you obtain rides from local farmers." He stopped to clear his throat and then gave me additional information, "After visiting with your parents you should go inland a short distance from Niigata to the village of Kitakata where you will find your temple Koetsu-ji."

"I don't know how to thank you, Roshi-san."

"No need to thank me. Just remember – in your travels you will meet the malevolent and the charitable. Accept both as a gift. It will open itself to the great life of humanity. *The human spirit is stronger than anything that can happen to it.*"

Somehow I got the feeling that he has given that sage advice to others before me. As usual there was no warmth between us. I left and headed to the kitchen quickly to bid farewell to the Tenzo. "Ah, good morning Tenzo-san, I came to say goodbye. I am leaving for my home in Echigo."

"Yes, I expected you, "He said with his cheerful voice. "Roshi-san told me of your pending departure. I wish you luck and happiness in your future life and your new venture." He then handed me a warm package saying, "I have prepared a package of cooked rice for you that will probably turn cold by the time you eat it but it will still be edible."

I thanked him and went to my room to retrieve my bag containing my meager belongings and made my way to the large front gate. As I approached the gate I remembered the first day that I arrived in the monastery waiting out side overnight before gaining admittance. Suddenly, I realized that a gauntlet was formed by the monks through which I had to pass. All I saw were their smiling faces and cheers of *"Goodbye Sweki"*. It was a wonderful feeling to hear the good wishes of my confreres. I kept walking between the two lines with my bag slung over my shoulder. My arm was raised and waving at the assemblage until I reached the road. I turned to face the crowd of monks and waved again. Then I was off walking down the road to Mutsu. The roadway down the mountainside was made treacherous due to the deposition in my way of rocks and large boulders by the recent earthquake. I continued downward avoiding, as best as I could, the detritus and by jumping over an occasional rill until I reached the bottom road to Mutsu. The roadway was now cleared of all hazards to my course. I began a steady momentum in my walking gait with a liberal pace. Along the way I passed people who kept me in view out of curiosity and sometimes I would wave to them. But they never waved back, perhaps regarding me as an oddity. After some time I arrived at the outskirts of Mutsu. I could now see buildings and hear an increase in the din of busy activity. I continued until I came to a fork in the road. I was in a quandary, which way shall I go to Nohesi? As if by magic, a farmer riding a dray being pulled by a pair of bullocks passed by me. "Ho there, farmer," I shouted after him, "Which way to Nohesi?" He stopped his heavily loaded wagon until I could reach him by a quickened pace.

"I am on my way to Nohesi," he said, "If you like you may keep me company, Reverend."

"Yes, yes, thank you very much." I then clambered on board his load of hay by catching hold of his calloused hand. He was a small man with a craggy, wind bitten face and gray hair creeping out from under his hat. He then asked, "Do you have business in Nohesi, *Shaku* (Reverend)?"

"No, no, I am on my way to Niigata but I thought I would stay the night in Hirosaki at the temple there."

"You mean the temple Shobo-ji?"

"Yes, that is the name."

"I see, well, I can take you as far as Nohesi but then you must continue your journey on foot to Hirosaki. I should caution you, *Shaku* (Reverend), not to walk alone at night. There are bandits and unsavory people roaming these roads at night preying on travelers."

"Thank you for the advice but I didn't intend walking at night. Indeed, I am too poor to become a victim of bandits. I own nothing of value. All I have is the robe on my back with a rakusu hanging from my neck as you can see. My bag only contains a spare robe, a spare pair of walking slippers and a Shobogenzo."

"Where did you come from, *Shaku* (Reverend)?"

"I have just left the monastery above Mutsu this morning"

"Where are you going in Niigata, *Shaku* (Reverend)?"

"I am visiting my parents who are farmers inland from the city of Kitakata where I shall preside over the temple there."

"Farmers, you say, well then we are brethren."

"Yes, we are brethren," I chuckled.

The banter continued this way until we reached Nohesi where I jumped off the dray and waved goodbye to the farmer. I then continued by foot towards Hirosaki. It was a lonely road going through some mountainous areas making the walking somewhat more difficult. I kept moving steadily as I noticed the sun dipping below the horizon. It was getting dusky and then it happened. I saw *Okami* (a wolf) at the side of the road. He had long, sharp, canine teeth which he gnashed at me with a low, rumbling, deep murmur emitting from his throat. He had silver fur spotted with black at the throat and muzzle. His jaw and mouth were projected and he strained as if to leap. I was frightened at the sight of him with his steady, fixed gaze of deep, yellow eyes. I thought he would leap at me at any moment.

I calmly put down my bag without unnecessary movements, and began speaking to him softly, "Are you hungry? I have some lovely cooked rice in my bag which I would be happy to share with you." He responded with a slow snarl while I reached into my bag to retrieve the package of cooked rice. I laid it on the ground and opened the package, "Here you are, come have some delicious rice," I said with a cautionary tone in my voice. The wolf did not move. He simply stared at me while the light of the moonrise sparkled off his white teeth. I repeated and pointed to the rice, "Have some, Mr. Wolf."

I waited and then I saw him lower his head. He closed his mouth and licked his lips with his long, wet tongue. He began moving very slowly towards me and so I moved back away from the rice. Still distrustful, he approached the rice sniffing and waited; then he lowered his head with open mouth while his eyes moved upwards as he kept me in his sight. With a few large bites he swallowed the entire amount of rice followed by the licking of his chops with his long, moist tongue followed by a snap of his jaws. He then sniffed the empty paper, looked up at me sorrowfully as if to say thanks and retreated to the side of the road under the protection of the vegetation where he resumed his sentry position.

I picked up the spent paper and put it in my bag which I shouldered and resumed walking again. He was alerted by my movements and began following me, more like accompanying me, along the side of the road as I proceeded. It was now the darker part of twilight so I attempted to hurry along and quicken my pace. This caused the wolf to pick up his pace as well. In a few hours we reached the temple Shobo-ji in Hirosaki by nightfall. The wolf waited outside, resting on his belly and haunches, while I passed through the temple gate. I opened the door to the temple anteroom where I removed my walking slippers. As I looked up I noticed a Zen priest looking at me. When our eyes met he said, "Good evening, *Shaku* (Reverend). How may I help you?"

"Good evening, Roshi-san, I am on my way to my temple in Kitakata. I was hoping I may stay the night?"

"Of course, of course, you may sleep in the Zendo after zazen."

"Thank you Roshi-san. I am most grateful."

"By the way have you eaten, are you hungry?"

"I have not eaten since breakfast and I gave away my food to a friend who was hungrier than me, Roshi-san."

"Ah yes, come with me to the kitchen and we shall find a meal for you. My name is Unzan. What is your name?"

I bowed with a gassho as I followed him, "My dharma name is Kosan but I am usually known by my birth name Sueki. My friends call me Sweki."

"I see, and then Sweki it shall be. Are you traveling alone, Sweki?"

I chuckled, "Ha, ha, I have been accompanied by a wolf for a short distance since I left Nohesi. Up until there I was given a ride by a farmer on his dray."

"I see, here we are in the kitchen, please sit. May I offer you *tabemono* (food)?" He presented me with a bowl of rice and a skewer of roasted fish.

"Oh, how wonderful, I have not eaten fish for the many years I have been in the monastery."

"Well then enjoy yourself," he said while handing me the steaming bowl of cooked rice and the fish skewered with a pair of *hashi* (chopsticks). "When you are finished you may go to the Zendo for zazen. I shall leave a blanket for you on your sitting place."

"Thank you for your kindness, Roshi-san," I said. He left so I began chewing the fish whole and stuffing my mouth with the cooked rice. It tasted a lot better than the fish I ate when stranded on the wet board in the ocean current. When I finished I placed the bowl and bamboo chopsticks in the sink and went to the Zendo. In the Zendo there were other practitioners. I sat zazen for one hour. By the time I finished the other practitioners had all left. I was completely alone in this dark room. I stretched out on the platform using my bag as a pillow, and covering myself with the provided blanket to ward off the night chill. Soon I was fast asleep. I dreamt the same recurring dream about my home and my parents.

In the morning the sound of a *rin* (bell) woke me up. It was time for zazen. I immediately folded the blanket and sat for an hour as the vital force of conscious existence slowly returned to me. At the completion of zazen I took the folded blanket and searched for Unzan, the Roshi. I found him in the Hatto, preparing for morning service. He took the blanket from me and invited me to stay for services, "After services, you may join us for breakfast and then you may go on your way to Kitakata."

I was overwhelmed by his kindness and could only say, "Thank you." At breakfast I was given a bowl of rice gruel and a hard boiled duck egg. It was delicious and now it was time to go. "Goodbye, Roshi-san. Thank you for all your kindness to me," I said with a low bow and gassho.

"Goodbye Sweki, have a good trip," he said as he handed me a package. "Here is some cooked rice for your long journey."

Tears came to my eyes at his thoughtfulness. This was the same parting gift bestowed on me by the Tenzo of the monastery. I placed it in my bag and went to retrieve my walking slippers. Then I left the temple as the first light of morning began to appear. I breathed in deeply the early morning clean air. I looked about me but the wolf was no where to be seen. I suppose he returned to his pack. I started down the road to Noshiro, a distance of about 160 kilometers. It should take me about six hours of steady walking to reach Noshiro which means I should get there in the early afternoon. As I trudged along the sun kept slowly rising producing a warming sensation in the atmosphere. The road kept dividing the trees like a tunnel. All I could see around me were the deciduous trees regaining their leaves and the coniferous trees which never lost their green and remained verdant through the harsh winter.

In two hours of walking I came to the town of Odate, the first sign of civilization after leaving the mountainous area behind me. I sat on a tree stump by the side of the road to rest. Then another stroke of good fortune – a farmer's wagon stopped next to me. "Hello, *Shaku* (Reverend), do you need a ride? You look tired."

"Yes, yes. I am tired. I am going to Noshiro. Are you going near there?"

"Reverend, you are in good luck that's exactly where I am going. I am bringing these fruits to the market there. Come up on board." With that he extended his hand and then with a clicking sound from his mouth and a slap of the reins on the horse's rump he made the horse pull the wagon forward. For a few minutes there was silence until he questioned me, "What will you do in Noshiro, *Shaku* (Reverend)?"

With a low impatient sigh I said," Actually, I am heading down the coastal road to Niigata. I am presiding over a temple inland from there at Kitakata."

"Oh, that sounds like a long distance."

"Yes, it should take me about a week of walking." Then, I hastily added, "Unless I meet good people like you to give me rides."

He laughed but continued, "Are you from around here, *Shaku* (Reverend)?"

"No, no, I was a member of the monastery above Mutsu."

After about two hours of this chitter-chatter we came to the outskirts of Noshiro. I debarked from the wagon with unceasing thanks to the farmer and continued on the road toward the coastal road. Suddenly I recognized the aroma in the air. It was the salty smell of the sea. How could I forget it? I am now coming close to the Japan Sea and the coastal road. I walked on the sandy beach until I could see the waves of water flowing up to the flat beach surface and spreading a wet stain. It was a sight buried deep in my memory of the time I was rescued by the Makah Indians from the beach in America.

I removed my clothes and ran into the surf nude. No one was around so I felt courageous. The water was icy cold but it was a refreshing experience to remove the smell of body sweat. I would then squeegee off the superfluous water with my hands and put back my robe on my damp body. I sat on the sand and decided to partake of the food given to me by the Roshi of temple Shobo-ji. On opening the package I discovered the same meal I had for supper – cooked rice and a roasted fish skewered with a pair of bamboo chopsticks. After eating this hearty meal I lay back on my bag as a pillow and allowed the warm sun to bake me like a lizard until I fell asleep. It seemed like a long time since I dozed off but in reality it was only a few minutes before I was woken. In my dreamy state I heard some one calling, "Are you alright *Shaku* (Reverend)?" I quickly jumped to my feet. "Yes, I am alright. What is it?"

"I am sorry to disturb you, *Shaku*; I thought you might have been injured."

"No, no, I was just dozing."

"May I help you in any way? I am a fisherman and my sloop is anchored off shore." He pointed with great pride to the most beautiful sea worthy vessel I have ever seen. He continued, "I just came ashore in my skiff to resupply my sloop. I am heading for my fishing village at Sakata. I have just returned from Matsumae with a load of cold water fish."

"Sakata, where is that?" I inquired with great interest.

"Let me see. Oh, yes, Sakata is about halfway from here to Niigata."

"You don't say." I said with surprise. "It happens that I am going to Niigata. My family and my temple are inland from there at Kitakata."

"Well then, come along with me. It's better than walking."

I hesitated but then quickly took up his offer. "Are you sure I won't be any trouble? I do not wish to interfere."

"By all means, it will be no trouble at all. Wait by my skiff while I get a carboy of fresh water."

I went to the water's edge where the skiff had been pulled up on the sand and then looked out to sea. There it was, stately and majestic. I could see the sloop off the shore anchored at sea. She was a fore-and-aft-rigged vessel with one mast and a single headsail jib, as well as a topsail, mainsail, and a spinnaker flopping in the wind. I knew from the look of her that she was fast and could slice through the water with a favorable wind. It seemed possible to me that I could reach Sakata in about ten hours or less. That would mean I would only have about 180 kilometers left to Niigata. I mused, *where did he get such a remarkable vessel? It is not of Japanese make.* In a little while the fisherman returned carrying the large carboy of fresh water enclosed in a wicker-work with handles. He placed the carboy in the skiff, turned to me and commanded, "Come along get in the skiff. We have little time to spare." Then he shoved the skiff into the surf and hopped in with great dexterity as it began floating. He mounted the oars and began rowing to the sloop. He questioned me as he panted, "What is your name, Shaku?"

"My name is Fumihiko Sueki. My friends call me Sweki. How did you know I was a Buddhist monk?"

He looked at me with a glint in his eyes, "I saw your robe and rakusu."

"Ah yes, that would certainly give me away. May I ask your name, fisherman?"

"My name is Watanabe Tamayo. Ha, ha, my friends call me Tami," he laughed as he put his broad back and thick arms into the rowing.

We finally reached the sloop. There were two others on board calling out to Tami, "Did you get the fresh water? We have to put up the fish stew."

"Yes, here it is," he said as he handed it up to the men on board. "We have a guest who will sail with us to Sakata. He is a Buddhist monk so be careful of your language."

I climbed up the rope ladder on the side of the sloop while Tami tied the skiff to the aft. When we were aboard introductions were quickly made and the men immediately weighed anchor and scurried about raising the sails. When the sails were unfurled we were on our way with the spinnaker ballooning out full with the wind. Tami was at the binnacle steering the helm. The sun was high in a cloudless sky and the sloop was gliding along as if on wheels. There were no choppy waves to cause drag and the sloop did not rock. Sea birds were following us with their screeches hoping to catch a meal.

Tami shouted to me, "It will be night time when we get to Sakata but we must unload our catch as soon as we get there."

"I'll be happy to help," I responded.

"Good, we may need you."

I reluctantly tried to satisfy my curiosity, "Tell me, Tami, where did you get this sloop. It is not native to Japan. It has a foreign look."

He turned and said, "I wondered when you were going to ask me that question. The story is rather simple. I had a junk which I inherited from my father. One day while plying the waters off Hokkaido we ran aground on some rocks and the junk began to sink. We were rescued by a Russian fishing trawler which took us to Sakhalin Island. It was there the Russian captain told me of the sloop and offered to sell it to me so that I and my crew could return to Japan. I arranged with him to pay a small amount after each catch hauled in. We still owe some money but the Russian captain is very patient."

"I want you to know that the only other time I ever saw a sloop was when I left Hokkaido on a ferry to Honshu. It brings back fond memories."

"I see, that sloop was also probably made in Russia."

"Yes, I can see that now. Well, I think I'll go aft and help the cook prepare the evening meal."

"That's a good idea," he agreed.

I walked to the back in time to help the cook lift the carboy of water and pour it into a large metal pot and place it on the cooking stove.

The cook had a slight limp which caused his right foot to drag almost imperceptibly with each step. After lifting the pot of water on the cooking stove he attended to the fire by placing more wood chips into the burner. He looked at me with a broad grin on his gaunt face and began thanking me profusely, "Thank you, Shaku, that pot was heavy. Now, I must eviscerate the fish and remove the skins." He took several small fish and disemboweled them throwing the entrails into the sea. I could see the sea birds diving to retrieve the morsels. Sometimes more than one bird at a time would fight over the meal with screeches.

Then the cook was able to deftly rip the skins off the fish's body in one fast movement as well as removing the head and spine. These were also thrown overboard into the sea for the sea birds to haggle over. The remaining sea birds soared overhead waiting patiently for more bits of food. He then took the long strips of fish fillets and chopped them into smaller pieces which he threw into the steaming pot of water on the cooking stove.

"We must allow it to simmer for about an hour until the fish is rendered producing a broth. At the end of that time I will ask you to help me take the hot pot off the cooking stove so that I can add the rice to the broth to help thicken the stew."

"Yes, of course, I will help you."

After about an hour the cook signaled to me that he was ready to take the hot pot off the stove. I grabbed the hot handle of the pot with a diffident concern and slowly we lifted it off the cooking stove and placed it on the floor board of the sloop. My hand was scorched from the heat of the handle so for relief I began blowing on the palm of my hand.

"Shaku," the cook yelled, "stick your hand in that kettle of sea water over there," pointing to a small vessel of sea water.

"Oh, yes, thank you, I shall." I thrust my hand into the vessel of sea water to my great relief. He continued speaking while I had my hand in the vessel of sea water, "I am now ready to put in the rice. You must mix the broth with this bamboo stick while I pour in the rice." I grabbed the bamboo stick in my reddened hand and began mixing the fish stew slowly while he poured in a cup of rice in a measured way. Within minutes I noticed that the fish stew began thickening to finally become somewhat lumpy. The cook got out four bowls and chopsticks for each of the crew members. He called out, "Stew is ready!"

The single other crew member came to the cook's area to receive a bowl of stew, which the cook ladled out of the pot. The cook approached me with a filled bowl and said, "Take this bowl to Tami at the wheel tiller. You will get your bowl when you return. Meanwhile, I will put a tea pot on the stove to boil water for tea." I brought the bowl of fish stew to Tami.

"Ah, well, isn't that lovely. Please hold the wheel steady while I eat. Be careful, I can feel the current getting rough."

I grabbed the wheel and held it steady to prevent the rudder from swinging back and forth at the whim of the current.

"Thank you," Tami said as he pushed the thick stew into his mouth with the chopsticks. "Hold the course, follow the shoreline."

When he finished I took the bowl and returned to the cook. "Rinse the bowl out, with the sea water in the kettle," he said pointing to the same vessel in which I cooled my hand. "Very good, Shaku, now bring the bowl to me so I can fill it with hot tea for Tami." I brought the bowl of tea back to Tami and placed it on the binnacle for him to drink in small sips. Returning to the cook we both ate our stew, followed by the hot tea while sitting on the floor boards of the sloop with the other crew member. The stew was delicious with its large morsels of fish floating in the thick, briny broth. After we all had second bowls I felt quite sated and was able to relax and partake in the small talk while sipping the tea with loud slurping noises.

After a while, the sloop began to bounce up and down due to a cross current. We had to secure everything. It was most important to get rid of the embers from the cooking stove before they spilled out and caused a fire. Two men lifted the cooking stove and brought it to the side of the sloop and tossed the burning wood chips and the ashes into the sea. The sea birds hovered over this refuse but never dived to retrieve any of it.

A slight rain began falling. I could hear Tami yelling, " I think we are heading into a storm, tie down everything." The two men and I went scurrying about the sloop securing boxes with ropes and making sure nothing was free to move. The rain was now beating down heavily on us, and the sky was becoming dark and overcast. It was apparent that we were heading into a squall. Suddenly, a gust of wind with rain and snow was blowing into us from the aft causing the spinnaker to billow fully like a massive balloon. Tami had his hands full trying to keep the tiller wheel steady. The stern of the sloop was slapping the water with loud noises as it lifted up and came crashing down on the churning sea. The keel along the center of the sloop was strong so there was no fear of it cracking during the upheaval. This weather condition continued for a while until the rain and wind slowly abated. The sky began clearing and I could see us traveling parallel to the shore. Everyone began to relax as the sailing became smoother.

I heard Tami call out to me, "Shaku, please come up here and relieve me on the tiller."

I rushed up and grabbed the wheel. "Just keep it steady and follow the coast but do not get too close to the shore there may be dangerous outcroppings," he explained. I did as I was told and followed the shoreline. By this time the sun was declining and the sky had a soft, orange glow. Soon it will be nightfall and we shall be traveling in the dark. As the sun set I could see shafts of crimson light rising from the horizon. The day was over. Tami came up to me and grabbed the wheel as he said, "Thank you, Shaku, you make a good coxswain. I needed that rest. I'll take over now for the remainder of the trip. We only have about two hours to Sakata in the dark if the weather stays calm. Please help the men light the lamps for the masts and the running lights."

As we breezed along, I could see us passing an occasional light on the shoreline. Eventually, I saw a whole group of lights and surmised that we were approaching a town. Within minutes, Tami shouted, "We are coming into Sakata, prepare for landing." The men knew exactly what to do, tossing ropes to people on the dock. The sails were all gathered and stashed. Then the fish catch had to be unloaded. It took a long time for all of us to unload the sloop. At the end of the work the men went home and it was then that Tami approached me saying, "If you like you may sleep aboard the sloop until morning when you can continue your journey."

"Yes, yes, that would be fine, Tami."

"In the morning we will breakfast together, Shaku; then you can be on your way."

"Thank you for everything, Tami."

"I'll be back with some blankets in a little while."

I sat down on the floor board waiting for Tami to return. I could feel the slow rocking of the sloop with each incoming wave. I felt tired from the long day but energized by the fact that I will soon be home, perhaps tomorrow. The sway of the sloop caused me to doze off for a little while in the sitting position. But soon I was woken by Tami's voice, "Here are two blankets, Shaku."

"Oh, yes, yes, thank you, Tami, you are so kind," I blubbered.

He dropped the blankets next to me and went back to his house. I flattened one blanket made of homespun and placed it beneath me as a sort of futon and then lay down with the second blanket covering me to ward off the cold. I soon fell fast asleep dreaming my ubiquitous dream of home.

TWENTY-THREE

At first light, the next morning, I arose to greet the rising sun. I stretched but felt sullied and sticky all over. I decided to bathe in the sea before anyone could see me. I removed my robe, rakusu, and *zubonshita* (under drawers) and slowly let my body slink into the water. It was frighteningly cold but in some way very refreshing. I rubbed my body with my hands as best as I could until I couldn't stand the icy feeling any longer, it reminded me too much of my time on the Kuroshio Current. I came out of the water and wrapped my wet body in one of the blankets until I stopped shivering, all the while thinking about soaking in a hot tub when I get home. I put my clothes back on and sat in zazen for what seemed like an hour. Not having any *ko* (incense) there was no way I could time myself. Each incense stick is made to burn between thirty and forty minutes so my usual habit is to sit zazen for the burning of two incense sticks.

At the moment I finished zazen, Tami arrived carrying a tray on which there were two bowls of congee, a plate containing two small roasted fish and an iron pot of tea. "Good morning, Shaku, I brought our breakfast. I hope I am not disturbing you,"

"No. no, not at all, I am glad to see you."

"Did you sleep well?" he inquired.

"Yes, very well indeed, come sit next to me and join me in breakfast."

"I shall, thank you that would be nice. It will give us a chance to chat a little."

We ate in silence for a while and then Tami started the conversation. "Tell me, Shaku, about your life as a Buddhist monk. I am interested since I never met a monk before."

"There isn't much to tell. I was recently ordained as a monk in the monastery near Mutsu. I have not practiced my calling yet but will start when I attend the temple in Kitakata."

"Well then tell me, why did you become a monk? I mean, what was your life before that?"

With a certain amount of restlessness I began to relate my story. "Six years ago I lived on a farm with my family. My father was getting old and I did not want to work for my elder brother when he inherited the farm; so I went to sea and became a sailor. One day my junk was shipwrecked and I floated on the Kuroshio Current for almost a year to America. It was while I was floating on a wet board that I entreated the Buddha, if he saved me I would enter a monastery as a penance. That's how I became a monk.

"You mean you were saved when you landed in America?" He questioned in disbelief.

"Yes, I was enslaved for a time by the Makah Indians but in time a wonderful Englishman rescued me and I returned to Hokkaido on an American whaling ship. I lived for almost a year with the Ainu people while in Hokkaido and eventually came back to Japan posing as an Ainu because I was afraid of being arrested by the police."

"Oh, oh, I am sorry to have to tell you that the Tokugawa seclusion policy is hardly exercised any more. In particular they now give sanctuary to shipwrecked sailors."

I was taken aback almost speechless. "Really, you don't say, *odoroku no hoka wa hai* (I can't help being astonished)."

Tami looked at me with wonder in his eyes, "Yes I can see you have had a strange but wonderful life."

I pondered his statement and then replied, "I have no regrets. I believe I am now a better person. I am anxious to get rid of my wandering and settle down."

He looked at me for a moment before speaking, "Well thank you for telling me your story. I am happy to tell you that I shall arrange for my cousin to take you part of the way to Niigata since he will be transporting our fish catch to the market down the coast road."

"I don't have the proper words to thank you, Tami. You have been most kind to me. I shall not forget you."

"Think nothing of it. I am glad to help. I'll return for you when my cousin is ready to leave."

In a little while the wagon loaded down with the boxes of fish pulled up to the dock by an old brown horse with a long hairy mane. I could see Tami and his cousin patiently waiting for me. I jumped out of the sloop and walked over to the waiting wagon and was introduced to Tami's cousin whose name was Seiji. Seiji bowed to me and explained, "When we leave Sakata we will be heading for Marakami where the fish market is located. This is a distance of about sixty kilometers and may take us about three hours to get there." He was obviously trying to be helpful and so he continued, "From Marakami to Niigata is not more than fifty kilometers."

He explained this in a pedantic way but I acknowledged, "Yes, I understand but I may not go all the way to Niigata. I am thinking about going through Shiibata and then directly to Kitakata."

"Well, certainly that is very possible and should save you some time. From Shiibata to Kitakata is only about seventy kilometers."

I climbed up on the wagon and immediately was accosted by the fishy smell of the cargo. Seiji came up after me and grabbed the reins. I turned and waved to Tami while yelling, "Thank you for everything, Tami. Have a good life. I shall always remember you. My temple is Koetsu-ji in Kitakata. Come visit me if you are able. Goodbye!"

"Goodbye, Shaku, thank you for the invitation." He waved back as we rode along in a trot. The freight we were carrying had an awful smell which became more pronounced as the wagon waggled with every impediment in the road.

Seiji looked at me and said almost apologetically, "I know the smell is terrible, Shaku, but it will decrease as we pick up speed."

"Oh, I don't mind it, Seiji. I am really grateful to have the ride. I am hoping to get home tonight at this rate."

"Maybe you will. Tell me how long have you been gone from your home?"

"I have not been home for more than six years, "I said pensively.

"Oh, yes, indeed, that is a long time."

After a time of small chit chat it remained silent during which time I was able to appreciate the vista to my right of the shoreline and the azure blue sea whizzing by. Every so often we would pass isolated houses where people would wave to us as a friendly gesture. I could see inland to my left that there was a forest nestled beneath rugged mountains. This area along the coast road is really beautiful. It gave me a blissful feeling to be back in my homeland. Seiji pulled me out of my musings. "Shaku, when we get to Marakami it will be lunch time. I would be honored if you will join me for lunch."

"Oh, thank you that would be nice. Tell me, Seiji, what kind of fish are we transporting?"

"It is a cold water fish known as Alaskan blackfish. People around here really like it. I am sure I will be able to dispose of the entire load."

"Is that so? Well, tell me how were they caught?" I asked with great interest.

"They were netted but sometimes the crew angle as well until the nets are filled; then they are hauled in and put in the boxes you see on board here."

"Have you ever gone out fishing with the sloop?"

"Yes, I did, even with the junk before it capsized, but now I am too busy transporting and selling the catch. Of course, we all share in the profit."

"Is it a lucrative occupation?" I asked cautiously.

"Well, we all manage to make a living." Is all he could say? I was satisfied with the answer and did not press further. The sun was coming up by this time and the weather was turning warmer. The sky had only a few scudding clouds and there was a slight breeze. We were trotting along rather swiftly now and I hoped this meant that we would soon be arriving in Marakami. My anxiety was stimulated by the thought of seeing my family once again. I wondered if they had changed much in my six years of absence.

"How are you doing, Shaku?"

"Very well, Seiji."

And so it went for most of the trip. There was nothing more than a litany of trivial conversation. As the sun rose high overhead, we arrived in Marakami. The fish market was in a field right off the coast road. The wagon pulled up to the open air house and several burly men came out to talk with Seiji. Several boxes were taken down and the content examined. Some haggling took place between Seiji and what appeared to be the fish house owner. At the completion of negotiations I noticed the passage of money and the removal of the boxes from the wagon. With the deal completed Seiji came over to me and gleefully called out, "Come down, Shaku, we can have lunch now." I descended from the wagon and walked with Seiji into the fish house. I noticed some people already inspecting the fish laid out in small bins. There were some people seated at tables and eating. We selected a table and Seiji ordered our lunch which consisted of fish cakes made of fish shredded, mixed with mashed rice and fried, accompanied by the inevitable cups of tea. *Oishi*, it was delicious. After lunch Seiji explained that he had to return to Sakata and so I made my way onward after saying a tearful good bye.

I began trudging along the road passing people who were arriving at the fish market on foot and in all kinds of conveyances. Some came in pedicabs, jinrikishas and horse drawn vehicles. They all seemed very anxious to acquire the fish. I turned and saw the people eagerly purchasing the fish we recently brought. Some were haggling loudly and the fish mongers were shouting their wares. I was glad that the fish catch became a valuable commodity and added money to the coffers of the Tami/Seiji family. I continued on my way occasionally returning a bow made by a passing person. It then occurred to me that my costume engendered the respect of the populace. I felt encouraged at this prospect since it meant that the opportunity of developing a parish would be easier with interested and knowledge people. Still, these people are many kilometers away from Kitakata and my temple Koetsu-ji, where things may be different. I looked up over my shoulder and saw the sun hanging midway in the sky which means I am nearing Shiibata and the turn off to Kitakata. I was suddenly very tired and decided to rest at the side of the road. No one was about so I found a grassy spot to rest upon my haunches. My eyelids, which were very heavy, closed and I began dozing being overcome by the sultry air.

I do not remember how long I dozed off as I felt someone tapping me on the shoulder. I opened my eyes to see an aged man with a long wispy beard standing in front of me. "Are you alright, Shaku," he said in a high pitched, unnatural sounding voice. For a minute I was stymied for an answer but then I rose off my haunches saying in a deliberate way, "Yes, yes, I am fine. I was just resting."

He squeaked, "May I help you in any way, Shaku?"

I was startled from my slumber, "No. no, I was just on my way to the Kitakata cut-off when I decided to rest."

"Well, then let me take you there," he insisted in his high almost falsetto voice.

"Oh, I'll be alright, there is no need to trouble you."

"It's no trouble at all, I can take you in my pedicab," he said pointing to a tricycle with a rear compartment and a pedaling seat on the roadway. I was stunned into disbelief and momentary silence by his offer.

"No, no, I cannot expect a man of your age to carry me in your pedicab. That would be too much."

Once again in his shrill voice he countered, "Nonsense, it would be my pleasure to pedal you to the Kitakata cut-off."

I reluctantly approached the pedicab and inspected the leather seat and overhead canopy. I turned and said, "I am sorry to tell you, *watakushi no tomodashi* (my friend) that I am poor and cannot pay you."

"What, what, who asked you for payment. I told you it would be my pleasure. Please get in," he screeched angrily.

I shook my head incredulously and ascended to the back seat in the pedicab. The old man mounted the front seat and began pedaling with his skinny brown legs. After a while, I could see him sweating. He had a dull, gray cotton cloth around his neck which he often used to wipe his brow and bald pate. I also noticed that he was breathing hard and would frequently spit out from the side of his mouth anything raised by hawking. Needless to say, I was very upset at his uncompensated labor. It was amazing to me how rapidly we were moving merely by foot power. The pedicab was really bustling along. He almost resembled a small horse, with the same force and energy. I was thankful when we finally reached the Kitakata cut-off. He stopped and dismounted. Turning to me he said in a gentle way, "We are here, Shaku." I was too embarrassed to merely say, thank you, so I held a very low bow to him. "My temple is the Koetsu-ji in Kitakata. Please come and visit me."

He looked at me with a twinkle in his eye as he fingered his wispy beard. "Thank you, Shaku, for allowing me to earn good karma." It was then I understood his motivation.

"I hope we shall meet again," I said. "Thank you very much." I then turned and took the road at the left which was narrow and in poorer condition than the main road. The walking was made difficult by the poor condition of the road. There were many potholes and ruts in the dirt and it lacked the general smoothness of the coast road. I found my slippers grinding the stones and gravel which whirled around my feet as I walked. It was unpleasant and limited my ability to make any substantial headway. Now, the road was passing through a wooded area which became increasingly darkened by the trees and verdant surroundings. I could see the sun flickering through the trees as I walked along but unfortunately it did not provide much light for easy walking. The weather was turning colder and I found myself pulling my robe tighter around my body. Several times I heard forest noises such as rustling leaves but as I left the shoreline and penetrated deeper into the forest it became eerily silent. I could hear my footsteps as I trudged along the road. I was somewhat frightened by the prospect of being attacked by a wild animal after hearing the glissando of an animal shriek. It became even darker as the sun began setting causing me some difficulty making my way. I almost tripped once adding to my consternation. But thankfully the road veered out of the forest and I came upon patches of farm land lit up by the moonlight. I somehow knew I was near home but I was completely confused by the changes that took place with time to the physical features of the land. After roaming around in a somewhat circuitous fashion I came upon a familiar-looking house at the edge of a farm. I knew it was my home. Something sparked within me and told me I was home. I approached the front door with some reservations so I did nothing. I just stood still to collect my thoughts and sort out the proper approach. Finally I knocked on the door. In a few minutes the door slowly creaked open revealing a tall man holding a candle-stick.

His face was very tawny and his head sported long black hair. He held the candle high in his left hand as his eyes searched me, the intruder. "Who is it?" he said in a firm voice.

"It is I, Sueki, *Niisan* (Elder-brother)," I responded with a little doubt in my voice.

"Sueki, Sueki, I can't believe it. What are you doing here?"

"I came home to visit."

"Come in, come in, welcome, it has been a long time. I hardly recognized you."

I stepped over the threshold and he closed the door behind me as he examined me from top to bottom while holding the candle-stick high. I kicked off my tattered slippers and put on a pair of soft house slippers.

"You look bedraggled and disheveled. Where have you come from?"

"I have been gone over six years, *Niisan* (Elder-brother), and the story is a long one. I will be happy to tell you everything tomorrow. May I stay the night? I am very tired."

"Of course, of course, you may sleep in my room. Come with me I shall prepare a futon for you."

I turned to face him and asked, "Tell me, how is mother and father?'

His face turned solemn as he slowly answered me, "Father is dead. Mother is very sick in her room and *Imotosan* (Younger-sister) is now married to a gentleman living in the city of Niigata."

I was shocked by the news. "Father is dead? How did it happen?"

"He died one day while working in the rice paddy. It must have been his heart. His gravestone is at the burial corner of the farm with the graves of the grandparents. We will go there tomorrow if you like."

"Oh, how sad it is. What about mother?"

"Mother got sick two weeks ago. A local midwife came to attend to her. She said it was *korera* (cholera) after examining her vomitus. She has been throwing up her food constantly. We expect the worst."

"Oh, oh, I am so sorry to hear this bad news."

Then Elder-brother rallied and closely inspecting me said, "I see you are wearing a priest's robe. I thought you went away to become a sailor."

I readily responded, "I am now a Buddhist monk and I have been assigned by my Roshi to take over the temple Koetsu-ji near here."

"What, that broken down barn, it will take a lifetime to fix it up again."

"I looked at Elder-brother questioningly and responded with a seriousness of purpose, "We can talk about it tomorrow. Right now I must get some sleep."

TWENTY-FOUR

In the morning I woke, sat zazen and had a bowl of congee ladled from the pot on the stove. After washing it down with a bowl of tea I went outside to find *Niisan* (Elder-brother) in the vegetable patch. "Good morning, Elder-brother. How are you?"

"I am fine. Did you sleep well?"

"Yes, very well. May I see mother now?"

"I was just about to bring her some breakfast. You may come with me."

We went inside where Elder-brother prepared a tray with a bowl of congee and a bowl of tea to bring to mother for breakfast. As we entered the room I could whiff the stale air which conveyed a scent of sickness to my nostrils. There she was, lying still on her back with her mouth open, exhaling foul air. "Hello, mother, I am home to visit you," I exclaimed softly as I kneeled at her bedside.

"Who is it?" she muttered weakly in her scratchy voice. "Oh, Sueki, you wonderful boy. Thank you for coming. I am happy to see you." She seemed to recognize me with a steady immobile stare. She continued staring but nothing more was said. She became rigid. What was happening? Elder-brother put his hand on my shoulder, "She is dead."

I looked at her in disbelief and suddenly began crying with a heaving of my shoulders. I kept looking at her in a wonder not well understood, not really believing my eyes. Is this really happening? How could this be? Her face is yellow and waxy, a thickened, oddly bloated image. The lips nearly colorless are set in an expression of uncharacteristic haughtiness. Below the cover, I realize, my mother is unclothed. This fact shames me, and causes me to turn briefly away. When I look again I study the face more closely, still thinking that perhaps it is a mistake, that a tap on my mother's shoulder will wake her. After a few moments I realize that a chair has been brought by Elder-brother for me to sit in. I sit down. I wonder if I should touch my mother's face, lay a hand on her forehead. And yet I feel terrified to do so, unable to move. Eventually, with my index finger, I graze her lips, an eyebrow, a bit of hair on her head, those parts of her, I know so well. I rose from my seat saying, "I would like to visit our father's gravestone now."

"Alright, first let me get a pail of water."

"Yes, yes, that would be proper to clean the stone. I'll say a prayer," I hastily agreed.

"You see I have been so busy with working the farm alone and caring for mother that I didn't have time to clean father's gravestone," He added apologetically.

I lowered my head in shame knowing that I have been the prodigal son who squandered his life instead of remaining home to help his father. "Well, let us go then." I commanded with renewed conviction.

Elder-brother grabbed a pail of water and a brush. We started walking along the dike of the rice paddy until we reached the clump of trees which surrounded the three gravestones. Elder-brother scrubbed and washed the gravestones until they lost their gray coating and the moss growing on them. At the conclusion of his labor, Elder-brother stepped back and I began the chant of the Heart Sutra beginning with *Mahaprajnaparamita* (The great perfection of wisdom) and ending with *Gate, gate, paragate, parasamgate, Bodhi svabha* (Gone, gone, gone beyond, gone utterly beyond, enlightenment, so may it be). I lowered my gassho and turned to Elder-brother to say, "Now let us make arrangements for our mother."

"Yes, I shall make the arrangements for a horse and wagon to transport mother to the crematorium. The midwife will notify the local people and gather them as mourners. I have always had a casket provided for mother's demise which I kept in the shed. We must have the midwife dress her in a white shroud and then we can place her in the casket. I have done all this before for our father."

Late in the afternoon, *Imotosan* (Younger-sister) arrived with her husband. There were introductions made with the usual expressions of condolence. The ceremony began after all the mourners gathered in front of the open casket. The body in the casket had been brought out from the house. Those present were invited to join in the thrice-repeated formula of faith, *Namo tasso bhagavata Arahato samma sambuddhasa* (Homage be to she who is Arhat, the enlightened one). After the recitation, water is poured into a bowl placed before the casket, as it fills and pours over the edge, I recite, "As the rains fill the rivers and overflow into the ocean, so likewise may what is given here reach the departed. May the wealth of merit acquired by this effort be accepted by all the gods, and may it result in her welfare in every way."

The coffin was then closed and placed on the wagon to be removed for cremation. The mourners then returned for a funeral meal. The simple meal was prepared by Younger-sister while tears were flowing from her eyes. I had changed into the new robe made for me as an ordination gift by the female monks of the monastery and the walking slippers made for me as a departing gift by Ichi. I suddenly burst out crying, not so much for my sorrow but because of the awakening memories of the tribulations I encountered in my life. I removed myself from the gathering of people to control my affliction of grief. It would not do for a monk to exhibit distress and adversity. Monks are supposedly a pillar of confidence and immune to emotion.

After a short visit with Younger-sister and her new husband they returned to their home in Niigata with an empty promise to visit again. Most of the mourners left with bows and good wishes. I was then left alone with Elder-brother.

"I have the urn containing mother's ashes. When shall we bury it?" he said in a sorrowful manner.

"We can do it tomorrow or if you like we can wait until her gravestone is ready," I answered thoughtfully.

"Yes, perhaps that is best. Let us wait until the gravestone is ready," He agreed.

Then there was silence. We both looked down at the ground. Finally, I said, "May I stay for a few days until I can wash and repair my old robe and provision myself for occupation of the temple."

"Yes, of course, we are brothers and I intend helping you restore the old temple to a sound state. You may take the futon and anything else you may need."

"Thank you," I said sincerely with a lump in my throat. Then in great contrition I offered, "Let us clean up mother's room and put it in livable order."

"Yes, good idea let us begin."

We both walked into the house and began cleaning up the room, removing unwanted items and airing out the smell of death. When we finished, Elder-brother approached me, "Sweki, I have some under drawers and work clothes for you. You have so little you will need these items in your new life. You should not spoil your fine robes when you do manual labor."

"Thank you, Elder-brother, that is very kind of you."

He continued, "Also I will lend you some tools and farming equipment as you need them."

I looked at him with moist eyes, "Thank you, Elder-brother. I intend to make a success of the temple, not because of my commitment to my Roshi but because it is the only meaningful thing left in my life."

"Well, I expect to help you," he said firmly.

I couldn't answer. I was all choked up. So I just shook my head affirmatively.

Elder-brother had to go to the rice paddy to do the weeding. I, on the other hand, washed and repaired my old robe. I then donned the work clothes given to me by Elder-brother. The trouser legs were too long so I had to roll them up otherwise they were very comfortable. It seemed appropriate for me to start making dinner. I put up a pot of water to cook some vegetables which I took out of the garden. I expected to use the hot vegetable water to cook some rice. When Elder-brother was finished weeding in the rice paddy he came in to bathe. We both soaked in the hot tub together as we did when we were youngsters. We began frolicking in the tub like we did as children. It was a real friendship between two men that is nonsexual but intimate and even loving. Now that I am back home I can see the resurrection of the close mutual friendship we had many years ago.

We sat down at a table in the kitchen to the dinner I had prepared. When we were finished eating we sat for a long time, sipping tea and talking.

"Tell me, Sweki, what happened to you after you left the farm to go to sea?" he questioned.

I told him the whole sorry story of my shipwreck, floating on a board for almost a year to America, being enslaved by the Makah Indians, then rescued by the Englishman, and my return on an American whaling ship to Hokkaido, the life I led with the Ainu people and my eventual stay and ordination in the monastery.

He looked at me wide-eyed in rapture and disbelief." I am surprised you survived such a terrible life.

"It was not only a struggle for existence but I knew that by lifting up my heart I would attain a great value of merit. Now I intend using that merit to build a temple of distinction for the people of the Echigo area."

Elder-brother looked at me in wonderment. "Ah, yes, you have changed. You are no longer the small restless person of your youth. I admire the way you have grown. I look forward to what you will accomplish in the future." Then he was silent for a while but continued, "When will you leave?"

"I am thinking of going to the temple tomorrow. I am anxious to get started."

The next morning, I put all my belongings in my old shoulder bag plus the few tools such as a hammer, nails and a pull-saw as well as the few clothes and futon given to me by Elder-brother. In a second bag I took some rice, dried beans, and lentils for my sustenance until the time I could grow my own vegetables. I then bowed and said goodbye to Elder-brother. He returned the bow saying, "I shall try to visit you soon."

"Yes, it is only about sixteen kilometers from here. Come when you are able." I felt secure and confident knowing that Elder-brother was nearby. I trudged off down the roadway to whatever uncertainties awaited me.

TWENTY-FIVE

In about a half-day I reached the temple building. When I arrived I stood outside, in shock, looking at the run down building with windows dulled by dust. The building was made of permanently darkened wood from the burning of coal. Yet there was something majestic about the building which cast a shadow over the gloomy little neighborhood. I entered apprehensively, to discover animal nests and feces in the corner. "Seedy" is not the word for the temple; better "prehistoric". Inside, the place was old and vintage – exposed beams overhead, with greenish lacquered walls darkened by oil and soot. I looked about me while standing in the center of the room with a feeling of discouragement. This will take a lot of soap and water, I thought. Putting my things down I scouted around and found a small hand broom. The first thing I did was to clean out the animal nests and to sweep an area where I could place my belongings. Suddenly I rose from my work and turned to find an old lady staring at me intently. She was small but wiry. She had wispy, thinning hair on her head revealing her scalp. Her face was craggy and lined with eyes that kept darting in sharp movements. She called out to me in a squeaky voice, "Who are you?"

It was obvious she did not detect my status since I was not wearing my robe. "My name is Kosan; I am the new Sensei of this temple." I bowed and asked her, "May I ask who you are, dear lady?"

Her demeanor changed immediately and she seemed to tremble at the sound of my voice. "Please forgive me Sensei-san. I did not recognize you. I mean I did not expect anyone of your stature to arrive here. My name is Yamabashi Utako. I am the *Onna-shitsuji* (Deaconess) of this temple."

"I see, I am happy to meet you," I said with a bow. "We have much work to do before we open this temple to our good neighbors."

"Yes, you are right, Sensei-san. I shall help you all I can. I am too old for heavy work but there are many important things I can do such as cooking."

"Of course, I am happy to have your help."

"Well, Sensei-san have you eaten yet?"

"Not since breakfast," I replied quickly.

"Well then let me bring you a casserole."

"Thank you that would be nice. I am very hungry."

She left hurriedly with a waddle-type gait. In the meantime I kept sweeping the area where I expected to reside temporarily. There was a bedroom and a kitchen at the rear of the large central room. I decided not to use these living quarters until I could thoroughly clean them. That I could start on tomorrow. In about a half hour, Utako returned carrying a large chafing dish covered by a towel. "Here is your dinner, Sensei-san," she sang out in her squeaky voice.

"Oh, thank you, it looks wonderful. Would you like to join me?"

"Oh, I am honored, Sensei-san."

"No, no, the honor is mine," I offered with a smile. We sat on the floor and she joined me in partaking of the food. When we finished eating I thanked her and she left saying, "I shall return tomorrow to pick up the empty casserole dish."

Being all alone in the silence of this cavernous room I decided to unroll my futon for sleep. Removing my clothes I wrapped myself in the blanket and fell fast asleep. I thought tomorrow I shall begin the clean-up work on the temple starting with the bedroom and the kitchen.

Next morning I woke with a start from my agitated sleep, drenched in a cold sweat despite the noise of the rain hammering furiously against the windows, throbbing with ancestral fear. I caught my breath with a dull, hoarse wheeze. I cleared my throat and narrowed my eyes. Yellow light pierced the gloom of early morning. It was time for zazen. Afterwards I went outside to inspect the condition of the building which was battered by the rain. Rain-drenched, I was swallowed up. I hastily pushed forward to get to the door and return to the safety of the inside which already exhibited many leaks from the roof. After rolling up my futon, I quickly finished the cold remnants of last night's casserole followed by a bowl of hot tea.

When the rain stopped I decided to walk to the beach for a morning bath. When I reached the sandy beach I noticed the wind stirring the tufts of grass on the low dunes, like beards on the chins of giants. A miracle seems to hold up the little shed where the fishermen's boats are kept, battered as if by storms and sea water. The sun is about to rise, night is over and day has not yet begun. A pinkish light falls upon the gulls as they wheel placidly about, occasionally fighting with the crabs for the dead fish that have fallen from the night's nets. Slow backwash, low tide, a fine mist hides the edge of the beach from north to south. Not a soul about. So once again I remove my work clothes and head into the cold surf completely nude. The reminder of my drifting on the current has never left me. I was able to wash the grime and sweat off my body.

Far off I noticed some men approaching. There were three of them walking slowly and talking rapidly. I came out of the surf and put my clothes on my wet body. When they saw me they stopped abruptly in their tracks and stared at me questioningly. The tall man walked slowly ahead of the other two. "What are you doing here?" he challenged me severely. "Who are you? What do you want?" he added.

I walked slowly to face them saying, "My name is Kosan, and I am the new Sensei of the temple. I just finished bathing." I bowed low in deference.

"What temple" he inquired further.

"Why, temple Koetsu-ji, of course." I said in surprise.

"You mean that old building that's about to fall down?"

"Ha, ha, yes, that's the one," I laughed but with greater bravado I added, "But in a short time, with some help, it will be a place for the local people to practice."

They looked at me in apparent diffidence. The tall one became interested. "Are you serious?"

"Yes, I shall work on that building until it is ready," I said in great confidence.

He responded respectfully, "Shaku, these are my brothers," pointing to the other two men. "We are the Hashimoto brothers. I am Noriko, and this is Akira and Toshiki, my two brothers."

"I am glad to meet all of you," I said with a low bow and gassho.

He continued after returning the bow, "We are fishermen but we would be happy to help you if you will allow us."

I was taken aback at this kind offer, "Certainly I would appreciate any help you can give me. There is so much work to accomplish before the temple will be ready." I hesitated for a moment but then continued in an ingratiating regard for his wishes, "Would the three of you consider painting the outside of the building?"

"Of course, of course, we will scrape off the soot and whitewash all the boarding and siding."

I clapped my hands and said in delight, "Wonderful, you may start any time at your leisure."

"Alright then we will start tomorrow afternoon. We fish in the mornings but return in the early afternoon. It is then we are free until evening; that's when we will paint."

For the next three days, the three men scraped the wooden siding and whitewashed the entire exterior. They also repaired the few holes in the roof through which water leaked during a rainfall. I was extremely grateful and gathered them in a group during the afternoon of the fourth day when they returned to retrieve their tools. "I would like very much to express my thanks," I said in a solemn voice as I bowed low with a gassho. I raised my hands over their heads and began to recite a passage from the *Avatamsaka Sutra* (The Flower Ornament Scripture).

Full of virtue and great knowledge, gone to the goal of enlightenment practice.
Givers of security to all worlds – behold these, the offspring of Buddha,
Intelligent, with boundless wisdom, and well-concentrated minds,
In the realm of boundlessly deep and broad knowledge.
They are the miraculous transformation of the autonomous Buddha.
By the power of which these enlightened beings have come.

By this time I had cleaned the bedroom and kitchen as well as the large room which will become the combination Zendo and Hatto. I occupied the bedroom and was grateful for the help given me by Utako, the deaconess, despite her advanced age and frail condition. Not only did she help with the cleaning but she also made dinner for me every night. She would say in her squeaky voice, "Please allow me to prepare your dinner, Sensei-san. You must be very tired from your daily labor."

I could only answer, "Thank you." It was true that the daily work of cleaning and repairing was grueling and fatiguing and made me too weary to prepare food, so I relented after much discussion and allowed her to putter in the kitchen. The days went by rapidly but I could see the results of our work producing a worthy building. One day the Hashimoto brothers came by to present me with a parcel of fish. I thanked them and then noticed that Noriko had a long board in his hands. He then raised it into view and presented me with a sign bearing the Japanese Kanji characters *Koetsu-ji*. He was shy and blushing as he handed it to me, "This sign is for the temple, Sensei-san. The characters mean Temple of Revision and are meant to tell people to come inside and revise their lives." We all laughed, but I became very serious, "Yes it is a very beautiful sign. We can place it on a post at the entrance path. For those who read the sign and come in it is a chance for a new beginning; it is an opportunity to discard destructive habits. I thank you for this wonderful present for the temple."

And so time went by. The temple became increasingly reestablished as a place for people to congregate and to practice. There developed a small group of steady attendees who helped with their time, energy, and donations of money and sometimes food to keep the temple growing. These people were mostly women since the men worked during the day. They were ordinary simple folk. The families were mostly fishermen and others were farmers. All were interested in using the temple as a place to interact and socialize in addition to practicing their religious obligations. They were all tirelessly hard-working people, capable of standing up to natural adversities and overcoming them. Many years ago the Echigo area was known as a place where exiles used to be sent, to be dispatched to the dismal lands of the great beyond, far away from the civilization of the Japanese Shogunate. Echigo in those days was a wilderness and attracted bandits and other offensive and unsavory characters. But with time farmers and fishermen came to establish a civilized community by intermarrying with the indigenous people and eventually becoming upstanding productive citizens. Some of these lands became large estates and eventually Niigata became a large, important port and city.

Temple Koetsu-ji was located on a large tract of land which I leased to a tenant farmer. I kept a small plot for my personal vegetable garden. The tenant farmer donated a large bag of rice and a large bag of lentils once-a-year for my well being in addition to the rent for use of the land. He was able to clear the weeds and till the soil and establish a rice paddy encompassed by a dike for annual flooding. In this way I was able to keep the temple thriving as I began to form a small parish.

Utako, the deaconess, continued to make my meals and life began to adopt a routine. The large room used as a Hatto/Zendo combination was now occupied by a sizeable number of practitioners for daily morning zazen and services. The men came at 4:30 am on their way to work. I was very gratified to see their participation. The temple was beginning to satisfy the needs of a significant number of families.

One day while busily working in the vegetable garden tilling the earth with an adz-like ploughshare, I became aware of someone standing behind me. I slowly turned, thinking it was one of the parishioners, to face an apparition. The sun was shining directly in my eyes so I could not make out who was standing there. I raised my hand to shield my eyes from the fiercely burning sun and slowly I could make out a female figure. *Can it be?* I hesitatingly spoke, "Is it really you, Ichi?"

"Yes, it is I, Sweki; I just arrived from a long trip to visit you."

"Oh, I am so happy to see you."

"I missed you, Sweki," she demurred.

"And I missed you, Ichi," I replied.

I stood up and threw convention to the wind by grabbing her hands and pulling her toward me. She began laughing with delight. "Be careful, Sweki, someone may see us."

"I don't care. These are good people and they won't mind. Come let us go inside." We sat down in the kitchen and started talking with a flurry of questions. "How did you get here?" I asked with unabated interest.

She began in a narrative way, "First, I must tell you that the Roshi was sending a delegation of monks to Eiheiji Monastery in Fukui for special training as priests. When I learned of this I thought it was a real opportunity to go along and visit you. I was concerned that the Roshi would not permit this but I took my courage in hand and approached him to see if I could go along to visit you. He not only allowed it but also suggested that you may be able to use me as an assistant." She stopped with a flushed face and with heavy, bated breath as she looked at me anxiously.

On hearing this I was nonplussed. "What do you mean by assistant?"

"I mean if you will have me I will stay with you and help you with your work."

"I see." I was silent and pensive for a moment but then I rallied out of my quandary. "What a wonderful idea," I exclaimed with enthusiasm.

She added, "Yes, it is a beautiful temple. I can do many things to help with the renovation work as well as help with morning services." She looked around with approval.

"Yes, yes, of course you may stay. I am so happy you are here. There is much to be done but we have a good start and I certainly could use your help. For one thing I want to start a class on the Shobogenzo."

Just then, Utako came into the temple calling, "Sensei-san, I am here to make your dinner." She came into the kitchen and stopped in her tracks at the sight of Ichi. Her jaw dropped and with an open mouth she blubbered, "Hello, hello."

I got up and quickly started speaking to avoid any embarrassment, "Utako, I want you to meet my new assistant Noguchi Ichi." I turned to face Ichi, "She just arrived from the monastery." Then I turned to face Utako "Ichi, this is Utako my deaconess." Utako beamed as they both bowed. "I am glad to meet you, Ichi, welcome to Koetsu-ji," Utako said with grave reverence and bowed low a second time.

"The pleasure is mine," Ichi quickly responded as she returned the bow.

I quickly rejoined, "Utako, will you join us for dinner? We are now the three officials of this temple."

Utako's face shined with happiness, "Thank you, Sensei-san. I would be most honored to join you. Now, let me get started with dinner."

Ichi rose saying, "May I help you?"

"No. no, I am able to do it all myself, thank you." After saying that, she turned and became busy in the kitchen. Ichi sat down once again and we continued our conversation out of earshot of Utako.

TWENTY-SIX

After dinner, Utako went home with much fanfare and greetings for Ichi. We were left to clean up and straighten up the kitchen. Then we headed for the bedroom hand in hand. As we entered together I turned and spoke to Ichi, "I will have to make the futon larger to accommodate both of us."

Ichi giggled, "I am sure we can both fit in the futon."

Despite her assurance I proceeded to add another blanket to the existing one so that we could have more room. "Tomorrow I shall get another futon so that we can join both at sleep time."

Ichi had brought a small canvas bag containing her personal things which she began unloading and distributing some of the items for easy access. There was no furniture in the room and everything was at floor level. Then she began disrobing and I undressed as well. We both crawled into the futon and reached out to each other. I hugged her close to my nude body. "Now, my life is complete," I said in a quiet voice into her ear.

"I love you, Sweki. I want to be with you forever," she said as she placed her arms around my torso.

"My life is like an *enso* (one stroke painted circle)," I said, "with no beginning and no end."

She was quiet for a while then she said, "There are no happy endings in life only happy moments."

Afterword

Sueki's adventures took place between 1863 when he was shipwrecked to 1869 when he took charge of the Koetsu-ji temple. He was born during the Tokugawa Ieyoshi Shogunate (1837-1853) and left home to be a sailor during the Tokugawa Yoshinobu Shogunate (1867-1868). He then settled at the Koetsu-ji temple during the Meiji Regime (1868-1912) when the imperial power was restored.

To put things in perspective the following events occurred:

Commodore Perry opened Japan for the United States in 1853.

Herman Melville wrote "Moby Dick" in 1851.

The American Civil War was raging between 1861 and 1865.

The great ukiyo-e style (woodblock prints) ended with the death of three of its greatest masters Hokusai in 1849, Hiroshige in 1858, and Kuniyoshi in 1861.

In 1871 there was an abolition of feudal clans and the establishment of prefectures throughout Japan. This may be considered the time of modernism for Japan.

A NOTE ON USAGE

The spelling of the Japanese terms in this book follows the Hepburn system of Romanization. Person's names are given in Japanese order with family name preceding the given name. Dates are approximate because of differences between calendars. Measurements are metric as is the present case in Japan.

SUEKI'S NAMES

Fumihiko Sueki —— Birth name

Sweki ——Nickname

Kosan—Dharma name (ordination name)

Shaku ———Reverend

Sensei ———Teacher

Adding –san to his name (Sueki-san) is an honorific

Finally, it must be stated that this story is completely fictional and a product of the author's imagination. The names of the people and certain places mentioned in the story do not actually exist; to discover otherwise is purely coincidental and unintentional. There are, however, certain facts behind the fiction on which events this story is based. There are records of Japanese castaways who landed on the shores of America. Seafarers from Japan have been drifting eastwards on crippled vessels for hundreds of years.

The Kuroshio (black) current was named after the deep color of its waters. The Kuroshio is the north Pacific Gulf Stream for it brings warm waters from the tropics up east of Taiwan, north-eastwards along the Japanese coast and on towards the polar regions, sweeping east below the Aleutian Islands and down the American coast. To this day Japanese fishing floats and even monk's wooden sandals are washed up on the shores of the Pacific Northwest.

The Ainu were the original inhabitants of much of northern Japan, while related groups had long settled Sakhalin and Kamchatka. They are fair-skinned and very hairy and look more Caucasoid than mongoloid. Modern day Hokkaido was settled by Japanese émigrés much like America's settlement of the western territories. Today, only vestigial communities of Ainu survive.

Escape From Exile Island

Preface

Exile is the banishment of an individual (or group of individuals) from a society as a form of punishment of that individual for offences against the society. In addition, exile is to be away from one's home while being explicitly refused permission to return. There have been many noteworthy exiles in history which have been preserved in literature and politics such as:

- The exile of the Jews in the Old Testament of the Bible during Babylonian captivity.
- The exile of Cubans since the 1959 Cuban Revolution.
- Men of politics, high rank soldiers, administrators, and intellectuals of the Ottoman Empire who were sent to exile in Malta.
- The Marian exiles consisting of more than 800 English Protestants who fled to Germany, Switzerland, and France to join with reformed churches.

These are just a few of the many that have occurred including such individuals as the Norwegian playwright and Nobel Prize winner, Henryk Ibsen, was forced into exile because his countrymen failed to understand the meaning of his great dramas and Emperor Napoleon Bonaparte who was exiled to St. Helena Island from 1815 to 1821 and Nichiren (1222-1282), the head of the Buddhist sect that bears his name, was banished from Kamakura to Sado Island from 1261 to 1263 for admonishing the rulers. Exile can even take place in one's home for very long periods of time as is evidenced by the confinement of Aung San Suu Kyi, the courageous leader of Burma's democracy movement.

Islands have more frequently been used as exile communities. The Exile Island in this narrative is depicted as an isolated penal colony about 250 miles southeast of Tokyo in the Pacific Ocean. For 200 hundred years between the seventeenth and nineteenth centuries more than nineteen hundred men, women, and children were banished there. Among them were defeated soldiers, dissident priests, arsonists, whores, gamblers, smugglers, pick-pockets, murderers, rapists, adulterers, sculptors, and poets. Their crimes were often simply disagreement with the Tokugawa government.

Exile Island in this story became known as the place where exiles used to be sent, to be dispatched to the dismal island of the great beyond, the away from the civilization of the Japanese Shogunate. It was often used as a place to separate individuals and sometimes their families from interfering with societal matters.

This is the fictional story of one such individual, Katsuko Okada, the courtesan, who with the aid of some men took part in a bloody escape attempt from Exile Island.

This story is also a testament to the courage and survival skills of the exiled people who made a life for themselves under the most arduous conditions of anarchy. The islands are now permanent domiciles often used as resort areas and fishing outposts. Regular ferry service brings groups of tourists and others to these strange, somewhat primitive outposts of the Japanese archipelago. Exile as a punishment is no longer used in Japan. The names of persons and places in this narrative are all fictional. The story, however, is based on actual events.

I

The boat was plodding along as it rocked in the rough sea. In the hold a voice rose from the lee side, immediately below. Or so it seemed. It was difficult in the total darkness and the monotonous hum of the wind, to judge distance or direction. It was difficult, at any rate, for someone like Katsuko Okada, who was sitting on the starboard side. Her life, until some weeks ago, had never been touched by the necessity for making such judgments.

"Yes?" she asked and waited. There was no answer. She said sharply, "Who wants me? Who is there?"

The voice rose again, but the words seemed to disintegrate under pressure from the wind. Katsuko, moving toward it, pushed back the sleeve of her kimono in order to reach out to the voice.

"Who are you?" she inquired carefully.

"My name is Toshiki Otsumi," the voice replied in a low, nasal manner.

It took Katsuko by surprise. "Yes, I heard," she said, and the unmistakable rasp of irritation in her own voice made her hesitate. She was not an irritable person. More accurately, she had never before considered herself as such. Considering it now, and finding the result distasteful, she made an effort. She said evenly, "What can I do for you? What do you want?"

The voice with its nasal quality responded "I am very thirsty. Do you have any water?"

Katsuko was taken aback by this request but answered forcefully,

"No, there is no water down here." She could barely make out the image of a person in the dark hold of the boat. "You said your name is Toshiki Otsumi. Is that right?"

"Yes, that is my name. How long do you think it will be before we land?"

"I do not know," she said irritably but continued, "I suspect it will be some few hours." Then there was silence for a while before the conversation continued. The only sound was the wind howling outside and the boat occasionally slapping against the rough waves. The atmosphere in the hold was stifling and hot.

With a tear in his voice, Toshiki asked, "Where are we going?"

She was surprised and almost whispered incredulously under her breath," Don't you know?"

"Yes, I know," he said dejectedly. "We are on our way to Exile Island."

Suddenly the hatch opened with a loud noise as a piercing, white, bright sunbeam came streaming in. The voices of two men could be heard as they came down the ladder slowly, talking to each other. "Where are you?" one of them said as he held a lantern high searching the dark hold.

"Over here," Katsuko answered while turning to face the men.

"Ah, yes, there you are. Are you both enjoying your trip?" the guard said mockingly in a sarcastic tone. "Get up! Get up! You both must be on deck immediately in order to receive your daily meal. Ha! Ha!"

Katsuko and Toshiki got up and shuffled over to the ladder under the watchful eyes of the two guards. Climbing the ladder caused their eyes to squint from the burning light of the noon day sun. They were placed in a line with several other male prisoners to receive a bowl of rice gruel. All the men turned their heads to observe and leer at Katsuko. She was the only female prisoner in the line and, in addition, was outstanding as a beautiful woman. She was tall and slender like a lily with auburn hair and green eyes which gave her a haunting appearance. The men were whispering to each other as they inspected her lustfully. She became self-conscious but kept looking ahead standoffishly as if unaware of the staring men. Toshiki Otsumi was right behind Katsuko on the line. He was bobbing from one foot to the other, sort of dancing with an obviously nervous gesture. He was an average height for a Japanese man with long black hair and deep set eyes. His facial skin was reddish and bore the pits and scars of smallpox. Every once in a while he would raise his cupped hands to his mouth and blow into them with a slight whistle. The line proceeded along to a server who was ladling hot rice porridge out of a pot into wooden bowls and handing them to the passing prisoners. Katsuko and Toshiki took there filled bowls to the aft of the boat deck where they sat. Katsuko tolerated Toshiki because she needed his presence as protection. They drank the porridge from the bowl edge by frequently raising the bowls to their mouths.

Suddenly, Toshiki addressed Katsuko as he looked into her eyes, "What is your crime? Why are you here?"

Katsuko was momentarily stunned but answered him angrily, "How dare you address me like that? I am not one of your criminals."

He answered hastily, "Oh, I am very sorry. I meant no disrespect. All on board are exiles. I just thought ———. She interrupted, "Well, next time be careful how you address me. I am not some broken down whore."

He continued hastily, "Please do not be offended. I meant no harm. I was just trying to be friendly.

Katsuko accepted his lame excuse with a shake of her head and kept eating the rice porridge. "This food is vile," she grunted and continued, "If you must know. I was a courtesan for a very rich merchant since I was fourteen years old. I am now eighteen. After he got tired of me and replaced me with another he accused me of stealing some of his jewels. The magistrate who heard my case condemned me to exile to get me out of the way. I am sure they were in cahoots. But, I am innocent, I tell you. I never stole anything. I now must find a way to escape from Exile Island."

Toshiki was listening with rapt attention to her story. "If I can help you I would be pleased to complot. I, too, would like to escape."

She looked at him with disdain and spoke with a curious but haughty way, "What was your crime?"

He quickly answered, almost proudly, "I am a thief. I was caught for the third time burglarizing a rich man's home. Instead of prison they condemned me to a lifetime sentence as an exile. I think I can help you with any plans you may have to escape."

She looked at him carefully as they sat eating, "I have no plans. I shall begin making plans as soon as we land and I understand the lay of the land."

"I just want you to know that as a thief I know how to steal useful things and I can handle a boat quite well," he insisted.

She said nothing but looked at him pensively, "That's very interesting."

He sycophantically offered, "Now that we are partners we should get to know each other better."

She shouted in a huff, "We are not partners. I don't know you and don't want to know anything about you. My feminine wiles will be used as a tool to get me off the island, not to be wasted on a fool like you." She rose to return the wooden bowl.

He followed her hurriedly, "I am sorry. I did not mean to insult you. I only wanted to be part of your plans."

She turned, "Shush you fool. Someone might hear you." Everyone was looking at the two in wonderment. Meanwhile, the wind was blowing in great gusts and the boat was rocking unsteadily causing all to bob and trip from side to side. One of the guards approached saying, "You two don't have to go to your suite below deck. Ha! Ha! You may stay on deck with your fellow shipmates until we land."

"When will that be?" Katsuko pondered.

"Are you in a hurry? Do you have an appointment to make?" he asked in his usual sarcastic manner.

"I'm just curious. This boat smells terribly," she shot back, to the astonishment of the guard.

"Well then, it may be about two hours. Of course, there will be a welcoming committee and a military band to greet you when you debark, your highness."

"I see you have your fun in the misery of others," she commented.

"I always enjoy seeing law-breakers get what they deserve," he rejoined forcefully.

As the guard turned to leave, Toshiki came to soothe her ire, "Never mind him, Kat, he's only a stupid policeman."

"What did you call me?" she asked.

"I called you Kat. You may call me, Toshi. In that way we can be friendlier," he explained hesitatingly.

"Oh, alright, I agree, Toshi." She laughingly said with a lilt in her voice, "But remember there will be no intimacy."

In the next two hours the wind gusted evermore forcefully and the boat seemed to rock from side to side with every gust of wind. Kat and Toshi were sitting in the aft of the boat with their heads in their hands trying to steady themselves from the incipient dizziness. Toshi got up suddenly to lean over the side and vomit the rice gruel into the turbulent ocean. The silence was broken by someone shouting, "Land ahead!' Yes they were nearly approaching Exile Island.

II

After the boat tied up in the port, the prisoners debarked and stood on the dock waiting for someone to come over with instructions. Some of the island people gathered in a group and stood silently on dockside looking the prisoners over like chattel. In a little while an officious looking man in a brass buttoned uniform came off the boat and addressed the prisoners, "You are all free to enjoy this lovely island unconfined and unfettered. You may notice some of the islanders observing these festivities," he pointed to the crowd and continued, "These people have living facilities and food which they are willing to share with you for work. Please make your arrangements with them otherwise you are on your own to survive as best as you are able." With that he turned and boarded the boat with the guards. For a little while nothing happened until some of the islanders broke ranks and approached the group of standing prisoners chatting and talking in a loud din. Many men approached Kat. She shooed them all away until a kindly looking, little old lady came shuffling over. "I need a housekeeper to help with cooking and cleaning. If you come to live with me, I have sleeping quarters in the barn for you and will provide three meals a day."

For Katsuko this was a great challenge. After all she never did housework and always lived an opulent life. But there was something about the old lady that she found empathetic. After all what was she to do? She was interested first in personal safety and did not want to become involved with men. She asked the old lady, "Will you be patient with me until I learn?"

The old lady quickly replied, "Of course, I shall. You will learn quickly, I am sure."

Then, I shall come to you." She turned to Toshiki and reluctantly said, "First, is there room for my friend, Toshiki?"

The old lady hesitated for a moment then said after carefully looking him over, "Yes, I will take him for work on our farm if he is willing."

Toshi quickly agreed, "I have never worked on a farm but I am willing and anxious to learn."

"Well then it is settled," the old lady said with a bow. "My name is Hashinaga Yukuri. You may call me Yuki." At the conclusion of their talk they all bowed to each other then the two exiles followed the old lady to her house.

Her house was a comfortable old farm-house having a projecting gable-wing to its right. The roof was thickly thatched. At the end of the wing was a triangular latticed opening from which thin blue wreaths of smoke were curling. The building contained a few rooms, including an unusually spacious kitchen. The kitchen opened directly into a larger unfinished portion of the house, having earth for its floor and used as a woodshed. A huge pile of wood cut for the winter's supply was piled up. Yuki informed them that the farm-house was nearly one hundred years old and that she and her husband were the second owners. To the left of the farm-house was a high wooden fence, and passing through a gateway they came into a smaller yard and vegetable garden. In this area was the barn quite independent of the farm-house; this was where hay and barrels of comestibles along with farm tools such as rakes, shovels, and the customary utensils of a farmer's occupation were scattered about.

Its conspicuous feature consisted of a thatched roof, surmounted by an elaborate and picturesque ridge. Within were two large rooms opening upon a narrow verandah. This was to be their sleeping quarters. Communication with the old farm-house was by means of a covered passageway. While inspecting the two rooms, Yuki's husband came in – a fine old gentleman, dignified, and courtly in his manners. He was slightly bent over but was able to bow repeatedly. He was bald with thick, gray eyebrows which seemed to cover his eyes. He wore a perpetual smile on his face and had a toothless grin.

Kat and Toshi followed Yuki back to the farm-house, trailed by the old man who shuffled along rather slowly. Everyone removed their street shoes and placed them on a shelf in the vestibule. The interior of the farm-house is so simple in its construction, and so unlike anything to which one is accustomed that it is difficult to find terms of comparison in attempting to describe it. The first thing that impresses one on entering the farm-house is the small size and low stud of the rooms. The ceilings are so low that in many cases one can easily touch them, and in going from one room to another one is apt to strike his head against the *kamoi*, or lintel. The *tokonoma*, a recess in the best-room, contains a vase with flowers and a hanging scroll of a mountain landscape scene. The group all gathered in the best-room and sat on the *tatami* covered floor to listen to Yuki give instructions.

"Your sleeping quarters are in the barn which we just left. There is one room for each of you. You will find a paillasse for each of you in the two rooms. You should replace the old straw with fresh straw. You, Kat, will make breakfast every morning for the four of us, wash the dishes, and clean the rooms. Then you will prepare lunch and dinner. I will work with you until you learn the routine and can work alone." She hesitated a moment expecting a comment from Kat. None came so she continued, "You, Toshi, will work on the farm which is adjacent to our property. Right now we are growing lentils, soy beans, and we have a small wet farm for growing rice. These are all cash crops, some of which we sell and barter. Also, you will care for our small vegetable garden outside the farm-house. My husband will show you what to do so don't be alarmed or concerned. You will meet him everyday after breakfast." Once again she waited for any questions or comments, but none came. "You may rest for the remainder of the day and make ready your rooms. We will start at first light tomorrow morning," Yuki said.

Kat and Toshi got up and bowed. They then retired to the barn where they busied themselves replenishing the straw in the paillasse and cleaning the two rooms. On completion of their work they both sat on the small verandah and slowly reviewed their situation.

"Well, what do you think?" asked Kat, casually.

"First, I want to thank you, Kat, for including me in this venture. I am grateful and I now know we are friends." Toshi hesitated for a moment and then remarked, "I think we're both amateurs at this domestic work and it will take us sometime to learn how to perform properly."

"No. I think it will go smoothly. The two old people are very nice and will be patient with us. Meanwhile, we have a berth and we will be plotting and scheming in preparation for our breakout."

"Do you really think so?

"Yes, yes, I do. In a little time we will learn the whereabouts of everything. We must find the best point to leave from and locate an available boat. We must also prepare and store food for the journey back to the mainland."

"You're really serious, aren't you?

"Yes, of course, I am," Kat stated flatly without fanfare.

"Together, I am sure we can do it, "Toshi agreed convincingly.

"Well, tomorrow is our first day of work so let's get a good night's sleep," Kat rose as she spoke and entered her room.

"Good night, Kat."

"Good night, Toshi. See you early tomorrow."

III

A shrill, screech of a rooster woke them up at first light. Apparently, there is a brood of domestic fowl on the premises of which this screaming cock is the dominant male. To Toshi's mind this call of the rooster meant eggs. His mouth watered at the thought of eggs for breakfast. But that was not to be. When he and Kat arrived at the kitchen of the farm-house, Kat was congenially instructed by Yuki in the proper method for making rice gruel. The rice gruel was served with pickled *daikon* (radishes). Pickled vegetables became a staple of early morning rice gruel. These vegetables, such as *daikon* (radishes), *botan-na* (cabbages), *adzuki* (beans), and *kyuri* (cucumbers) were marinated in brine barrels containing sea water and rice bran.

Kat and Toshi sat down at breakfast joined by Yuki and her husband. Looking at Kat, Yuki said, "You did very well Kat. You seem to take to cooking."

"Thank you, Yuki. You are a good teacher."

At this point, Toshi broke into the conversation, "A rooster woke me up this morning. Do you have a chicken coop?"

"Yes," said the old man. "It is located in back of the barn. You must have missed it yesterday. We have one rooster and seven chickens. The rooster has a joyous time with his harem. Ha! Ha! He makes love and we get eggs, Ha! Ha!"

After breakfast, Toshi and the old man departed for the farm while Kat was left to clean up and prepare for the day's meals. The old man told Toshi to grab a hoe and a shovel from the barn. He slung these tools over his shoulder as they continued walking to the farm. The old man walked bent over and proceeded very slowly apparently hindered by arthritic legs, but he was able to speak slowly in rhythm with his gait, "We bought this house and land from a wealthy, exiled merchant who lived here with his wife and infant son. His wife and son died from a cholera epidemic which ravaged the island some years ago. They are buried on the gravesite in the south corner of the farm. I'll show it to you when we reach the farm. Yuki and I would like to be buried there as well when our time comes. Well, we came here two years ago after the epidemic and really liked the place even though it had fallen somewhat into ruin. The owner offered to sell it to us provided that we let him occupy and live in the guest-house until his death."

"Did you say guest-house?"

"Yes, what we now use as a barn was formerly a guest-house. The owner became a permanent resident of Exile Island even though he was pardoned years before."

"I find that hard to believe," exclaimed Toshi with an incredulous tone.

"Yes, there are some who have remained here to make a new life – never to return to the mainland. The owner would invite his extended family to visit him and stay over in the guest-house." He stopped speaking for a minute to gather his thoughts then continued, "There is a luxury boat that brings visiting family members here for the exiled residents."

"I see," said Toshi with great interest.

In time they reached the farm and Toshi was able to see the gravesite. The old man told Toshi, "I would like to show you the small waterfall where I wash every morning. You may join me today, if you like."

They walked in single file along the dike of the wet rice paddy until they came to a small rivulet which fed water to the rice paddy. As they followed the rivulet they came to a craggy outcrop of rocks at the base of a mountain. Water came streaming down softly but unrelentingly. The old man was removing his clothing which startled Toshi at first but was relieved when he saw the old man begin to shower himself under the waterfall.

"Come in!" the old man shouted.

Toshi hesitated but eventually removed his clothing and began to join the old man under the cataract watercourse. "This is my place for water bathing," said the old man. "I clean myself here every morning. You should do this routinely every morning before you start work on the farm. You will find it very invigorating and a good start of the day."

"Yes, and it is freezing cold," Toshi cried as he slapped his body with his hands.

"We have a hot-tub at the back of the farm-house which I usually fire up at the end of the day for all of us to soak in after dinner," explained the old man with some pride.

The waterfall cascaded down to a pool where there were several white, showy, flowered aquatic lilies at the edge. From there the water flowed downhill watering the farm as a natural irrigation. They both dried their bodies and dressed in their clothes.

The old man alerted Toshi breathlessly, "Now, I will show you how to paddle the furrows by uprooting the weeds with the hoe. In the meantime, I shall begin cutting new furrows using the shovel as a plowshare."

They worked at this chore in silence for several hours. The old man worked slowly but steadily making new furrows to receive seeds while Toshi continued hoeing the old furrows. He straightened up from his bent over position every once in a while. The work was hard and they were beginning to sweat even though the sun had not yet reached its zenith. Toshi stopped to rest when he saw that the old man was resting. He called out, "What happened to the owner of the farm-house?"

The old man cupped his ear with his hand in order to hear well. He returned the answer with a shout, "What, what, oh yes, one cold, frosty morning when I went to the guest-house to get some tools, I found him lying dead in his futon."

Toshi came over to the old man to continue the conversation, "You found him dead?"

"Yes, I then went all over the island looking for a Buddhist priest. There was none to be found but a Buddhist practitioner came and helped me build a pyre with a heap of logs and wood and other combustible materials in order to burn the dead body as a funeral rite. At the conclusion of the cremation I buried his ashes at the gravesite and built a cairn out of stones as a memorial. In addition, for the want of something better to do I chanted the Heart Sutra which I had learned and memorized as a child."

Prajna Paramita Hrdaya Sutra
When the Bodhisattva Avalokitesvara
was coursing in the Deep Prajna Paramita
He perceived that all Five Skandas are empty
Thus he overcame all ills and suffering
Oh Sariputra, form does not differ from the void, and
the void does not differ from form. Form is void and
void is form. The same is true for feelings, perceptions,
volitions and consciousness.
Oh Sariputra, the characteristics of the voidness of
all dharmas are non-arising, non-ceasing, non-defiled,
non-pure, non-increasing, non-decreasing.
Therefore, in the void there are no forms, no
feelings, perceptions, volitions or consciousness.
No eye, ear, nose, tongue, body or mind; no form,
sound, smell, taste, touch or mind object; no realm of
the eye, until we come to no realm or consciousness.
No ignorance and also no ending of ignorance, until
we come to no old age and death and no ending of old
age and death.
There is no wisdom and there is no attainment
whatsoever.
Because there is nothing to be attained, the
Bodhisattva relying on Prajna Paramita has no

obstruction in his mind.
The Buddhas of the past, present and future, by
Relying on Prajna Paramita have attained supreme
enlightenment.
Therefore, the Prajna Paramita is the great magic
spell, the spell of illumination, the supreme spell
which can
Truly protect one from all suffering without fail.
Therefore he uttered the spell of Prajna Paramita
saying - gate, gate, paragate, parasamgate, bodhi svaha.

Toshi looked at the old man with wide eyes and a startled expression, "what does it all mean?'

The old man winced but answered forthwith, "I don't really know. I learned it as a child from my parents, who were devout Buddhists. I thought it might be appropriate to say." Toshi shook his head and went back to work. By this time the sun was high in the sky so Toshi and the old man dropped their tools and started back to the farm-house for lunch. Toshi noticed the old man shuffling along slowly while moving his arms back and forth to give him balance. His bent frame was necessary to prevent him from falling over. Then he suddenly stopped and looked up saying, "Toshi, I am sorry I am delaying us, but I must stop for a minute to catch my breath."

"Oh, think nothing of it I am tired as well."

While standing still, the old man asked Toshi, "Tell me Toshi how involved you are with Kat?"

Toshi was apparently taken aback at this query, "What do you mean?"

"Forgive me for presuming but I thought you might have an amorous relationship with Kat."

"You mean – are we lovers?"

"Yes."

"Oh, no, nothing of the kind, we are only friends. I just met her on the boat which brought us here."

"I see. The reason I asked is that you seem so compatible."

"It is true that she requested my presence when Yuki selected us but I believe she only wanted me along as protection."

"Yes, you are probably right," he said as they began walking again.

Toshi continued the conversation by asking, "Did you do all the farm work by your self?"

"Oh no, when we first arrived I used to hire day laborers who worked for food. There is no money exchanged on the island. All transactions are bartered. The people I hired were usually bad workers. Most of them had committed serious crimes before they came here and were not inclined to honest work. We even had some thefts of tools and food. In the last two years I became arthritic and could not do the whole farm so I only planted half the farm and, of course, the rice paddy. Rice is the staple of the island and is worth much at times of barter. I exchange rice for fish at the fishing village at the nearby coast."

"I wondered about that. I would like to visit the fishing village."

"Well that certainly would be possible the next time we go for fish."

Eventually, they reached the farm-house. They washed up and went into the kitchen with greetings for Kat and Yuki. While sitting down at the table, Kat brought out a large bowl of *gohan* (boiled rice) and a platter of small skewered roasted fish together with pickled *daikon* (radishes). The old man couldn't help calling out enthusiastically, "Kat you did a marvelous job in making lunch."

Kat blushed slightly but responded, "Yuki is a wonderful teacher. I am learning a lot from her. Tell me, how did Toshi do on the farm?"

The old man said, "Toshi is a good worker. It is a pleasure working with him. He took to the work very easily."

After lunch was finished, the old man told Toshi, "I am going to take a nap now. You go back to the farm and complete hoeing the furrows. If you have time you may start on the new furrows. I'll join you later."

"Alright, I can work alone. I know what to do."

Toshi worked all day weeding the furrows and making new furrows which the old man had started. The old man never returned. Working alone Toshi found the silence to be soothing and comforting. It gave him time to reflect on his life. *Being a thief was never very productive. I prefer the satisfaction and tranquility of this kind of work even though it is very difficult.* The weather was extremely hot and Toshi was sweating profusely but at the end of the day he decided to shower in the waterfall again before returning to the farm-house. Afterwards on reaching the farm-house he found the old man stoking a fire in the fireplace under the hot tub. The hot tub was a very large iron vessel sitting on top of a stone fireplace.

"Hello, Toshi, have you finished your work for the day? I couldn't join you because I wasn't feeling well."

"Yes, I finished the furrowing. What are you doing?"

"I am building a fire for the hot tub so that we can soak after dinner."

"I see. What shall I do tomorrow?"

"Tomorrow, you will plant the seeds for *horenso* (spinach). The seeds are kept in a wooden locker in your room to prevent the rodents from getting at them."

They both went inside to join Kat and Yuki at the dinner table. Dinner consisted of the usual fare of *gohan* (boiled rice), fish and pickled *kyuri* (cucumbers). This was followed by a beverage made of hot water laced with a mixed berry preserve. Apparently the forest has many vines of wild berries which are gathered in the late spring and made into a mixture of berry preserve. The island is relatively free of large bears which might feed on the berries. Thus they are left untouched and available to all.

The Japanese diet is seriously lacking in dairy products such as those made from milk, butter and cheese. This is true of the mainland as well. There isn't enough pasture land for cattle grazing and cow husbandry any where in Japan with the result that the Japanese people had serious spinal and bone problems resulting in being "bent with age", a condition known as *koshi ga magatte oru*. This condition is obviously what caused the infirmity of the old man. In addition, the Japanese do not raise wheat and so no bread or cake products are consumed aggravating their naturally shortened stature. They do, however, raise other grains such as the cereal grasses sorghum, barley, and, of course, rice. The staple of foods in Japan as well as the Exile Island is rice and fish. There is only one item in serious default on the island and that is the lack of tea bushes thus causing a high price for the tea which must be imported.

While sitting at the table and sipping their berry infusion the conversation began revolving around the planting of the rice seed grasses. All four members of the household, Yuki, the old man, Kat and Toshi will have to participate in the planting of the rice seed grasses. The old man said, "I saw the rice seed grasses ready in one corner of the wet rice paddy yesterday. It is time to flood the paddy with water from the rivulet and separate the bundles of rice grasses and begin planting. Tomorrow we shall all go up to the farm. Toshi and I will go up first to prepare the paddy Yuki and Kat can come up after breakfast and clean up. Each rice grass must be planted individually by bending over and sticking them into the mud in a regimented layout. It is tedious work so let us have a good bath and retire early to be fresh in the morning."

After dinner the four left the kitchen and went to the back of the farm-house for the evening bath in the hot tub. Each participant removed clothing and placed it on hooks provided on the farm-house wall. The old people, Yuki and her husband, exhibited wrinkled skin at the arms and torso but Kat had a beautifully young, smooth body with sensuous curves that set Toshi's eyes bulging. He looked at her lasciviously and smiled as their eyes met. All entered the communal hot tub and relaxed as their bodies were suspended in the warm enveloping water. Cares and tribulations seemed to melt away as they floated in silence. Sometimes their toes would touch causing giggles to ensue. Yuki tried to make conversation but talk seemed to be a suspended for a while. After fifteen minutes, Kat and Toshi left the tub leaving the old people behind. They dried off with previously prepared towels, said goodnight, and headed for their rooms in the barn.

Toshi and Kat sat on their small verandah for a while discussing events of the day. Kat pulled out a sheet of paper from her kimono and showed it to Toshi. "I have been making this map after speaking with Yuki. She told me that the island is shaped like a teardrop with two main roads, one going north and south about twenty miles and the other going east and west about fifteen miles. We are located almost at the cross roads. The one going east and west is called the lateral road. The lateral road connects the two main ports *(minato)*. We came in on the east *(higashi)* port and the large port on the west *(nishi)* of the lateral road has more fishing villages with small boats. Also, leaving from the nishi port has better currents going north; that is why fishermen like to depart from there."

"My, my, I see you have been busy getting information," Toshi said in a surprised tone.

"Of course, the old lady likes to talk and is a fountain of information," Kat responded quickly. "I don't intend staying here more than I must," she said while folding the paper and slipping it into the sleeve of her kimono.

Toshi added to the events by relating his experience with the old man and suggesting that he would be able to look-about the area if he went with the old man to the fishing villages for bartering.

This seemed to confuse Kat very much. "That's a good idea," she said with complete consternation. "I hope you'll be able to make some contacts. We'll need some help in escaping." She got up to indicate that their conversation was over and then both went into their separate rooms to sleep.

IV

After breakfast the next day, Toshi and the old man headed for the rice paddy with tools slung over their shoulders. It was a very long trek for the old man who stopped at the paddy dike breathing hard and coughing once or twice. "Are you alright?" Toshi asked.

"Yes, yes, just slightly out of breath," he answered with a wheeze. After a moment of rest and as the old man caught his breath he said to Toshi, "Break the dike at the rivulet edge and direct the water to flow into the paddy." Having done this, Toshi caused the water to gush into the paddy and stir up the muddy bottom. "Very good, Toshi," said the old man with beaming pride. "Now the paddy will be ready to receive the rice grass seed." As soon as the paddy contained about a foot of water, Toshi repaired the dike thus sealing in the water. A few minutes later, Kat and Yuki wearing head coverings arrived. These head coverings looked like old fashioned bonnets with long visors and peaked tops. Japanese women who work on farms are very careful about exposure to the sun which might darken their skin. Housework is Kat's entire day, she begins as soon as the men leave for the farm in the morning – sweep the floors, tend the little garden, do the laundry, cook the meals, and wash the dishes. This extra service on the farm will come up from time to time.

The old man picked up several bundles of rice grass seeds and handed them to the three people. Saying, "Line up in a straight .line across the width of the paddy and begin transplanting rice into rows on the flooded paddy as you back up." They stand in the muddy water, backs bent as they stab the rice shoots into the wet earth, their hands unerring. All complied and seemed to work in unison by bending over and pushing a sliver of grass seed into the mud below. The three workers are bent over the earth in aching, backbreaking labor. The sun was very high in the sky at this point and the work was very exhausting. They were sweating profusely and the sweat kept running into their eyes. Toshi kept rubbing the sweat out of his eyes with the sleeve of his arm but this only made his eye irritate more. This kind of heat is to be expected since Exile Island is tropical. It took more than two hours for the paddy to be completely seeded at which time all straightened up and kneaded their back muscles. It was hard work but there was a sort of satisfaction to see the paddy with slivers of rice grass poking up in a regimented manner.

The old man said to Toshi, "This is our most valuable crop. The rice we gain from this planting will be exchanged for fish at barter time. We get three rice harvests a year and so we will be doing this again in the future."

Toshi responded with a broad smile, "Very good, I'll be ready." Kat looked at him strangely as she and Yuki retreated back to the farm-house. The walk back was done in silence. They were both very tired. At last Yuki said, "We must prepare lunch because the men will be coming back as soon as they are finished." Kat said nothing and only shook her head in assent. At the kitchen Kat immediately put up the boiling water for the rice. Yuki said that they will have rice and peas for the main dish followed by a soup made of bonito flakes, sea weed, and green onions. All of this had to be prepared by Kat who was learning the cooking part of her housework like an expert. She never expressed any satisfaction in her learning skills. Indeed, it was obvious she was not suited for this kind of work but she accepted her lot in silence.

The men arrived in somewhat of a jocose mood, sitting down at the table with constant chatter. The old man said to Toshi, "After lunch go back to the farm and finish planting the spinach and start a new furrow for soy beans. I'll join you later"

"Yes, I will," answered Toshi with enthusiasm knowing full well that the old man will probably take a nap and not come.

The days passed quickly, the rice growing higher in the paddy and the vegetables maturing to a near harvest. The clouds were thickening with the coming monsoon.

One morning, the old man enlisted the two women to begin weeding the rice paddy. Kat and Yuki were busy weeding the rice paddy, Kat tried to think about this labor that will feed families, these works and days of hands, the feeling of mud between the toes, water up to the ankles, the sun on the back of the neck – it is useless she can only think of someday escaping.

Suddenly, lightning splits open a cloud and all became drenched in rain. The monsoon unleashes itself in a dark, cloudy fury. There is thunder but it fades, the clouds and rain remain. All are enlisted to harvest the vegetables that are full grown before disaster strikes from the pelting rain. The rivulet has now become a flowing stream bringing down rocks and detritus from the mountain top. They all work feverishly to salvage the vegetables. Those tubers in the underground are left behind; the leafy vegetables are collected in wooden boxes and brought down to the farm-house. When they arrive at the farm-house water was collecting in the cistern but the old man directs them to collect the rain water in prepared receptacles. Then they all go inside to change clothes and partake of hot water laced with mixed berry fruit preserve. The rain continues in a steady down pour.

Toshi exclaims, while sitting at the table with the others, "Oh, what I would give for a hot cup of *ryokucha* (green tea)."

The old man answers, "Maybe after this harvest of the rice we can barter for some green tea." He reflects for a while but then continues, "After the rain abates we will have to dig an underground cellar to store the vegetables otherwise they will perish. An underground cellar is very cool and preserves the vegetables for a long time."

It rained continuously for a week without a let up. During that time Toshi and the old man busied themselves with repairs to the farm-house and straightening up the barn to make it more livable. The old man kept hinting at Toshi and Kat living together and so to free up one room for storage of tools, seeds, and farm equipment. But this was to no avail. Toshi gave the same answer to each suggestion, "She doesn't want to live with me. I would be happy to share my bed with her; but she doesn't like me enough to agree."

"I think she would agree if you married her."

"I don't think she would marry me."

"Have you asked her?"

"No, I haven't but it is no use."

"Why not ask her?"

Toshi stopped his work for a minute and looked up, "You must understand she is not some peasant, farm girl. She was a trained courtesan living an opulent life of luxury before coming here. I could never give her the life to which she is accustomed."

The old man was startled, "I can't believe what I am hearing. That old life is all over. You and Kat are exiles. You both are lucky to have been chosen by us to survive. You will be here until you are pardoned, if ever. Right now Kat is learning to be a farm girl. It really is time to make a new life. You have that opportunity here and now."

Toshi was stunned at these words but answered forthrightly, "I am grateful to be here. My life before this had no purpose. I really enjoy farm work. I think it is best to give Kat some time to think about her lot and perhaps she will eventually come around."

"You may be right. Let's wait and see."

After a week of steady rain the clouds began moving north to hammer the coast of the mainland. The sun peeped through the scudding clouds to begin the long dry out process. Toshi and the old man went to the farm to inspect the state of the plantings. All seemed to be saved, especially the rice paddy which was filled to the brim with water. Toshi had to break a channel in the dike to allow the water to flow out. The rice paddy was stuffed with green shoots like a carpet after the water receded. Now, it was time for the sun to do its work in ripening the kernels.

Toshi and the old man returned to the farm-house where the old man sited a place behind the farm-house near the chicken coop to dig a vegetable cellar. The old man sat on the ground directing the operation while Toshi dug a deep hole about six feet deep and six by nine feet wide. All the dirt had to be carted away in the pull wagon usually used for carrying comestibles to the fishing village for barter.

That night after dinner Kat and Toshi sat on their verandah discussing the usual plans for escape. Toshi spoke reluctantly, "The old man thinks we should get married."

She burst out laughing, "He does? Ha! Ha!, what a silly idea."

"Why silly, I really like you."

"Oh, you're nice enough but I don't want to get married."

"Why not? We could have a good life."

"I told you. I only have one thing on my mind. I want to escape this island. I am willing to risk my life on that. I want to live on the mainland." Then she hesitated for a moment to inquire, " Are you still with me in that endeavor?"

'"Yes, yes, of course."

"Then why do you bring up marriage. I get it all day from Yuki. She follows me around as I work - saying to me, "If we got married, in a little time, we could live in the farm-house and she and the old man would move to the barn and then we would eventually inherit the property when they die."

"She said that?"

"Yes, so what, I don't want to live here. I hate this life. I am nothing but an indentured servant. I want to return to the mainland where life is beautiful, sophisticated and cultured." She stopped to lower her voice questioning, "Don't you want that too?"

Toshi lowered his head and mumbled, "I guess so."

"What do you mean – you guess so."

"I mean – I would go with you and help you escape but I want you to know that I really enjoy farming. There is nothing on the mainland that I miss – returning there only offers me a life of crime." They then separated and went into their rooms for the night.

V

Days became weeks with nothing but work. There was no diversion, no entertainment, only work. Each day was the same as the previous one. Kat was becoming crucially bored with the daily company of Yuki. The old lady kept after her with constant criticisms and opinions to the point that Kat would sometimes scream at her. Meanwhile, Toshi was enjoying his work on the farm and was interested in everything the old man had to say. In fact a sort of father/son relationship was budding between them. Toshi liked the old man and would often seek his advice and would not allow him to do any heavy lifting. In time, the farm became very fecund and with each harvest was producing an excess of vegetables and rice. In particular the rice accumulation was plentiful due to the multiple plantings. The old man addressed Toshi, "It is time to go to the fishing village at the east end of the lateral road to trade our surplus vegetables and rice for fish."

Toshi asked, "When shall we go?"

The old man looked at Toshi with a twinkle in his eyes and said, "You may have to go alone without me. I don't feel strong enough to make the journey. It is too far to walk for me."

"But, I have never bartered before."

"Oh, you'll do alright. I have every faith and confidence in you. Tomorrow would be a good time to go while the vegetables are still fresh. In the morning I'll help you load up the pushcart and explain certain mannerisms and conditions that will be helpful to you."

"Alright, I'll do my best."

They left the farm for dinner and bath taking with them the day's harvest of vegetables. Toshi put most of the vegetables in three iron vessels and with the large box of rice kernels loaded up the pushcart for the morning's journey.

In the evening he and Kat sat on their verandah talking. Kat said, "I admire your ability to get along so well with the old man. I am jealous that you are going to the fishing village to barter. At least it will be a change from the boredom of the farm."

"I do not find my work on the farm boring."

"Well anyway, this may be your opportunity to learn some way to escape this island. Keep your eyes and ears active for ways to help us. Remember the most important thing is we will need a boat."

"Yes, I know, that is uppermost in my mind."

"Are you still anxious to escape with me?"

"Well, to be honest, I like it here. I have learned how to be a farmer. For the first time in my life I have been able to do something useful. But, I understand why you want to leave," he hesitated for a moment and then continued, "You want to return to your old life. You have not found a reason to be engrossed in your work as I have. Life here is of no interest to you. You believe that life on the mainland will excite you and engage your attention."

Kat immediately interrupted him, "Wait, wait, my life here is pure drudgery. It is nothing but wearisome toil. The exertion of my strength in cleaning and cooking accomplishes nothing. It is dull, irksome, and distasteful work. I yearn for diversion, recreation, and relaxation. I find nothing redeeming about the two old people. They mean well and in their way are very nice but they bore me to distraction." She rested to catch her breath and then continued her diatribe with her head held high, "You forget that I am an intellectually sophisticated person trained in the arts of music, dance and refined living. Merely to survive is not what I want. I am willing to risk my life in order to return to my world of humanity and pleasure. It is that important to me."

Toshi listened in silence but after a moment breathed a sigh with a deep audible breath, "Yes, I understand."

"Do you really understand?"

"Yes I do and I am willing to help you."

She was puzzled by this remark. With a creased forehead she inquired, "Why would you help me, if you are happy here?"

He resisted answering but finally blurted out, "Because I love you."

She was jolted backwards, "You mean you are willing to forsake the life you found and enjoy here to help me because you think you are in love with me?"

"Yes."

"I never gave you any reason to feel that way, but in that case we can discuss it when we reach the mainland. Right now I want to focus on the escape."

"Alright Kat, I must get up early tomorrow morning to bring the vegetables and rice to the fishing village for barter."

"Good night, Toshi. Good night, Kat.

They went into their separate rooms for the evening retirement. In the morning Toshi rose early to get the pushcart ready. He spoke at length with the old man, seeking his advice regarding the art of bartering.` After eating a breakfast of a bowl of boiled rice with a raw egg on top and a side dish of pickled radishes; he departed for the fishing village along the east lateral road.

The sun was beginning to rise as he trudged along pushing the pushcart. The weather became warmer as time passed by and Toshi was beginning to sweat and had to pause for breath. Suddenly he noticed a man following him. As he rested and wiped his brow the man approached. He was a pint-sized brown-haired gentleman with an evenly tanned sympathetic face. With his brown wavy hair and nut-colored face, with large, pointed heart-shaped ears and dangling Buddha-lobes, and dark ear holes that looked as though they'd been dug to a burrow by a mouse; a nose of impressive length that broadened as it descended, so that the nostrils, each a sizeable crescent, were just about hidden by the wide, weighted tip; and eyes that were ageless, polished brown protruding eyes surrounded by epicanthic flesh.

"Good morning," said Toshi.

The gentleman approached saying, "Good morning to you, kind sir. What have you there in the pushcart?"

"I have a load of rice and vegetables which I am taking to the fishing village to barter for fish."

"I see. Have you bartered before?"

"No, this is my first experience."

"Well then, please let me help you."

Toshi hesitated and looked intently at the gentleman whose eyes radiated like two refulgent lignite coals. A shudder went up his spine as he answered, "No thank you. I can manage by myself."

The gentleman smiled with an upward curving of the corners of his mouth. "Very well," he said, "I was just trying to be friendly."

"Of course, my name is Toshi," he said as he bowed with palms together.

The gentleman did not return the bow as his smile turned into a smirk, "My name is Natas. I am glad to meet you. May I walk with you as you push the cart along?"

"Yes, indeed, I would enjoy the company."

After a few steps of walking, Natas slowly inquired, "Tell me Toshi would you like to escape from Exile Island?"

Toshi was shocked to say the least, "What do you mean?"

Natas turned his head to confront Toshi more directly, "I have sources to accomplish an escape, if you are interested."

Toshi stopped in his tracks and turned to face Natas, "What makes you think I am interested. Can't you see I am just a poor farmer trying to barter my vegetables for fish? Who are you that you can speak to me like this. I don't know you and I don't understand your motive."

"Now, now, Toshi, don't be offended. Most people on this island want to escape. They are plotting all the time. I just thought you might want to escape also."

"No, no, you are wrong," Toshi hastily answered. "I am not interested."

"Alright, Toshi, it was my mistake. I shall leave you now." He turned and fled away swiftly as from danger or evil.

Toshi was shaken for a moment but then recovered quickly from weakness and pushed on. He could not help thinking about Natas. *Who was he, was he wrong in dismissing him? He was exactly the kind of resource Kat was looking for.* As he thought more about this incident he mumbled to himself, "I better not tell Kat about this incident she might get angry at the missed opportunity."

It was mid-morning when Toshi reached the fishing village. It was not really a village – more like a few houses on a water inlet. The houses all had their own boat docks and every so often one could see a variety of small skiffs bobbing up and down in the water. The big boats were apparently out to sea - and have not come in yet with the morning catch. Toshi set his pushcart at the front of the largest wooden dock and prepared to wait for the boat to arrive.

He went to get a pail of fresh water from a nearby pump to sprinkle on the vegetables to prevent wilting in the hot midday sun. While doing this a woman came out of the house to greet Toshi, "I am waiting for my husband to bring in the catch. When he arrives we can barter with you for your rice and vegetables. I want you to know that we have many large pieces of *himono* (dried fish) hanging in the backyard. Fresh fish is only good for a few days but dried fish can last for a long time. If you like we can examine them while you are waiting."

"Thank you, I shall wait for your husband to come in," Toshi said with some suspicion. He did not have to wait long as he spied the fishing boat coming into the dock. It was a single mast boat with a yardarm containing an unfurled square sail which was flopping in the wind like a flag. The shipmaster was bellowing orders to the crew as it neared dockside. A rope was tossed to the dock which was caught by the ship owner's wife who then tied it around one of the piles on the dock. Having been secured the crew began unloading the boxes of squirming, slithering fish. By this time a small crowd was assembling at the dock to inspect the catch. There began a din of a steady hum made by the observers coupled with the voices of the shouting crew. The ship owner/captain waddled off the boat on a gangplank still bellowing orders. As he approached Toshi and his pushcart he bawled, "Ah yes, fresh vegetables!"

Toshi responded, "I am here to trade."

The captain's wife came over to join the fray. Toshi pointed to the three iron vessels containing the vegetables, "I am ready to replace these vegetables with fish."

"Ha! Ha! Do you think bartering is that easy?"

"Yes, it's that easy."

"Do you really expect me to replace your vegetables with fish? I must first give one box of fish to each of my crew for their labor in catching the fish."

Toshi paused undecidedly and began to stammer," Well, if you don't replace the vegetables with fish then we do not have a deal and I shall leave. Fish spoils – vegetables can be eaten."

"Wait; hold on, we need to talk about this. We must barter," shouted the irate captain.

Toshi stuck fast and did not falter, "The vegetables for the fish and the rice for several pieces of *himono* (dried fish), that's my barter."

The captain demurred but with a hearty laugh finally agreed, "Alright let's do it."

The vegetables were carefully removed from the iron vessels and were replaced with live squirming fish and then covered with sea water. The captain's wife brought out four long dried fillets in exchange for the box of rice kernels. This was all placed in the pushcart. "Thank you very much," said Toshi as he was about to leave.

The captain raised his arm, "Please join me in a drink to your good health. I would like to learn more about you. I have never seen you before and assume that you are a new arrival."

"Very well," said Toshi, "But only for a minute. I would not want my fish to spoil."

They went into the house and the captain's wife brought two large tankards of a sweet drink for each of the men. They sat at a table and toasted each other. They made small talk as the captain's wife kept filling their tankards with the unusual drink from a large wicker covered carafe. Toshi was getting slightly dizzy and his eyes were intermittently closing. He was looking through a haze as he looked up slowly to see the face of Natas sitting next to the captain. He became frightened by this sight and rubbed his eyes in disbelief. He suddenly let out a shrill, sharp sound, "Mr. Natas what are you doing here?"

Natas answered in a deliberate manner, "I came to help you push the cart home. Now that you have finished bartering it is time to leave."

"Yes you are right; people are waiting for me."

The captain shook his head and spoke in an incredulous manner, "Who are you speaking to?"

Toshi got up and bowed crudely to the captain, "It was no one. I am slightly dizzy. Thank you for your good wishes. I shall return for bartering after the next harvest of rice and vegetables." He left the captain's house followed by Natas, who accompanied Toshi without assisting him in pushing the cart. They trudged slowly back to the farm.

Toshi and Natas approached the farm by midday. All the while Natas was confiding his thoughts to Toshi, "Did you see that boat with the single mast?"

"Yes, I saw it."

"It would be perfect for our escape."

"What do you mean OUR escape?"

"I mean, I am going with you."

"No you're not. You have not been invited."

"You will not be able to do it without me."

"Why not? I am perfectly capable."

"You need me to help you get the weapons in order to kill the captain and his wife."

Toshi was shocked, "Why do we have to kill them. Why not just steal the boat."

At the moment of making this statement Toshi came to the farm house where all stood and waited to greet him. The old man and Yuki came over to the pushcart and admired Toshi's achievement. "Oh, how wonderful, Yuki exclaimed as she held up the dried fish. "Now we can make *sakana tempura* (fried fish with rice flour) or *aburu tempura* (broiled fish with soy sauce) but first this dried fish must be soaked in fresh water for a day to restore the flesh."

Toshi took down the three iron kettles containing the live fish from the pushcart. He looked around but saw that Natas had disappeared. The old man said, "Why do you look so strangely?"

"Didn't you see the other man who accompanied me?" he said as he looked around furtively.

"No, I saw no one."

Toshi shook his shoulders, "Never mind, it's not important."

The old man looked at Toshi with a dubious eye. He was not able to fathom Toshi's change in comportment. He quickly said in a peremptory manner, "Toshi, I am very proud of your first day of bartering. This quantity of fish will last us a long time – certainly until the next harvest."

Toshi blushed and lowered his head, "Thank you for your confidence in me." He raised his head to see Kat beaming at him with folded arms just before she left to join Yuki with the dried fish. There was an obvious message in her eyes. *Did you learn anything about our escape?*

After dinner that evening, Toshi and Kat left for their barn. Kat was immediately surprised to see Natas sitting on their verandah. "Who are you?" she exclaimed. "What do you want?"

Toshi immediately intervened, "Wait Kat let me explain and introduce Mr. Natas. He offered to help us with our escape plans."

Kat calmed down as she made her way to the verandah. "Can you really help us?"

"Yes, of course I can. I have a plan for the three of us to escape."

Kat became extremely interested. She was no longer engrossed in Toshi. She now displayed an excitement of feeling for Natas and devoted special attention to him. She tempted him to sin, using all the devices at her disposal, glances, caresses, and gestures as they walked together into her room. Toshi was vexed and felt hurt that he would not partake in the conversation. But he understood Kat's wiles and ways and finally decided with a shrug of his shoulder to retire for the night.

The next morning, he and Kat went to the farm house for breakfast. Natas was nowhere to be seen. There was a moment during clean up that Kat was able to whisper in Toshi's ear, "We will escape in two days when the tide is high. I will speak with you further this evening on the verandah."

Toshi was working all day on the farm with Kat's voice still ringing in his ears, *"We will escape in two days." But how will we escape and, in what way? We need a boat, food, water. Where will we get all of this?* It was a long day until the evening meal.

He was afraid the two old people might get suspicious at their change in manner. Toshi lived in wild anticipation. He needed to speak with Kat. Eventually this came to pass. They were seated on the verandah. Kat was speaking with a keen and ardent voice, "Natas told me that the captain and his wife have a boat that would suit us. They also have food and water. All of this would be available to us for our journey to the mainland."

Toshi was irritated on hearing this but in exercising reasonable judgment asked, "how do we get these things?'

Kat, in her fanatic way said, "We take them."

"Take them. Are you blind to reality? They will not give them up without a fight."

Kat was deliberate, "Exactly, they must be killed."

Toshi raised his hand to stifle a groan. He thought, *"Am I hearing correctly?"* He was silent for a long time before speaking, "They are nice people who have not harmed us. Why must they be killed? Wouldn't it be better to borrow them or buy them?"

"Don't be silly, "Kat miffed. "They would not lend it to us and we cannot buy the stuff. The only way is to kill them and take the stuff. Then we can take our time in loading the boat and slipping out of the harbor."

"But their bodies will be discovered the next day."

"No, with the boat gone people will think the captain went fishing in his usual way."

Toshi did not want to enter into a petty quarrel with Kat so he said, "Let me think about it."

"What is there to think about? Didn't you say you wanted to help me escape?"

Toshi felt trapped by his promise to her. "Yes, I want to help you escape but I did not think it would involve murder."

"What's the difference? Once we reach the mainland we can disappear in the maze of the population."

"That's easy for you to say. You probably have a rich sponsor who will take you in. I have no one to help me or hide me. In no time I will be captured and they will hang me."

Kat looked at him with sympathetic eyes and held his hand, "Fear not, I shall take you with me. I know a place on the Yoshiwara Embankment where we will be safe."

Toshi hesitated for a moment then he spoke very slowly, "In that case, I will help you." He removed his hand from Kat's and felt very dejected. His love for Kat exceeded his ability to reason beyond justification for the act he was about to commit. He breathed quickly then exhaled heavily in fatigue, "Good night, Kat." He went into his room and dwelled on the coming events in an overwhelming depression. He slept little, tossing and turning all night.

VI

In two days, Kat and Toshi rose very early being very careful not wake the old people. They took their meager possessions and walked down the east lateral road to the fishing village. It was very dark and no one was about. It was as silent as a graveyard. Eventually they came to the home of the captain and waited outside in a crouched position to observe the house. No one spoke. All communication was accomplished by gestures. Suddenly Natas appeared and joined them at their waiting post. "I came to tell you how to kill the captain and his wife," he said matter-of-factly. Toshi gulped, the very thought of killing these innocent people disturbed him no end. Then Natas continued speaking in an impertinent and impudent way, "The captain has a collection of samurai swords displayed on the wall in the main room. Toshi you go in and carefully take down one of the swords. Kat, you and Toshi, sneak into the bedroom. Kat hold the captain's wife with your hand over her mouth while Toshi kills the captain with the sword. After that Toshi kill the captain's wife with the same sword. Then we can get the provisions for the journey."

Toshi felt sick but he controlled himself. He and Kat stealthily opened the front door to the house. They could hear the snoring of the captain in the bedroom. Quietly, they searched the main room for the sword collection. When it appeared to Toshi he methodically made a selection and took it off the wall. It was heavier than expected but he lifted it to his shoulder in anticipation of its use. Toshi and Kat walked into the dark, musty bedroom on tip-toe. It is there they found the two victims sleeping in a large double size futon. They hesitated. Toshi went around to the captain's side holding the sword high in the air in a ready-to-strike position. Kat was at the wife's futon side waiting surreptitiously to pounce on her. At a sign from Toshi to incite action, Kat leaped on the wife and holding her fast clasped her hand over the wife's mouth. The eyes of the poor woman bulged out of her head as she witnessed Toshi swing the sword like an axe chopping off the head of the captain. Blood spurted out everywhere like a fountain. Blood covered the bed clothes and on the poor, frightened wife. Suddenly, Toshi turned to Kat saying, "Let her go and move back." With the release of Kat's hand from the wife's mouth came a scream in a shrill voice. Toshi prepared to strike when the wife uttered a sharp outcry in a terrified voice, "Why, why?" This was muffled by blood rising in her throat after Toshi stabbed her in the chest with the point of the sword. Then there was silence. No one spoke. Nothing was said. Toshi was sweating but did no more than lay down the sword on the bloody bedding. He lowered his head and did not move for some time inspecting his hands and thinking of his dastardly deed.

It was Natas who came walking softly into the room saying, "It's done, now let's get the provisions and bring along the sword. Kat reached over and took Toshi by the arm. They rampaged through the house looking for provisions and a change of clothing for Toshi's bloody garments. They found a pot of cooked rice on the stove apparently in readiness for the next day's meal. Also, two large jars of fresh water. All was quickly brought to the boat.

Weary and, now that the hour of departure had come, more frightened than he would admit, Toshi crouched beside one of the water jars while lashing it amidships. Earlier in the day he and Kat had helped push the boat out to sea as Natas, who was seated in the boat, watched with his curious facial grin. Before that Toshi and Kat had been kept busy stowing supplies on board. Toshi had carried aboard sacks of cooked rice and as much fresh foodstuffs as would not spoil in the heat before it could be used. This was stowed below deck where there was space for cargo. A few weapons were stowed there also.

High above the deck, on the yardarm holding to the mast was the unfurled sail. Kat crouched on the prow with a sounding line. In the stern, Toshi stood up giving orders while steering the boat by its tiller. With a sudden lurch the wind caught the sail and it ballooned out to move the boat quickly into the sea. Toshi managed the sail with a long rope attached to the yardarm. He navigated the vessel by catching the wind as the sail puffed out. They were on their way out of the inlet, heading north to the mainland. Toshi was aware that he had no compass but once out to sea he kept the sun to his left before the noon hour and to his right after the noon hour. At night, he intended to use the stars to steer the boat by. After the first day at sea Kat's demeanor seemed to change. She was no longer sullen and even came to Toshi at the tiller with great enthusiasm. In an exuberant voice she blurted out, "I am so happy that we are finally on our way to the mainland. I intend showing you my gratitude when we get there."

Toshi grumbled, "Well Kat we are not there yet. We still have a great ocean to cross. It will take us many days. Anything can happen and even landing on the mainland could be a problem."

She listened carefully but reiterated, "Yes, I know but I feel so good that I am sure we will make it."

The sea was calm and the day seemed placid with the warm sun overhead and the few scudding clouds dotting the blue sky. Toshi, at the tiller, was deep in his thoughts. *Yes, all was right with the world. It was time to forget past delusions. Ah, but can they be forgotten?*

297

VII

Toshi could see the open sea – an unending view of water. As he looked ahead he could make out a dark, growing squall in the distance. *What to do?* He decided to furl the sail and alert Kat to be sure to secure everything standing freely. Natas was still seated amidships smiling in his usual way. He did not respond to Toshi's concern. Kat began tying down all loose objects. They were now being pelted with gusty wind and rain as they were approaching the squall. The sea became choppy and the boat began bobbing with each wave's rising and swelling. Without the unfurled sail there was no forward motion of the boat. But if the sail was unfurled it might rip to shreds in the storm leaving them without a source of future power. They were like a cork bobbing up and down in the churning waters at the mercy of nature. Toshi could do no more than hold the tiller steady to prevent the boat from capsizing. Kat went aft to speak with Toshi. She slipped and tripped unsteadily until she got there. "What are we to do?"

"I don't know. There is a severe storm ahead and all we can do is riding it out."

"Can't we sail around it?"

"No the storm is too big and I had to furl the sail to preserve it – so we would be adrift in trying to avoid it."

She looked around hastily saying, "Where is Natas?"

He answered her with annoyance, "I don't know. He comes and goes. One never knows about him. I hope he's gone forever."

By now, the waves were like giant mountains. Even the furled sail began to flutter as the gusty breeze increased. Rain was beginning to fall harder. The boat was being moved to and fro as the waves became higher. The boat was shaking and vibrating as it swung and swayed to the undulating motion of the boiling sea. The water swelled and crested with the rising and falling of the wave intensity. Kat was beginning to totter and reel as she sought shelter below deck. Toshi was still at the tiller holding it steady with rigid arms and hands which quivered with every slap of the keel at a wave. He almost faltered at these occurrences. The rain was now falling in biting pellets and the wind gusted so hard that the boat was indiscriminately projected deeper into the storms vortex. Toshi no longer had control over the tiller. It swung freely indicating that the rudder broke off.

They were now at the mercy of the weather. The intensity of the storm increased causing the boat to lift out of the sea and crash down with a loud thud into a water valley. The boat immediately broke apart littering the sea with a myriad of wooden parts and debris. Toshi was thrown overboard. As he began sinking into the murky depths he thought to himself, *I deserve this outcome. I killed the captain and his wife for no good reason. I did a terrible unforgivable thing for which I have great remorse. I am truly sorry.* His lungs began filling with water with stifling pain. His eyes were bulging and his blood ached in his head. *I have been a thief all of my life. Instead of being punished by lifelong exile I was given a chance to become a farmer and turn my life around. I even enjoyed the life of a farmer. It was like a gift. I almost requited evil in my life with good. But I didn't have the strength or the will to live my life in quiet desperation.* Then all went black. There was no more resistance. His arms and legs were splayed as he floated beneath the sea.

Among the debris in the water, Kat held on to a wooden deck which she grabbed with both hands until they turned blue. The water was still churning but the storm was beginning to move on. Finally, the storm abated and the sea became relatively calm once again. The water was icy cold. Kat was shaking and shivering as she hung suspended from the wooden deck by her hands. She kept spitting out the water that got into her mouth from the rolling waves. Occasionally, she would cough when water reached into her esophagus. She kept this up until her fingers and arms ached into numbness from hanging at the edge of the wooden deck. After a while the waves subsided altogether.

Then a new terror arose. While hanging from the wooden deck she felt something nibbling at her legs. She screamed and kicked her feet. This only caused her fingers to slip off the wooden deck. With a great show of strength she heaved her body up to her armpits and hung that way for a little while to catch her breath. But again she felt a sharp bite on her leg. She screamed and with a full force she pulled herself onto the wooden deck. As she sat breathing hard she inspected her leg to discover blood running out of a small wound in her calf. She rubbed her leg as she looked about at the endless watery desert. Strange thoughts appeared in her mind as she drifted along. *Where am I? What is to become of me?* She suddenly felt tired and exhausted as she slumped back into a heavy slumber. There was no sensation of feeling, just a natural torpor of dreamless sleep.

The sun grew hotter which caused her a fever of protracted lethargy with weakness and occasional tremors. She reached down to her calf to rub the wound.

She found it to be swollen and puffed up in a bulge. She became faint from the sweltering heat and began to sweat profusely. There was no doubt she had an infection from the bite on her leg. She was affected by dizziness and vertigo causing her to sway back like a sagging bundle until she lay in a semiconscious state on her side with her arms protruding overhead.

The wooden deck drifted with her aboard in a north easterly direction for several days. She kept going in and out of consciousness with no awareness of her surroundings. Her delirium was accompanied by confused and disordered mumbling. Finally, after a short crisis, all of this dissolved gradually resulting in a slight recovery. She began to sit up disheveled and disordered but was able to reach down to her calf and found that the swelling of the wound had receded somewhat with a residual exudate of a pus-like liquid. With a presence of mind she immediately washed the wound with sea water and began to be aware of her surroundings. She felt an unusual dryness of her mouth and throat and had an ardent desire for a drink of water. Despite her thirst she knew enough not to drink the sea water but she did apply small portions of sea water to her face and parched lips with her cupped hand. She was hungry not having eaten anything for days since the shipwreck. Her clothes were torn and her hair was matted. She was beginning to experience incipient sunburn. Still the wooden deck drifted on with Kat unaware of anything more than night and day.

She could see the debris of the boat surrounding her. Certain items would pop up from the ocean; others would sink to oblivion. There was splintered wood all around her but nothing edible. She thought about Toshi. *Poor man, he gave his life for me. I am the cause of his death. He only wanted to be a farmer. Now he is food for the fishes. What have I done?* This was not delirium. She was being quite rational. She had a lot of time to think about her life. After a week of drifting, the wooden deck carrying Kat became caught in the Kuroshio Current and rapidly started heading north. The weather and the water were getting colder. Kat began shivering uncontrollably and had no idea where she was going. She only surmised that she has left the tropical waters.

Her infirmity seemed to be gone. The wound on her calf was repairing itself with repeated treatments by Kat with sea water flushing. She had a wanton thirst and severe hunger pangs in her stomach. She thought: *can this be retribution for what I did to that captain and his wife on Exile Island? Am I on my way to death?* She fell back on the wooden deck holding her arms in folded position around her body to keep warm. She began to cry. She cried with stifled speech as she began a litany out loud, "Please, great Amida Buddha, save me. I want to live. Do not let me die. I promise to overcome my evil ways." She began a hysterical convulsive mixture of laughter and sobbing. She eventually quieted down and began to slap her arms back and forth to keep warm. She made sounds suggestive of sighs with an occasional heaving of her breast. With nightfall she sobbed herself to sleep.

Daylight brought a cold wind and a rolling fog which made her shiver. She noticed that more debris of a foreign nature was accumulating around the wooden deck. She searched the area as best she could for something to eat or drink. There was nothing of value among the rubbish. By now the fog was burning off by the rising sun. She sat up with her legs folded beneath her being careful not to irritate the wound on her calf. The sun was rising steadily to its zenith as she looked across the wide expanse of ocean. The sunlight was dancing on the flowing water like sparkling diamonds. *What's that coming toward me? Can it be a floating vessel? Yes, it looks like a ship.* A large schooner was making its way up the Kuroshio Current toward Kat. It was a fore-and-aft-rigged vessel having two masts, with the smaller sail on the fore mast and the mainmast stepped nearly amidships. Kat could hear some crew members shouting and waving a white flag. She returned the gesture with waving arms in an explosive vigor. Her mouth and throat were so dry it could only emit a hoarse squeak. As the ship neared Kat's wooden deck, it lowered a small skiff to retrieve her. Several sailors grabbed her off the wooden deck and eventually took her aboard the ship. They fed her a hot bowl of indescribable soup and covered her with a blanket. She could not make out the language they spoke but thanked them profusely for the rescue and their kindness which they seemed to understand. Shortly thereafter a large, burly man with a well trimmed, black beard came to see her. He was wearing a blue uniform with brass buttons on the tunic and a peaked cap on his head. He spoke kindly in faulty Japanese, "How are you? My name is Captain Dmitri Velsikov." He held out his hand in a friendly gesture as he spoke. "We are sailing from the Ryukyu Islands to our home base in the Kurile Islands. We came into the Kuroshio Current to make faster headway to our home with our cargo. That's when you were spotted by the lookout on the yardarm of the main sail." He pointed upwards of the mainmast as he spoke. "Don't bother speaking now. I will get all the details later after you have rested. He turned to one of the sailors and shouted orders in a strange language, sometimes pointing at Kat. The sailor ran away and hastily returned with another bowl of hot soup which Kat devoured voraciously. After sating her fill she leaned back and fell fast asleep. Unbeknownst to her the sailor covered her with an additional blanket. She was quite warm now as she fell into a stupor of heavy slumber. She began to dream of senseless weird images. She and Toshi were running and being chased by Natas. Suddenly, Toshi stopped running and turned to meet Natas. Toshi began to beat Natas until he crumbled into a little ball and eventually disappeared into nothingness. Kat's eyelids fluttered as she woke with a cry on her lips, "What does it mean?"

VIII

After a sound sleep Kat woke the next day to partake in a breakfast of hot gruel and several pieces of hardtack provided by the same sailor who helped her previously. Kat seemed to be regaining her strength and sat up still clothed in blankets. She reached down to her calf unconsciously only to find that the formerly swollen wound had subsided. She now relaxed after the sailor removed the used dishes with a deferential attitude. The soft breeze generated by the swift sailing of the schooner gave her pause as it rippled through her hair. Later, in the morning, Captain Dmitri arrived to assess her condition, "Well, you look better today. How do you feel?"

"Yes, thank you. I feel much better. I am most grateful to you for saving me."

He looked her straight in her eyes and began questioning. "Where are you from? First, tell me your name," the captain inquired.

She thought for a while before answering but then decided to be forthright. "My name is Katsuko Okada. A friend named Toshiki Otsumi and I escaped from Exile Island in a stolen boat. We were ensnared by a storm at sea. The boat capsized and was wrecked – my friend drowned. I survived by hanging on to a piece of wooden deck. I would have perished if it were not for your rescue."

"Yes, yes, tell me what your offense to be exiled was."

"I was an entertainer in a café. The proprietor wanted to get rid of me in favor of another entertainer and so he accused me of stealing. The magistrate ruled lifelong exile, but I swear to you I am innocent."

The captain listened intently to her tale and then assured her in a soft voice, "I believe you but, in any case, it does not matter. We are headed for our home base on Shumshu in the north Kurile Islands. Japan does not claim this island so you are safe there. When we arrive at Shumshu I shall make arrangements for you to stay with my sister and her husband until you are fully recovered; then you can decide what to do. There are no officials on this island so there is no need to have any fear."

Kat looked at Captain Dmitri with tears in her eyes and could only say, "Thank you."

"Do you have any questions?"

"Yes, I do. What language do you speak with the men?"

"I am Russian and speak Russian to my men who also speak Russian. Shumshu is a territory of the Tsar of Russia. I also speak Japanese as do some other of my people because we do business with the Japanese. Some of the lower Kuriles are occupied by Japanese fishing villages. Is there anything else?"

She moved the blanket off her leg to show him the wound on her calf. "I was bitten while floundering in the sea."

He bent down to look at the wound. "It may have been caused by a barracuda or some other voracious pike. It seems to be healing. We will treat it after we land. Is there anything else?"

She lowered her head and said, "No, thank you, there is nothing else."

He turned abruptly then hesitated to say, "I shall provide you with sailor's clothes before we land." With that he turned and walked away.

Kat was left to muse on her situation. *Well it appears I have escaped from Exile Island as I wanted. But what lies ahead for me?*

By the next day, land was spotted by the lookout. The schooner traveled along the east coasts of the chain of Kurile Islands until they reached the island of Shumshu. Eventually the schooner docked with great fanfare from people lining the shore. It seemed as though all the people of the island were out to greet the ship. Captain Dmitri, at the binnacle, could be seen barking orders for certain designated sails to be furled on their yardarms. It was an exciting time for Kat. She had never seen such activity. After docking the crew and some helpers from shore tied up the schooner and unloaded the cargo from below deck and from the deck on which Kat was resting. This work was finished in about two hours at which time Captain Dmitri approached Kat with a bundle. "Here are some clothes. You may use my cabin to change. There is a water basin with which you may wash up."

Kat got up with the blanket pulled around her and followed Captain Dmitri to his cabin. "When you have finished dressing please come on deck and I will take you home to my sister's house."

In the captain's cabin Kat removed the blanket and folded it neatly, placing it on the bed. Next, she removed her torn dress and began scrubbing her body with the sponge in the water basin. She dried herself with a provided towel and slipped on the sailor's trousers and tunic. They were much too large but she was able to fold the cuffs on the trouser legs and the sleeves on the tunic. It was adequate and she felt a sort of renewal of spirit with her new finery. She met the captain on the deck who commented, "You look like a different person. Come along, I'll lead you to my sister's house."

Kat howled occasionally from stepping on stones. She had no shoes and was not used to walking in bare feet. As a result she would knee-jerk when stepping on a sharp object. Captain Dmitri was patient with constant apologies. He walked slowly to help her maneuver the roadway. Finally, they reached Captain Dmitri's sister's house. Once inside the formality of introductions ensued. "This is my sister Galina she can speak Japanese." Galina was a somewhat plump woman with a round, flat face and a ruddy complexion. She had blonde hair in a bun and large blue eyes with a winning smile. Captain Dmitri spoke with her for a little while in Russian with occasional hand gestures. Kat assumed Captain Dmitri was explaining to his sister the events of the rescue. Kat hung her head in embarrassment. Galina broke into a low laugh and thrust her hand out to Kat saying, "Welcome to my home, Katsuko, I am glad to know you."

Kat was stunned by the welcoming speech but responded, "Thank you, I am glad to know you. Please call me Kat." They all laughed at her innocent simplicity. Captain Dmitri broke in, "You may call me Dmitri. There is no need to continue calling me captain." Then Galina spoke without duplicity, "You may stay here as long as you want until you make plans to leave."

Kat hurriedly suggested, "Thank you, but if I stay I want to work for my keep. I can cook and clean, a faculty I learned in exile." Once again, they all laughed in friendly merriment.

Captain Dmitri bade them goodbye and took his leave. Galina then showed Kat to her room upstairs. She also provided Kat with more suitable women's clothes. "I hope you'll be happy while you're here Kat. You've been through so much."

Kat was so touched by this kind gesture that she began to cry. Galina took her in her arms and hugged her with a constant pat on the back. The two women became instant friends.

IX

After several days of familiarity Kat found herself in the kitchen chopping vegetables and filleting a blackfish for supper. Galina spoke up, "I know you are used to rice but we can only import it since it does not grow here. For that reason we eat it sparingly. We consume lentils in its place."

"It does not matter; I like lentils as well as rice. A good way to stretch rice is to mix it with lentils or beans."

"Yes you are right, maybe we can try it one day.'

The two women shared the work in the kitchen and the clean-up duties in the house. One day Kat mused, *I hated cooking and cleaning when living with Yuki and the old man. Now I'm glad to do it. When one is near death a life can easily be altered. I no longer want to be the sophisticated lady I thought of while in exile. That life was meaningless. My life here with Galina has real meaning.*

And so life went on for many weeks for Kat. By now she sewed a new wardrobe and managed her hair into a pleasant looking coif. She was known and became part of the community having learned a few greetings and a modicum of the Russian language. Galina's husband Ivan, a fisherman, left before dawn in his boat to do fishing everyday. He didn't return until evening and had no real opportunity to partake in family life. It was Kat who filled the void left by Ivan in Galina's life. Kat tried to avoid too much contact with him except at the dinner table. She deliberately did this to prevent any resentment by Galina. Still Ivan and Kat were civil and pleasant to each other. Captain Dmitri would visit his sister on his return Voyl` ages. At these times, he would spend time speaking with Kat about his adventures as they sipped tea. Russian tea was from Darjeeling and differed from Japanese green tea in appearance and taste. For Kat it was another new experience with this unusual culture she was fast becoming a part of. Moreover, Captain Dmitri would bring presents for Kat and his sister from the Ryukyu Islands where he went frequently. Kat particularly treasured the cloth he would bring because it would make wonderful dresses for her wardrobe as well as for Galina's use.

One evening she climbed the steps to her bedroom. She found on entering the room that Natas was sitting on her bed. She shouted out loud, "No, no, get out. I don't want you here. You ruined the lives of many people. You ruined Toshi and you almost ruined mine. I want you out of my life right now. Go! Go!" Then a wonderful thing happened. Natas began shrinking right before her eyes and disappeared. Just then Galina came bounding up the stairs and busted into her room, "What is it Kat? I heard you shouting."

Kat was startled but quickly made light of it, "Oh, I just had a kind of fright. It really was nothing. I am sorry to have troubled you." Galina seemed to accept the explanation and left the room with a sympathetic grin. After Galina left, Kat sat on her bed and held her head in her hands. *I am so ashamed of my previous life. I did such terrible things. I am going to change.* She then undressed and prepared for bed thinking *tomorrow is another day.*

X

Captain Dmitri Velsikov returned from his latest voyage and came visiting his sister Galina. He dispensed gifts for all and eagerly gave a bear-hug embrace to his sister Galina with much frivolity. He then turned and gave a buss to each side of Kat's cheeks. There was much talk of his visit to a foreign land. What was it like? Are the people there kind and nice? How is the weather? How is the food? After the excitement died down, Dmitri approached Kat in a steady voice, "Would you like to go for a walk?"

"Yes, indeed," she replied, "I would like that very much."

"Well then, let's go."

Kat turned to Galina out of deference and excitedly said, "Dmitri and I are going for a walk. We'll be back soon."

"Of course, go and enjoy yourselves."

Kat and Dmitri left the house and began walking down the road toward the center of town. At first they were quiet and furtive but as they walked along the road they began talking in a desultory fashion, jumping from one subject to another. Finally Kat asked Dmitri demurely, "Do you live in town?"

"Yes, would you like to see where I live?"

Without hesitation Kat answered, "Yes, I would."

They walked passed the waterfront where one could see many boats moored from bow to stern. There was also a long wooden pier stretching out into the surf from which people were fishing with long fishing rods. Casually, they stood in front of a large two-story building. The ground floor was occupied by a ship's chandler with a sign in front painted with an anchor and written in letters of the Cyrillic alphabet. Dmitri pointed to the building, "I live there on the second floor. Would you like to see my apartment?"

"Yes please, I would like that very much."

They moved like a shadow across the road to disappear into the house. Dmitri followed Kat up the broad staircase and through the gloomy reaches of the upper hall. As he closed the door behind him, Kat wheeled about in the center of the bedroom. Her eyes were wide and her breathing audible in the still room. As Dmitri came toward her, she clutched at her flat stomach. It was a kneading, frantic gesture, and her hands moved convulsively about her pelvis. Short, impulsive cries escaped through her parted lips, and then, with a single savage movement, she slipped from her dress and stood naked before him, barbaric and eager, while the feral odor of her body, a pungent sweet musk, took possession of the room.

For a moment she stood there waiting for Dmitri to touch her. "I love you," she almost sobbed the whisper, "I love you, Dmitri." She shivered under his hands and then without another word went to the bed and flung herself down on the counterpane, a cat-like animal whose thighs twitched with a jerky circular motion. With one forearm stretched across her temple, she lay there fixing smoldering and unseeing eyes on the ceiling while behind her Dmitri slowly undressed. He took her with aggressive animal instinct, their bodies clamped in a beloved and serene embrace. When all was done they both lay back exhausted and sweaty saying nothing for a while. Dmitri leaned over and kissed Kat full on her lips as his tongue sought the wetness of her mouth. It was a pleasing and agreeable sweetish taste. He pulled back and spoke, "I love you Kat. We were made for each other. It seems like I have waited for you all of my life."

"I love you, too, "she answered softly. "I belong to you. After all you fished me out of the sea."

They both laughed in hilarity as they stirred on the bed. Rising in continuing merriment they dressed and left the room holding each other around the waist. When they reached the street they made there way back to Galina's house, laughing and talking almost childishly while walking hand in hand. Galina greeted them with raised arms and a loud shout as they entered the house, "I am glad you both came, supper is ready and we are just going to sit down."

The two lovers walked into the house smiling and greeting everyone with expressions of kind wishes. They all sat down at the table as the food was brought in. Ivan was busy pouring an amber fluid into small glasses at the various table settings. Every time he finished pouring he would raise his head and look at Kat with a smirk on his face before going on to the next person. At first Kat thought nothing of it and acknowledged it with a slight bow of her head but after a while she found his gesture very disconcerting. Dmitri, who was seated to Kat's left, noticed the exchange between them but raised his glass for a sip. He explained to Kat, as a means of diverting Ivan's gaze, "This drink is made from malt-barley. It is a favorite drink on special occasions. We usually drink vodka made from potatoes but since we are all together today it is most appropriate to have this special drink."

She answered, "I am not familiar with either beverage, I only know the taste of sake`, a wine made from rice."

In order to continue the small talk Dmitri said, "Ah yes, I have imbibed sake` at drinking parties on some of my travels to Japanese islands."

"You have?" she asked in credulously.

"Yes, I have," he answered quickly.

Then, Ivan rose holding his glass high declaring, "Let us drink to the health of our guest, Katsuko."

"Yes, yes," everyone shouted, holding their glasses high and looking at Kat, "to your health."

Kat blushed while acknowledging the good wishes with a bow of her head. Meanwhile, Dmitri was beaming at the recognition and acceptance accorded Kat. After the toast they began eating. All through the meal, Kat noticed Ivan looking at her with facial gestures. She tried averting her eyes but was afraid his attention to her was becoming too obvious. Certainly Dmitri noticed this with displeasure. When the meal was over, Dmitri went to speak to Ivan, "Why do you flirt with Kat. Don't you realize Galina is watching you and is probably unhappy at your trifles?"

Ivan made a quick rejoinder in a huff, "That is none of your business.".

"Yes, it is my business. I have designs on Kat myself. Besides you are married to my sister and this behavior in front of the family is unseemly," he blustered with anger.

A swell of sudden arrogance and petulance came over Ivan who raised his fists in a stance ready to render blows to Dmitri. On seeing this, Dmitri turned around giving Ivan his back. He called to Kat to join him outside. "You cannot stay here tonight Kat; Ivan is in an ugly mood."

"What shall I do?"

"Stay with me tonight and we shall leave tomorrow on my schooner for the trip to the Ryukyu Islands."

"But, I just can't leave without saying goodbye to Galina."

"Yes, I understand. You will have time tomorrow morning before the tide comes in to explain things to Galina. I will accompany you to help."

The next day Kat and Dmitri went to Galina's house to render an explanation of the previous day's events and bid Galina goodbye. On entering the house, Galina came hurriedly forward. "Oh, I am so glad to see you both. I want so much to apologize for Ivan's behavior yesterday." She hugged Kat. She then kissed Kat on each cheek. Just then Dmitri interrupted, "I must tell you Galina that Kat and I are in love and want to marry." Kat was stunned by this announcement and could only reach for his hands as her perplexed eyes sought Dmitri's.

Galina's face lit up and she clapped her hands, "How wonderful. "She hugged Kat again and then Dmitri in turn, "This is very wonderful news. Kat is now one of us. I am very happy."

Dmitri continued officiously, "We are leaving, at high tide, on my schooner for the Ryukyu Islands and hope to marry on our return. I wanted you to know that I am not angry with Ivan. He did not know of my intentions."

Kat quickly interrupted and said in a sardonic way, "No one knew."

Galina grabbed each of their hands and softly murmured, "Go with God. I shall help by looking for a priest, you know they are hard to find since we have a chapel without priest here.

For the first time Kat found her natural voice. In a low sibilant voice she said, "Thank you very much Galina. You have been like a sister to me. Dmitri and I have much to talk about and make preparations."

Dmitri said nothing' he was gloomily silent knowing that he announced his marriage desires without consulting Kat. They left Galina's house holding hands and strolling towards town. Kat looked up into Dmitri's face. "Well that was a surprise!" Dmitri hung his head. Kat continued in a huff, "It would have been nice if you asked me first if I would marry you."

"Well, will you?"

She laughed and squeezed his arm, "Of course, I'll marry you. I am so happy. I love you, Dmitri."

He stopped and looked at her. "I did what I did in order to settle any differences and let everyone know that you are now family and I won't tolerate any nonsense."

"Yes, I understand, Dmitri, I owe you and Galina my very life and even my dignity." She hesitated then turned to Dmitri raising her hand to his face, "I feel I have been given a new life. I want to remain here with you and make you happy."

He hugged her, "We can think of our trip to the Ryukyu Islands as a honeymoon."

"Yes, yes," she jumped up and down clapping her hands.

XI

Back in Dmitri's room they made preparations for their life at sea. The round trip and stay in the Ryukyu Islands will take about three weeks so they will need enough provisions to have a secure and pleasant trip. They brought their belongings on board while the seamen were still loading the cargo. Finally, the schooner eased out to sea from its berth. Dmitri was busy at the helm cleverly maneuvering the ship as it got underway. Kat meanwhile was rearranging things in Dmitri's stateroom to make it more livable for two people by removing the clutter and the bachelor image. When she finished it was cheerful and cozy. Kat went up on deck to watch the shore fade away until it vanished. The weather turned cold as the sky dimmed. A red sky began to appear on the horizon as the sun dipped into the calm sea. Kat watched the foam produced by the wake and shivered at the thought of her own experience in the water. She shook her head to remove the ugly thoughts and returned to the stateroom. After about an hour Dmitri came in with a great enthusiastic smile on his face. They hugged and kissed holding each other for several long minutes. Dmitri spoke in a spirited voice, "My love, we are underway. I gave guidance of the helm to my first mate so we can have the whole evening together.

They sat on the cot and spoke with each other in hurried segments about their future life. Dmitri, with a quizzical look on his face suddenly said, "You know, my love, I really don't know anything about you. What was your previous life like before we met?"

Kat's face became ashen drained of its blood. She stared at Dmitri in a bristled dread. I'd rather not talk about that. I now have a new life and I want to forget the past."

"But, I should know something about your past. After all when I rescued you from the sea all you told me was that you escaped from Exile Island. It is only fair that you at least tell me why you were put there."

Kat hesitated and became very pensive. "I see my past cannot be forgotten." She cleared her throat and said, "I shall tell you my life from the beginning. I shall not leave out anything. I want to have an honest life with you and a clean slate."

Dmitri looked at her with some apprehension, "Very good, please begin."

For a moment she hesitated while trying to recall. Then she took a deep breath and calmly told her story.

"I was born in a very poor family in the *Kansai district* (region between Osaka, Kyoto, and Kobe). I never knew my father. My mother was an itinerant farm worker in the rice paddies. As an infant she would take me with her and place me in the rushes of the vegetable fields where I would play. We never had a permanent home; most of the time we would live in a barn or a shack provided by the farmer for whom she worked. At the age of eight she took me to the *okiya* (geisha house) in *Heian-kyo* (Kyoto) for training. That was the last time I saw my mother."

At this time tears began welling up in her eyes. She suddenly burst out crying with a great heave of her body. Dmitri was startled, "Please, my dear, do not go on."

"No, no, now, that I have begun I want to tell it all," she cried. So she began again. "In fact, I became a servant to the *Maiko* (full apprentice geisha). She was a beautiful lady. I admired her and it was my dream to become just like her. I admired her wardrobe and the way she walked and talked. I learned the ways of the geisha from her and hoped for the day when I would become a *Maiko*. That day arrived when I turned sixteen years of age and became a *shikomi* (first stage apprentice geisha). I was obligated to perform domestic services until I was fully accepted as a *Maiko*. At the end of my apprenticeship at the age of eighteen, I was forced to live in the Gion district in Heian-kyo. It was common and considered elegant for a man in the public eye to "keep" a high-ranking geisha, an extremely expensive proposition. That is how I met Shingei Gakuso, a politician and financier who took me on as part of his "standing". He admired me so much that I even became a confidant and advisor to this man of power. I was in charge of entertainment at his parties for upper-class men. Thus, my life continued as a courtesan, a mistress to Shingei Gakuso, for two years until twenty years of age."

Dmitri interrupted her running commentary, "Did you have sex with him?"

She stopped speaking abruptly and looked Dmitri in the eyes, "Of course, that was part of my job." There was silence then she continued, "I noticed that he was beginning to change toward me. At first it was small, minor things and then I was sure he was tiring of me. It was obvious that he had another mistress who shared his ardor. I thought nothing of this; since it is not unusual for a powerful man to have more than one mistress. I was soon to learn how he would solve this dilemma. One day two policemen came to my abode, arrested me and took me to jail in irons to be confined in lawful custody until I would face the magistrate who would determine my fate. It was not long before I was brought into court. I was told the charge when I faced the magistrate for the first time. He convicted me of theft of some jewelry from my patron and sentenced me to exile in Exile Island as punishment. This was not true. I never stole anything. It was just a convenient way for Shingei Gakuso to get rid of me. I never did anything sinful or wicked in all the time I was with him."

Her eyes were red now as she coughed to clear her throat. "Would you like some water?" Dmitri asked.

"Yes please my mouth is dry," she quickly answered.

Dmitri reached over to a wicker-covered demijohn and poured some water into a ceramic tea mug.

"Thank you," she said as she sipped the water with zest. Placing the mug down next to her she continued, "When I arrived in Exile Island I befriended a weak-minded, petty thief named Toshi. Since I was a single girl, alone in this cruel world, I needed him for protection. We obtained work at the home and farm of an old couple. The old lady named Yuki and the old man named Koban. The old man did not want us to call him Koban because Koban means police station in Japanese so we simply called him "old man" which he preferred. Unfortunately for Toshi, he fell in love with me; but this was fortuitous for me because I was able to manipulate him to do my bidding. I was intent and completely focused on escaping from Exile Island. I would hear of nothing else from the moment I landed on that foreboding island. Toshi, on the other hand, seemed to find solace in farming and came to some resolution about his life. I had to use all my feminine wiles to keep him on course. When he told me that he had once stolen a boat and became quite proficient in its use I knew we had a chance to escape."

She stopped speaking, looked down as if examining her fingers and said nothing. Dmitri looked at her oddly, "What is it Kat?"

Kat raised her head questioningly, "Do you really want me to continue?"

"Yes, unless you have qualms."

"What I am about to say is so shameful that I am afraid you will detest me."

"What can it be?"

"I do not want your love to turn to hatred."

"Kat, I love you and that will not change no matter what you tell me."

She took a deep breath and slowly continued in small detached portions. "A fisherman on the island owned a boat which gave us the opportunity to steal the boat and escape." She rested for a moment.

"Yes, yes, go on," Dmitri exclaimed impatiently.

"Well, Toshi asserted and assured me that he could handle the boat effectively without trouble."

"Yes, yes, please go on."

"He said that the only way to steal the boat without being discovered was to kill the fisherman and his wife."

"What, what, did you say kill the fisherman and his wife?"

She did not immediately answer Dmitri but looked him straight in his eyes, "It was almost as if he was being pushed by the devil."

Dmitri was nonplussed as he muttered, "Did you kill the fisherman and his wife?"

"No, but I participated in their death – for which I am very sorry and thoroughly penitent," she hastened to add. She began to cry again and as she sobbed she said, "Dmitri, I am so ashamed. Toshi killed the fisherman and his wife but I am guilty as well because I made him do it. He was a petty thief all his life and finally in exile found a new life that made him happy. His only fault was falling in love with me. If I wasn't present, I am sure he would have turned his life around. I made him do it. *I made him do it.* He was innocent of any cruelty before this incident. He never harmed anyone. He was only guilty of thievery and burglary in his life for which he was being chastised by exile on the island."

"What happened to him? Where is he now?"

"He drowned when the boat capsized in the storm."

"A fitting retribution for his sin," Dmitri pondered aloud.

"Yes, but even that is my fault as well," she mumbled humbly.

Dmitri looked at Kat's tear-moistened face and said, "Enough Kat, I don't want to hear anymore. I am satisfied with your remorse and contrition. He moved over to her and took her in his arms as she sobbed. He slowly, softly spoke with a soothing gesture, "I love you, Kat. Your life with me will change everything. I will make you forget the past."

After her confession, Kat fell asleep sobbing. Dmitri quietly undressed and got into bed next to her. He held her close while she was sleeping in a fetal position. He kissed her numerous times as he muttered, "Poor girl – she was possessed by a demon." He then fell asleep only to wake up early in the gloomy, dismal, small morning hours and began lurking in the dark to eventually arrive at the tiller wheel in order to relieve the First Mate. He grabbed the wheel and waved the First Mate goodbye. Looking to his right he saw the light of the rising sun glimmer with long bands of light like a curtain opening. *Another day is beginning until we reach the port of Naze on the island of Amami in the Ryukyu Islands,* he thought. Dmitri and the First Mate, whose name is Vladimir, had arranged their usual alternating schedule of four hours on and four hours off for duty at the tiller wheel. The remainder of the crew is kept busy taking orders to adjust the sails in the most favorable way to capture the best prevailing wind.

They were doing about eight nautical miles per hour or loosely about eight knots per hour. At that rate they would be traveling an average of 221 miles per day. If there is no adversity from the Kuroshio Current, which was flowing against them, and with good prevailing winds they might reach their destination in record time. The Ryukyu Islands are about 2500 miles from the Kurile Islands. Dmitri had expected the trip to take about twelve days having made this trip many times in the past.

At 8:00 o'clock he was relieved by Vladimir the First Mate. It was a bright, sunny day and the schooner was cutting through the water at a breakneck speed of ten knots helped by an east-southeast wind at about 5 – 8 knots and seas around 1 foot. Dmitri gave over command to Vladimir and hurried to see Kat. She was just putting on a fresh kimono, which was a loose, colorful robe tied with a sash. Kat still made and retained her Japanese wardrobe. Dmitri came bounding in with great humor and outstretched arms, "How are you? Did you sleep well?" he inquired.

"Yes, yes, I slept very well, the rocking of the boat made me sleep like a baby." They kissed and hugged. Just then a knock on the door announced the arrival of breakfast, which consisted of *congee* (rice gruel), hard tack, and warm *kvass* (a sour fermented barley drink). "I hope I did not disturb you too much by my ill comportment last night. I don't know what came over me I just wanted to be honest with you and not have any secrets," she explained demurely with her head down and her eyes averted.

Dmitri held her head in his two hands and slowly looking in her eyes said in a compassionate voice, "I fully understand. I do not care about the past. We are together now and we will create a new life." He hesitated for a minute but suddenly kind words erupted from his mouth, "I love you Kat, that's all that matters to me. Let us try and forget the past." He then took a sip of the warm *Kvass* and looked into her tearful eyes.

She accepted his words with a long kiss on his lips. Nothing more was said until Dmitri explained, "I must get some sleep in the next four hours after which I have to relieve Vladimir the First Mate. You may join me at the helm at that time." And so their life on board was routinized according to the schedule of alternating every four hours between sleep and duty at the tiller wheel.

XII

By the early morning dawn of the eleventh day they reached the outer banks of the Naze port. It took expert seamanship to avoid the rising ground around the shoals and elevations under the sea. Dmitri knew exactly what he was doing as he listened to Vladimir who was taking soundings of the sea topography with a line plummeted at the end. Eventually, with slow and careful maneuvering, Dmitri guided the schooner into port. At this time, Kat was standing beside him and admired his nautical dexterity. A large rope was heaved ashore by the ship's crew to waiting arms. The schooner was finally docked and a long wooden gangplank was placed across the divide of the dock and the schooner.

A small, rotund man came aboard to speak with Dmitri. Meanwhile, the ship's crew began to unload the cargo located on deck and in the hold. The man who came aboard was obviously Asian having tawny skin and mongoloid features. He was small in stature like the Japanese but was so fat as to cause him to waddle by walking with short steps, swaying from side to side, like a duck. He wore a long-sleeved black, silk caftan which reached to the ground. On his head was a matching round cap which apparently marked his station or rank as a dignitary. He bowed low to Dmitri with his hands folded and hidden by his sleeves. Dmitri did not return the bow rather saluted by raising his hand to the visor on his cap.

"Welcome to Naze, Captain Velsikov," the small man said in a high-pitched, hissing voice which sounded like a squeaking door. "I hope your trip was pleasant and uneventful."

"Thank you, your honor," Dmitri replied. He then turned and introduced Kat. "This is Miss Katsuko Okado, my fiancé`," he said with some pride. "Kat, this is Jukichi Shatka, the magistrate of the Amani Prefecture," he continued with a pointing hand. Kat bowed low in the Japanese manner and seemingly whispered, "I am happy to meet you."

Jukichi returned the bow and said in a querulous voice, "Thank you, Miss. Are you Japanese?"

"Yes, I am Japanese by birth." Then she added in haste, "But I will soon be Russian when I marry Captain Velsikov."

"Ah, I see. Good luck to you both."

She pondered her next small talk, "It is good of you to meet us, you honor."

"It is nothing of the kind. It is my duty," he rocked his head as he spoke in an officious manner.

Dmitri chimed in, "While they are unloading the cargo, Miss Kat and I will go ashore to stretch our legs."

Jukichi piped in, "Please join me for lunch. I would be most honored for your company."

"Thank you, your honor, that would be very nice," Dmitri said deferentially. They then left the schooner. Dmitri gave final instructions to Vladimir who was on the shore supervising the removal of the cargo. They walked along the esplanade until they reached a magnificent building decorated in the Chinese style with a tiled, pitched roof. The structure was simple: twelve exterior pillars and *mitesaki* (bracket sets) above them support the roof frame. Inside are nothing more than ceiling beams. It could be entered only through the front door and had windows only at the front. On entering there was a large *boshan* (incense burner) on each side of the door giving off a somewhat nauseating sweetish odor.

As they entered they were greeted by a sycophantic host who bowed low multiple times as he led them to a private alcove. The alcove had a low table and chairs, which required criss-crossing one's legs after sitting down. Jukichi began speaking in his high-pitched voice, "This restaurant was formerly a Buddhist temple but was abandoned some years ago during the indigenous uprising against Japanese domination. There was a lot of Buddhist persecution by the local people at that time but things have since simmered down."

"Are there any Buddhists left on the islands?" Dmitri asked.

"Yes, there are some who have survived, but Shinto is the most popular religion."

Suddenly, a young lady, dressed in a kimono came to the table carrying a tray with earthenware sake` urn and three cups. She poured sake` into each cup before placing it on the table in front of each seated person, then she placed the urn in the center of the table and quickly departed with the swish sound of her slippers.

Jukichi held up his cup and said, "*Kampai* (cheers)." The two others complied by raising their cups with a responsive shout of Kampai." Jukichi lowered his cup and asked, "How long will you stay in Naze, Captain Dmitri?"

"I intend leaving right after I take on my return cargo. It shouldn't take .longer than three days."

"Do you have any plans for your time here?"

"No, not really, I would like to show the sights to Miss Kat, however."

"Well then, please allow me to help you. May I show you the Shinto temple in Naze?"

"Did you say Shinto temple?"

"Yes, it is very beautiful."

Dmitri looked at Kat for approval and then answered, "Yes indeed, that would be very kind of you."

Jukichi assented by saying, "You know, of course, that the Shinto religion is Japanese spiritual roots."

"What do you mean?"

"I mean there are many religions in Japan but somehow the people think of Shinto as the basis of all these religions. There is a belief in Shinto that all people and things deserve our profound gratitude; the remarkable understanding of the healing power of nature to radiate in human life."

"I see."

"Yes, It would be hard to imagine Japan without Shinto."

"But, are these islands really Japan?"

"These islands, as you say, have been occupied for centuries by explorers, land speculators, fishermen, businessmen and mostly those who were desperate to get away from the four main islands of Japan. They brought Shinto with them. Shinto is Japan's oldest religion and over the centuries it has been at the very heart of the native Japanese spirit, a persistent background to the shifting patterns of Japanese culture and history."

Dmitri looked at Jukichi before returning a question, "I belong to the Russian orthodox religion, which is a form of Christianity. How does Shinto differ from Christianity?"

Jukichi hesitated in thought before answering. "Unlike a moral religion such as Christianity, Shinto is wholly devoted to life in this world and emphasizes man's essential goodness. The Shinto Gods cooperate with man at every stage of his life."

Just then the young lady, our waitress, returned with a plate of comestibles and a charcoal burner on which was placed a pot of boiling oil. While the waitress was setting the table, Jukichi hurriedly explained, "I have ordered for all of us. I hope you do not mind. This food is the specialty of the house. In fact that is all they serve here." The waitress while on her knees placed the plate containing the various fish on the center of the table. She then placed a plate in front of each person and filled each cup with a second portion of sake`.

Jukichi continued, "The Kurile Islands are famous for the variety of fish we catch in our waters. I have taken the liberty of introducing you to a special way we have of preparing the fruit of the sea."

The diverse species of fish on the central plate were all eviscerated with their fins and scales removed. Each person was able to snare a morsel with the provided *hashi* (chopsticks) and dipped into the boiling oil for one minute and, thereafter, placed on the individual's plate to cool. This was then eaten over a bowl of *gohan* (cooked rice). Finally all was washed down with cups of *ryokucha* (green tea). Kat was so starved for the tea that she quaffed repeated cups.

At the conclusion of the meal the three people left the restaurant where they found a *jinrikisha* (pedicab) waiting for them in front of the building. It was a small three-passenger, two-wheeled, hooded vehicle drawn by a half-naked man wearing only short pants. It seemed to Dmitri so inhuman for a man pulling the cart to undergo such laborious affliction with such solemn fortitude. The man literally took the place of a draft-horse.

Arriving at the *Ota Jinja* (Ota Shrine) they saw before them an ornate building in the style of the Hachiman cult. The sweeping thatch-covered roofs of the shrine, linked to the idea of reincarnation, seem to have been borrowed from Buddhist architecture. In front of the shrine is the distinctive figure of the fox. The fox frequently wears a red bib. Worshipers will sometimes place fried bean curd before him to gain his favor. As the trio walked up the stone inlaid pathway they passed underneath a large, wooden *torii* gate. *Torii*, the formal entrance to shrines usually vary in size but this gate was not too large allowing the three persons to pass through without being inhibited and thus they became purified. The gate consisted simply of four pieces of undressed wood with two cross members sitting on two posts. Shinto shrines are located on sites chosen by the *kami* (mythical deity), that is to say, on sites that emanate a clear sense of the sacred. This shrine, Ota Jinja, was built near a sacred mountain where a sense of reverence was engendered. It is natural for a *kami* to be identified and revered in such a place.

On walking inside they were greeted by a monk dressed in white robes and wearing a pointed, black hat resting precariously on his head. He bowed low with a *gassho* (palms together) in apparent recognition. "Good afternoon, your honor," he declared with assurance. "May I be of service?"

Jukichi remarked like an angered goose, "I am only showing my guests this beautiful shrine. There is no need to bother you."

"By all means, your honor, may I help you in any way?"

"No, that won't be necessary."

He lowered his eyes and bowed, "Very well, your honor."

Just then, a Shinto priest came out of his alcove to greet the visitors. "Ah yes, welcome dear folks. Welcome to Ota Jinja."

"Thank you," responded Jukichi pointing to Dmitri and Kat he said, "my friends have come from the far away Kurile Islands. They just arrived today."

"I see, I see, we don't often get foreign visitors but you are most welcome. Please enjoy the peace and tranquility of our shrine." He then turned with an insouciant air walking backwards and bowing at the same time. After he left they continued for some minutes inspecting and examining the inside of the shrine. Suddenly Jukichi stopped in his tracks to face Dmitri and Kat. "I have an idea." He seemed very gleeful as he turned to face them with a sincere tone amid the merriment in his voice," How would you both like to be married by the Shinto priest?"

Dmitri was stunned, "What do you mean?"

"I mean, I could arrange a wedding ceremony for both of you here in this Shinto shrine."

There was silence while Dmitri looked at Kat questioningly. "Well Kat what do you think. Of course, we will still be married by a Russian orthodox priest when we return."

Kat was astonished. She became very pensive and was much confused. "What would such a ceremony mean; would the ceremony be recognized everywhere? I do not want to disappoint our family at home. They are expecting us to perform a wedding ceremony when we arrive home."

Jukichi looked at both of them with saddened eyes and answered, "It would probably only be recognized in Japan." He hesitated for a moment and then continued, "I don't really know. I am not sure. However this can be overcome when you marry by a Russian priest at home." He swallowed and then exuded, "I just thought you might find the ceremony interesting and that you might enjoy the symbolic custom. If I have presumed too much or offended you I am truly sorry and ask your forgiveness."

Dmitri hastily remarked, "No. no, there is no need to be sorry. Indeed, it's a very good idea." Holding Kat's hand he faced her questioningly, "What do you think, Kat, should we do it? If you have any doubt we certainly will get married by a Russian priest when we return home."

Kat smiled broadly, "Yes, let's do it. It might be fun."

Dmitri faced Jukichi with a solemn expression on his face. "Can you make all the arrangements?"

"Yes, of course, I will approach the *shinshoku* (priest) now."

The Shinto priest returned with Jukichi. They both appeared to be engaged in friendly conversation as they shuffled toward Dmitri and Kat. The priest looked at Dmitri and Kat, from one to the other, in a grave manner before he spoke; then in a solemn disposition he said, "Is it true that you both want to enter into marriage?"

Dmitri and Kat assented with several nods of their heads. It was Kat who hurriedly expressed compliance, "Yes, yes, we want to be married."

This acquiescence was followed immediately by Dmitri, "Yes, we wish to be married."

"I see," the priest acknowledged. "Do you wish me to officiate?"

"Yes, of course," they both agreed after looking at each other. Dmitri added, "That is, if it is possible?"

"It is possible," the priest answered forthwith, "However, there are conditions. You must prepare certain necessary matters beforehand."

"What matters do you mean?" Kat asked with a slight fright in her voice.

The priest began to enumerate an itemized list of necessary articles for the ceremony. "First you, Miss Kat, must wear a kimono containing a predominantly red design. Mr. Dmitri may wear his official naval uniform instead of the traditional Japanese *hakama* (a kind of pleated skirt). Miss Kat, you must also wear a special ornamental headdress. Mr. Dmitri will not need a head covering and, indeed, should remove his cap at the time of the ceremony. *Jukichi-kun* (Mr. Jukichi) will take you to a merchant in town who will provide Miss Kat with the Kimono and headdress." He was silent for a while and then after searching their eyes continued, "If this is agreeable we can perform the ceremony tomorrow morning at ten o'clock."

Jukichi abruptly interrupted, "I shall act as the go-between during the ceremony." Dmitri and Kat thanked him for all his help as they left the priest with a low bow and gassho.

Outside the shrine they all looked at each other with smiling faces and laughter. "I can't believe it," said Kat. It's really happening.

"Is it really true?" asked Dmitri.

Jukichi explained, "Yes, it took some doing but I convinced the priest that this was very important for both of you. In addition, I explained that Captain Dmitri was an important envoy from Russia." They all laughed with mirthful satisfaction at hearing this comment. This sportive burlesque was followed by an exciting statement from Jukichi, "Let us be off to the merchant who will provide the items for Miss Kat." Each of them mounted the waiting Jinrikisha in turn, which took them to the merchant's abode. It was a house in a residential area. The front room contained two garment workers and a seamstress. There were shelves which contained bolts of cloth made of fine cottons and silks in a myriad of colors and designs. On entering the work room they were greeted by the proprietor with a low bow and solicitous words, "Welcome, your honor, it is good to see you again. How can I help you?"

"Thank you, Shinichi, "responded Jukichi with a bow. "These are my friends from the Kurile Islands," he said pointing to Dmitri and Kat. "They are to be married tomorrow in the Ota Jinja. The young lady is in need of a red kimono and a garniture for her head. Can you help us?"

The proprietor seemed undaunted by the request and responded positively. "Oh, I see, yes I can help you. I have a lovely kimono which is made of white habutae silk with a picture of a *sakura* (cherry blossoms) tree. Let me fetch it for the young lady's perusal." He went to a pocket-door closet which contained many hanging robes and kimonos. After taking one kimono out he returned with a broad grin on his face. "Here it is," he said as he spread it out on the worktable.

Kat and Dmitri were struck speechless at the beauty of the graphical portrayal of a cherry tree in blossom. The image was almost a *tableau vivant* (living picture) of a landscape produced by stitches with thread and needle.

Kat exclaimed, "It is very beautiful."

The proprietor said, "Try it on."

Kat put the kimono over her shoulders and carefully inserted her arms into the massive sleeves. She held the material against her slim body and looked down at the floor.

"It is slightly too long," said the proprietor, "but, I shall alter it and it will be ready tonight." He then proceeded to mark off the necessary portion to be altered.

Dmitri helped Kat remove the kimono with an amorous dalliance. "You are beautiful, Kat and the kimono brings out your beauty."

The proprietor then told Kat, "The garniture for your head will be made of a stiff, white cloth for a crown and brim adorned on top with cherries and flowers. The needlewoman will measure your head shape for the brim. This will also be ready this evening."

"Oh, how wonderful; I am delighted beyond words." She turned to Jukichi saying, "These items must be very expensive."

Jukichi waved off his hand, "Let us not talk about that now."

Dmitri interrupted, "But it is important that we settle the price."

Jukichi looked at Dmitri, "Please trust me there will be no price to discuss."

"Why not, what do you mean?"

"Alright, I am arranging for the kimono to be borrowed – not sold. Whatever cost evolves from the proprietor's service will be borne by me as a wedding gift to you. It will be my greatest pleasure. Please do not deny me." He hesitated for a moment and then continued," One of my servants will pick up the completed kimono and headdress tonight. I shall bring it with me tomorrow morning when I pick you both up in time for the ceremony."

Dmitri was slightly tongue-tied, "But, but, but."

"No, please trust me Dmitri. I would enjoy doing this very much."

Dmitri looked down then slowly raised his head as he looked into Kat's eyes. We both appreciate your kindness very much." After this discussion they left the proprietor's shop and all ascended into the waiting Jinrikisha and headed back to the ship.

"Good day to both of you, dear friends, I shall pick you up at nine o'clock tomorrow morning," said Jukichi in a playful mood.

"Thank you again, Jukichi," Dmitri said with a salute to his cap visor.

Dmitri and Kat walked up the gangplank to be met by the First Mate, Vladimir. "Hello Captain and Miss Kat, we will be finished loading our cargo tomorrow afternoon Captain.

"That's very good, Vladimir. By the way, Miss Kat and I are to be married tomorrow by a Shinto priest in a Shinto shrine. We would like you to join us as a representative of our family."

Vladimir was taken aback but readily expressed his feelings in a happy voice, "I shall be honored, Captain."

XIII

At exactly nine o'clock the next morning Jukichi appeared with two Jinrikishas to accommodate Vladimir and the servant who carried the items from the garment shop. Everyone then left for Ota Jinja. On arrival at the shrine a single file of the people passed under the vermillion red torii and approached the colorful building of Ota Jinja. These colorations show the influence of Chinese tastes in design. Nevertheless, all shrine structures share the essential feature of being made out of natural materials. Ota Jinja like all shrines is made out of wood. Generally, shrines face the east, but never north, which is associated with death, or the west, which is considered unlucky.

As everyone entered the shrine, the priest performed *oharai*, which means removing polluting spirits and presences. He waves his *haraigushi*, a switch made from a sacred tree and with white linen cloth streamers attached, as an act of purification. Kat, who changed into the traditional kimono and headdress brought by Jukichi's servant, together with Dmitri wearing his uniform walked together into the memorial hall of the shrine. The couple sat before the priest. Vladimir, representing the family, sat on the side. Jukichi, the go-between, sat in back of the couple. All those present received some sake`, Japanese rice wine, as a sharing of a holy feast with the protective *kami* who have been invoked. The *miko*, the priest's female assistant served the sake`. Finally, there is a reception with food offerings to the *kami* including rice, rice cakes, sake`, vegetables, fish, chicken, fruits and candies. The priest recited sacred texts which were acknowledged and confirmed by the wedding couple sipping sake` alternately from the same container. The ceremony ended with everyone recognizing the married couple with good wishes and partaking of the food offerings. Thus, Kat and Dmitri were married.

Kat removed the kimono and headdress and gave it to the servant to be returned to the garment shop. "I can't thank you enough for your kindness to me, "Kat said turning to Jukichi. "The ceremony was beautiful and I shall always remember your effort in helping us enjoy this wonderful day."

"It was no great effort," said Jukichi, "But I am glad you enjoyed it. Now let us have a farewell luncheon." He raised his arms in a gathering gesture.

"Good idea, your honor, our cargo is loaded and we shall be able to leave with the tide today," he then turned and looked at Vladimir, "Please join us, Vladimir, you are now family."

"Thank you, Captain, I would be most honored."

They went to the same restaurant as yesterday where they were greeted with exclamations of praise by the staff. Obviously a section of the restaurant was reserved beforehand for the wedding party with thin ribbons and colored streamers floating down and waving from the ceiling joists. Everyone enjoyed the fun and playful action. The meal was special and unforgettable. Vladimir had to leave the party a little early to prepare the schooner fore-and-aft. Not too much later Kat and Dmitri arrived at the base of the gangplank with Jukichi to say goodbye. They waved as they strolled up the gangplank and eventually disappeared into the stateroom. After entering the stateroom, Dmitri closed the door and turned to reach out to Kat, "My little wife," he said as he kissed and hugged her.

Kat laughed and countered with, "I love you, Dmitri. I shall be your wife always." They then changed clothing after which Dmitri left to supervise the final preparations for the schooner to debouch the dock. Kat eventually joined him at the helm where Dmitri was relaying orders through Vladimir to remove the gangplank and restraining ropes for-and-aft. The jibs and foresails were unfurled to catch the wind; slowly the great schooner eased out of the port and headed into the open sea with the help of several oared tug boats. Finally, the remainder of the sails was unfurled allowing the wind to propel the vessel through the water. When in the clear sea, Vladimir and the crew saw to it that the ship was full-rigged under all sails.

Dmitri holding the tiller in his left hand and with his right hand around Kat's waist exclaimed, "Well Kat, we are on our way. If all goes well we should be home in less than ten days." Dmitri and Vladimir returned to the four hour on-and-off schedule for the return trip. For the next four hours Dmitri and Kat at the helm watched as the sun set to their left indicating that the ship was heading in a northeast direction to the Kurile Islands. Dmitri said to Kat, "We are heading for the Kuroshio Current, my dear, which should propel us faster on the voyage home." She shivered at the thought of the Kuroshio Current.

Just then Vladimir came up to the poopdeck aft of the mizzenmast, where the tiller was located. With a formal salute he said, "I'll take over now, Captain."

"Thank you," said Dmitri with a return salute. "Come Kat let us return to our cabin," he said taking Kat by the hand and leading her down below deck. "I'll relieve you in four hours, Vladimir," he said to Vladimir who grabbed the tiller. In their cabin, Kat and Dmitri relaxed on the small cot and reviewed the day's events with each other.

It was Kat who initiated the conversation, "Dmitri I know that we will be married again by a Russian priest but I must tell you I already feel married to you."

"I know what you mean. I too have that feeling but because of convention and out of respect for my family we must be married by a Russian priest in accordance with the laws of the Tsar."

"Yes, of course, otherwise we will disappoint Galina who is probably working very hard right now putting a wedding party together."

"I would suspect the whole town will be part of the nuptials."

"Yes, it should be a lot of fun after the ceremony. I am looking forward to the wedding feast and the singing and dancing to the tunes of the balalaika and accordion," she said with a repeated clap of her hands.

XIV

It took nine days for the schooner to reach the Kuriles. Dmitri, in his skilled seamanship maneuvered the tiller to bring the schooner into dock with the help of several tug craft. The shore was lined with people and family members waving scarves and hats and shouting greetings to the crew. Some of the shore people mounted the gangplank across the gap between the ship and the embankment. The crew then began unloading the cargo under the tutelage of Vladimir. Some men carried cargo on their shoulders while others used hand trucks for large boxes. Kat and Dmitri went ashore in the midst of this melee`. They hailed select people who came out of this confusion to welcome them with expressions of kind wishes. They then escaped the crowd and walked hand-in-hand to Galina's house. At Galina's house a small crowd was gathering at the entrance. One could hear the herd-laughter as the couple, Kat and Dmitri, arrived. Suddenly, Galina ran forward, waving wildly, grasped Kat's hand, smiling, half-hopped-and-skipped keeping up with Dmitri and Kat for a few paces. Then she fell back and exclaimed, "Welcome home. Come in. Come in. We are all waiting for you." The foyer was filled with relatives and close friends. Dmitri exclaimed joyously, "How wonderful to see you all here to welcome us home."

Galina interrupted, holding Kat's hand and looking at Dmitri, said, "These people are all our family members and close friends who are here to welcome you both home and greeting you both before your marriage. I have contacted an orthodox priest who will be here in our church next week to officiate at your wedding."

Dmitri and Kat both laughed and participated in the whooping and hilarity of the crowd. Dmitri shouted above the noise, "You are all invited to the wedding but now please leave us in peace and quiet so that Kat and I can relax and recover from our long journey." At this statement, people started filing out of the doorway with goodbyes and much well-wishing. Kat and Dmitri joined Galina in the next room. Galina faced them with a broad facial grin, "So tell me about your trip to the Ryukyus?"

Dmitri answered, "It was a wonderful trip. We had no untoward incidents in sailing either way." He hesitated for a moment and then licking his lips and looking straight at Galina said, "While we were in the Ryukyus we got married by a Shinto priest."

There was deathly silence in the room. Dmitri held Kat's hand. Galina's face became reddened as she blurted out, "What did you say? Did you say married?"

Dmitri hastily answered, "Wait, wait, it was a sham wedding. It meant nothing. It was not real. It was only a way for Kat and me to express our love for each other. Naturally, we are still looking forward to being authentically married by an orthodox priest."

Galina drew in her breath, "Ah yes, I see."

"Yes you must remember that Kat was born a Japanese subject and Shinto was part of her culture. It is true that she now speaks Russian and has melted into our community and that she will soon be married to a Russian man but we must not forget to respect her rearing and nurture. She has declared to me her willingness to practice Russian orthodoxy as my wife." He held her around the waist as he spoke.

Galina demurred and said, "Of course, my dears, I was just a little startled. I am happy for you both. Besides, no one need know of your little escapade."

Dmitri concurred, "Alright, we will continue with the necessary wedding arrangements for our marriage next week."

Kat added in her childlike way, "I love Dmitri and we are both looking forward to our wedding. We are grateful to you for making all the arrangements."

Galina went over to Kat and hugged her warmly with a buss on her cheek. "You are like a sister to me and I only want what is best for you and my brother. Of course, I shall continue with the arrangements for the wedding next week."

After a modicum of small talk, Kat and Dmitri left Galina and walked to Dmitri's apartment above the ship's chandler store. Kat asked as they climbed the flight of stairs to his apartment," Will we always live here, Dmitri?"

"No, of course not, this place was satisfactory for a bachelor mostly because I was away for long periods of time on my trips. But now, I think we should look for a house near Galina where most of my family lives. What do you think?"

"Well, I'm glad to hear we will not live hear long. I like the area near Galina. Do you think we can find something suitable over there?"

"I am not sure but my family will help us in the search. I believe we will find something nice."

They entered the apartment and saw that someone, probably Vladimir, had brought up their luggage. They began distributing all their possessions and made ready for bed. The next morning they arose and went to a local restaurant where they consumed a breakfast of cabbage soup and bread. After being sated, Dmitri advised Kat, "I think we should go to the Department of Public Services this morning and register for our marriage."

"Is that necessary?"

"Well we might as well do it now while we have the time. It is important to make our marriage official. There is a close relationship between the Russian Orthodoxy and the government – births, deaths and marriages are recorded by the clergy for the government. Remember you are an alien but when you marry me you will automatically become a Russian citizen."

"Oh, how wonderful," she said.

"Yes and this will protect you from any problem with the Japanese authorities."

"I see, I almost forgot about my former life. My past will always haunt me."

"Not to worry, my love, No one will seek you up here in these forgotten islands."

"Well anyway I shall be your good wife and you will protect me," she said as she jostled his arms childishly.

They left the restaurant and walked to the municipal building to register their marriage in the office of the Department of Public Services. Upon completion of the task they made their way back to Galina's house for a second breakfast. It turns out Galina was anxious to speak with them. "I just heard from the priest. He would like you to visit him tomorrow at the church for instructions. Also, I forgot to tell you that my husband Ivan will supply the two gold rings for the ceremony. It will be his wedding gift to you both."

"That's very nice," said Dmitri. "Please thank Ivan." Kat assented with a nod of her head as she held Dmitri's arm. "We will go to the church tomorrow and speak with the priest."

The next day Dmitri and Kat walked up the hill to the church. It was a weather beaten, old, wooden building with a tall steeple to one side and an orthodox patriarchal cross in front. Inside, the walls were decorated with painted icons and the floor space was occupied by heavy, hewn, wooden pews. There was a bema in front containing the altar, the Bishop's throne, and clergy stalls. The priest came out of his office on hearing them enter. He was wearing a white robe and a white, flat-top, high hat on his head. His face was almost totally covered by a white, flossy beard. He wore a heavy, dangling, golden crucifix around his neck. The fingers of his hands were interlocked in embrace as he spoke, "I am Father Constantine. I am happy to meet you. So, you two have decided to get married in the Russian Orthodox Church."

"Yes Father," they both answered simultaneously.

He looked at them with sharp, penetrating eyes as he instructed, "You will need two *svideteli* (witnesses)."

Dmitri quickly answered, "My sister and her husband."

"You will need two gold rings."

"We have them."

"You must first register your marriage with the Department of Public Services."

"We already have done that yesterday."

"Very good, now please allow me to speak with you about the religious aspects of the ceremony. Let us sit over here," he said as he pointed to the pew. He looked at them, clasped his hands together in front of his protruding belly, cleared his throat and spoke very didactically," Holy matrimony is one of the mysteries of the Holy Orthodox Church in which a man and a woman are united by the Holy Trinity. Your conjugal union will be blessed by our Lord Jesus Christ through the church." He stopped for a minute to catch his breath and then continued, "God's grace is imparted to both of you to live together in his love, mutually fulfilling and perfecting each other. The mystery of the marriage of the Holy Orthodox Church is steeped in ritual and symbolism. Each of the following acts will be performed at your wedding ceremony for its special meaning and significance: the rings, the candles, the joining of the right hands, the crowning, the common cup, the walk, and the blessing. Do you understand all of this?"

They looked at each other in wavering doubt and hesitation. Dmitri eventually said, "We understand, Father."

"Don't be dismayed. It sounds complicated but it will all turn out well. Go in peace and God bless you both."

They left the church, holding hands and smiling at each other. Kat looked up to Dmitri, "It sounds formidable."

"No, my dear, as the priest said it will go smoothly."

They reached Galina's house in a bemused, happy mood. "It was very nice to meet the priest. He gave us instructions and a pleasant discussion of marriage," Dmitri said with tongue-in-cheek.

Kat reached out to Galina saying," It will be a beautiful and breathtaking ceremony. I am sure."

The day of the marriage ceremony came quickly. Family members and invited guests were gathering at the front of the church at the appointed hour. Dmitri and Kat came dressed in their finery. Dmitri wore his naval uniform and Kat wore a long, white gown loaned to her by Galina. People were congratulating the couple as they entered the church and approached the priest up the aisle. They stood before the priest stiffly while Ivan, who was in back of the couple with Galina, hurriedly placed the two gold rings in the hand of the priest. All was ready.

The rings were blessed by the priest who took them in his hand and made the sign of the cross over the heads of the bride and groom saying, "The servant of God is betrothed to the maid of God … in the name of the Father, of the Son, and of the Holy Spirit." The couple then exchanged the rings, taking Kat's ring and placing it on Dmitri's hand and vice-versa. The rings, of course, are the symbol of betrothal and their exchange signifies that in married life the weaknesses of one partner will be compensated by the strength of the other, the imperfections of one by the perfections of the other. By themselves, the newly betrothed are incomplete: together they are made perfect. Thus the exchange of rings gives expression to the fact that the spouses in marriage will constantly be complementing each other. Each will be enriched by the union.

The wedding service began immediately following the betrothal service. Kat and Dmitri were handed candles which they held throughout the service. The candles are like the lamps of the five wise maidens of the Bible, who because they had enough oil in them, were able to receive the Bridegroom, Christ, when he came in the darkness of the night. The candles symbolize the spiritual willingness of the couple to receive Christ, Who will bless them through this mystery.

Next, the right hand of Kat and Dmitri are joined as the priest reads the prayer that beseeches God to "join these thy servants, unite them in one mind and one flesh." The hands are kept joined throughout the service to symbolize the 'oneness' of the couple.

The service of the crowning follows next. It is the climax of the wedding service. The crowns are signs of the glory and honor with which God crowns them during the mystery. Dmitri and Kat are crowned as the king and queen of their own little kingdom, the home which they will rule with fear of God, wisdom, justice and integrity. When the crowning took place the priest held the crowns above the heads of Kat and Dmitri and said, "The servants of God, Dmitri and Katsuko, are crowned in the name of the Father, the Son and the Holy Spirit. Amen." The crowns refer to the crowns of martyrdom since every true marriage involves immeasurable self-sacrifice on both sides.

The service of the crowning is followed by the reading of the Epistle and the Gospel. The Gospel reading describes the marriage of Cana of Galilee which was attended and blessed by the Lord and Savior Christ, and for which He reserved His first miracle. There He converted the water into better wine and gave of it to the newlyweds, in remembrance of this blessing, wine is given to Dmitri and Kat. This is the "common cup" of better life denoting the mutual sharing of joy and sorrow, the token of a life of harmony. The drinking of wine from the common cup serves to impress upon Dmitri and Kat that from that moment on they will share everything in life, joys as well as sorrows, and that they are to "bear one another's burdens." Their joys will be doubled and their sorrows will be halved because they will be shared.

The priest then leads Dmitri and Kat in a circle around the table on which are placed the Gospel and the Cross, the one containing the word of God, the other being the symbol of our redemption by the Savior, Jesus Christ. The husband and wife, Dmitri and Kat, are taking the first steps as a married couple, and the Church, in the person of the priest, leads them in the way they must walk. The way is symbolized by the circle at the center of which is the Gospel, and the Cross of the Lord. This expresses the fact that the way of Christian living is a perfect orbit around the center of life, who is Jesus Christ, the Lord. During this walk around the table a hymn is sung to the Holy Martyrs reminding the newly married couple, Dmitri and Kat, of the sacrificial love they are to have for each other in marriage – a love that seeks not its own but is willing to sacrifice its all for the one loved.

Dmitri and Kat return to their places and the priest blessing Dmitri said, "Be thou magnified, Oh bridegroom, as Abraham, and blessed as Isaac, and increased as Jacob, walking in peace and working in righteousness the commandments of God." And blessing Kat, Oh bride, be thou magnified as Sarah, and glad as Rebecca, and do thou increase like unto Rachael, rejoicing in thine husband, Dmitri, fulfilling the conditions of the law; for so it is well pleasing unto God." Thus they were married in the Russian tradition.

Dmitri and Kat walked back down the aisle while people sprinkled them with flowers and rice. Everyone gathered outside, men shaking hands with Dmitri and women bussing Kat. Music struck up and people started dancing on the freshly cut grassed ground. Then it stopped as all looked to the side where Vladimir was holding up a glass of wine. "A toast, a toast," he shouted. All turned to listen, "To the bride and groom, much luck and happiness." Everyone shouted in agreement and the music started up again. Someone was playing a *garmoshka* (button accordion) and another was playing a *balalaika* (Russian lute). Dmitri, in tradition, kept his eyes on Kat so that she would not be 'stolen' by his friends. It was a game which would require him to pay ransom for her if she should be 'stolen'. The wedding reception was very loud and includes a lot of Russian music, singing, dancing, long toasts, and an abundance of food and drinks. Galina brought over to Dmitri and Kat bread and a container of salt as a symbol of health, prosperity and long life. Both Dmitri and Kat took a bite of the bread. Since Dmitri took the largest bite he became the head of the family or so tradition has it. These festivities and traditions were all unknown and unusual to Kat but she delighted in the fun and frolic.

At the end of the long day, Dmitri and Kat were carried on the shoulders of several select bearers to their apartment. The festivities continued into the wee hours of the morning. After the bearers left with good wishes, Dmitri and Kat climbed the stairs to the apartment door. Dmitri with good humor carried Kat over the threshold of the doorway. They kissed passionately before he let her down. "Now, our life will begin," he said to her as he placed her on the bed. He began removing his clothes and Kat did likewise. They stood before each other in their nakedness, Kat said, "I love you, Dmitri, now it is time for us to produce a family."

Dmitri held her close as he whispered in her ear, "Yes, I would like my own family."

They hugged flesh to flesh and each began hand exploration of the other. They kissed and hobbled to the bed where they plunked down laughing. They began entwining their legs and arms as they sought each other's wet mouths. Dmitri's member stiffened as it lay against her inner thigh. Kat grabbed Dmitri's stiff member and thrust it into her lubricious vagina. After a few minutes of steady gyrations they were both spent and sweating. They moved apart to fall asleep. Dmitri held Kat very close with one hand on her small breast and whispered into her ear, "It was a beautiful wedding ceremony."

She murmured, "Yes, it was lovely. We must thank Galina tomorrow. They then both fell asleep to encounter Morpheus, the God of dreams.

XV

Dmitri stirred restlessly. Sleep, he clung to it and strove to shut out everything else. A siren rose and fell again, gathering in intensity. There was a fire someplace. It didn't matter much. He pressed his face against the pillow. His arm hurt, and when he shifted it his hand lay on cool, satiny flesh. A little at a time he drew in the line of consciousness. He must have fallen asleep. He felt with his hand again, Kat was beside him. He remembered now. What was it that had awakened him? The siren shrieked. That was it. The fire alarm was shrieking.

He licked his teeth with his tongue. They were rough and coated. His nose was sore, too. Kat was asleep; he could hear her breathing, like a baby. The windows made gray patches in the wall. It was a good thing that the siren had awakened him. What the hell made the inside of his nose so sore? He took a deep breath and his body whipped itself taut. There was smoke in the room, sharp, stinging smoke. That was why his nose hurt. He was fully awake now. Someone was yelling in the street below. The fire was in the building.

He tore the covers away with a single sweep of one arm and shook the sleeping Kat roughly.

"Kat!" he yelled at her. "Kat!"

She turned over reluctantly, eyes half open and not focusing. She blinked a couple of times, straining to see.

"Kat!"

Her mouth curved in a happy, childish smile. She could see him now.

"Dmitri." It was a caress.

"Kat," he continued to shake her. "Kat, you don't understand. The building is on fire."

She was incredulous after that horror filled her eyes. Then she moved swiftly, turning on the bed and crouching there on her hands and knees.

"The whole damn place is on fire," he yelled angrily. When she didn't move he slapped her. "We've got to get out of here."

She cringed and whimpered beneath the blow.

Dmitri found his trousers and drew them on. Then with a wrench he opened the door leading from the room to the landing at the top of the stairs. A swirling, black, and menacing billow of smoke and fire enveloped and seared him. Half blind he slammed the door shut and stood with his back against it as if to keep the terror out. The staircase and lower floor was ablaze. Above the confusion outside he could hear the crisp, wicked crackle of the flames. He heard the shouts and screams of persons in the street. There was the tinkling crash of glass at the front of the store.

He turned to the bed. The floor was so hot now that he couldn't keep his feet still, and they moved in a little, humorless jig. They would have to get to the window where the firemen could see them.

"Now listen, Kat."

Kat had seen what swarmed up the steps when the door was opened. The smoke and heat were unbearable. Then she screamed, shrill and hysterically. He lunged at her, but she slipped through his fingers. For a moment she was framed in the window, one knee resting on the sill, then her body tipped forward and she was gone.

"You fool. You God-damn silly little fool," he threw futile curses at the empty window. It was only thirty or thirty-five feet to the ground. He could have held her hands and dropped her, and she wouldn't have been hurt, But to go that way!

He looked out. The crowd was packed in the street, but he could see a tight knot of men and women. They were bending over something, and the rest of the mob was pressing closer. He swung himself over the ledge and as he did so a ladder touched the sill. A fireman stood at the bottom and looked up.

"Come on, Dmitri," he called. "It is all right. Are there any more there?"

Scorning the rungs, Dmitri grasped the side of the ladder and slid down, the wood searing his hands. Then he dropped to the street and battled his way through the almost solid front of the crowd. It was hot as hell. He wondered how they could stand so close. Cursing and shoving he fought his way between ranks.

On the width of hard-packed earth between sidewalk and curb, Kat was a pitiful huddle. One leg was tucked beneath her fine, young body. The other had an ugly twist. No one was doing anything.

He leaned over Kat's mangled body and found she was not breathing. Kat was dead.

Epilogue

So there you have it; three tragic stories, two ending in death, all three of an existential mode.

The protagonist of *The Japanese Castaway*, Sueki, learned like Job how to accept the life which was conferred on him. In the end he was the only hero of the three stories.

The Buddhist priest, Jiun, of *The Roshi*, could not turn his life around even when given a second chance.

The escapee, Katsuko, of *Escape from Exile Island* did try to turn her life around after committing the most heinous act but to no avail. It was inevitable that she would pay for her crimes with her life.

What does it all mean? Is one's life guided by some supernatural force? Or is it the individual's karma which is the driving force of our actions? According to karma theory every action has a consequence which will come to fruition in either this or a future life; thus morally good acts will have positive consequences, whereas bad acts will produce negative results.